IRONWOOD RIDGE

ALSO BY BARRY WOOD

Invented History, Fabricated Power
Nonfiction Authors Association Award

Malcolm Lowry: The Writer and His Critics
Ontario Arts Council Award

The Only Freedom

The Magnificent Frolic

BARRY WOOD

IRONWOOD RIDGE

Barry Wood

Vanguard Press

VANGUARD PAPERBACK

A CIP catalogue record for this title is
available from the British Library.

ISBN 978 1 80016 146 7

Vanguard Press is an imprint of
Pegasus Elliot MacKenzie Publishers Ltd.
www.pegasuspublishers.com

First Published in 2022

Vanguard Press
Sheraton House Castle Park
Cambridge England

Printed & Bound in Great Britain

For Vickie

Prologue

Broc O'Neill was too much in shock to think, too paralyzed to feel anything, furious to the point of rage, yet, he had to find whatever small window to survival might open in the next few minutes.

The minister went on with his final words over the polished walnut casket ready for lowering into the ground — a casket that contained the remains of Darcy.

Remains. The scattered bits and pieces of human life blown over an acre of pavement in an explosion intended for him — Broc O'Neill. He shuddered to think of the mutilated remains mercifully hidden within the closed casket. The atrocity had torn him apart for the past three days, sending him into a fury of pounding furniture and tearing through his home like a caged beast.

Darcy… His wife, the only woman he had ever loved, everything he had worked and lived for. And now she was gone. O'Neill clenched his fists as he stared at the casket, the homilies of the minister making no sense. He saw no one, though he was surrounded by the shocked community of colleagues — faculty and staff from Jefferson State University and more from the community, hundreds of people in shock from the tragedy of Darcy's death.

Struggling to control himself, O'Neill tried to think. The attempt on his life, which had ended in Darcy's death, had made everything clear. Someone wanted him dead. No, the effort and planning told him it wasn't someone; it was many. But who? And why? He did not know, but he knew he would be dead within hours if they had their way.

He imagined he could feel their eyes. Not the eyes of the graveside mourners, but hidden eyes — perhaps in one of the parked cars just beyond the iron fence or in a restaurant across the street, or perhaps behind the half-drawn curtains of an apartment down the block. Eyes, watching him. Eyes of unknown enemies who had somehow decided to take his life away. They had failed this time. They might not fail again.

He hardly heard the final words of consolation. A few people began to move off. In minutes he would be exposed, vulnerable, a target for those he was sure were watching him. But he had to survive. He had to slip through whatever net was closing in; he would have no second chance. If he was going to enact revenge, he had to survive, suppress his grief, and think more clearly than ever before.

They were lowering the casket. He watched it descend — fighting back the knots in his stomach, feeling as though some deadly beast were stalking him, ready to spring, ready to maim and kill.

The minister beckoned to him. He gathered up a handful of moist soil and scattered it into the grave. The dull sound of earth falling on the casket jarred him with its finality. The minister offered a final benediction and then stepped back.

O'Neill stared into the grave. A little girl stepped forward: Brittany, a colleague's daughter, five or six years old. He watched her throw a bouquet into the grave and then saw the tears on her cheeks as she turned and looked up at him. Reaching out, touching her shoulder, he felt the hot wetness of her tears, the shocking and terrible softness of her hair brushing his hand. He turned slowly, nodding his gratitude to those who had come to Darcy's burial.

"Broc, if there's anything we can do—"

He closed his eyes for a few seconds and then nodded understanding.

"— Just call. Please, Broc, just call, or come over—"

"Thanks, Mary. Thanks, Tim. I'll… I'll be okay." He wanted to flee into the arms of friends. But he had to risk everything — for Darcy's sake — alone. No one else could help.

He moved slowly, thanking people. He felt their hands on his shoulders. Trying to think what was next, he struggled against the agony of their tears. People drifted toward the driveway, the iron gates, the boulevard fronting the cemetery. Aware of parked cars, curtained windows across the street, O'Neill moved with them. He had to separate himself from the others. He had to escape. He had to get revenge.

Chapter One

Jefferson, Indiana
One week earlier
Thursday, May 16, 1996

"This is the scariest thing I've read this semester."

Broc looked up. Christelle Washington, a graduate student in political science, stood in the doorway of his office in a soft green cotton dress.

"All those readings you assigned on the history of intelligence, Dr. O'Neill—they were pretty unnerving," she said as she walked in holding the latest issue of *American Documentary History*, "but this is worse. I found your article this morning. It's bound to upset some people in Washington. Dr. O'Neill, where on Earth did you find this?"

"In the library where Harry Truman grew up," he answered as Christelle sat down. "Boxes of uncatalogued papers from his early presidency. God knows how they got there." She laid the journal on the edge of his desk like a sacred object. "But the semester's over. You can put off reading academic journals until next fall."

"This issue just arrived in the Poly Sci reading room." She looked at the buff-colored journal, then at him. "It's pretty upsetting. It makes me go cold just thinking about it."

"I wish all my students were as attentive." O'Neill smiled with pleasure. He pulled a stapled sheaf of paper from a half-opened bundle on his desk. "Here, fifty offprints came in this morning's mail. Good thing, or I wouldn't have received them until I got back in September. Would you like one?"

Christelle beamed as only a student can who has been recognized and favored by her mentor, her teacher in two history seminars and now a member of her newly-formed dissertation committee. "I'd love one, Dr. O'Neill." He passed it across the desk. "But —would you sign it?" Broc took it back feeling like a celebrity as he wrote his name under the title of the article. "Good! Now I can say I knew you before you testified before the Senate." She fingered the offprint as though it were a string of expensive pearls.

Broc smiled. "I think it's about as interesting as an old shoe — speaking from a layman's perspective. After all, it's from the Truman years. That's half a century ago."

Christelle thumbed through the offprint. "That's the historian's perspective. But I'm sure some in high places would prefer this document never saw the light of day."

Broc shrugged. "We historians get hardened up after a while. After Watergate and Oliver North, nothing in Washington seems surprising. New forms of deception, new examples of corruption." Broc smiled. "And the dirty tricks change with every administration. Clinton has had it easy so far even with Republicans in control of both Houses. Of course, they're no worse than Democrats. Just new rules for dirty games just as we managed to figure out the old ones."

Christelle listened to him attentively, then opened her handbag. "Is it true that you won't be back until September?" She laid a stapled sheaf of pages on his desk.

"Darcy's been with her law firm six years, she wants a long vacation. She's working out plans for the summer. Ten weeks."

"So, that means no more rummaging in old presidential documents."

He nodded. "Darcy's demanding a clean, research-free, brainless vacation."

Christelle smiled at his description. "Dr. O'Neill, I love that wife of yours. She's a woman after my own heart." She paused, wrinkling her forehead. "As for me, I can't imagine a whole summer off, not with this dissertation to plan. Where are you going?"

"A grad-school buddy has a place out by Chesapeake Bay. He's invited us to use his guest house, but I expect to spend some time in DC." O'Neill picked up another copy of the offprint. "There's more to it than this, more documents never examined."

Christelle smiled at him across the desk. "It doesn't sound like a research-free, brainless vacation to me. What does Darcy say?"

"She says I can do what I like in Washington, but never to say a single thing about it to her, not unless I come home with theater tickets or venues for classy sight-seeing. But she's ruled out the Native American and Holocaust Museums."

"Well, I thought she was interested in all that kind of stuff."

"She is, but she says I'll get distracted and start chasing some wild hare into the politics of broken Indian treaties or activities still unknown about Hitler and the Nazis — which I have mentioned from time to time."

"So, are you planning to poke around in the Library of Congress?"

"Some things are possible. Staying out of libraries for ten weeks is not. Darcy says research is an academic disease. I can prowl the stacks as much as I want, but the cabin is an academic-free zone. She's a lawyer. She's threatened to write out a legal contract listing off-limit topics and penalties if I break the rules."

Christelle smiled in amusement, then pointed at Broc's article. "Academic sleuthing seems pretty intriguing. Nobody in Poly Sci does anything interesting. They just sit around and argue about the election in November. Your summer sounds more interesting."

Broc shrugged. "It could be interesting if anything turns up, but it won't be much of an adventure. Have you ever been to DC in the summer?" She shook her head. "It's awfully hot. Five-showers-a-day weather. You may not know about this. California has a sensible climate."

Christelle nodded. "You're right: it's pretty nice in San Diego. Anyway" — she patted the pages she had laid on his desk — "this is a first draft of a dissertation proposal. Something to read when you're not sleuthing. My first and second readers have it — Dr. Bailey and Dr. Jones."

O'Neill glanced at the stapled pages. "How soon do you need a reply?"

"Oh, there's no rush! I need to do a lot of reading. This is only a first draft, a sort of work-in-progress. I'll try to define the topic more exactly over the summer. So September is fine." She watched Broc glance at the title. He lifted the lid of his briefcase and slid the proposal inside. "But I would like to have your summer address so I can send a card. You and Darcy have an anniversary soon."

Her memory caught him by surprise until he recalled how well Christelle had taken to Darcy at joint faculty-student gatherings — not surprising considering that Darcy, at age thirty-two, was probably only three or four years older than Christelle. On the fifth of August they would celebrate ten years of marriage.

"That's awfully kind, Christelle, but don't feel you need to remember all the important dates in the lives of your dissertation committee, especially your third reader."

"I'm sure Darcy would appreciate it. Lady lawyers are as sentimental as the rest of us."

Broc squeezed his lips together, acknowledging her point. "Well, you can send things care of the History Department at Georgetown University." He opened a notebook and thumbed through. "It's Washington, DC. Zip code, 20057." Christelle jotted down the address. "Also, I'll be calling here every couple of days to get my phone mail. Just leave your number and I'll call back. Where will you be?"

She stuffed her pen and the offprint into her purse. "I've borrowed my sister's cabin in Vermont for the summer. She and her hubby are off to Europe. I need to be away from distractions if I'm going to get any reading done. There's Internet but no video player, not even TV, nothing except a walk in the woods every day."

"Sounds idyllic. We've got a place like that. It belonged to Darcy's mother. Completely isolated. But it doesn't seem like we'll even get there this summer."

He watched Christelle stand up and close her handbag. Her green dress set off her hazel eyes and auburn hair, which fell in spreading waves halfway down her back. "You look like you're on your way somewhere."

She glanced at her watch. "The airport. I've got a flight in three hours. I'm spending a couple of weeks with Mom and Dad, then a drive across the country. I'm looking forward to that. And then, I'll be holing up in Vermont."

Broc stood and gathered up his spring-semester paperwork. "I have to hand this in and then I'm gone for the rest of the summer! Can you wait? I'll walk you to your car."

Standing in the parking lot, they enjoyed the spring air and smell of honeysuckle blossoms from the bordering hedge. "I know your proposal is a work-in-progress, but how close are you to pinning down a topic?"

"It's going to be something about double-agenda politics — federal bills that appear to be one thing but are put forward to build party power in ways the public may not notice. Politicians do things with devious intentions that no one realizes until later."

Broc gazed across the parking lot. "It makes a lot of sense, especially now with Republicans trying to neutralize a fairly effective president. There's manipulation at every level, slanted news releases, closed-door deliberations leaked to *The New York Times*. There's such duplicity and subterfuge in Congress. How does Dr. Bailey feel about the topic?"

"He says I should focus on one or two administrations or this will become a multi-volumed tome. He says you would know the period that will yield the best results."

Just about any period will give examples. "Whatever you come up with will probably do. But is September early enough?"

"Oh, definitely early enough! I need to explore major bills over at least the past forty years, maybe everything since FDR, before settling on a specific period."

He nodded again. "Look, Christelle, this whole topic is fascinating! It's such an interesting twist on legislation. If you get it mapped out — you know, a chapter outline, whatever — e-mail it. I'll get back to you."

"Will Darcy allow you to read academic stuff during your vacation?"

"She'll be okay because she knows you're trying to finish your degree."

Christelle smiled her thanks. "I don't understand everything in your article. It assumes a lot of complicated background that I'd like you to explain, but that will have to wait until September. And it's separate from my summer dissertation project." Broc nodded. "Anyway," she said, glancing at her watch, "I have to go or I'll get caught in traffic."

Broc weaved through the parking lot to his car, an aging Honda Accord, and opened the door, which he never locked. As he got in, he remembered his task for the rest of the afternoon. He set the briefcase flat on the seat, opened it, and pulled out the cell phone. The damn thing had gone haywire two days ago, but he knew he could get it replaced free of charge since it was still under warranty.

Christelle's car passed by — a new Pontiac Grand Am SE with cross-laced wire wheels that communicated the kind of muscle more typical of the seventies. Steel-gray, elegant. A price tag of something around thirty-six thousand hovered in his mind; he wondered where today's graduate students found the money to live in luxury while working full time on a degree. O'Neill backed out and followed her car to the parking lot entrance, then along the boulevard. The black detailing and low-lying, rear-deck spoiler radiated understated elegance. He caught a glimpse of sunlight on Christelle's hair as she turned left under the freeway and headed up the ramp to Highway 40. She waved as he continued south toward the mall.

Broc set his briefcase on the table, examined his new phone and punched in Darcy's office number. The voice came on after the first ring: "This is Sanderson and Sanderson, Attorneys at Law. Please listen carefully as our menu has recently changed."

He punched in Darcy's extension and waited while the phone rang twice. "This is Darcy O'Neill," she announced in the same telephone voice that had entranced him for a dozen years.

"Well, Counselor, how are things in the law patch?" he asked, thinking of something like an urban cabbage patch. He admired Darcy's competence in her chosen profession. The days of hardship while he put her through law school were behind them, and now the dollars were rolling in. Hers from Sanderson and Sanderson were rolling in at about double his from Jefferson State University.

"Hello, Professor. Hey, you were gone a long time this morning. I missed you."

"Today was my last day at JSU. I decided to get my vacation started the right way, so I ran an extra couple of miles. But I saw you drive off just as I turned onto our street."

"Health nut! Hey, where are you?"

"The food court at the mall. I just traded out that defunct phone for a new one. Do you want the new number?"

14

"It looks like it's on my phone, but I'll write it down anyway and put it beside my office phone. Just a minute." He waited, imagining Darcy pawing through her drawer for a pad of sticky notes. Across the open space at the edge of the food court, he caught the eye of the Chinese salesman sixty feet away, standing in the doorway of the Worldwide Communications store, a booming new franchise that had set Wall Street buzzing when it went public a few months ago. Broc raised his thumb to signal that his new phone was working; the salesman waved back.

Darcy's voice came floating back. "There, now I can find you even if I misplace my cell phone. So, you're on vacation now, huh?"

"Filed my grades a couple of hours ago and thought maybe we could celebrate."

"It's Thursday, Professor, I've got to be up at six tomorrow morning."

"Why so early?"

"Brushing, combing, primping, the usual sorcery. Anyway, that's not the point."

"What's the point? I wasn't planning an all-nighter, just dinner at the Skyscape." The rotating restaurant thirty stories above the city was one of Darcy's favorite spots.

"That's all?"

"We won't be out all night, just long enough for dinner. We could be home by nine thirty."

He listened to the silence at the other end. "That's all?"

"Oh, maybe some Irish Cream afterward at my place."

"Hey, Professor, I have to get up at six. How do I know you'll behave?"

"I always behave at my place."

"But this time, maybe you won't. You're on vacation; you can sleep in."

"Well, if you're nervous about my place, how about your place, Counselor?"

"Sounds wonderful!"

"Why the hell will you never do it at my place? It always has to be at your place."

"Just a quirk. How does six thirty sound?"

Broc's watch showed four thirty. "Fine, I'll pick you up at six."

"So long, Professor. But remember — since it's my place, you bring the Irish Cream."

"Done!"

He pushed the off button and thumbed through his notebook for another number. *Her place, his place*: it was crazy. They lived at the same place, shared the same bedroom, slept in the same bed. But every date had to end up at "her" place, not "his." You bring the Irish Cream. That was the standard ritual. He couldn't remember whether they had any at home; he should go by the liquor store down the mall.

O'Neill punched up Alan Creighton's number, directed his new phone to save it, then waited while the network sorted through its millions of customers. Creighton lived a couple of hundred miles away, one area code west, and taught at a branch of the University of Illinois at Edwardsville. He was in the same academic field as Broc, American history, but Alan had followed two tours of duty in Vietnam with graduate school at Berkeley and four books on high-tech military warfare.

While the phone rang, Broc eyed an offprint of his article. The bold-print title spread over three lines with the excessive but precise wording required in the scholarly community: "An Early Policy Directive from President Truman: The Origins of Clandestine Domestic Operations by the National Security Agency."

The scariest thing I've read all semester— O'Neill smiled to himself. She was young with a pristine innocence his generation had missed. He calculated: in her late twenties, born toward the end of the Vietnam War — too late to be saddled with the disillusionment and guilt that had obsessed a whole generation of young Americans. He read his article title again. *Makes me go cold just thinking about it.* O'Neill supposed it could be disturbing from one point of view. After all, the document he had found and analyzed was a hitherto unknown directive from President Truman establishing the ground rules for a new intelligence-gathering operation that had soon become the most secret branch of the federal government.

Alan Creighton answered on the eighth ring — out of breath.

"Alan, my article on the founding of the NSA just came out. I'm going to mail you one. Also, sections of a couple of Truman documents plus some notes of analysis. I'm wondering whether you could read my analyses for the usual, glaring errors, jumps in logic, my tendency to theorize before all the facts are certain."

"Sure, Broc, but I've got a fax modem in my new machine. That'll be quicker."

"Busy weekend ahead, but I'll get it to you by Monday.

Chapter Two

Darcy O'Neill followed the waiter as he led her and Broc through the maze of tables toward the west-facing windows where the evening sun lit up a stack of pink and yellow clouds. The waiter seated Darcy in the most elegant style of service available anywhere in the city. Broc pulled in his own chair.

He thanked the host. Darcy noted how his dark eyes caught the candlelight as he touched the silverware and glanced at the sky. Then he turned to her and she felt the force of his presence, the thick shock of chestnut hair across his forehead, his eyes moving from her hair over her face to her lips, then to her eyes.

"This was such a good idea!" Her eyes moved from the brown-suited width of his shoulders to his hands, his gold wedding band, his gold watch, a gift bought with her Christmas bonus. She wriggled in her chair and pulled off her gray tweed jacket.

"My God. Do you go to work in things like that?" he wondered, his eyes on the plunging neckline and frills around her bodice.

She touched the fine gold chain at her neck and saw his eyes follow it to the hanging emerald against her skin. "You like it? So do all the guys on my floor." She felt a little devilment as she watched his eyes. The fact was she had laid out a nondescript blue blouse with her jacket for today's work. She reached across the table and put her hand on his. "But the goodies are just for you, Professor."

"When did you have a chance to get home and change?"

"I didn't," she confessed, fluffing the ruffles. "I bought this a couple of months back. Left it in my office closet for emergencies."

"This is an emergency?"

"When your hubby wants a date, it's always an emergency." She watched his eyes, and the knowing smile, feeling a little flutter of excitement. She reached across the table, beckoning him to lean forward, and proceeded to adjust the handkerchief in his jacket pocket. "You should talk, Professor. This getup wasn't what you wore this morning. Do you keep extra suits at your office to dazzle all those sweet co-eds?"

"I had time to go home and change."

She ran her fingers down the collar, admiring the tie, then caught his eyes again. She squeezed his hand and they gazed together over the city as the restaurant turned almost imperceptibly toward the darker northern sky.

Broc ordered ice water and a bottle of German Riesling, three-year-old vintage, which they sipped while watching the restaurant fill up. A quarter hour later the waiter took their order. Broc was acting relaxed and wealthy as he always did, facing three months of summer vacation. He ordered pepper steak with baked potato and snow peas; she ordered a lighter meal of seafood and dinner salad.

"So you're on vacation! Does that mean you're going to loaf all through my last week of slavery at the law patch? If so, I just want to say it's disgusting!" She loved to remind him he had a soft job with too many afternoons free and obscenely long vacations while she put in a respectable day from nine to five. Even if she stayed home, she'd put in more hours shopping and cooking. Once she told him it was another male plot to keep women in bondage, and he countered with his usual accusation that temptresses signing up for university courses — "As you did!" — was an equally sinister female plot.

"Actually, while you're slaving away next week, I've got to run into Indianapolis." Darcy waited while he sipped his wine. "I got a call today from Samuel Whiterock. He's invited me to meet him next week."

"Whiterock?" Her memory worked. "Where have I heard that name before?"

"It took me a minute, too," Broc admitted. "He was a Democrat in Congress until he got booted out in the Republican housecleaning of '94."

"I don't remember a thing about him. Fill me in."

"There isn't much to remember. I think he's from Virginia. He served one term in the House."

"What's he doing now? What's he want?"

"I don't know much," he said, distracted by the lights of Jefferson's skyscrapers slowly passing their window. "He's running some sort of consulting firm or foundation, no idea what. He says he wants to make an offer."

"An offer! Hey, Professor, are you going to take it?"

Broc moved his hand in a gesture of finality. "I'm going to drive up to Indianapolis next Wednesday out of courtesy and see what's on his mind. That's all. I doubt that anything he could offer would be more interesting than the next ten weeks."

Darcy used his reminder as her cue. "Okay! Here's what we've got! She opened her purse and pulled out a packet of envelopes, which she laid out in a row on the table. "I finish up here a week Friday. I figure we need a weekend to get organized." She opened up one of the red, white, and blue envelopes. "I've got us tickets to Washington for the following Tuesday. American Airlines, nine in the morning. You think you can get up early enough to make it?"

"Depends. Where are we staying the night before, your place or mine?"

"It better be yours," she advised; "you might not be able to handle that much excitement right before we fly."

"I vote for your place; I'm on vacation and by then you will be, too. You'll just have to deal with the situation."

"Then you'll have to bring the Irish Cream."

"Again? We haven't even opened today's bottle and you're putting in orders for the week after next. Don't you know that drinking before flying is not good for you?"

"Maybe not for pilots," she quipped. "Anyway, we better enjoy ourselves while we can. I hereby issue an invitation. No more nights at your place, every night till we fly at my place."

Broc appeared confused. "You're acting a little nutty! What's going on? And what's this about while we can?"

"I got a phone call from the doc today."

"What about?"

Darcy felt little bubbles of excitement inside. Broc hadn't even known she had an appointment. "You're going to be a father, Professor; that's what!"

Astonished, he was unable to speak. It was all she could do to keep from laughing out loud. He was such a handsome devil, but right now he looked like a dumbfounded kid.

"So that's what I mean, while we can. I've been reading up on this. Apparently, we're supposed to be celibate for six weeks before and six weeks after."

"Before and after what?"

"Before and after the baby comes, silly. So we haven't much time. Apparently, I'm three months pregnant, the doc says the baby is due in November. We can play all summer but have to be good starting at the end of September."

Stunned by the news and struggling for words, he ran his fingers through his hair. She reached across and cradled his hand again. "Don't men ever think to hold a lady's hand?"

"My God! A baby. Diapers in the washer, pablum on the floor, Legos on the driveway. How can you be so calm?"

"What's this about Legos in the driveway?"

"Dad once ran over my Lego castle. I'll have to train him to build inside."

"Him? What makes you think it's a him? I built great Lego castles when I was a kid. And I was better than my brother. You could have a daughter."

"This is really going to disrupt everything."

"What on Earth did you think? That we would go on leading this Yuppie lifestyle forever?"

"But we've been married without kids for ten years."

"That's the point, Professor. It's time! Anyway" — she pulled her hand away and started rearranging envelopes on the table — "we've got these flights out of here on the twenty-seventh. I've booked us into the Ritz in Washington for five days. That will give us time to walk around the Mall, meet your friend at Georgetown U, and maybe see the Smithsonian, which you've been lusting after for years."

Broc didn't quite appear to be concentrating, but it didn't matter. It would be fun telling it all twice. "Then" — she touched his hand to get his attention — "I've rented a car for thirteen weeks, all of June, July, and August. We can head out to the cabin first of June and — vacation begins!"

"Cabin?"

Darcy smiled at him across the table, feeling as amused at his confusion as she was excited about the summer. "I've been studying the map. I've booked a cabin down on Choptank Bay. Right on the water! There are all these quaint little towns with British names like Tilghman and Oxford and Sherwood and Christ's Rock. And you can ferry into Washington whenever you can't stay away. Me? I don't plan to budge from the beach the whole summer!" She felt a little like a romantic adolescent.

"A car for three months, and a cabin," he paused, "that's a bunch of money."

"Never mind, Professor, I got a huge bonus from that oil litigation we settled last month. Twenty-six thousand extra dollars!"

"My God, I'm in the wrong profession!"

"So, I've decided to book a little vacation."

"Little! A waterfront cabin for three months? That's a vacation to end all vacations?"

"Not quite!" She lowered her eyes and then up at him mischievously. "Choptank Bay is just for starters. I've fixed us a little getaway in the middle — last week in July, first two weeks in August." Darcy picked up another envelope. "See, here it is." Beaming from ear to ear, she passed the ticket across the table.

Broc read the ticket. American Airlines. Washington to Los Angeles... L.A. to Singapore, July 22nd. Astonished, he looked up at her.

"See, Professor, we're going to have this baby in November. After that, it's all Pampers and rocking a baby in the middle of the night. So we need to have one big fling. You always said you wanted to see Asia. From what I hear, Singapore's a world-class city."

The waiter arrived with a tray and steaming plates. She watched him moving his wine glass and flatware to make room, his thick hair falling a little farther down his forehead as he examined everything. But even the pepper steak could not quite distract him from all the news. She watched the waiter sprinkle cheese on her spinach salad.

Broc was looking at her when she looked up. "What a summer! I thought I was making a big splash booking a table up here" — he waved his hand to take in the candlelit tables, now all full — "but nothing like the splash you've planned." She smiled and held up her wineglass. He raised his and clinked it against hers.

"You know, Darcy, you're in the wrong profession. You should have gone into tourism."

"You've forgotten," she observed, her fork poised, "but it was before we met; it's no wonder you forgot. Two-year program, Franklin College, remember — in Travel and Tourism."

Broc sliced through his steak and she dug into her salad. She had met Broc twelve years ago when she enrolled at Jefferson State University with two years of transfer credit from New Jersey. She had taken one American history class from him, majored in business, and they had been married in August the summer after she graduated. Then she had gone into law school, completed bar exams three years later, and joined Sanderson & Sanderson, a low-key law firm with a dozen partners at a beginning salary of eighty-five thousand, plus bonuses. Their savings account had started to grow. It was time, she thought, to celebrate. She had worked hard and he had supported her ambitions in every way. Both of them deserved a big splashy vacation.

Broc followed her BMW — last year's Z3 affectionately known as "Beemy" — which fulfilled her need to play the role of the big-time attorney. He felt full and well fed, and he was very much in love with his wife. He remembered her dark eyes glittering across the table and her midnight black hair framing her face. Pregnant! Of course, he shouldn't be surprised, the way they spent all their spare time.

He pulled his Honda Accord into the driveway beside Beemy and turned off the motor; it was nine fifty-five. She leaned her head on his shoulder as he found the key.

From somewhere in the distance — a dozen blocks away — they heard a muffled volley of pops. They paused, listening. It was difficult to tell the direction of the sound.

"I thought Chinese New Year was over." Darcy turned toward the house. Another burst of pops sounded like firecrackers.

Broc followed her in and flicked on the lights. She dropped her jacket on the hall chair and walked to the middle of the living room. She was a picture of beauty. A memory flashed across his mind: he remembered the first day he had met her; she had come up to the podium at the end of class and asked a question about an assignment. He remembered how she turned afterward, and how she had looked as she walked toward the door. Tonight, twelve years later, she still looked that way, as slim and fit as that day when she was barely twenty-two.

Darcy flung her arms out and spun around in the middle of the room, stopped, and pointed at the crooked lamp shade beside his reading chair. "See, Professor, your place is so messy, like that package on the chair–"

"It's my new license plates for Honda."

"It's been there for three days."

"So my place is messy because I'm waiting till the weekend to put them on the car?"

"So messy. That's why we can't do it at your place. But observe my place." She walked behind the couch patting the pillows neatly lined up, then turned and ran her finger along the mantle. "I keep everything so nice and neat!" She turned toward him, her dark eyes beckoning. "This could be an emergency. You want to come upstairs and fix it?"

He walked toward her and wrapped her in his arms. She met his lips with the full softness of her own, clinging to him, her hands moving on his back. They kissed for a long time and then stood in front of the couch holding each other.

"I'd love to fix it, Counselor." He held her to him again, and then the phone rang.

"You get it," she said, "I'll be upstairs." She gave him a lingering look over her shoulder as she crossed the carpet. "And don't forget the Irish Cream."

He picked up the phone after the third ring as he emptied his pocket and dropped a couple of pens on the desk. "Hello—" The line was silent. "Hello, hello. Who is this?" He listened, watching as one of the pens rolled off the desk. Holding the receiver to his ear, he stooped to pick it up.

The room filled with deafening sound. Somewhere beyond the front window a weapon hammered away. The glass shattered behind the drapes. O'Neill heard the hiss of flying debris, the crash of splintering wood from the desk as he rolled onto the carpet. Sudden pain in his arm. The whole room seemed to come apart, torn and ripped by a barrage of flying steel. He heard Darcy scream.

The noise died away, but the sound of gunfire continued down the street for several seconds. He heard a distant scream, and then several hysterical voices shouting somewhere at the end of the block.

He lay still, feeling the pain in his arm.

"Broc! Broc!" Darcy was crying. "Are you all right?"

Slowly he moved his head, seeking her out. Darcy was gripping the banister halfway up the stairs at the far end of the room, her eyes wide with fear, flooded with tears. Slowly, cautiously, he got to his knees, dazed by the shattered glass and debris across the rug. Pain shot through his arm above the elbow; his hand came away with blood. He turned toward the window. The drapes were shredded, their tattered remnants drifting in the breeze blowing through the broken glass.

"Broc!" She came down the stairs, eyes startled, paralyzed by terror. "Broc, you're hurt!"

He moved his arm. "There's blood, but it moves. I think it's just a flesh wound. Darcy, you better call the police."

Somewhere in the distance gunfire like fireworks sounded again, and then died away.

Thirty minutes had passed. Beyond the shredded drapes the police cruiser's red and blue lights flashed, painful to the eyes, nerve wracking, like a surreal dream from a bad TV program. O'Neill had taken off his shirt and was holding his arm, which Darcy had wrapped with three-inch gauze. Red was leaking through, but the bleeding was momentarily stilled.

"A lot of gunfire," the officer was saying into his radio. "One casualty, flesh wound. Front of the house shot up. A lot of property damage."

The officer listened for a few seconds, then signed off and turned to O'Neill. "There's been a bunch of drive-by shootings the last half hour. Six blocks from here, over on Sumac Street, and Wayside. And three or four houses down the block. Nobody hurt, just a lot of broken picture windows. Looks like we've got a carload of drunks out on a joyride. But that's the way it goes — nothing for weeks, then three or four in one night. They go crazy in spring."

"A drive-by with automatic guns?" Broc queried.

"It's happening more and more," the officer explained. "They get their hands on an automatic, maybe one that dad smuggled out of training camp, and they have to try it out."

Darcy's eyes were wild with fear. "My God, what's the world coming to?"

"You're lucky to be alive, Mr. O'Neill. Your front wall is a mess, but those loaded file cabinets stopped a lot of steel. Hope you don't need the files; they'll have to dig out the bullets. Evidence, you know. There might be a couple of dozen rounds buried in all that paper. But Jesus" — the officer examined the wall across the room — "if you had been standing up, you'd have been mincemeat. Anyway, you're safe now. Those guys are gone, so you might as well forget it till morning."

The officer passed a slip of paper to O'Neill. "This is the investigation number; your insurance agent will need it. In the meantime, you might as well get a good night's sleep."

"If you think we're staying here tonight," Darcy blurted out, "you're wrong!" Stunned by her outburst, O'Neill just looked at her.

She glared from the officer to O'Neill, then at the torn curtains. She pulled out her cell phone. "I'm going to reserve us a room downtown."

Chapter Three

Broc glanced in his rearview mirror, then at his watch, as he crossed Loop 465 driving east on Interstate 70, heading into Indianapolis. He had left Jefferson at 10:40 a.m. and driven at the speed limit all the way. His watch showed eleven fifty-four; his appointment was at twelve thirty. He watched the Indianapolis skyline in the distance as the highway ran northeast a few miles, then veered east. The day was heating up, a harbinger of long hot summer afternoons by the water on Choptank Bay.

It had been a rough week. Neighbors up and down their street were outraged at damage to their homes; the papers were sensationalizing a "new crime wave" in the city. There were calls for a law enforcement crackdown.

The police had come back the next day and spent most of the morning digging bullets out of walls and file cabinets. O'Neill had filled out forms and answered questions. The insurance adjuster arrived at the house as the police were pulling away. Everything had gone well: the plate glass windows had been replaced Friday afternoon, making the house at least secure. Similar repairs were going on all down the block. Monday morning the carpenters arrived. As O'Neill left this morning, two workmen were finishing the new siding across the front of the house while two more were replacing the knotty pine paneling across the back wall.

O'Neill shifted in his seat and slowly pulled his shoulders up toward his ears. His left arm throbbed where the flesh had been sewn together five days ago. It would be uncomfortable, the doctor warned, for a couple of weeks.

Darcy had not taken any of it well, but after an extended weekend at the best downtown hotel, she had reluctantly agreed to move back into their house Monday night. By Tuesday, she had more or less put things in focus and called Macy's for custom drapes, which would be hung later in the week. That would give them four days in their newly restored quarters before leaving for Washington.

O'Neill drove a few miles and then took the Downtown Destinations exit, following a route he knew well toward the research library at Purdue University. He glanced in his mirror for perhaps the hundredth time. The events of last Thursday night had set him on edge, like an aggravating noise that wouldn't stop. The whole incident was just too close to fatal to forget easily. But Darcy needed to be calmed down, so O'Neill suppressed his own anxieties and attended to her needs. A phone call on Monday to the officer in charge of the investigation turned up nothing. O'Neill willed himself to put his life back in order.

Once the chaos at home had been cleared away, O'Neill had turned his thoughts to the invitation and his appointment some thirty minutes hence. He had found basic information on Samuel Whiterock in *The Almanac of American Politics*. Before his election to the House in 1988, Whiterock had spent years hovering around the edge of the federal bureaucracy, though in what capacity was not entirely clear. The 1990 and 1992 editions of the *Almanac* revealed that he had done little more than warm a seat in the House of Representatives for six years before being swept out of office in the Republican landslide of 1994. O'Neill's resources at home were inadequate for further research, and he could not get online; his computer had been disabled by the gunfire. Annoyed at the loss of time and general chaos of the past six days, O'Neill swore under his breath.

Several blocks before the Purdue University campus he turned off and slowed, watching street signs. A few minutes later he spotted the brick building, a branch annex of numerous federal buildings in the city. But the building was a landmark only. Eight blocks beyond, he found it — an older hotel, newly renovated.

As O'Neill parked and got out of his car, he spotted a man on a third-floor balcony. He recognized Whiterock from magazine photos. His hair was graying; he appeared a little tired; but the forceful stature that had commanded the attention of the Virginia electorate was still evident.

Whiterock beckoned him across the street. The hotel clerk motioned him toward the elevator as though he had had been expecting him for some time.

Whiterock shook O'Neill's hand and introduced himself, then led him toward the bar. Two men came out of a bedroom with drinks and sat down while Whiterock talked. "We'll have sandwiches brought up in a while, Dr. O'Neill. In the meantime, would you care for something liquid?"

O'Neill sensed an inside-the-beltway protocol unfolding, the first step being adequate lubrication. He motioned at the Cutty Sark. "About half and half." As Whiterock chipped ice into the glass, O'Neill glanced at the others. One watched the weather on the TV, which was muted; the other was smoking and gazing through the open curtains toward the balcony. Both were dressed in standard department-store suits. Government people, he thought. Compared with the well-suited Samuel Whiterock, they were underlings.

Whiterock handed him the Scotch-and-water and led him toward the chairs. The others sat across the large coffee table. "I'd like you to meet two of my colleagues, Wayne Boatwright and Jim Sawyer." Both men held his eyes as they leaned forward and shook hands across the table.

"I'll get right to the point, Dr. O'Neill. I run a small institution — probably one you've never heard of — The Whiterock Foundation on Foreign Policy. Nonprofit. Wayne is my vice-president, Jim is secretary. I'd describe us as a think tank."

"Foreign policy?" O'Neill queried. "What's your connection to The Council on Foreign Relations?"

Whiterock gazed at O'Neill; his heavy brows shadowed his deep-set eyes. "The Council on Foreign Relations has never been more than a government retirees' club. Most of them are frustrated intellectuals who don't understand politics and play it badly when they try."

O'Neill said nothing, hiding his disagreement.

"For instance, when they advised President Carter to admit the Shah of Iran to the U.S. for medical treatment. That's a good place to begin. The taking of American hostages at Tehran was the result. Over a hundred Americans were held for over four hundred days."

O'Neill nodded agreement, though he preferred to consider the causes of the 1979 crisis as slightly more complex. "What's the mission of your foundation?"

"We are beginning a complicated investigation — a secret investigation, if you will, Dr. O'Neill — into the wrongdoings of the Republican Party since the sixties."

"That would take us back to the Nixon administration."

Whiterock held O'Neill's eyes as he nodded. "A little earlier, actually. But we'll make a full disclosure of the rigged election of 1980 our first item of business."

O'Neill looked at him noncommittally. The suspicion that Ronald Reagan's people had somehow manipulated his election to the presidency had simmered for years.

"There have been rumors for years, but nothing conclusive," Whiterock hinted. "It's been alleged that the Reagan National Committee negotiated with Tehran through the summer and fall of 1980. The American hostages were sweltering under Muslim captivity and tropical heat for over a year. President Carter worked desperately to free them by October — to get himself re-elected in November. Remember that abortive rescue attempt?"

O'Neill nodded, recalling the shock of colliding American aircraft crashing somewhere in the Iranian desert in the spring of 1980. Then, as the election neared, everyone had wondered whether Jimmy Carter would be able to pull off a last-ditch 'October Surprise,' get the hostages home, and guarantee his reelection. But it had never happened.

"We're close now, we're close to a detailed picture of what happened. The evidence suggests that the release of the hostages was delayed — deliberately delayed — until Ronald Reagan was safely elected."

"There were a couple of books on it as I recall," O'Neill volunteered. "A Reagan intern wrote one — *October Surprise*, I think it was called." Whiterock nodded. "And then a Senate investigation dismissed the whole thing—"

"That book made a start, but it missed crucial pieces of evidence. And so, yes, the smoking gun eluded the investigators and Reagan got away with it!"

O'Neill listened, remembering the startling cut-and-paste on American television on Reagan's inauguration day in 1981. As the ceremony went forward in Washington, the news anchors kept cutting to the Middle East where the hostages were being released and flown out to Greece, then to Germany. The effect had been surreal. And every thoughtful observer wondered whether it was all coincidence. But a congressional investigation years later turned up nothing. O'Neill wasn't convinced there was any 'smoking gun'.

"The full evidence will show, Dr. O'Neill, that the Republican election committee cut a deal with the terrorists in Iran, arranging for a delay in the release of the hostages until after the election. Isn't it highly suspicious that they were released on Ronald Reagan's inauguration day? What a coincidence! Great theater. We believe it was orchestrated to the hour."

"For what purpose?"

Whiterock leaned forward, his eyes intense. "It was a powerful piece of symbolism. It suggested that foreign terrorists who had the audacity to toy with a Democratic president, especially a peace-at-all-costs peanut farmer like Jimmy Carter, should never dare play the same game with the new Republican President, Ronald Reagan. Their release at the very hour when he was sworn in symbolized what every Republican wanted Reagan to stand for: the Great Warrior Hero standing victorious over the barbaric heathens of the Middle East."

"So you think it was planned down to the hour?"

"We are sure it was." Whiterock searched for O'Neill's response.

O'Neill suppressed his urge to challenge Whiterock. Two books had detailed Jimmy Carter's inability to mount an 'October Surprise'. Both had alleged that Reagan's closest allies had made such an October Surprise impossible, thus guaranteeing Carter's loss. But neither had uncovered decisive evidence. The possibility, however, could not be ignored, but a congressional investigation failed to prove wrongdoing, and so the issue was dismissed.

"The whole 'October Surprise' investigation was a whitewash!" Whiterock's anger was growing. "And I wonder why! George Bush was vice president under Reagan; he would have known about any negotiations of Reagan's henchmen with Tehran. But Bush had become president when it was investigated. If it really happened, it was kicked under the carpet; there's no way Congress would have indicted a sitting president! But it needs to be scrutinized again."

31

"It happened sixteen years ago."

"It was only the beginning. Reagan was the president who played fast and loose in foreign policy. Or his lackeys played fast and loose for him — his campaign manager William Casey, and Admiral Poindexter, and Oliver North." Whiterock tilted back his glass of Scotch; it was half empty when he set it down. "Believe me, Dr. O'Neill, the rigging of the 1980 election and Irangate are only the tip of the iceberg. We've got evidence of all kinds of travesties in foreign policy, including evidence that casts a shadow over most of George Bush's alleged accomplishments in Desert Storm."

"It's history." O'Neill wondered what the evidence could be.

"It's reality, Dr. O'Neill. And it's one of the keys to our own times. The Iranians played along with Reagan's election committee but realized later how Reagan had manipulated history with their unwitting assistance. You'll notice that no one in the Middle East is willing to negotiate with us on anything any more. Now they strap on bombs and blow things up. A lot of it is revenge for all the times they were gulled in the past."

O'Neill was silent for a minute, mulling over a spin on past events that varied a good deal from what he had concluded. "Maybe, but it seems unnecessary to debunk the Republicans all these years later. After George Bush showed himself incompetent on domestic policy, we got Bill Clinton, who looks okay. Democrats are a minority Congress now, but we'll probably see the pendulum swing toward the Democrats again soon."

Whiterock leaned forward, his eyes blazing, angry. "You're right, and I'll be happy — no matter which Democrats pick up seats, because presidents mean nothing. It's Congress that makes or breaks this great nation. We elected a Democratic president and a Democratic Congress in '92. That was promising. It shut out a party that is still on a right-wing, ignore-the-poor, creation-science runaway train, and nothing is changing. Then everything went down the tubes in '94. The voters gave away both House and Senate to the Republicans, whose last term controlling both houses was during the Eisenhower administration! Think of it! For forty years Democrats occupied both houses! That's the secret of American prosperity today — solid Democratic control, election after election, most with huge Democratic majorities. But now, see what's happened since '94. Hillary Clinton's health care initiative, a program fully in keeping with Democratic ideals, was voted down, killed within the first year of the new Republican Congress. Their ideology is hostile to the people and their needs. It's a good index of what is to follow."

"And the Whiterock Foundation aims at... aims at what?"

"We are conducting an intensive investigation. First of all, think of all the ridiculous governmental scandals during Republican administrations. Senator McCarthy's witch hunts in the fifties... a Republican move to discredit young Democrats who were thinking about how to prevent more wars, thoughtful about capitalism, attempting to work out other plans for a just government. Or Watergate. A crooked Republican president trying to guarantee a second term in office. Or the Iran-Contra arms-for-hostages exchange... another Republican plan to undercut the less dramatic but ultimately more ethical Democratic policies.

"But we are ready to deal with these things more effectively than ever before. We've collected the most sophisticated equipment. The Whiterock Foundation has gathered great minds. But what we expect to do will involve intelligence. Your expertise in the field of intelligence is well known. We've been collecting evidence for years. We've got a backlog — thousands of hours of coded messages between the most secretive departments of our government. We've got encrypted material from the last six federal elections.

"What little we've been able to crack says that the great Republican 'revolution' of 1994 was also based on all kinds of manipulation and illegal activity, things that would make Watergate pale. Corruption everywhere. We want to break it all open, bring it out into the clear light of day. Discredit the entire Party. Our government should be Democratic, without exception, and it was for decades. The entire Republican platform is mired in error. It always has been. The only way they gained power in '94 was by fraud and deception. We've figured it out and we aim to expose it all."

O'Neill watched Whiterock. Boatwright and Sawyer sat impassively, watching him. They were sincere in their beliefs —

fanatically, frighteningly, alarmingly sincere. They had veered into an outrageous ideology of their own; they seemed to have lost any sense of the inherent strength of a two-party system, the defining feature that set the American system apart from the single-party politics of Russia, China, Cuba. They were building a huge edifice of wrongdoing on a smattering of clues, and much of it was circumstantial. None of them was objective enough to assess the facts. And they were fanatically resentful of the Democratic loss in 1994.

A knock. Wayne Boatwright moved to the door. The food service waiter wheeled in sandwiches and another bottle of Scotch.

O'Neill sat in his car in the parking lot outside the Purdue University library. He pulled the phone out of his briefcase and punched in his home number. It was 6:25 p.m.

The phone rang twice and then Darcy answered.

"How does the new wall paneling look?"

"Hey, Professor, I've been home only five minutes. Let me see." There was a pause; O'Neill imagined her standing by his desk while surveying the back wall. "Looks like new. The workmen were gone when I got home and everything's cleaned up. A new desk and file cabinets were delivered today. Nothing left to do here but get a new desktop computer."

"That can wait till September. Anyway, are you feeling a little better?"

"Much!" She declared it with definitive enthusiasm. "I got a call at work today. The police have picked up three guys they think were behind the shootings. Local losers, unemployed, previous records. They found automatic guns and a lot of ammunition. They said they'll let us know."

O'Neill felt a wave of relief. They had after all been accidental victims. Accidental or not, it wasn't nice to be a victim. Random vandalism was disturbing.

"Hey, what's going on in Indy?" Darcy asked. "Did you meet this guy Whiterock?"

"I spent a few hours with him."

"What's he want?"

"He wants me to take over a major role on his research project."

"Sounds great! Are you going to do it?"

"It would mean three years of leave from Jefferson State."

"Three years. There ought to be some big bucks in that. Are you going to do it?"

"His foundation is in Alexandria, Virginia." There was a long silence on the other end of the phone. "You'd have to give up your practice at the law patch."

"No way! I'm not giving up my practice!"

"That's what I thought. So I'd have to commute. A flight home every second weekend."

Another long silence.

"Are you going to take it?" Darcy wondered aloud, her voice completely nonchalant.

"Hell, no! I don't mind doing it only at your place — but every second weekend?"

"You're a victim of testosterone, Professor. So, when will you be home?"

"If I had my way, tonight. But Whiterock insisted I not make up my mind today. He wants to talk again tomorrow morning. So I'm going to get a room."

"You'll probably give in."

"I probably will not give in, not after a night in a lonely hotel room. I'm quote-unquote a victim of testosterone. Remember, I was going to spend every night this week at your place."

"Why don't you just say no and come home now? I could make it worthwhile."

"This guy flew all the way from Virginia to meet me. He deserves to be heard. And I want to find out more about the Whiterock Foundation."

"So you'll be home tomorrow night?"

"Earlier — by noon."

"Hey, Professor, that's great. In time for lunch?"

"Name the place."

"Well, Beemy's got some sort of trouble. Vibration in the front end. Also, he needs his three-month checkup. Going to the BMW dealership for servicing is more expensive, but easier. And there's that place just down the road — the Jefferson Chicken Diner."

"So, how about I meet you there. Then we'll drop off Beemy, I'll drive you back to the office, then pick you up after work?"

"Sounds nice. Can you make it?"

"I'll get out of Indianapolis by eleven. How about I meet you at twelve forty-five?"

"Done! Sounds great. Can't wait. And, sorry about tonight. What can I say?"

"You can say 'yes' tomorrow night when I suggest doubles."

"You know what, Professor, you're a victim of your lust."

"No, Counselor, you're a victim of my lust."

Chapter Four

O'Neill filled up at a convenience store just outside Loop 465, tucked the latest edition of *USA Today* into his briefcase, then headed west on Interstate 70 toward Jefferson. The sky was a brilliant blue; the first foot of corn was standing tall in the fields. He set the cruise control at sixty-two miles per hour and let his mind wander over his second meeting with Samuel Whiterock.

"You know, Dr. O'Neill, you're a Yale man; you ought to appreciate the importance of intelligence. Yale was the birthplace of intelligence — Norman Holmes Pearson, Nathan Hale, heroes all."

"You're right, Sam. There's that statue of Hale — 'The First American Spy' — out there on the campus. We were supposed to salute him every day. And I knew Robin Winks. I took classes from him. Winks never let us forget about all the Yale boys who had served in the OSS and the CIA."

"Then, Dr. O'Neill, why the hesitation?"

Broc walked to the kitchenette and poured himself another cup of coffee. He turned and watched Whiterock, who waited for his reply, his eyes immoveable, his body taut. O'Neill was amazed at his intensity.

"The intelligence you're talking about, Mr. Whiterock, borders on the illegal. If you've collected encrypted materials from the whole Reagan-Bush era, as you claim, and from the last dozen elections, it's been done illegally. The status of domestic intelligence gathering was cleared up by the Rockefeller Commission on CIA Activities, if memory serves, back in '75. *The Rockefeller Commission Report* laid out ground rules to be followed on intelligence collection — after years of abuse by both Republicans and Democrats."

"Come on, O'Neill; you know as well as I that domestic intelligence is being gathered every day. My God, the Department of Defense—"

"And the CIA," O'Neill snapped, "and the Justice Department, and the FBI, and who knows what others? They're all full of 'plumbers.' But it's still outside the law. The questionable activities of both parties include abridgements of civil liberties that have created a ground swell of opposition by good American citizens, at least half of them Democrats, yet you seem to feel that utilizing the same illegal tactics of secret surveillance is okay."

"Sometimes you have to adopt dirty methods to keep up with the enemy."

"And," said O'Neill, trying to hold his temper, "the moral foundations of civilization are compromised. We may be technologically advanced, but ethically, most of the world is stuck somewhere in the Dark Ages."

"You don't think what they did was legal!"

"If the Reagan-Bush National Committee did delay the release of American hostages — even by a day, let alone weeks or months — then it was one of the most unconscionable acts in American history. It was a terrible and despicable abuse of power and grounds for a massive legal suit against the Party. Maybe a revolution. But such travesties won't be eradicated by stooping to the same methods—"

Whiterock was annoyed at the suggestion. "I can't believe you academics live in this ivory-tower world!"

"Maybe it's you living in an ivory-tower world, Sam. You're not a faculty member in a university, but everything you say indicates you do the same kind of in-depth research we do in the ivory-towered academy. But your research is all skewed one way. Democrats are perfect; Republicans are criminals. You seem to forget travesties committed by Democrats."

Whiterock turned to him. "Like what?"

"Have you forgotten? In the 1930s? Roosevelt was fed up with a Supreme Court overthrowing his New Deal legislation. He proposed adding judges to gain a Democratic majority. It never happened, but the stupidity of even thinking it is stunning."

Whiterock waved his hands as though to dismiss the point.

"Or what about Kennedy's failed invasion at the Bay of Pigs?" Whiterock shrugged. "Or Johnson's bombing of North Vietnam, allegedly because of a nighttime attack on a ship in the Gulf of Tonkin.

No one knows to this day whether that was real or fabricated. Like your theory of the Reagan election, there's no decisive evidence."

"Your published articles suggest Democratic leanings," Whiterock observed. "Isn't that the Party you support? Isn't that the way you vote?"

"I vote that way because I don't want to waste my vote on candidates like Ralph Nader or Ross Perot, who don't have a chance of winning. But my leanings are usually toward Independents. The reason is because both parties are mired in corruption that appalls me. You seem to want to ignore this side of the Democratic Party and exaggerate Republican travesties. Democrats are as prone to stupidity as anyone else. I voted for Clinton and so far, he's looking good, but there's this controversy over something called Whitewater. It's not very clear what it's about yet, and no one knows where it's going, but it could turn out that Clinton is just as bad as any of your Republican villains."

"Shit! It's not the same thing." Whiterock pounded his fist on his chair and stormed out to the balcony. After a few minutes, he sat down in an aluminum chair and O'Neill joined him. They sat silently, facing the street for several minutes. Between the apartments, they could see children running on a school playground. Morning recess.

"You know, Professor O'Neill, I don't think the younger generation of intellectuals understands what's been lost." Broc listened, hearing the deep tone of despair in the man's voice. "You had to know my father to understand."

O'Neill waited, saying nothing.

"Dad was born a few years after World War I. He grew up in the twenties and then got caught, as so many young men did, in the bleak days of the thirties. The day he turned sixteen, he had to quit school. That was in 1936. His father was out of work. So, Dad went out to support a family of five at age sixteen."

Whiterock pulled out a pack of cigarettes; offered one to O'Neill, who declined; lit one up; and went on. "It wasn't long before Dad had work. He got in on one of Roosevelt's New Deal civil-works projects. They built highways and repaired bridges." Whiterock turned to O'Neill and caught his eyes. "You know, even though he suggested stacking the Supreme Court, FDR was the greatest damned president this country has ever seen!"

This might qualify, O'Neill mused, as the first really sound judgment Whiterock had uttered. O'Neill watched him as he dragged on his cigarette and flicked the ashes off the balcony. Whiterock sat for a minute, his face expressionless, his eyes staring toward the schoolyard. O'Neill was vaguely aware of a school bell in the distance.

"Then came Pearl Harbor and the mobilization for taking back half a dozen countries that Japan had seized. Mom and Dad got married in March 1942. Three days later he left for the War. He served for three and a half years in the Pacific, fought at the Mariana Islands and Okinawa, survived Iwo Jima. Cited for bravery twice. And then, you know what? He got in on the American Dream! Came home, took advantage of the GI Bill, went to college. In four years, he made up for years of high school lost and entered Virginia Tech. It was an all-male military school in those days. He graduated in 1951 at age thirty, then went into business, founded his own company." Whiterock sucked a long drag on his cigarette and blew smoke so violently it whistled through his teeth, then turned his head slowly and stared at O'Neill.

"And then, you know what, O'Neill?" Whiterock's eyes were like pools of blue ice. "Six years later, he started to forget things."

Feeling the weight of the question, Broc turned toward the schoolyard and the distant skyscrapers.

"You know what he had, O'Neill?"

Broc paused, afraid to speak, though he knew he had to. "Alzheimer's."

"—Only in 1957 they didn't call it Alzheimer's Disease. It was called senility." Whiterock flicked his cigarette over the balcony rail. "Senile at thirty-six. I was three years old. Never knew my father any other way, just a forgetful, wasted, gray-headed old man. That's all I ever knew of him the whole time I was growing up."

O'Neill tried to grasp what Whiterock's life was like, what went on. "How long did he live?"

"He lived forever. He broke nearly every record for early-onset Alzheimer's. Longer than Rita Hayworth. He lived like a vegetable for another twenty-four years! Died in 1981."

Whiterock lit up another cigarette, and then leaned forward, jabbing it in O'Neill's direction. "But you know what, O'Neill?" His face twisted in a grimace of irony. "He got the benefit of the American Dream, in sickness and in health! Unfortunately, mostly in sickness when he was too far gone even to know or understand. Eighteen years in a VA hospital. Those were the days when we looked after our walking dead!"

He puffed on his cigarette three or four times as though he were trying to blacken his whole insides and blew smoke until the still air of the balcony was blue. "But not any more!"

Broc waited, his mind racing, trying to grasp his meaning.

"Not any more! The whole damn thing's shutting down. And now Earl is wasting away."

"I'm sorry, Sam, you've lost me. Who is Earl?"

Whiterock turned toward O'Neill again. His face was ashen. He radiated an icy hatred Broc could not comprehend.

"Earl is my brother." He took another drag and then dropped the cigarette on the cement, where it lay, smoke curling up and spreading into a blue mushroom. "My older brother. When Dad left for the Pacific — it was just three days after he was married — he left my mother pregnant. Earl was born in 1943, thirteen years my senior. Bloody brilliant kid. Followed in Dad's footsteps. Got in the reserves as soon as he was eighteen, just in time for Vietnam. Went to Southeast Asia in 1965, did three tours of duty, survived the Tet Offensive in '68, Purple Heart, accomplished as much as Dad ever did."

"His father would have been proud of him—"

"Would have, yes! But Dad was already a vegetable. He missed it all! He sat like a bloody zombie when they loaded Earl up with more decorations than any three men." Whiterock stood up and pounded the rail.

O'Neill watched him, feeling the rage in the air. "What's Earl doing now?"

Whiterock turned, his face a mask of rage. "When he was forty-two, Earl started forgetting things. That was 1985. He's been rotting away now for a decade, probably a candidate for another record for longevity as a vegetable. It appears that my family has two things: first, a genetic propensity for early Alzheimer's Disease, and, second, robust constitutions that guarantee we will live under this curse far beyond the average, which is about eight years."

41

O'Neill leaned forward and ran his hands through his hair, then stood up and walked to the rail near Whiterock. "He was a war hero; he ought to be getting the best of care—"

"Damn it, O'Neill! What do you think this is all about? You don't think anything is intact. It was fine when Dad was admitted to a VA hospital way back in '63, but not so fine when we admitted Earl in '87. It was fine when the Democrats still controlled Congress. But you know what's happened? We've got a Democratic president. Clinton is likely to win another term later this year, but he can't get any social reforms off the ground with Republicans in control of Congress. Veterans are beginning to languish and wither. It's all coming apart. Half a century of the American Dream — everything that FDR started and the Democrats have spent decades building — it's all falling into ruin. They're dismantling it."

"You talk as though it's a done thing, Sam. Legislative trends are not forever. The Democrats have retained a lot of their strength, in some states increased it. And some of the problem is not political at all. It's increases in costs, building construction, utilities."

"Democratic strength, even new Democratic initiatives, won't reverse the damage. Republican rhetoric has set a mood, with Newt Gingrich at the helm. He led the way for the Republican takeover in '94. Then they made him Speaker of the House and *Time* magazine named him 'Man of the Year.' What a travesty!"

O'Neill watched, taking in the rage.

"Welfare is under attack. The care in VA hospitals is eroding. Newt and his Republican disciples have primed the public for tax cuts. That means less money for social programs that matter."

"It doesn't make sense. American veterans have always—"

"The Republicans don't give a damn about veterans or anyone else. Sad to say, many vets are school dropouts from underprivileged Democratic ghettos. Many Republicans come from moneyed backgrounds. Their net worths, are way higher than what Democrats can show. They do their quote-unquote 'military' service in the National Guard or the Merchant Marine. Or they get a doctor to come up with a medical excuse for not serving." Whiterock pounded the balcony rail and swore. "They don't care about anything we've held sacred since the 1930s. And they sure don't care about our veterans!"

They stood facing the school yard for a long time. In the distance the glass buildings of downtown Indianapolis stood gleaming in the sun. Broc felt the weight of cynicism and defeat in the air. "You never got to serve," he deduced, "or did you?"

Whiterock turned sideways and leaned against the rail as he slowly shook his head. "I would have, but I was in elected office during Desert Storm. It's one of the things I didn't get to do. But I'm a gunman, you know. I spend hours every week at the range. So, when I line up the sights, I always remember what Earl said. He was old enough to remember Dad talking about the War. You know what he said? He said when you've fought for weeks and months against an enemy like the Japs; when you understand that they have threatened the way of life you stand for; when you've seen the men beside you shot up, bleeding from their lungs, gasping for breath; when you've lost the people that mean the most to you, you want one thing, just once. You want to look down the barrel of your own gun, you want to see the whites of the eyes of just one of them, you want to see the fear, and then you want to feel yourself pull the trigger. You want to see them die in the same agony your buddies went through, protracted, unremitting, painful, excruciating."

Broc was stunned, shaken by the hatred.

"Earl said he understood. He said he got the chance in Nam. Looked down the barrel into the eyes of a bloody gook, saw the terror, and then pulled the trigger." Whiterock turned toward the rail and the distant buildings. "It's not a pleasure I've ever known."

"There are more civilized pleasures," Broc suggested.

"Hell, yes! The pleasures of tracking down the bastards who are dismantling our world!"

"Your fuse is burning," O'Neill cut in, speaking for the first time like a father chastising a son, "like a bomb ready to explode. Do you do anything other than harbor hatred toward political enemies?"

Whiterock faced O'Neill for a moment, then looked away and drew a deep breath. "A couple of vacations a year in Curaçao."

The name rang a bell. A beautiful island in the Caribbean, also a tax haven — one of the most effective places for wealthy Americans to hide their accounts. Undoubtedly, Whiterock had enough money to make a tax haven worthwhile.

Whiterock mumbled on. "I try to enjoy other pleasures. The pleasures of — Shit! The bloody pleasure of getting up and actually remembering what I've got to do that day, still knowing where my car keys are, and finding them where I know they are, and turning on the ignition and knowing why I'm in the car and where I'm supposed to be going, counting the days when I know that I can still know, knowing that one day I may not know."

Broc parked in the lot of the Jefferson Chicken Diner at twelve thirty. Darcy had reserved a table by the back window where they could gaze out on a piece of vacant woods, but he was a quarter hour early and she had not arrived yet. Broc pulled out his newspaper and waited near the front entrance.

At twelve forty-five on the dot, he saw Darcy's black BMW cruise past the jam of cars near the entrance of the restaurant, then circle to a spot where there were still parking spaces. Swinging her purse, she came down the wooden boardwalk a couple of minutes later. She was dressed in a black business suit; the white of her blouse made a deep V at the front. She looked as happy as he had seen her since before the drive-by. As she came in, he rose and hugged her. She was wearing blue sapphire earrings — his favorites because they matched her eyes.

The waiter led them to their table and ran through the specials.

"I'd like a glass of white wine." Broc added he'd like the same.

"Well, what happened? Did you give in?"

Broc shook his head. She caught the strain he was feeling. "I put him off last night till this morning, then put him off this morning till some indefinite time in the future."

"Does that mean you're going to give in?" Her face was expressionless as she watched, trying to read his thoughts.

"No, I'm not going to give in, but I couldn't tell him that. He said the offer was good for six months. I couldn't face another interview in the middle of our vacation, so I told him nothing would happen before the fall."

44

"Well, that's a relief! I wasn't looking forward to canceling our vacation. But why didn't you just tell him you weren't interested?"

The waiter arrived and set out their glasses of wine. Darcy opened her menu, skimmed it, and ordered a salad. Broc ordered a Reuben. They raised their glasses and nodded in their traditional toast reserved for celebrating good times and drank together. Broc gazed pensively out the window; Darcy waited.

"It's a futile project, Darcy. I don't want to participate. I prefer to watch what happens like a disinterested observer. Whiterock's foundation is working to discredit the entire Republican Party."

"Well, you know where I stand on that," she said, pushing her dark hair away from her face. "He can dismantle them piece by piece for all I care."

"I know, I know. I guess we're like everyone else of our breed. I told Whiterock I had leanings toward Independents, which is not quite true. I vote for Democrats, and I think you do, too, though I'm surprised you haven't shifted to the right. A lot of attorneys do. Anyway, Whiterock wants to scour up manure that's decades old. Not just the Reagan election but Irangate and the politics of Desert Storm. Who knows? We think we know everything about Watergate. Maybe we do. But Whiterock says Nixon was guilty of stuff all the way back to his days as vice president under Eisenhower. If Eisenhower did something questionable, Whiterock wants to find it. He wants to excavate the Dark Ages. I just can't see it. Real evidence of fraud today might be relevant, but unearthing corruption half a century ago when a lot of the principals are now dead can't lead anywhere."

"Then why didn't you tell him?"

"Well, I did, but Darcy, the guy is on the edge. His brother's a sick veteran. He's raging against a system where budgets are being trimmed. He thinks the VA hospitals are letting veterans rot. It's classic conspiracy theory. In his eyes everything is going to hell; he's a fanatic. As I see it, it doesn't matter how much Democratic legislation has been undermined in the past few years; it can't be as bad as Whiterock says."

"He's an intelligent man, isn't he? Didn't he serve in Congress?" Broc nodded. "Then how's he got everything so twisted up?"

"His father and his brother were war heroes. His father got early Alzheimer's, then lived for another twenty years. His brother got it, too, and he's heading for another record as a living vegetable. Whiterock said the average survival time after diagnosis is eight years, and it runs in families."

Darcy sipped her wine." How old is he?"

"Fifty-four."

"My God—"

"He's scared as hell. He says he thinks the same thing got his grandfather and two uncles. He's terrified."

"So today was not the time to turn him down."

Broc nodded. "Decidedly not the time. I'll let it ride over the summer. I told him I'd be in touch in September. Maybe I can work from home and send him stuff from afar without leaving Jefferson."

They ate in silence. Broc caught the slight distraction in Darcy's eyes. She was turning over what she had heard, contemplating the tragedy of a family ravaged by an incurable hereditary disease.

"I hope we don't get it. You won't ever forget me, will you?"

"I will always remember climbing up to your balcony to propose."

She nodded, smiling. "Rapunzel never had it so good."

When the waiter came back, Broc ordered another round of wine. Her eyes met his and her smile spread. She reached across the table for his hand and gave it a squeeze.

"You're wearing a new tie."

"A specialty for the occasion. It's symbolic."

"Symbolic? It's just like any other tie."

"You don't like my tie?"

"It's a beautiful tie, just right. Why is it symbolic?"

"It's made in Singapore."

Darcy's smile slowly spread. Her eyes shone as she nodded her approval. "Oh! That reminds me," she said, fishing in her handbag and pulling out a bundle of envelopes. "I've been carrying these for a week. Why don't you safeguard them?"

He shoved the packet of airline tickets in his jacket. "You finished? You want some dessert?"

She shook her head and rubbed her hand across her waist. "Can't indulge in this condition."

Wrinkling his forehead, Broc noted her waist, as trim as it always had been.

"My God! You've forgotten already! We're going to have a baby!"

"I haven't forgotten. It's just hard to believe. It doesn't show."

"Well, it will! Soon I'm going to blow up like a balloon. I'll be fat, so fat, and even fatter if I eat like we've been doing."

Broc waved to the waiter, who brought their bill. It came to twenty-six dollars and change. He pulled out two five-dollar bills for a tip and stuck them between the salt and pepper shakers.

"Look, Darcy, I'll take Beemy down the road to have his wheels straightened; you drive my car back to the office. BMW has a courtesy service; they'll drop me off at the house."

"I don't know about that, Professor. Driving a car like Beemy could soon spoil you. You might want one, and our budget couldn't stand it."

"What's so good about him?" he quizzed. "He's got a shimmy—"

"If you take Beemy, I'll have to drive Honda."

"That won't hurt you."

"Honda's old."

"We went on our first date in Honda."

"That's what I mean, really old. Anyway, the back seat was too small."

"Your legs were too long—"

"Hey, Professor, let's not get personal!"

"But there was room enough for your legs on the balcony."

"You are so bad!"

"Anyway, we'll be at your place tonight."

"My place is a long way from the office. Honda might not make it."

"Honda made it all the way to Indianapolis and back."

"The back seat is full of library books and Coke cans."

"Homo neanderthalensis didn't have them. They're a sign of intelligence, national symbols for enlightenment."

"The Coke cans are national symbols for trash."

"You just have to take one more ride, Darcy, then we can put Honda in the garage for the summer and drive a rental car for two months."

Darcy checked her watch. "Okay, but we'd better go." They stood up and headed toward the cashier.

"It's going to be a busy afternoon," she said as they stood at the front counter. "I'd like to leave by five, but I've got three days of work to clear up this afternoon and tomorrow."

The woman ahead was chewing out the waitress at the register because her VISA card had been rejected.

"You might as well go," Broc suggested. Darcy fished in her purse and they traded car keys.

"Have them change the oil and give Beemy a lube, too," she requested. "He's overdue."

"See you tonight. And drive Honda carefully. She's a precious antique."

Darcy rolled her eyes and headed through the glass doors. Broc watched her crossing the pavement and swinging her purse. The woman ahead fished in her purse, slapped down cash, and fumed at the cashier as she counted out change; then she marched out in a huff.

Broc handed over thirty dollars with their lunch bill. A baby! It was hard to believe. They had lived together for ten years without children. It was hard to imagine what a baby would do to their lives. It was hard to visualize her roaming the house in a negligee with a baby following her around.

"Sir, your change." The cashier counted coins into his palm.

Pocketing it, he pushed past waiting diners and exited the restaurant door as Darcy was opening the door of the Honda. Watching as she pulled the door closed behind her, he started across the pavement toward the BMW.

The car exploded. The blast hit him like a tsunami, blowing him backward onto the pavement. He felt the sting as he rolled, frantically trying to gain control. He scrambled to his knees and watched, stunned, as the Honda erupted into a huge fireball, and everything he had loved and lived for was suddenly gone.

Chapter Five

Green Mountains, Vermont
Saturday, June 15

Christelle Washington turned at East Middlebury and headed east on Highway 125, past the pine-clad slopes. At Ripton, she turned, following the curves of the mountain road north, heading toward Bread Loaf Mountain and Mount Grant, yet seeing nothing. A quarter hour later she turned onto the side road and headed up the slope of the mountain.

And then she began to cry.

It was a week and a half since she had flown from California, landed at Jefferson Airport, unlocked her apartment, opened her mail, and then gone out to the campus to borrow some books. She heard the news within minutes of reaching the Political Science department: Dr. O'Neill's wife, Darcy, had died on the 22nd of May. Unable to believe it, Christelle had dashed across to the History Department, where the secretary confirmed the news. Professor O'Neill's wife had died in a car explosion; the funeral had been held on the 25th. Closed casket.

"The casket was a waste," the secretary imparted. "There wasn't anything left of her."

Christelle ran across the square to the library. She was half blinded with tears as she sat down with last month's newspapers and began searching. She found the story on the front page of *The Jefferson Mail* for Friday, May 24th. The photograph showed the charred and twisted remains of the O'Neill car in the parking lot of a restaurant out on Beacon Road. She read the first paragraph through twice:

> Dr. Broc O'Neill, professor of history at Jefferson State University, and his wife Darcy, attorney for Sanderson & Sanderson, had just eaten at the Jefferson Chicken Diner when the O'Neill car,

a 1985 Honda Accord, exploded, killing Darcy instantly. Dr. O'Neill suffered cuts and bruises from flying glass. Police are investigating.

The story continued on page 4. There was another photo, this one of Dr. O'Neill.

Through misted tears, Christelle peered at the photo. Dr. O'Neill stood with two policemen. He was holding a cloth to one side of his face; his eyes were lowered. She read the whole article again, and then ran out of the library and back to the History Department. She went to Dr. O'Neill's office; it was locked up, with the same things as always stuck to his door: his spring class schedules, newspaper cartoons.

The History Department secretary said Dr. O'Neill had been at his wife's funeral but then had disappeared. His campus mailbox was full of the usual publishers' catalogues, campus mail, and a thank you note from a student. He had not been back or heard from since he turned in his grades on the 16th of May.

Christelle paced her apartment and tried to make sense of it all. The whole campus was in shock; everyone knew Darcy O'Neill. No one could believe it. Christelle phoned her friends, who knew nothing beyond what was in the paper. She rang Dr. O'Neill's home; his answering machine was full.

She wandered — around the campus, through the mall, in the park — for three days. She looked up where Dr. O'Neill lived and drove out to his house. No one in the neighborhood had seen him since his wife's funeral.

"It's such an awful thing," the woman across the street said. "Those poor O'Neills — such nice people. First their house gets wrecked when some gang of hoodlums drives by and shoots it up. Everybody on that side of the street was shot at. Then no sooner was that repaired and Mrs. O'Neill gets blown up. It just makes you wonder."

The neighbor showed Christelle news clippings of drive-by shootings the night of May 16th. *The day we talked in the parking lot—* She emptied the O'Neill mailbox and carried the mail to his back porch, piled it inside on a wicker chair, and then peeked in the garage window. Darcy's BMW was gone.

Christelle struggled nearly a week to get herself back on track. Her main task was to get to work on her dissertation. But Dr. O'Neill had disappeared. She wondered whether she might have to find a new reader next fall if he was not able. What she needed to do now was get out of town, put the shock of events behind her, and somehow get herself in focus.

She gathered up her dissertation books and piled them in the trunk of her car, packed up all her summer clothes in two suitcases, loaded them into the back seat, locked up her apartment, and headed east on Interstate 70 toward Indianapolis, and beyond. Vermont.

Christelle pushed open the cabin door. The place was cool under a grove of pine trees. She pulled back the curtains, opened windows, then went out to the car to unload the groceries, her suitcases and books, and her laptop computer. She found the note by the bedside table:

Dear Christy *(I hate that nickname—)*
Hello Sis. Hope you enjoy it here while Roy and I are enjoying sunny Spain. Towels in the closet. Hot water heater switch behind the washing machine. Don't worry about electricity, phone, the bills are paid by automatic withdrawal. We'll straighten it out later.
Love, Joyce & Roy

Christelle stashed everything in the pantry and refrigerator and then changed into her shorts. She found a cold Michelob and went out to the deck, where she found a folding chaise lounge. She leaned back and gazed out over the valley. The cabin was 1,500 feet above sea level; the pine-clad summit was another two-mile drive up the mountain at 3,800 feet. On the slopes a mile or two away she could see mountain cabins in the trees. She scrunched down on the chaise lounge and took a long drink, thinking she must be in the most beautiful place on Earth. Thank God for Joyce and Roy's cabin at a time like this.

Her mind had been in a turmoil as she drove from Indiana to Vermont. *Cars don't just blow up—* Not unless they're already on fire and the heat gets to the gas tank. But it had blown up. The explosion had blown out the windows of the restaurant. *Professors don't just disappear*— Not after a death, not after a funeral. He has a house. He had gone, left it empty.

Then she remembered the O'Neills had planned to go someplace for the summer. Christelle jumped up and ran for her purse. His summer mailing address was there. She picked up the phone and asked for information. Thirty seconds later she was dialing Georgetown University. In another minute she was connected to the History Department.

Yes, Dr. O'Neill was well known — a good friend of one of their faculty members in the department. No, Dr. O'Neill had not been heard from for several weeks. No, they had not heard the news of his wife's death. The secretary would pass on the news. Christelle hung up. A month had passed. Maybe Dr. O'Neill had surfaced back in Jefferson. She found his number, dialed his home, and waited. After twelve rings she hung up. Christelle went back to the porch and picked up her beer. Where on Earth was he? Why wasn't he at his house?

House. Houses don't just get shot up— Well, they do, occasionally. The news clipping Dr. O'Neill's neighbor had shown her said there were a dozen houses around Jefferson shot up that night. The lady across the street had said the police had picked up some suspects.

She gazed across the valley and picked out the half-hidden roofs.

Something had gone on four weeks ago in Jefferson, something dangerous and deadly. Christelle jumped up and ran into the cabin. After a couple of minutes of scrounging through her boxes, she found her class notes from Dr. O'Neill's seminar on the history of the Cold War. She thumbed through the lectures from last spring. He had told them something. It was a story, something about a friend. Dr. O'Neill had collaborated with somebody on a research project.

A minute later she spotted it, a reference to an article by Dr. O'Neill's collaborator at Southern Illinois University. She had written it down and starred it in her notes.

Information gave her the area code for Southern Illinois: 618. She dialed up information. "Do you have a number for Alan Creighton in Edwardsville? I don't have an address." She waited.

"I don't see any listing for an Alan Creighton. Are you sure it's Edwardsville?"

"No, I'm not sure. All I know is he works at Southern Illinois University. I think that's in Edwardsville."

"Oh, I'm sorry, Miss; he could live anywhere—"

"Listen, I need to reach Dr. Creighton. A friend of his from Jefferson State University may be in a lot of trouble. They're old friends, but this professor-friend has disappeared."

"Oh, my! This is serious! Well, let me see what I can do."

Christelle waited, watching the time. The telephone bill would be paid out of her sister's account. *We'll straighten it out later—* That was all fine and dandy, but she guessed Joyce could access her account by telephone from Spain. She was uptight about everything. It would not be good for her sister to discover a string of long-distance calls made the very day her kid sister arrived at the cabin.

"I'm still looking, Miss I've checked everything out as far as Litchfield and Centralia. Nothing so far. A lot of professors from that campus probably live in St. Louis. That's what I'm checking now." There was another long pause. "Miss, this might be it — A. R. Creighton in Clayton. You think that's it?"

"Are there any others? I have no idea where Clayton is."

"It's a ritzy area in St. Louis. You want the number? There's nothing else that comes close."

"Please!"

The operator read out the number; she wrote it down. "Look, Miss, let me save you some money. I'll dial it for you." Christelle thanked her profusely. She hoped he was home to pick up.

A minute later, she had Alan Creighton on the line.

"No, I haven't heard a thing from Broc, not since he phoned—"

"When was that?"

"Let's see; it was the day I filed my grades, May 20th." Two days before Darcy died. "I talked to Broc a few days earlier about that article he published. He faxed some things he was working on and mailed the article. Damn fine stuff. He's really cracked into the National Security Agency. You say you're a student of his?"

"Dr. O'Neill is third reader on my dissertation. I'm spending the summer reading. But I can't seem to locate him."

"Well, I wouldn't worry about it, Miss; I sometimes don't hear from him for months. He and that classy wife lead a pretty busy life."

Oh, God! He doesn't know!

"Dr. Creighton, Dr. O'Neill's wife died last month. She died in a car explosion." There was a long silence on the other end of the line. "Darcy O'Neill was buried on the 25th of May. Then Dr. O'Neill vanished."

"My God—"

"And I have reason to think his life is in danger. That's why I think he's disappeared."

"This is disturbing, but I don't know what I can do—"

"I don't think any of us can do anything, Dr. Creighton. I'm just trying to see whether I can locate him, trying to see whether he's okay."

"Listen, Miss, I'm sorry; I didn't catch your name."

"Christelle. Christelle Washington."

"Well, Miss Washington, I will watch out for Broc. And, if you hear anything, will you let me know? In the meantime, I'm going to reinspect the stuff he sent. It's a good thing I made a copy at my office because the article disappeared when my house was burglarized. A bunch of stuff was taken from my study."

"That's too bad, Dr. Creighton. Anyway, I'll get back with you as soon as I find out anything."

Christelle went to the refrigerator and got out some food. Rye bread, sliced beef, Swiss cheese. She forked out a dill pickle and sliced it while the bread toasted, cut up a tomato, and carried the finished sandwich to the deck with another beer. She set it all down and realized she was packing food in like a mercenary trooper. She spread her arms and eyeballed her waist, thinking she detected an extra half inch, then gathered a couple of big pinches of flesh on her behind.

She eyed the sandwich and pickle, meditated on her second beer, and decided she would worry about proper dietary habits tomorrow. She had too many things on her mind to think about her figure right now. She needed some comfort food.

The sandwich was good. She ate it with sips of beer between mouthfuls while staring at the forested mountainside across the valley.

She was halfway done when it occurred to her that Dr. O'Neill had deliberately disappeared.

Maybe he knows something. All that shooting up and down his street — maybe it was a cover-up — an attempted murder disguised as random vandalism. Maybe they were really after him! But that seemed all too bizarre. It sounded like a conspiracy theory and Christelle was pretty skilled at recognizing them. That was a necessary part of understanding politics.

The Jefferson newspapers said Darcy was killed when his Honda blew up. Why was she in Dr. O'Neill's car rather than her own? The question hung for a minute, and then the truth struck her. The explosion was meant for him. This was no conspiracy theory. This was real. Now she realized why he had disappeared, and how: Darcy's car was not in their garage. He had gone into hiding. He was trying to stay alive.

But where was he? She sat for a minute, slowly eating the rest of her sandwich and dill pickle. Then she carried her beer inside and sat down by the telephone. She had already spent several dollars on long distance. Joyce would not be pleased. But she had one more call to make, the only one left that could possibly get her in touch with Dr. O'Neill.

Chapter Six

Kenwood Acres
Washington, DC
Monday, June 17

John Orchard glanced up from the markets section of *The Wall Street Journal* to his watch when the phone rang — once. It was 10:55 p.m. He went back to the article and finished the last three paragraphs. Thirty seconds later it rang again. He moved to the padded leather chair by the telephone table and glanced down the length of the hall to the master bedroom. No light under the door; his wife was asleep.

He picked up the phone before the third ring. "Orchard here."

"Good evening, John." It was Joe Terrence from the State Department. "Are you alone?"

"Lucy went to bed a while ago."

"We've got some confirmations. From Brasler this evening. They've been haggling for a week over that Senate bill on mining regulations; he's pretty disgusted. Anyway, he's got confirmation from Alaran Development in Atlanta. It looks good."

"How good?"

"A deposit of three million in the Houston account. I checked it about an hour ago." Orchard wrote the number on a yellow note pad. "The other five million will go in next week. Seems like Alaran's on board now. Starting in July, monthly deposits of eight million on the twentieth—"

"What about the others?"

"I've checked the accounts in Washington, New York, and L.A. in the past twenty-four hours. New deposits of forty-six million, and change."

"Good, nine new clients on deck. What about the regulars?"

"Everything looks good. In my sector, twenty-nine long-term clients were on time. Over seventy monthly deposits since January without a break. Same good news from all other sectors."

Orchard gazed out the picture window across the room. The Potomac River ran black beyond the trees; across the river headlights moved along the George Washington Memorial Parkway. A mile away the highway ran from Virginia into the District of Columbia, seat of the greatest concentration of power on Earth.

Orchard was impressed with Joe Terrence. His reports were always on time and complete. "I'll pass it along, Joe. The General will be pleased. Anything else?"

"Calls from Thompkins and Spiker. We're getting some disclosures from Kennelin Industries, also Warden & Sands. Thompkins estimates three or four weeks to get everything in place. But Spiker reports resistance from Pennsylvania Produce."

"Bloody bastards. They've been dicking around for months."

"Spiker expects some softening up soon. He's provided some incentives. Check it out: page forty-four in today's *Post*."

Orchard smiled to himself as he drew a row of jagged designs on his scratch pad. He had already seen the notice of the warehouse fire at Pennsylvania Produce. Six million in damages. Softening up, indeed. Likely, there would be a response from PP within seventy-two hours.

Orchard leaned back and swiveled his chair. "What about this mess out in Indiana?"

"Nothing yet. O'Neill could be lying low in the area, but he hasn't shown up at home since the funeral. They've got a tap on his phone and a bug in his garage. His wife's BMW has disappeared. If he's on the road, they'll get him."

"What about his department at the university?"

"Not a sign of him, but that's no surprise. He's off for the summer, won't be back until September. Blakeney's checking with secretaries every couple of days. It's doubtful he'll show up anywhere near Jefferson."

"Damn! How could this happen?"

"O'Neill got the jump on us. We didn't know he had escaped the car bomb until his wife's obit showed up. Everyone figured O'Neill would stay around town after his wife's funeral, but he never went back to his house. None of his neighbors saw him. Blakeney figured he must be staying with friends, everyone expected he'd show soon. It took Blakeney a few days to realize he had bolted."

Orchard scribbled, blackening in the triangles. And now Professor O'Neill had been out of sight for more than three weeks. "What have you found out about this guy, Joe?"

"O'Neill's a straight arrow." Orchard heard the faint sound of shuffling papers over the telephone. Terrence went on: "Grew up in Wisconsin, went to school in Green Bay, graduated in '81. Went to Yale on scholarship, PhD in history. Accepted a position at University of Wisconsin, stayed a year, then moved to Jefferson State. He's an associate professor, tenured."

"Why the move? He must have family in Wisconsin."

"Evidently not, no siblings. He left Wisconsin the year after his mother died. Met his wife at Jefferson State — one of his students. They were married in '86."

"Where else is he likely to go?"

"One of our agents talked to someone at University of Wisconsin. He spent summers running white water for one of those river-touring outfits in Idaho. A lot of backpacking in the mountains — wilderness stuff."

And now his wife was in her grave. John Orchard duplicated the design on his pad with parallel strokes.

"Hell, Joe, he could be sitting in the top of a pine tree in the Sierras for all we know. Sounds like there's not much we can do but wait. I'll pass it on."

Orchard poured himself a Scotch on ice. Back at his desk he dialed the number, with an 800 prefix, and waited until the female voice started with the recorded menu, then punched in extension code 494.

He waited. There was no way to tell where the phone at the other end was located; it could be anywhere in the country. Or Canada. Maybe the Caribbean. He waited; nearly a minute passed. Somewhere in the labyrinthine bowels of the telephone company a connection was made and a call forwarded to yet another unknown location. A brief message came on: State your name, leave your number, stay by your phone. The call was over in seven seconds.

Two minutes later the phone rang. "Hello, John, this is the Admiral."

Orchard had no idea who he was, only that 'The Admiral' had been his only contact with the higher command for several years.

Briefly, he reported the deposits and other news, then summarized the disappearance of Professor Broc O'Neill. "He's evaded Blakeney for more than three weeks. We don't know how. He's an academic; he has no experience in dealing with professionals. We don't know how he's staying out of sight."

The silence on the other end of the phone was deadly. After a minute the Admiral spoke. "We can't let him get away; we can't allow him to organize a Senate investigation. This situation is intolerable, John."

"I'll pass on your displeasure to—"

"What resources has Blakeney deployed?"

"Low profile so far. State Police in Indiana, Illinois, Ohio, Missouri"

"Blakeney ought to know they're incompetent."

"Usually they are, but the FBI makes them jump—"

"The net's not wide enough, John, or we would have had him by now! He's been out of sight too long; he could be anywhere. We need a nationwide watch."

Orchard waited; the silence on the line was ominous. He had ideas of his own, but he knew his role now was to wait until instructed.

"This situation is virtually out of control. We're into an 'absolute termination' scenario, John, and it must happen now or there will be soldiers all down the line who will find their careers wasted. Do you understand?"

"The message is clear. What do—?"

"I suggest you bypass both Terrence and Blakeney. Take down this number." Orchard scribbled the eight-hundred number on his pad. "That's a clean channel. You'll connect up with someone you'll know only as Veil. He's got connections in the National Security Consortium. Tell him; he'll know what to do. He's got lines into the best surveillance networks available."

Orchard felt his skin crawl. Veil! Mention of Veil and the National Security Consortium could only mean top-secret, below-the-horizon surveillance within the Office of SIGINT — Signals Intelligence — where the most advanced technology on Earth was linked to the labyrinthine network of COMINT, Communications Intelligence, and ELINT, Electronics Intelligence. And all of it was buried deep within the most secretive of all intelligence institutions with the Consortium buried even deeper. He recognized the penetration of the Admiral's Committee into every branch of government, every agency. O'Neill wouldn't be able to pump gas or buy a beer without being spotted.

"Let's plan to make contact on this," the Admiral said, "in the next seventy-two hours. I need to pass on some better information before the weekend."

"I'll call Friday, let's say by 9 p.m." Orchard paused, then asked, "What the hell do we do if Professor O'Neill evades us, if he escapes and does what he threatens?'

There was a long silence on the other end before the Admiral spoke. "That can't happen, John. That just can't happen. This is not a minor problem. Everything's at stake. Every possible resource has to be deployed."

Orchard waited. The Admiral was not threatening; he was simply communicating that the cost of failure would be too great to tolerate.

"I can delay seventy-two hours," the Admiral went on, "then I'll have to pass the information on, all the way to the director at the top. Carry on, John; we'll be in touch."

Orchard considered what that meant. He stared across the darkness of the Potomac Valley at the night lights around the huge complex of the Central Intelligence Agency, which was neatly tucked into a sweeping curve on the west side of the river. Whoever he was, the director at the top could be there, right across the river in the darkness of the CIA. But, then, he could be anywhere. Somewhere out there in the darkness blanketing the vast forests and plains and mountains of America, he sat, the center, the lynchpin, the man no member of the Committee knew but who knew everyone. Within seventy-two hours the Admiral hoped he would be able to report to someone higher, to Ironwood, that someone called Broc O'Neill had been terminated.

Ironwood. Code name for the head of the Committee. A man and a network. And now Orchard knew something else: that the Committee included someone in the National Security Consortium called Veil. He wondered what resources Veil could draw on to capture the fugitive professor from Jefferson State University.

Chapter Seven

Land o' Lakes, Wisconsin
Tuesday, June 18

The evening sun had disappeared behind the trees as dusk descended over the forest. Suddenly, the trees appeared to shake, and the forest lit up as the sun exploded. O'Neill's whole body heaved into life, awakened by a blinding flash of light that gradually faded away, replaced by the waning light of dusk settling over the land. He lay back, feeling clammy, staring toward the window and the gathering darkness under the pines.

He lay still for a long time. His head ached. He squeezed his eyelids together. The red disc of the sun was falling toward sunset, dropping into the night. It shuddered — then it exploded, making his body shake again. The sound was deafening. Waves of fire blew him backward onto the pavement.

Slowly, O'Neill rolled over and slid his knees off the bed onto the floor. Something fell over, a bottle. His head ached, blinding pain. Vaguely, he knew he had consumed enough liquor over the past week to float a battleship. Waves of nausea rolled over him. He knelt on the floor, his head on the edge of the bed for several minutes, his head throbbing, eyes squeezed shut, locking him in darkness.

Be careful with Honda, she's a valuable antique—

Darcy rolled her eyes and went through the glass doors. He turned to the waitress and peeled off the bills, two tens, two fives. The Honda door opened; Darcy sat in the front seat. The explosion was blinding; he felt the pain in his head as he hit the pavement. He rolled and scrambled and saw the car break into pieces, and everything he had lived for and loved was gone.

O'Neill slipped to the floor. Another bottle fell over. He lay still, squeezing his eyes shut, closing out the light. He gritted his teeth against the pain in his forehead. Then out of the darkness he saw the red disc of the sun coming toward him, shuddering, slowly breaking apart.

No! He shielded his eyes against the inevitable explosion, rolled in agony on the floor. He opened his eyes and saw a foul-smelling whiskey bottle with a garish label. His arm lashed out, sweeping it away. It slid across the floor, rolled into the darkness, and smashed against the wall. A puddle of whisky was slowly spreading under his hand.

See, Professor. It's so messy. That's why we can't do it at your place. But look at my place. I keep it so nice—

He felt the slowly gathering rage, the fury of days and nights, the blinding pain of exploding metal and fire. His fingers clenched into fists.

Somewhere nearby he heard a sound. He rolled over and sat up, looking into the gathering dusk. Through the screen door he saw a movement. He watched. Something banged, the metal lid of a garbage can. Carefully, he got to his feet. He walked across the room and reached into the corner of the closet, his eyes still focused beyond the screen door. He felt the rifle, a Ruger 10/22.

He glanced at it, pulled the lever back slowly, quietly. It was loaded with standard target-practice bullets. He raised it, sighting through the blurred lines of the screen door. He saw something moving. He aimed, his hands shaking, his head aching. Then it turned toward the screen door and O'Neill saw the eyes. He fired.

He heard the growl as he ran to the door and switched on the outside light. The animal — a huge raccoon that had been coming around the cabin for years, as long as he could remember — was standing in the path; stunned, confused, its body racked with a new presence under its skin.

O'Neill felt the rage. One shot would not kill it. He raised the gun, aimed, held it steady for a few seconds, and fired. The shot blew the raccoon backward. It scrambled to its feet, shaking, and then started down the path. O'Neill opened the screen door and aimed. He heard the guttural growl as the bullet hit. The raccoon staggered, then dragged itself up.

O'Neill went back to the bureau and found the pistol and a box of shells, dumped six into his hands, and loaded them into the cylinder. He walked outside; the raccoon was clawing at the ground and dragging itself down the slope. He walked up to it. He heard its ragged breathing, the rasp of breath, the gurgling of blood. He stood over it for a minute, watching it die, feeling the rage, the fury.

The last wave of pain along its fur subsided. It lay still. There was no sound. He considered it for a full minute, knowing it was dead, feeling the rage rolling over him, feeling the fury. Then he pulled back the hammer and slowly fired all six bullets into the carcass.

Dawn. The sun was moving up the sky. It exploded in a white fireball. O'Neill was jolted from his sleep. He lay still for a minute, feeling the heat of the morning sun streaming in the window.

When your hubby wants a date, it's always an emergency—

Broc rolled over, his body damp, sheets sticking to his skin. Slowly, he sat up on the edge of the bed, a heavy piece his father had crafted of oak forty years ago. His power tools in the nearby shop had not been used for years. Broc sat gazing blankly at familiar things for several minutes, the long rows of shelves lined with his mother's Book-of-the-Month-Club selections from the sixties, the pot-bellied wood stove, the wide varnished pine floorboards, the dark walls built of massive pine logs, the ancient dishes on open shelves. He looked at the green curtains; they were new a few summers ago, Darcy's handwork.

Look at my place. I keep it so nice—

The cabin was hidden in a deep forest on more than a hundred acres of wild land with eighteen hundred feet of shoreline circling the whole end of the lake. His mother's parents had bought it sometime in the 1930s for next to nothing. There was no other access to the lake, no one within miles to hear the gunshots last evening. O'Neill gazed through the trees at the crystalline water and gray rocks on the opposite shore. A mile away, the water opened out to a maze of linked lakes straddling the Wisconsin-Michigan border on the edge of the Ottawa National Forest.

Darcy… Darcy—

O'Neill moved across the room to the kitchen counter, opened the refrigerator, poured a glass of orange juice, and stared up the roadway into the trees, then into the thickness of the forest, a mix of pine and tamarack, with occasional patches of white birch and a stand of oak almost out of sight. The wind from the lake was rattling the leaves of a bigtooth aspen that alternated between glossy green and gray. The carport on its heavy pine posts sheltered Darcy's BMW. Its glossy black exterior was now steel-gray. The paint shop twenty miles outside Jefferson had finished the job in three days while he holed up in the local Holiday Inn. Using her obituary, he had changed the registration of the BMW to his own name, bought new plates, then deliberately dropped them in the trunk and screwed on his new Honda plates instead, making the car superficially untraceable.

Broc rubbed his hand across his forehead; it came away wet. He stood for a minute steadying himself against the counter, then poured water into the coffee maker. The drive from Indiana to northern Wisconsin, wilderness country beyond the Northern Highlands State Forest, had taken him three days, mostly on secondary highways. He slept at rest stops on little-used roads outside non-descript towns. It was only four hundred fifty miles, but it might as well have been ten thousand. The Land o' Lakes seemed as remote as the far side of the Moon.

He climbed into the shower. The water came in waves, a minute of blasting spray as the well pump built up pressure, then half a minute of dwindling flow. He listened to the pump cut off as he dried himself. It was a miracle it was still working. It was a nuisance to drain every fall and prime every spring. Maybe he would put in a submersible before winter.

He went to the bureau, pulled out a clean pair of shorts, then dried his hair while the coffee maker worked its morning magic. He fixed up a sandwich with mustard and three slices of beef and cheese; sitting on the front deck, he drank coffee and stared out at the blue water through the pines. The air was warm; it was the first day in three weeks that he had not had to light a wood fire to drive away the chill of late spring in the north woods.

See, Professor, we're going to have this baby in November. After that, it's all Pampers and getting up in the middle of the night. So we need to have one big fling—

This was a fling that would never happen.

He set his empty cup on the deck and walked down the rocky path. Hidden in the trees, almost invisible from both cabin and lake, the dark brown, steel-roofed boathouse stood, so far unopened. He pulled out a key, undid the padlock, and pulled out the canoe, a lightweight aluminum craft fifteen feet long, and launched it. Quietly paddling around the edge of the bay, he watched the leaf-speckled sand under the keel, golden brown in the morning sun, and the untamed thickness of the brush along the shore. It was a pleasure unchanged since he first canoed the shallow bays a quarter century ago. Sunfish and perch cruised above the sandy bottom; chipmunks chattered in the maples. Three hundred feet away, a loon floated, then disappeared. It was gone for half a minute then surfaced a hundred feet farther away.

Darcy... Darcy—

Two summers ago, they had spent a month here, paddling in the early morning, watching the fish, listening to the loons after dusk, watching the stars from the window at night. She had leaned against him in the middle of the canoe; he felt her presence, her warm mouth on his.

It's too dangerous, Professor; we can't make love in a canoe. Maybe we should go back to my place —

The trouble is your legs are too long—

Hey, Professor, let's not get personal—

O'Neill gave the paddle a furious pull, and then another, pointing the canoe across the bay. He lined up its bow with a tree on the far point and began a steady pull, long strokes, with a slight outward curve of the paddle at the end of each stroke to keep the craft aligned. He pulled, each time with more strength, throwing every fiber in his back and arms into each stroke. The fury rose in his stomach and gathered in his chest, and he drove the paddle deeper, hurling his rage against the water, speeding across the lake, driving ahead.

You're a victim of your passions, Professor—

He was halfway across. Aiming the canoe at the tree two hundred yards away, he gritted his teeth and narrowed his eyes. He thrust the paddle, throwing his strength into every stroke, feeling his muscles ache as they stretched and tightened, feeling the cold fury in his neck and jaws. His teeth were clenched, locked together like welded iron.

A huge blast erupted ahead of the canoe, a slow-motion explosion of steel and glass, a blinding fireball soaring into the sky, and everything that he loved and lived for was suddenly gone.

He gripped the gunwales, his knuckles white. He drifted, staring at the towering pines and gray rocks and the fireweed exploding on the sunlit shore. He had paddled these waters as a boy during the long summer afternoons when he visited with his grandparents; he knew every tree. They stood as they always had, great masts that had survived the snows and storms and the passing of a thousand seasons. He knew every rock; he had climbed them all. They lay as they always had, great blocks of Precambrian granite dragged down from the Canadian wilderness by moving glaciers — pieces of the Earth that had hardened two billion years ago. Permanent. The same. Always.

You think we can go on living this yuppie life forever—

Broc paddled the canoe along the shore toward the landing. He paddled slowly, letting the everlasting permanence of the world settle in, the permanence that made a mockery of everything changeable and human.

When your hubby wants a date, it's always an emergency—

Darcy. He wished she were here; he wanted her; he needed her. He wanted another day with her, another evening, another night.

He saw her spinning around in the living room, walking behind the couch, patting the pillows, turning by the fireplace, her dark eyes beckoning.

You want to come upstairs, Professor? This could be an emergency—

He hauled the canoe up the bank and into the boathouse, locked it up, and walked up the path. The raccoon lay on the pine needles darkened with blood. He looked at it, remembered the summers he and Darcy had set out bread and pieces of fish hooked out of the lake, and then watched as this same raccoon came out to feed in the gathering dusk.

O'Neill stooped and ran his fingers through the dark fur at the back of its neck, the only place on its body that was not torn apart and matted with blood. He felt a surge of sorrow and pain in his stomach. Poor misbegotten creature. Hurled into eternity by being in the wrong place at the wrong time, a victim of rage.

The morning was warming up; the cool of the cabin was welcome. The coffee maker was still on; he poured himself another cup. Life had to go on, but the way was not clear. If he forced things out of his mind, the quiet of this place would do its work, as it had been doing for three weeks. He was better now, able to stand up and move around, able to get out of bed in the morning, able to behold the water, able to paddle the canoe. But when he tried to look back, when he tried to bring into focus his life at Jefferson State, his work, the human history he had followed and lived for and written about, everything fell apart. There was no way through, no road out. Something was wrong out there, and he was powerless to set it right.

He sat by the table drinking the last mouthfuls of coffee and gazed around. His briefcase stood where he had set it three weeks ago, a reminder of the life he had left behind. He had opened it once and found the newspaper bought the morning Darcy had died, the final record of a life that had ended.

Drifting, he was drifting. He felt the need to stop drifting, to make some tiny connection with what was once meaningful. He drank another cup of coffee, emptied the coffee maker, rinsed his cup, then stood for several minutes by the window. Finally, he went to the phone, one of the earliest pushbuttons made, and dialed Jefferson State University. When the menu came on, he pushed the pound sign and then 6949, his campus extension. A few seconds later, he heard his own voice, "Broc O'Neill," and then a request for his password. In agony, he slowly punched in 32729, the numbers corresponding to DARCY on the telephone dial. He waited a few seconds, heard a beep and then a message:

Dr. O'Neil, Dr. O'Neill, I heard when I got back into town. It's awful, I can't believe it. I'm so sorry.

There was a long pause, the sound of paper crinkling, and then he heard her crying:

Dr. O'Neill, this is Christelle. I can't reach you. But I'd like to know whether you're alive. I guess you know I don't have a cell phone, but you can write to PO Box 674 at Middlebury in... That's in Vermont... Zip code is... 05... 753.

Chapter Eight

Broc settled into his seat by the window; thankful no one was seated beside him, he watched the rows of buildings and houses roll by as the airplane, an Embraer Brasilia turboprop, climbed and banked away from the Kent County International Airport southeast of Grand Rapids. The western Michigan sky was overcast. In a few minutes the wings leveled out while the plane continued climbing to its cruising altitude of twenty thousand feet on its way to Cleveland.

Broc watched the ground, dark under the clouds, for twenty minutes, until the gray of smog over Toledo appeared in the distance. He read the headlines of the *Grand Rapids Press*; then, unable to concentrate, he threw it on the seat and gripped the armrests, feeling the waves of fury rising, as they had a dozen times a day for the past month. As the rage swept over him, he clenched his teeth, feeling the pain in his jaws — pain that merged with the pain of grief and shock and overwhelming helplessness. Somewhere out there something lurked, something malicious and deadly that had destroyed Darcy and was waiting to rip out the center of his life.

Somehow — after he put his life together, after he could think without being blinded with rage — he would go after it, whatever it was, go after it and find it and destroy it as it had destroyed everything he had lived for and loved.

The connecting flight on the MD 80 jet airliner from Hopkins International Airport at Cleveland was over eastern Ohio when food was served. Through the clouds he caught flashes of the south shore of Lake Erie as he ate the last of his lunch. He watched the gray water slipping away to the north as the plane headed east. The gray sky circled overhead like a great iron dome, closing in the world. He watched the farmlands of Western Pennsylvania unrolling below, his mind numb.

After a few minutes the stewardess came by and collected garbage. O'Neill lifted his briefcase onto the empty seat and rifled through the papers. It was the first time in a month he had pondered the remnants of his academic life.

Christelle Washington's essay, which would eventually become a full-blown dissertation proposal, ran a neat four pages, with a two-page appended bibliography. He glanced over the books, noting at least four studies for each of the past four presidential administrations, and a dozen more books on economic policy from 1968 to 1992. The paper was titled 'Notes on Double-agenda Party Politics in Recent Administrations'. He read her introduction:

> Power is traditionally conferred through the electoral process according to the constitutionally defined terms of office for the President and members of Congress. Traditional wisdom says that after the term has been completed, the political power of elected officials ceases.
>
> There are, however, ways by which political power is extended beyond the term of office. The best known of these, also constitutionally defined, is the extension of presidential power, often for decades, through partisan appointments to the Supreme Court. Within Congress, political power is extended through specific acts of legislation, which continue to shape federal policy far beyond the terms of those who framed them. The most obvious example is the massive New Deal legislation of the 1930s, which extended Democratic power and shaped American life for the next half century.

Broc had not read anything for a month. Christelle's words were a reminder of his previous life surrounded by books and ideas. O'Neill lay back and closed his eyes. The world of Washington seemed so far away. The maneuverings of thousands of people, all jockeying for attention and influence and power, was a world apart — a strange and unreal realm that had no part in his life. He felt the burden of it like the iron weight of the sky, locking him in. There was so little that could be done. One person's wants and wishes, one person's life and loves, were lost under the gray dome of higher powers. He read on:

The past three decades have been particularly volatile in terms of power. A continuing budgetary crisis has pitted both political parties against one another, the specific issue being power, the specific arena being control of the budget.

Democrats have traditionally favored social legislation. In broad social programs, they acquired power, not only by expanding the percentage of the budget allocated to social programs but also by extending their influence through an enlarged bureaucracy set up to manage these programs. Some divisions of the federal government employ tens of thousands.

In recent years, the Republicans have sought to limit Democratic power. One mechanism has been to cut taxes, thus making less money available for expanded social programs. Another has been to divert major segments of the federal budget into alternate areas, most often the military. This became a specific strategy during the Reagan presidency when the Administration refueled fear of communism and expanded Republican power through the growth of a massive military bureaucracy.

Following the upset of 1994 when the Republican Party gained a majority of seats in both the House and the Senate, there has been a sharp rise in 'double-agenda' politics. This may be defined as policies framed with an ostensible purpose that can be 'sold' to the public while, in fact, serving another purpose. Most often the hidden agenda of such policies is aimed at expanding bureaucratic power, limiting the influence of the opposition, or attracting voters — with these goals achieved through manipulation of the budget. Almost all plans to appropriate funds, reduce the deficit, balance the budget or reform the federal tax structure involve 'double-agenda politics.'

There was more, all of it persuasively worked out. It seemed a responsible use of available data to support a philosophically intriguing theory. O'Neill was impressed, though he was not surprised. Christelle Washington had proven herself an astute observer of the passing political

72

scene. Her observations were always clearly focused. It would be a good dissertation.

The plane landed at 6:38 p.m. at Newark International Airport, a few minutes early; it was over two hours until his connecting flight. O'Neill retrieved his luggage and headed for the restroom, where he locked himself in a stall and checked the contents of his suitcases. He realized he was paranoid, but he had never had this much money in his hands before. Darcy's life insurance policy, one of the fringe benefits of employment with Sanderson & Sanderson, had been paid into his account in Jefferson: an even two million dollars. He was carrying ninety-thousand dollars in cash.

Driving across the northern peninsula of Michigan, then south, he had reached Kalamazoo on June 26th, found an apartment, signed a lease under a fictitious name, paid twelve months advance rent, and ordered furniture for living room, kitchen, and bedroom — paying cash for everything. He had stocked the refrigerator and food cupboard with sodas and general supplies that would remain intact for months. At a local second-hand bookstore, he had picked up a couple of years of back issues of *National Geographic*; a Dallas Cowboys Cheerleaders calendar for the current year, which he hung in the kitchen; a few innocuous paperbacks, Westerns and detective mysteries; and enough randomly-chosen props to make the apartment appear occupied should the manager prove nosey enough to take a tour.

On July 2nd he drove to Lansing, withdrew cash, and opened a bank account. Back in Kalamazoo, he bundled the cash between heavy cardboard the size of hardback books and divided the bundles into two suitcases mixed with several newly purchased hardbacks. If asked at the airport, which it turned out he was not, he would be a professor on a research trip to major university libraries in New England. A self-storage facility next to the Kalamazoo apartments provided the main reason for his choice of location. He had rented a garage-sized unit far to the rear of the complex, which featured 24/7 gate access, and paid a year's rent in advance. During the evening of July 7th, he had pulled Darcy's newly washed car into the garage, removed the battery and locked it in the trunk along with a battery charger from Walmart that would allow him to get the car started weeks or months from now. Finally, he added a case-hardened padlock to the storage-unit door. The vehicle, disguised with a new paint job and new plates registered to his non-existent Honda, was now so well hidden that all material traces of his former life had vanished.

On the morning of July 8th, O'Neill walked two blocks and caught a nine-a.m. bus for the fifty-mile ride to Grand Rapids. Assured ahead of time that he was certain to find a seat on the plane on the mid-afternoon flight, O'Neill found the sales representative correct; he paid cash for a 3:40 flight to Cleveland with a connecting flight to Newark, New Jersey. Scheduled arrival, 6:49 p.m.

O'Neill left the restroom stall. Satisfied that his suitcase contents were intact, he checked them through from Newark for the final leg of his trip, a flight to Burlington, Vermont; bought himself a copy of *The New York Times*; and found a table toward the back of the airport diner. After a ham-and-cheese sandwich and two cups of coffee, he read most of the paper, including various articles and speculative editorials on the political conventions coming up next month when the parties would make official their candidates for the November election. Clinton was fueling Democratic fears with warnings that Dole, in company with Newt Gingrich and the Republican Congress, would slash taxes and trim long-standing social programs.

O'Neill gazed out the huge glass windows, watching the blinking lights of planes landing and taking off in the gathering darkness. It seemed that Dole would be the candidate for the Republicans, Clinton for the Democrats.

At twenty-five minutes to nine, O'Neill folded the newspaper and opened his briefcase. Christelle's desperate message on his university-office voicemail had brought him back to reality. He had thought about it for a couple of hours, then typed a brief reply, found an envelope, and driven from the cabin to mail it at Eagle River, twenty miles from the cabin. O'Neill's mother had died more than a dozen years ago, but he had kept her postal box open. The key hung by the back door of the cabin. He used her P. O. box number as his return address and paid the annual fee to keep it open for yet another year, leaving it, like the property, in her name, which was not 'O'Neill' but the name of his grandfather, who had passed away decades ago. His note to Christelle advised printing rather than writing her reply and addressing the letter to his deceased mother; and he included a likely arrival date for a flight to Vermont. He asked her to confirm by mail.

Broc pulled out her reply, which he had carried ever since opening it in Wisconsin, and reread the last paragraph:

> With your likely arrival time in mind, I'll plan to spend two days, July 7th and 8th, at Burlington, at the Fletcher Library, from around two o'clock each day until about nine. There is a good selection of books useful for my dissertation. I'll go out for supper at five and be back by six and I'll make sure I'm sitting within sight of the reference desk. The library telephone number is 802-865-7217. Just tell the librarian what I look like. I'll pick you up at the airport.
>   All the best,
>   Christelle

He was not sure whether it had been wise to contact Christelle, but she wanted to talk to him and he needed to talk to someone. He knew he could not hide forever in the Wisconsin woods. He was reluctant to burden anyone with his grief, certainly not an innocent student, but Christelle was different. Her words on his voicemail caught him by surprise; he was momentarily lifted out of his grief by her concern, by the realization that someone cared. Christelle had known Darcy well and sent her birthday cards. Once he and Darcy had met her in the mall; after that, Darcy and Christelle had gone shopping together two or three times. Darcy had approved of her; she would have been touched and moved to hear the plaintive grief in Christelle's words.

I can't find you, but I'd like to know whether you're alive—

O'Neill dialed the Fletcher Library. He had chosen to arrive late, giving Christelle the full two days of research she had planned. A thin little voice came on the phone; O'Neill pictured a little old bespectacled lady managing a sleepy reference desk.

"Auburn hair? Oh yes. Mister, I can see her from here. She's been here all day. Awfully nice girl, and she's got the prettiest hazel eyes. Are you her father?"

O'Neill hesitated, and then on impulse said yes.

"Just a minute, Mister, I'll get her. What's your name?"

"O'Neill. Broc O'Neill."

Christelle came on the phone a minute later. "Oh, Dr. O'Neill" — she giggled — "this funny little librarian called me Miss O'Neill. Anyway, I've been looking at my watch. I was afraid you wouldn't call."

"Well, Miss O'Neill, I'll be boarding in ten minutes, but, look, I'm pretty sure you should not get mixed up in this. I just want to say ahead of time, if you change your mind, I'll move on tomorrow. I'll understand—"

"Dr. O'Neill, there is not a chance in the world I would change my mind!"

O'Neill was silent for a few seconds, moved by the sincerity of her voice. "Okay, I'll be landing at Burlington International in ninety minutes; the ticket says I'll get in at ten minutes after ten."

"Just come out the private pickup exit. You know my car."

Christelle saw Dr. O'Neill, wearing denims and a light jacket, come through the glass doors at 10:25 p.m. He had a suitcase in each hand and his briefcase tucked under his arm. Why didn't he get himself a buggy? As soon as the thought crossed her mind, she knew it was silly; he was over six feet tall and handled the luggage with ease. He was pretty rugged looking. She remembered he had some kind of framed award in his office for a mountain climb, someplace out West, she thought.

She tooted the horn; winding among cars and taxis, he started toward her. He looked the same except for the shock of his chestnut hair, which was longer than she remembered. She had known him casually for over two years, but she had a sudden sense that she had known him much longer. Maybe it was the boyish flop of his hair over his forehead. As he came closer, she thought he seemed a little worn.

She pulled the lever to pop the trunk and got out, smiling as he set down the suitcases. "Hi." Feeling awkward, she shoved out her hand and he shook it, and held it limply for a few seconds. He smiled at her— as though from a great distance. They packed the suitcases into the trunk. As he walked around to the passenger side and she got in, Christelle felt a sudden wave of sorrow. Darcy was dead. It seemed impossible. She turned toward him for a few seconds and then, unable to control herself, she buried her face in her hands and burst into tears.

"I'm sorry. I just can't believe... I can't believe Darcy... is... is gone." She sobbed, unable to hold back the sudden surge of grief. "I can't... believe... all this has happened."

After a minute, she sat up and wiped her eyes and looked at him again. She shouldn't have done that. Dr. O'Neill looked shaken. He lifted his briefcase over the back of the seat and put it in the rear of the car. "Believe me, Christelle," he uttered tonelessly, "I can't believe any of this either." He seemed to be holding himself in another world.

She watched him as he stared out the windshield, but she could tell his eyes were not seeing anything. She started the car, dried her face on her sleeve, and pulled out into the traffic. In a few minutes they were out heading east on Highway 89.

"That place in Wisconsin where you were staying — is that the place you and Darcy used to go sometimes?" She felt guilty for mentioning Darcy again.

"It's a cabin in the woods. It belonged to my mother, and her father before that. There aren't any neighbors. The nearest house is more than a mile away. I needed someplace to be alone for a while."

He also needed some place to hide, Christelle thought, but the time was not right for bringing that up. Instead, she said: "It sounds wonderful, peaceful and nice. I hope I didn't drag you away."

His head was turned toward the side window. "I guess I needed to be dragged away. Being alone is no way to deal with grief."

Christelle signaled right and entered the ramp onto Highway 116, a picturesque road that wound south into the hills. The summer dusk was settling over the land; the last rays of the sun lit up the summit of Camel's Hump.

"Since you like those sorts of lonely spots, you'll like my sister's place. The neighbors are a little closer than a mile, but none of them are around except in winter. It's a mountain village for skiers. It's kind of peaceful and nice this time of year. We'll be there in about half an hour."

They drove on quietly as the darkness settled. She slowed for Hinesburg, and another ten miles down the road for Starksboro.

Broc stared out the window toward the darkening western sky. He felt dead, beaten down by events of the last five weeks, unable to bring anything into focus. He glanced over at Christelle; her profile was barely visible in the soft light from the dashboard. He thought he should talk, but he didn't know what to say. He stared again into the darkness, wondering why he had come. Innocent kid. He had no business imposing on her. He had simply written that he was coming. She hardly had any choice but to say 'yes.' If he'd thought it through, he would have stayed in Wisconsin.

The western sky was dark over the valley. He would stay a few days. It would be nice to have someone to talk to, and then he would disappear again. Where, he wasn't sure. Maybe Kalamazoo. Maybe the Wisconsin woods again—

"Damn!"

Christelle's eyes were lit up by light reflected from the rearview mirror. He felt the car surge ahead as she hit the gas.

"That car's been following us for miles."

O'Neill turned in his seat. The headlights were half a mile back. "You've made only one turn. Maybe it's just on the same road."

"Maybe, but I had this strange feeling at the airport. There was this guy standing near the door."

O'Neill watched ahead as their lights lit up the road. Her Grand Am must be cruising at seventy. A minute later he saw a sign; abruptly, Christelle was braking.

"I guess we'll find out," she said, heading into the left turn at the last instant, tires screaming. O'Neill felt himself pressed against the door. The car surged up the road as it began to gain elevation.

"Is this the way?"

"No, this heads back toward the ski hills. Glen Ellen, Sugarbush. I just want to lose him." O'Neill turned and stared out the back window.

"I knew it! That car made the turn; it is following us!"

The Grand Am roared into another turn and headed uphill into a series of switchbacks. Christelle pushed the car to fifty on every straightway, then slowed to forty at the curves, a cautious thirty-five if she had to. O'Neill watched the headlights behind, which came into view, then disappeared; they were holding their distance at a little more than half a mile.

"I hate this!" He heard the anger in her voice. "I hate these guys that watch you, and stalk you, and follow you in their cars. I hate it!"

The car came out of a turn onto a straightaway and Christelle hit the gas. The big motor — it had to be an eight cylinder — surged ahead. O'Neill pulled the end of his seat belt a little tighter across his chest. The car roared uphill.

"Holy blazes! You know where you're going?"

"Every road, trail, and squirrel run within fifty miles. I spent all my summers here with Sis."

The road ran straight for a good mile, a steep hill rising on their left, a dark embankment on their right. The Grand Am roared up the grade like a plane ready to soar into the sky. He guessed they were hitting seventy-five and still accelerating. He monitored the back window. Christelle had taken the other car by surprise; the half mile had lengthened by a couple of hundred yards.

She headed the Grand Am into another leftward turn. He heard the tires screaming; the following headlights were out of sight. He caught his breath as he sensed the blackness and the drop-off over the right shoulder of the road.

Christelle began braking. A hundred yards up the next straightway she switched off the lights and did a sudden U-turn, pulling the car to a stop in the middle of the road. For a few seconds they sat facing downhill in complete darkness. What on Earth was she doing? She let off the brake. The car began to roll slowly down the road.

"I'm going to teach this guy a thing or two!"

O'Neill tensed and gripped the armrest as he watched the lights coming up the road, hidden by the high embankment now on their right, brightening as the car came up on the turn. Christelle hit the gas pedal; the tires peeled, and the car roared down the center of the road. The pursuing car came around the bend, but before its headlights could sweep around, Christelle tramped her car into overdrive and turned on her high beams.

O'Neill gripped the door and seat. The other car was big and heavy and going too fast; Christelle's headlights must have blinded the driver. Its right tires slipped onto the gravel and it began to slide. As it roared past, they heard the staccato crack of an automatic weapon and the metallic clunk as bullets tore into the side of Christelle's Grand Am. A second later, the pursuing car, out of control, went over the embankment.

Christelle braked and skidded to a stop. She opened the door and O'Neill caught her wide startled eyes in the sudden light; and then she was out of the car — they were both out of the car — running back up the pavement.

They stood at the edge of the embankment. Three hundred feet down the jagged rocky slope, the car lay on its side against a huge pine tree, its crushed roof glinting in the red glare of flames shooting from under the sprung hood. Stunned, they stared at the wreckage. The only sound was the crackle of fire catching the pine needles above. It flared as spilled oil caught fire.

"Let's get out of here, Christelle. That car's going to explode and set the mountain on fire."

Chapter Nine

They stood in the lighted garage, the trunk of the Grand Am open, O'Neill's luggage on the floor. O'Neill ran his finger along the rear fender on the driver's side. The gray metal was punctured by bullet holes, three on the fender, three on the rear door, all six spaced about eight inches apart along a line just below the window. A seventh bullet had smashed the taillight.

O'Neill opened the back door. The foremost bullet had entered just behind the front door, torn through the vinyl interior, and entered the backrest of the driver's seat. It had missed Christelle by less than an inch. He broke into a cold sweat. He turned to Christelle, who was leaning against the workbench. Her face was drained of color; her eyes were wide with terror; her lips were trembling.

O'Neill took her arm and led her into the house, found the light switch, and guided her to the couch. He watched her for a few seconds as she stared blankly into space. He went back to the garage, turned off the light and opened the garage door. He stood for a minute in the darkness, then crossed the grass to the edge of the cleared ground. The lawn ran to the edge of a hill that fell away to pine-clad slopes. In the darkness he could sense the bulk of nearby mountains. Off to the left, a dozen miles away he guessed, he could see a red glow where their pursuing car had exploded and ignited the trees; above, he could see the flashing lights of an emergency helicopter circling. A police cruiser on the road flashed preternatural blue and red.

O'Neill closed the garage door and hauled his luggage inside. "I ran him… ran him right off the road." She stared at him, biting her lip. Then her eyes began to well with tears and her voice broke up.

"They're going to… to come after me. They're going to… take me in for murder."

O'Neill sat beside her on the couch; he felt the need to stay calm, to allay her fears. "Christelle, we were lucky to get away with our lives.

There were two in that car; there was somebody driving and someone else with an automatic weapon. The car window was open; the gun was loaded; the gunman was ready. He tried to kill us."

Trying to take in what he said, she looked at him, her eyes terrified, her hands shaking.

"Whoever they were, they would have chased us to the ski lift and filled us with bullets under a ski tow. Your daring little escapade saved us—"

"They're going to come after me. They'll want me for murder. Does Vermont have the death penalty?"

"Don't think so. One state east, New Hampshire, yes."

"I'll be in prison forever—" She was shaking.

"It was an act of self-defense. Anyway, there's no sign of anything up on that road other than a car going too fast and skidding out of control. We were at least five miles away before it exploded. No one saw it happen, and we didn't pass another car all the way here."

"They'll find the bullet holes in my car."

She wasn't thinking clearly. Her car was in the garage. O'Neill got up and looked around. On the kitchen counter stood a bottle of Bacardi. "You want something to drink?"

She nodded mechanically; he went and found some Coke and ice, mixed her a drink, and put it in her hands. Expressionless, she looked at him as she swallowed a mouthful.

He spoke calmly. "We'll keep your car out of sight until we figure out what to do. Then we'll find somebody who does body work, no questions asked. I don't think it would be a good idea to put in a claim on your insurance."

"Oh, God! Daddy will kill me!"

"It's his car?"

"It was his graduation gift when I got my master's. He says he'll pay the insurance until I get my doctorate. But I can't tell him. He already thinks I was crazy for moving from California to Indiana. He says it's full of NRA militia and right-wing survivalist camps. He'll be sure some of them shot my car. He says I'm living in Midwest Redville."

O'Neill was reminded once again that intelligent people sometimes have Neanderthal parents.

"He's going to wonder what kind of life I'm leading."

"You could point out that your car collected bullet holes in Vermont, not Indiana."

Christelle shook her head. "If it's not California, it's guerrilla country."

"I hope his political views are not hereditary." O'Neill went outside. The red glow was almost gone, the circling helicopter lights were gone. Standing in the dark, he wondered what the hell was going on.

Christelle wiggled her head and arms into the holes of a pale blue cotton blouse and ran a brush through her hair, still damp from her shower. The morning air was chilly; she pulled on a pair of long white socks and found her sister's après-ski boots in the closet, pulled the legs of her jeans down over the boots, and then buttoned up a baggy leaf-green sweater with a British label in the collar.

She walked softly down the hall to the kitchen. The door to Dr. O'Neill's bedroom was still closed. They had stayed up talking late in the night, but she had awakened after only four hours of sleep, lain in bed for an hour, and then decided she was not destined to sleep again until sunset. It was eight twenty. The sun was up; it was going to be a brighter day than yesterday.

Christelle drank down half a glass of orange juice; feeling hungry, she decided to wait until Dr. O'Neill got up. She went to the cupboard and got out a mixing bowl. Within a quarter hour she had preheated the oven and whipped up a batch of wheat muffins. Then she filled the coffee maker with water and shoveled five level scoops into the filter for ten cups worth according to the marks on the glass, enough for five big mugs.

The machine was gurgling when she sat down at the table with Dr. O'Neill's article offprint. Looking at it for the first time since he had autographed it in his office, she read the title: "An Early Policy Directive from President Truman: The Origins of Domestic Clandestine Operations by the National Security Agency."

She had skimmed through most of it when the screen door opened and Dr. O'Neill came in wearing denims and a plaid cotton shirt. "Something smells awfully good."

"My goodness! I thought you were still sleeping. Where were you?"

"Took a run up the road. Beautiful mountain."

"Do you do this every morning?"

"Well, my schedule has been a little disrupted. But, yes, I started again over the Independence Day break in Kalamazoo. I feel better after a little running." He paused a few seconds, then observed, "You seem better this morning. You were pretty rattled last night."

"I think you are right. All they could find was a car driving too fast on a mountain road. There's no evidence another car was there. And my car is hidden, so I guess we are safe for a while."

"Safe in a really nice place." Broc swept his eyes around the room. "Cedar paneling, granite fireplace." He motioned to the huge front window. "Great view, too."

"I love it!" Christelle declared. "I spent many summers here with Joyce when I was a kid. She's my big sister."

"I noticed a rack of skis in the garage. Do you spend winters here, too?"

"Christmas vacations when I was in high school." Christelle walked to the front window and pointed. "That trail leads to the ski slopes. It's about a quarter mile to the chair lifts. You can ski out in the morning, and in the afternoon ski down another trail that comes in behind the house."

"Pretty convenient for your sister and hubby."

"Yes, Joyce and Roy both work from home, so they live here all year round. Almost everyone else goes back to the city in the summer. The neighbors next door live in Burlington; others are from Amherst and Boston." She headed to the refrigerator and brought back butter and marmalade. "For the muffins," she said, opening the oven and bringing out the steaming pan. She set it on an iron trivet on the table. "I've got some cream here, too, Dr. O'Neill." He sat down at the table as she brought two mugs and poured the coffee.

"Since we're grounded here for a while, Miss Washington, perhaps you should call me Broc."

She smiled. "Okay, Broc. First thing, have a muffin."

She watched as he pulled one from the muffin pan, then a second, which he offered to her. The smell of the fresh baking filled the air. "No doubt about it," he assured her, gesturing with a muffin and his knife, "we've got some formidable talent here."

"Maybe if I live long enough, I'll learn how to do spaghetti."

Broc glanced at her; he realized she was still thinking about last night's shooting.

"Second thing," she said, breaking open a muffin and spreading marmalade, "this whole thing is very scary."

Broc nodded slowly. "It's the second time I've been shot at in six weeks. And in between, my car blew up."

She saw the sudden grief come into his eyes. *Oh, God! He's been through a lot—*

She watched him until the look passed, and then she saw the coldness in his eyes, a fleeting rage that made her realize how events had shattered his life. And then it, too, passed.

"I meant this," she clarified, holding up the offprint of his article, autographed in his office more than a month ago. "I've read it twice. It's a complicated history, and I don't know whether I understand all of it."

"The journal where you found it — *American Documentary History* — is pretty specialized. It assumes readers with a lot of background."

"Well, yes, I guess you'll have to fill me in. All I'm sure of is that it is pretty scary."

"The history of intelligence is depressing. What don't you understand?"

"Well, the Harry Truman connection, for one thing."

O'Neill swallowed a mouthful of coffee. "Truman came into office at a turning point in history. Spring 1945. Most people think of his decision to bomb Hiroshima, but there's more to it than that. The end of World War II pushed him into some very complicated decisions."

"Like what?"

"Probably, the Cold War was the main thing. That's what everything in the next several years boiled down to. Containing the Soviet Union, holding back Communism."

"And how's this connected?" Christelle asked, touching the offprint.

"It all has to do with intelligence. The most dramatic part, of course, has always been the breaking of secret codes. Not many people know the full story, but we've had a group of cryptographers working for the government for years, all the way back to World War I. And always top secret."

She watched him spreading marmalade. "With World War II, cryptography became big business. There were secret communications between the U.S. and England during the years of planning that went into the Normandy invasion. Monitoring and decoding enemy messages — German messages in Europe, Japanese messages in the Pacific, maybe even messages between Germany and Japan. President Roosevelt had a pretty good sense of new lines of power that were developing. He made sure that the whole area of intelligence was well funded. By the end of the war there were hundreds of personnel involved."

"And President Truman inherited it all."

O'Neill nodded as he spread more marmalade. "Inherited it without really knowing anything in advance, just like he inherited the atomic bomb. Actually, considering how little he had been told as Vice President, it's remarkable that Truman managed to get any of it in focus. Anyway, after the War, things got complicated. Wartime intelligence had been gathered in the field, so the Army was involved, and from ships, so the Navy was involved. There were false messages planted to fool Hitler: counterintelligence. New encryption technologies had emerged, which meant major commitments to research and development, and new facilities — listening posts, sensitive interceptors underwater and in the air. Covert operations came into the picture, activities that our government could not own up to."

"It's much more extensive than I ever imagined," she admitted.

"Huge, really big and complicated. Then the Cold War started, which tangled things even more. The Soviet Union became our enemy, and most of our intelligence was directed at intercepting Soviet messages. Then Mao Tse-Tung came to power in China, and the Cold War spread to Asia. Infiltration, spying, all kinds of clandestine activity. The whole thing soon became a Hydra monster with too many heads to count. It needed organization. That was where President Truman came in. He brought some order to it all and laid out the basic pattern of American intelligence still in operation today."

Christelle looked at the article, then at O'Neill.

He went on: "It started with the National Security Act of 1947. Then in 1949, the Central Intelligence Agency Act."

"The CIA!"

O'Neill nodded. "All of it top secret, part of the Department of Defense. But the most secretive was the National Security Agency that Truman chartered. It went into operation quietly, symbolically, at 12:01 a.m. November 4th, 1952, the day Dwight Eisenhower was elected as the next president."

"So it really was Truman's legacy for every president who followed."

"Yes, and it was as secret as they could make it. For years the CIA operated without people even knowing it existed, all through the Eisenhower and Kennedy and Johnson years, right through the Vietnam War and through the Nixon administration. It was twenty years later, when President Ford established the Rockefeller Commission, that the full range of CIA operations became known to the public. And a lot of the stuff the CIA was doing — covert operations, secret wars — was highly questionable. There was a big shakedown."

"What about the National Security Agency?"

"A whole different story. Absolutely secret. The NSA is so secret it's often called No Such Agency. Congress hardly knew what they did. Many people still don't. All we know is the NSA is supposed to intercept messages and decode them. And it's supposedly limited to international messages. Domestic surveillance is out of bounds."

"Well, why the secrecy? Why have we been kept in the dark?"

"It's hard to know, but it makes me think the NSA may be engaged in more than international surveillance. Most of the documents are still classified. And not just documents generated by the NSA. I mean the original founding documents. They're called NSCIDs: National Security Council Intelligence Directives. The most controversial one was NSCID No. 9, which stated that any government orders or policies concerning intelligence gathering would not apply to these agencies unless they included actual wording stating they applied."

"That's ridiculous! That's like a law I claim does not apply to me unless the congressional bill actually uses my name!"

"Exactly."

Christelle got up and poured some more coffee. "But, suppose Congress was just very careful. Suppose they made sure that any bill that could apply to the NSA named the NSA. Wouldn't that cover it?"

"It would if Congress knew precisely what the NSA was chartered to do. But with the charter documents classified, we don't know everything the NSA is authorized to do. It's difficult to write bills addressing or limiting powers that remain undefined."

Christelle sat down again, her eyes glancing down at the offprint. "Then, what you found among those Truman papers, what you call 'an early policy directive', is, you think—"

"An earlier draft of NSCID No. 9."

"And so it's not secret any more. Your article in *American Documentary History* has declassified it, hasn't it?"

"Not quite. You might notice I didn't print the actual text of the document. But calling for a congressional investigation might force declassification. And what would be declassified is an early draft, not the later one actually in force."

"But if I understand it, that early draft, if it had become official, would have allowed the NSA to do things that no one ever suspected, like conduct domestic intelligence operations."

"Yes. It's possible that President Truman's first idea was to monitor everyone, maybe with the idea of combatting domestic crime."

"Clandestine activity on American soil: phone tapping, eavesdropping, surveillance."

O'Neill nodded. "Without a court order. And this may have been going on for the past forty years. On the other hand, he may have changed his mind. But without knowing what the final document says, we don't know."

"But," Christelle said, digging out another muffin, "the Democrats have been screaming for years about domestic spying. You know, every so often there's a leak. They've been saying it's all illegal and any president who used domestic surveillance has broken the law and should be impeached. Does this mean that, after all, domestic spying would turn out to be okay?"

O'Neill paused. "It's not entirely clear. But If NSCID No. 9 were in force today and if it is anything like this early draft, then domestic spying without a warrant might be legally defensible; that is, until a case comes to the Supreme Court. They might rule it unconstitutional. Until then, it would be hard to prosecute. Meanwhile, it may have been okay all along. Complaints surfacing now sound like this is a new thing, but domestic surveillance could be the dirtiest secret of the past half century. If this is what we find, the American public will be outraged to learn that domestic eavesdropping has been going on, possibly legally, through the past eight presidencies."

Christelle shook her head, her eyes wide with disbelief.

"The one important fact, however," Broc continued, "is that we don't know whether that provision was expunged from NSCID No. 9 before it was passed because the final version is still classified."

He looked across the table at Christelle for a long minute. She was a political science major but had probably never explored the darker side of her field. Her eyes showed her disturbance as she cut another muffin in half and drank a mouthful of coffee.

"Broc, are you thinking what I'm thinking?"

"Maybe. What are you thinking?"

"First, that your finding could exonerate the whole intelligence community."

"I have misgivings about that. I hate the idea that domestic spying might be legal; it appalls me that an investigation might actually give the NSA a clean slate. What else are you thinking?"

"Have you considered that your article is a threat to the NSA. You're calling for a Senate investigation that might expose decades of spying? And you wrote in no uncertain terms that even if it is legal, it's not ethical. It looks like someone wants to squash your article and a Senate investigation."

O'Neill felt the same anger he always felt about powers that might threaten academic inquiry. He had always believed in free speech, in academic freedom, in the right of the intellectual — the scholar, the journalist — to investigate, to find, and to publish findings. And he had the legal right, too! The courts had established that when they upheld the right of *The New York Times* to publish *The Pentagon Papers*, excerpts from a classified Department of Defense history of the Vietnam War. Free inquiry, free speech was basic to America, a cornerstone of his profession, the foundation of his rights as a thinking citizen. But the evidence pointed in another direction. Christelle saw it, and he was forced to see it, too.

He looked across the table into Christelle's eyes. He watched her struggling with her words. "That's why," she said quietly, "that's why Darcy died, isn't it?"

He stood up; walked to the window; stared over the valley. *He saw Darcy roll her eyes as she went through the door; he saw her walk across the parking lot toward the Honda; he saw her — God! If he could only forget!* He turned and faced Christelle, his stomach knotted, unable to acknowledge what he knew was true.

"That drive-by shooting was no accident, either," she said. "And it was your Honda. That bomb in the car was meant for you, wasn't it?"

O'Neill nodded, unable to speak.

"And the burglary of Dr. Creighton's house—"

"What!" O'Neill turned, startled. "What did you say?"

"I phoned Dr. Creighton. I was trying to... I was trying to find you. He told me he had been burglarized. He lost all kinds of papers from his study, including your article — except he made a copy and it's in his office."

"Damn! How in the hell!" O'Neill flung himself around, flaying his fists in empty air. "How would anyone know he had my article?"

"You told the class you had worked on projects with Dr. Creighton. I wrote down his name."

After a minute of staring out the window, he turned to her again. She was watching him, calmly, steadily, coolly. "I just don't know what is going on," she said, "but we had better figure this out soon, or you — maybe you and I — will not be alive much longer."

Chapter Ten

"Is there any other possibility?"

O'Neill eyed the cell phone that he had taken out of his briefcase and set carefully on the table. Christelle eyed it as though it were a cobra. "How many times have you used it?"

O'Neill thought a minute. "I phoned Darcy from Indianapolis the day before she died. We made plans to meet at the Jefferson Chicken Diner. There's no other way anyone could have known I would be there."

"And you phoned me last night to say when you'd be landing. That's got to be how they knew where you were. Did you use it up there in the Wisconsin woods?"

"No, never took it out of my briefcase. I guess that's why they didn't find me. But I remember now: I called Alan Creighton to tell him I was sending the article. I phoned Darcy from the mall, and then Alan, right after I got the telephone."

"Got the telephone?"

"The day we talked in the parking lot. My first cell phone went bad a couple of days earlier. It was full of static... *Damn!* They did it! Somebody wrecked my phone. I had it for less than a month and then it went bad. So I had to trade it in for a new one! And the only replacement in stock, they said, was this model, available from Worldwide Communications!"

Christelle and Broc looked at each other, then at the telephone.

"Don't touch it!" she exclaimed, then turned to him. "I told you that article scared me!"

Broc shook his head, stunned. Could that be it? He had stumbled onto documents half a century old, and now he was running for his life. He had called for an investigation of current surveillance practices and somebody was very upset. His telephone calls had allowed them to track him so they could kill him. This must be a huge organization. He could get rid of the telephone, but there was little else he could do that would not leave a trail. One mistake, and they would get him, and maybe now Christelle, too. It was only a matter of time.

It was twenty minutes before midnight when O'Neill pulled the twenty-six-foot U-Haul into the parking lot of Robb Walker's Auto Shop just outside Waterbury. Two men came out from the lighted office and motioned him to turn. O'Neill backed the trailer into the open shop door. Christelle pulled up in her sister's Mercury Grand Marquis as he stepped out of the truck.

"Christelle! Wow! It's nice to see you again!" one of the men said as he walked toward her.

"Robb's folks have a cabin near ours," she said to O'Neill. "We used to pal around during summer holidays. Robb, this is a teacher from my university, Professor Broc O'Neill."

O'Neill shook his hand; Robb nodded and headed to the back of the U-Haul.

Robb's friend stepped up. "Dillon Shaver," he said, sticking out his hand. "Never went to university. I did a year at college, certificate in electronics. Your car shot up, eh?"

Eh...! Dillon Shaver must be from Canada— For a minute O'Neill thought he was looking at a younger brother. Shaver was Broc's height and build, with the same hair and eyes. He was wearing a vinyl identification plate above his pocket with the words 'Bell Communications' in blue letters under his name.

O'Neill shook his hand. "Then you may be the man we're looking for."

The whistle was shrill. Broc, Christelle, and Dillon walked to the rear of the U-Haul. Robb was inside, standing beside the Grand Am.

"This is a nice car, Christelle," Robb said, "but these bullet holes sure have messed it up. And gray doesn't seem to suit you." With eyebrows raised, he ran his fingers along the fender from hole to hole. "Getting into scrapes as usual?" She looked a little sheepish. Broc had never imagined her as an adolescent, much less getting into 'scrapes.' She had always seemed the perfect lady.

"I've already ordered a new rear door, quarter panel, and tail light," Robb went on. "They may be here tomorrow. We should have this fixed up in a few days. And don't worry: we'll keep this baby out of sight until we're done."

Christelle smiled at him, obviously relieved she did not have to offer an explanation.

"Any chance you need a color change on this baby?"

Christelle turned to O'Neill, who nodded. "Probably a good idea, just in case."

Robb brought out a color chart. "Gray was Daddy's choice. How about this?" She pointed to the forest green.

"Okay. That would be my choice, too. Suits you better. You want similar detailing?"

"That was Daddy's choice, not mine, so just plain green."

In another minute they had the rear ramps in place and Robb was climbing into the car. As he started up the engine, she brought the telephone out of her handbag.

"Mr. Shaver, we don't know what the story is here, only that this telephone may be bugged."

Dillon picked it up, turned it over, and swiveled a lever. "In that case," he said, sliding out the battery pack, "we better disable it, eh?" He turned it over two or three times. "Nice phone, a little like some of the new ones, but a little different, too." He picked up a flashlight and shone it where the battery pack had been. "Chinese writing. And a name, Hai Phong Electronics. No telling where that's located. You want me to go over it?"

"Considering what's happened to Broc and me, I think this is important. So, yes, see what you can discover."

O'Neill had been on Christelle's desktop computer all day except for an hour when they had eaten dinner. It sat on a desk with a printer near the window where he could survey the pines and a forested mountain a mile away. Cardboard packaging and diskettes lay beside the monitor. *Windows 95*, he noted. State of the art.

It turned out Christelle could cook — baked potato, pepper steak, and broccoli — served up with a bottle of Glen Ellen dinner wine. Broc could still feel the comfortable warmth in his stomach, which was fortunate because he had been wrestling with a maze of computer screens and files for hours. The endless corridors of the Internet were frustrating, but his life depended on finding something. What, he did not know. But somewhere out there in the web of electronic records there might be answers.

He glanced past the computer to the deck where Christelle was sitting, her feet resting on the edge of a cedar planter. A couple of overhead lights gave a dim glow. She was wearing what seemed her favorite garb, a pair of faded blue jeans, a baggy British sweater, and a forest green tam o'shanter. It was pleasant being with her; it was a welcome change after nearly a month of isolation in the north woods. They had taken long walks every day up the mountain and explored trails around the flanks of the mountain. He was glad he had come. She listened for as long as he needed to talk and then she talked about her own past, her life in California, her family.

Christelle jumped up as the headlights shone through the trees. A minute later the U-Haul pulled in and Robb Walker and Dillon Shaver got out. O'Neill struggled on with various screens, clicking from one to other, following leads. Finally, as Christelle's Grand Am rolled down the ramp, he got up and went outside.

The car had a gleaming new forest green paint job and no sign of the recent damage. Robb opened the back door; the upholstery had been repaired with liquid leather.

"It's beautiful! I can't believe it. It's like new." Christelle beamed.

"Here's a bunch of souvenirs." Robb poured six mutilated bullets into her hand. "These were in the door, the trunk, and your seat."

Christelle's hand shook.

"Here's something else." Robb handed her a pair of New Hampshire license plates. "They're from a car that came in last week. It was totaled. If you need to hide ownership or residency for any reason, get rid of those Indiana plates and use these."

"Okay, good idea. Now hang on while I get my purse."

As Broc heard the screen door slam, he stepped forward and pulled out his wallet. "I'm going to pay for this," he told Robb. "It was my fault it happened. What's the bill?"

"Twenty-eight hundred and thirty."

"You gave her a deal because she's an old friend, but let's calculate this job for me, a stranger." O'Neill peeled off thirty-two one hundred-dollar bills and handed them to Robb, then counted out another fifteen hundred and held the bills out to Dillon. "Did you bring them?"

Dillon Shaver nodded and passed him the envelope. O'Neill put it in his pocket. Shaver flattened the cash and shoved it in his wallet just as Christelle came out the door with her handbag.

"What have you found out?" O'Neill queried.

Shaver stepped over to the truck and retrieved the cell phone. "Where in hell did you get this?"

"A phone outlet in Jefferson, Indiana. Worldwide Communications. I think it's a nationwide franchise."

Shaver shook his head. "This is the most amazing thing. First of all, it's a bloody well-made instrument with some of the best electronics I've seen. I spent a good hour going over it and couldn't find a thing. Looks perfectly normal. But you said it might be bugged, eh? Well, it is."

Dillon moved the lever and slid out the battery pack. With another twist he had the earphone off. "First thing, when it's sitting on the table or riding around in your car, it's harmless. It doesn't have a tracking chip. They're pretty rare, though I suspect GPS trackers will be standard in a few years. This phone was not designed to track people, but to listen in on calls. Since you were tracked here, it must have been because you gave away your location during a phone conversation."

O'Neill nodded. In both attempts on his life, he had stated where he would be and at what time. He had not been followed to Wisconsin or the apartment in Kalamazoo.

"The moment you make a call, things start to happen." Dillon poked his finger at the knot of tiny wires. "Like I say, you can't see anything unusual here, even the computer chips appear standard. I had to hook them up to some pretty fancy lab equipment to figure out what was going on." He pointed. "A cell phone has a chip with your phone number programmed in. If somebody calls you, the signal finds your chip. If you phone somebody, the signal finds their chip."

Dillon looked at O'Neill and Christelle for confirmation; both nodded understanding.

"Okay, now the FCC — that's the Federal Communications Commission — has designated specific frequencies for cell phones. Altogether, there are six hundred and sixty-six. They range from 825.0300 megahertz up to 844.9800 megahertz. Advanced phones like this are chipped to use several frequencies so they can be used all over the country.

"But this phone has a little extra. Here's what happens when you make a call. It sends your call out on the designated frequency for this area, but it's also got some fancy twists in the chips, so they simultaneously beam your conversation out on two additional channels. The right equipment can pluck it out of the sky."

O'Neill shook his head. "Doesn't that take pretty fancy equipment?"

"Fancy is hardly the word, Dr. O'Neill. The extra channels work by rapid-frequency alternation transmission. What's happening is that your phone is continuously shifting through these three frequencies, with dozens of shifts a second. Anyone tuned in on one of these frequencies will hear only noise, nothing comprehensible. But someone with an interceptor with a matching chip that shifts between the same channels in perfect sync will pick up your conversation as though it were on a single frequency."

"Both ends of the conversation?"

Shaver nodded. "The chips are activated by both earphone and microphone. In the case of incoming talk, it comes down to your phone on the regular channel, then triggers the rapid frequency alternation. Whoever is tuned in can pick up both ends of the conversation."

O'Neill was astonished. "What's so special about the three alternation frequencies."

"I don't suppose anything, Dr. O'Neill, except this phone is hard wired for rapid-frequency alternation transmission on just these three frequencies. I suspect another phone would use a different three channels. Whoever's listening can identify the phone, and thus its owner, by which three channels are carrying the signal. Bloody clever, eh?"

O'Neill scratched his head. "Which means... which means what?"

"Which means there are probably a lot more phones out there with these special chips. There must be an awful lot of conversations being picked up. Which means whoever is eavesdropping must be monitoring every frequency. Which means an enormous listening network. The combinations of three channels from six hundred and sixty-six is in the millions. It would take astounding equipment to work with millions of combinations of frequencies, sort incoming signals, and put the right combinations together. And to be effective, it has to work almost instantaneously."

Shaver gazed around at the night sky. "I'd say that whoever is picking up messages on your phone is bloody big. And it's pretty amazing because I don't know of any outfit with the resources. Not unless you're talking about the U.S. Government itself."

O'Neill looked at Shaver, then at Christelle. So, she was right. He had uncovered evidence that the American intelligence community may have been authorized to spy on its own citizens for the last half century. It was a theory based on long-forgotten documents. But maybe they were in force. And now he had become a victim of his own findings. They were tracking him by his cell phone.

It was no longer guesswork. It was a fact.

Chapter Eleven

Sunday, July 14

Christelle was up at eight on Sunday morning. She needed groceries but was waylaid by the local newspaper thrown onto the front porch. The front page carried another story about the accident, the fire, and the deaths of three occupants, so far unidentified. Christelle read it carefully; there was no mention of any other vehicle. Maybe the glass on the road from her tail light had escaped notice, but she was still nervous. Nothing in the article indicated whether an investigation was underway. There was no mention of any weapon in the wreck, a puzzling glitch in the story both she and Broc had discussed, though that could well be information withheld from the press.

Christelle was eager to drive her newly repaired, repainted, and well-disguised Grand Am, but decided against it. They knew her at the grocery store; she was on speaking terms with a couple of cashiers. They knew her car, too — steel gray with Indiana plates. She would have trouble explaining her new paint job and New Hampshire plates. Christelle decided the risk was too great, and so she drove her sister's Mercury to town, cursing the whole way about the difficulty of driving a car on a mountain road with a hood the size of an aircraft carrier. She wished she could drive her own car.

It was ten fifteen when she got back. The coffee maker was still on, and still three-quarters full. There were no signs that O'Neill was up. Christelle unpacked the groceries and poured herself another cup, adding an extra dollop of cream. Feeling impatient, she drank her coffee while taking in the forested mountains across the valley. O'Neill's cocoa mug was by the computer, the one she had set there close to midnight the previous evening when she had finally given up on the day and gone to bed. Broc had been surfing the Internet since noon Saturday.

Broc had tapped into the main computer at Jefferson State University by using her graduate student computer account and password, and from there he had immediate access to *Netscape*. God! She would have to call her sister! Joyce would go ballistic when she saw the long-distance charges. A pile of paper by the printer was filled with little more than names of people and companies. She flipped through, then poured another cup of coffee, peeled a banana, and went out to the deck.

By noon, she could wait no longer. Standing quietly outside his door and hearing nothing, she knocked softly. A half minute later she knocked a little louder, called his name, and then slowly pushed back the door.

The bed was exactly as she had made it the previous morning. It had not been slept in. She surveyed the room; everything was neat and orderly. Then she saw the note on the end table and her heart skipped a beat.

Christelle — There's money in the drawer for yesterday's long distance. I really must thank you for everything; it's been a wonderful week. But I can't involve you in what must soon become a very dangerous business. Thanks for being so understanding. I'll be in touch. — Broc

Christelle felt a sudden desperation. She ran from the room and looked out the window down the road, realizing immediately it was pointless. He had been gone for hours, probably since the middle of the night. She raced back into his room and opened the closet door; one of his suitcases, the smaller of the two, was gone, but the larger one was there with his briefcase, and several of his shirts were still there.

Oh, God, what should she do next? She felt the panic rising. They were out there somewhere after him, seeking to destroy him, shoot him, blow him up, eliminate him from the face of the Earth. They had tried three times, almost finishing him each time. She felt her heart pounding as she ran to the window again. Where had he gone? Where would he go?

She ran to his bedroom and tore open the night table drawer. There was a wad of bills folded in the front. She counted them. Good God! Eight hundred. She read his note again, her hands shaking.

I can't involve you in what must soon become a very dangerous business—

Panicked, Christelle dumped out her purse until she found the business card for Robb's Auto Shop. Robb would not be at the shop; it was Sunday, but the card included his home number. After three tries, she could finally dial the whole number. Robb's wife came on the line, then went and got him.

"Robb! He's gone; he's disappeared!"

"Christelle, hold on; who's gone?"

"Broc, Broc O'Neill, you know, my professor."

"He was there last night when we brought back your car."

"I know, Robb; I know. He was here when I went to bed, but he's gone now, and I don't know where."

"Christy, what's the fuss about? Wasn't he just visiting?"

"Robb, I can't explain it all. It's just… just that he… Oh, God, Robb, where would he have gone? Do you have any idea?"

"Well, I'd say he could've gone anywhere with that passport—"

"What are you talking about? What passport?"

"Didn't you know? The passport he got from Dillon. Passport and driver's license."

Christelle's hands were shaking as she was trying to take it all in. "Robb, I don't know what you're saying. Tell me what you mean."

"You know what Dillon looks like. He's a dead ringer for your professor friend. Well, Mr.… Dr. O'Neill called him last week and paid him to borrow his passport and driver's license."

"Paid him… for…"

"Paid him damn good money! Fifteen hundred dollars."

Christelle stood stark still in shock. "Where did he say he was going?"

"He didn't say. Well, yes, he said he didn't know yet, not then. But he told Dillon he thought he would need his ID for only a couple of weeks."

Christelle thanked Robb, hung up the phone, and then stood by the picture window. Broc knew he was a hunted man. He couldn't use his own driver's license or passport to buy tickets, not if he wanted to stay alive. He packed Dillon Shaver's ID so his movements would not be traced. Maybe he was in less danger than she had thought.

Christelle felt the knots of panic in her stomach slowly letting go. She went to the refrigerator and pulled out makings for a ham and tomato sandwich and an apple.

As she ate, she went over to the darkened screen of the computer, then noticed the green light was on. She tapped the mouse and watched as the monitor slowly came to life, then read:

Worldwide Communications
1304 Columbia Boulevard
Philadelphia, Pennsylvania

Nathan Jamiessen, CEO, Brandeis Electronics, Harrisburg
William Kaiser III, VP, Kaiser Shipping Enterprises, York
Walter P. Monahan, CEO, Pennsylvania Produce, Allentown
John L. P. Randolph, CEO, GEO Corporation, Harrisburg

She was in the middle of some sort of long document. Tapping the arrows, she scrolled back to the beginning, then through to the end. There were scores of names, hundreds. The document ran on for eighty pages.

She scrolled back to the beginning where the heading said Worldwide Communications. Christelle remembered Worldwide Communications was the name of the outlet in Jefferson where Broc had bought his cellular phone. But the address on the screen was in Pennsylvania. Slowly, she scrolled. Every twenty or thirty lines she found the same words — Worldwide Communications — with another address in another state.

These must be cell phone customers. Fascinated, she kept on scrolling. She came to a page headed "Indiana." There were outlets in Bloomington, Indianapolis and — yes, there it was! — the mall outlet in Jefferson. And there he was: Broc O'Neill was listed, along with the address of the O'Neill home on Maple Lane.

Quickly, she scrolled through, searching. A minute later, she found the list for Missouri. Broc's friend, Alan Creighton, was on the list. They had burglarized his home after Broc's phone call and now they had decided to monitor his phone, probably hoping Broc might call and reveal where he was.

Suddenly, Christelle remembered she had signed out the journal with Dr. O'Neill's article from the Poly Sci reading room and never returned it. Oh, my God! She still had it. Or did she? She tried to think. No, she had accidently left it on Dr. O'Neill's desk in his office when he autographed the offprint. She let out her breath, glad she didn't have it. Maybe a secretary had found it and returned it to the Poly Sci reading room.

Christelle leaned back in her chair. Broc had found a customer list. People who owned phones like his. They must all be bugged! Thousands of them!

The blue bar across the top of the document read www.WWCustomerlist.org. Christelle quickly opened up the C-drive files. He had saved it. She glanced at the printer and printout, a continuous pile of paper folded at the perforations. Christelle bit a chunk of her apple and picked up the printout, which immediately fell into two parts. It had been torn apart after page 42. Page 43 was missing. She went back to the computer screen and scrolled until she found page 43, the page she had first seen on the screen.

She scanned the names again: customers of a Worldwide Communications outlet in Pennsylvania. There were twenty names listed, several in Philadelphia, the rest in various towns around the state, including York, Allentown, and Harrisburg.

Broc must have taken page 43 with him. That meant he was headed to Pennsylvania. She clicked on 'File' and printed out her own copy of page 43. She knew where he had gone, but it didn't make her feel any better. He had gone without her. She felt left out, abandoned, and then her hurt turned to anger.

She picked up the phone, dialed the number and waited, impatient, frustration building. The voice came on the phone, and she pushed the extension: 6949. A second later she heard his voice over the telephone lines from Indiana: "You have reached the office of Broc O'Neill. I'll be

available through the spring semester on Tuesdays and Thursdays."
Spring semester was past. He had not recorded a new message for the
summer or the coming fall semester.

She waited until the beep and then left him a scathing message. Then
she sat still for another fifteen minutes, collecting her thoughts. She
washed the dishes, walked around the house, picked things up, fidgeted.
She kept seeing his eyes, deep brown and steady. She remembered how
his eyes had captivated her, how she had found his eyes and his words
leading her from idea to idea, compelling, persuasive. But the past few
days she had seen new meanings as she watched his eyes. There were
moments of rage as he walked around the house or just stood by the
window, pushing back his thick shock of chestnut hair, and then there
were moments of sadness when he seemed bewildered, as though he had
wandered into some strange and terrible dream.

He had been there less than a week, but she missed him. She wanted
to know where he was; she wanted to know he was safe.

She had been in Joyce and Roy's bedroom only once since she had
arrived, but now she wandered, trying to distract herself. There were
framed photographs on the wall. One of them was a picture of herself, a
tiny tot of not more than two or three. Another showed Mom and Dad
the day they were married back in the fifties. Beside it was a picture of
Roy in his uniform; it must have been after he returned from Vietnam.

Vietnam. Christelle had a sudden recollection. She looked around
the room, and then went to the bureau. She explored each drawer, moving
clothes, carefully putting them back in place. Roy was a veteran; his
things were in perfect piles. She opened the closet; his shirts were hung
with the regulation three finger widths between each hanger. Two pairs
of shoes on the floor were polished to a mirror finish. She reached up to
the top shelf; there was nothing there except two new shirts still in plastic
wrapping.

She lifted away an ornament and a pile of *Guns and Ammo*
magazines from the trunk at the foot of the bed, then lifted the lid. Inside
were pictures and souvenirs, things Roy had brought back from Vietnam.
She moved aside a military uniform folded and wrapped in clear plastic.
There was more military-issue stuff, a paperback book by David
Halberstam, *The Best and the Brightest*, and another by Neil Sheehan, *A*

Bright Shining Lie. She remembered Roy talking about Halberstam; he always admired the journalists in Vietnam who risked their lives to bring the story to the American public. Roy had once dreamed of being a journalist.

Christelle moved the books aside and then lifted away two pairs of military pants. Slowly, she lifted it and held its weight in her hand, amazed at how heavy it felt and how the metal seemed so cold.

"My God, lady! You want to shoot this?"

Christelle looked down the firing range at the targets. Some were standard round targets with black centers; others were shaped like sinister looking crooks with targets on their chests. Every few seconds a gun went off; nine of the fourteen firing spaces were occupied by people firing various weapons down the range.

The range instructor examined the weapon. "This is a Colt 1911 A1. Standard military issue for officers in both World Wars, and Nam. Miss, this is a bloody 45; it's a man's gun. It's got a kick that will give you pain in your bones."

She glared at him. "You mean a woman can't shoot this!"

"Well, I'm not saying that. If a woman's trained, she can—"

"How many bullets do you have to fire to… to learn how?"

"You mean how many rounds? I'd say, the average guy shoots thirty rounds each time. Stays an hour, maybe two. I suggest a day off between. Pretty good shot at the end of two weeks."

Christelle did a mental calculation. She checked her watch; it showed 2:30 p.m.

"We're open until seven tonight," he said, "in case you're wondering."

"I'd like to shoot two hundred bullets — rounds — today!"

The instructor turned with an open mouth. "You won't make twenty, not with that bloody V-C killer. But I'll tell you what, we'll start you with a Beretta that fires smaller 22 shells till you get the hang of it, let's say the first forty rounds. Then we'll see if you can make another twenty with a Colt Python; it fires a 357 Magnum shell. I'll issue ammunition in twenty-round batches, pay as you go. Then, if your arm will still bend tomorrow, we'll go for another forty rounds and see if we can get you steady enough for the 45. I'll give you some pointers. Come back Tuesday, we'll get in another hundred. A hundred rounds in three days: you'll feel like you've been through a war. You'll be so bloody sore you won't ever want to think about this damn thing again. But you'll be able to shoot it."

"Issue the ammunition!"

Christelle gazed down the range at the target, gripping Roy's weapon in her hand, wondering how many Viet Cong had met their end from the barrel of this gun. She had gone through the preliminary rounds with smaller caliber weapons. Deep down in the pit of her stomach, she could feel a knot gathering, a tightening under the skin that she recognized. Her body was ready; her mind was nearly so. The target assumed the sinister shape of unknown enemies. She could feel her determination gathering.

I'm going to blow that target apart—

Chapter Twelve

Broc had been on Interstate 81 from Scranton for less than two hours when it merged with Interstate 78 heading into Harrisburg. He continued for a few more miles and then exited. A mile south the road intersected Pennsylvania Highway 22 and O'Neill turned west. A few miles farther brought him to the beginning of the suburbs; it was midafternoon Sunday.

He had been lucky. He had left the cabin Sunday morning at two o'clock, hiked down the road, and was picked up by the first car that came along. The driver, a woman, probably aged fifty, wanted someone to talk to rather than traveling alone. They shared the driving through the night, crossed lower New York State, and got into Pennsylvania mid-morning. She let him out at a farmers' market beside a car rental.

Broc filled up the rented Ford Tempo and checked the water and oil, then drove another mile to the Ramada Inn, arriving a few minutes after 5 p.m. Within ten minutes he had registered for three nights under the name of Dillon Shaver, paid cash, added a fifty-dollar deposit against long-distance charges he might accrue, and found his room on the second floor. In another ten minutes he had unpacked his suitcase, changed into casual slacks and jacket, and was on his way out the door with the Ramada phone number and his room extension jotted on a slip of paper.

It was a three-minute walk across a paper-littered field, under the freeway, and across the mall parking lot to a restaurant, the sign of which was visible from his room. O'Neill ordered an all-you-can-eat salad and ice water and sat at the front corner of the restaurant where he could see the buildings of Harrisburg a few miles away.

He took a full twenty minutes to finish a second helping of salad while perusing the sheet from Christelle's computer. He had located Worldwide Communications outlets all over the country but had brought with him only the list from Pennsylvania — twenty-two names with corporate affiliations in Philadelphia, Norristown, Scranton, Allentown, and York. There were three names from the Pennsylvania capital, Harrisburg, enough to warrant a stay of two or three days without facing a crisis of choice that the numerous names in Philadelphia would present.

Some corporations sounded vaguely familiar. They were all giants in the industrial life of Pennsylvania. He had spent an hour searching out the names on his list in the public library a few miles north with Dun & Bradstreet's *Million Dollar Directory of America's Leading Public and Private Companies*. The common denominators: each held a high, often the highest, position in his company, and each was the owner of a Worldwide Communications cell phone. He needed to find out why.

It had been a challenge. From Christelle's laptop, he had used her graduate-student account to go through the mainframe computer at Jefferson State University and logged into the Internet. Then he had phoned the largest Worldwide Communications outlet in the country, situated in Los Angeles, and asked about the best cellular phones available, requesting specifications: warranties, availability of parts, and the origin of components. His stated reasons were that he was in search of the best quality for a large order of phones. He listed several qualifications: his company was opposed to any instruments with Chinese components. "It's a thing our Board of Directors had voted on. They prefer to support the made-in-America electronics industry."

His story was deliberate fabrication. He wanted to avoid questions about Hai Phong Electronics; that could alert whoever was distributing Worldwide telephones. In addition, it would force an extended but probably futile hunt through U.S. manufacturing records and thus keep the phone connection open as long as possible.

The ruse worked. The customer service rep could not answer all of his questions directly and so had to search screen after screen for specifics. The call consumed twenty minutes, and while O'Neill was connected, Christelle's computer was at the threshold of Worldwide Communications' mainframe with a streamlined hacker program called Interwedge running through its millions of combinations. By the time O'Neill hung up, the combination had been found and he was into Worldwide's data banks.

From there it had been easy. Lists of Worldwide outlets around the country came up, then lists of inventories and purchases, and finally records of sales. It had taken O'Neill several hours, but by midnight he had located the forty largest franchise outlets with all of their sales for several years. Each franchise dealt in dozens of brands of cellular phones, including those supplied by Hai Phong Electronics. These made up a very small proportion of thousands of cell phones sold, not more than a fraction of one percent. Still, most Worldwide outlets had sold between sixty and two hundred HPE cellular phones over the past five years. That added up to hundreds nationwide. And every one was distributed as a replacement for other brands that had been turned in as faulty.

It was all crystal clear. Whoever was targeted for eavesdropping would find their cell phone developing problems, most likely annoying static. Once they showed up for a replacement, they would be steered toward an HPE model without knowing it was hard wired for eavesdropping.

By midnight O'Neill had downloaded printouts listing 4,160 HPE phones — every one in the hands of a powerful corporate executive. His seemed to be the only one in the hands of an ordinary citizen. It's flattering, he had mused, to own a phone reserved for the rich and powerful. And dangerous, he thought, though none of the other owners appeared to be running for their lives.

Lingering over the last few bits of salad, O'Neill examined his list. Two in Harrisburg interested him: Nathan Jamiessen of Brandeis Electronics and John Randolph of GEO Corporation. It was too late to get started tonight, but the Harrisburg Public Library would open at nine Monday morning. With luck he would have what he needed to know by ten thirty and would be on the trail by noon.

O'Neill cleared his table then found a public telephone. He pulled a handful of change from his pocket. He had been collecting quarters at every snack and gas stop along the way. It was 9:30 p.m. — eight thirty in Clayton, Missouri. He dialed the number from his address book. Twenty seconds later Alan Creighton was on the line.

Broc cut in immediately. "Alan, you'll recognize my voice, but don't say my name! Have you got another landline in the house — not your cell phone?"

There was a pause of a few seconds, then Creighton's reply.

"What's the number?"

Creighton recited the seven-digit number.

"Okay, get to it. I'll phone you in thirty seconds. And no names!" He hung up, waited half a minute, and then dialed the new number.

Creighton answered. Broc cut in again. "Okay, we've got a clean line at your place. Phone me in ten minutes at this number." He read the number of his hotel room and gave the extension, then hung up.

"Broc, where are you? And what's going on?"

"I'm in a motel in Harrisburg, Pennsylvania. Where are you?"

"I'm in the apartment over my garage. My student renter went home for the summer. This phone is under his name. But why not my cell phone?"

"Okay, let me guess. It's new."

"Right. How did you know?"

"Another guess. You got it in the past month."

"What on Earth? How do you know that?"

"Another guess. It's a Worldwide Communications phone."

"How…?"

"Okay, listen. That phone is bugged. Very sophisticated, very high tech, almost undetectable. Your previous phone probably went bad after the burglary. They were after my article, and they want to know whether you've read it and whether you agree with a Senate investigation. If they hear that you agree, you'll be target for assassination."

"Wow! I guess I should throw it away."

"No, just keep using the phone, innocuously, when you make a doctor's appointment or phone a bookstore. Just normal use. But do not try to phone me. You won't be able to reach me. Wait for me to call you on your safe line."

"Okay, but Broc, are you okay? It sounds like you're in real danger."

"I'm fine."

"I heard. I heard about Darcy. Your graduate student filled me in."

"It was real nasty, a car bomb; it was meant for me."

"I'm so sorry."

"Well, I've got to put it behind me, Alan, I've stumbled into something really big. Apparently, my article pushed the wrong button — or maybe the right button."

"Hell! This makes me so furious."

"Right, tell me about it! I've developed an acute sense of rage."

"So, what are you doing in Harrisburg?"

"I've got a list of heavy hitters, big CEOs, with rigged phones all supplied by Worldwide Communications. I'm about to do some snooping of my own."

"Listen, Broc, I know a guy who might be able to help."

"Who? What's his connection?"

"A guy from my Vietnam platoon. There are four of us. We had a reunion three or four years back. They're all over the world. One's in Hawaii, another in Singapore."

"And the one who might be able to help?"

"Springfield, Virginia. He's CIA."

"What the hell is he doing there?"

"Listen, Broc, we were the best hardware and munitions guys in Nam. We set explosives all up and down the Mekong River, places that are still classified. And the best guy in the platoon was Brentley Hagan. Brent could rig a bomb with pepper and a hairpin. He was so good the CIA picked him up after the war. Probably offered him six figures. He was good! The FBI wanted him, too."

"You trust this guy, Alan?"

"With my life, the whole platoon did!"

"The only thing. Whatever's going on is all tied up with surveillance. That's CIA territory. If we make contact with the CIA, we could be running right into the thugs who are listening in and chasing me around with machine guns."

"What a tangle! Well, there are numerous departments. And I know Brent's politics. If there's domestic surveillance going on, he won't be involved. The bureaucracy is huge; there are plenty of hot-doggers, but they still make up only a small percentage."

"I know: eighteen, maybe twenty thousand people supposedly employed in the Washington area alone. But what about his politics?"

"Brent Hagan came out of Nam in '73 — he was among the last evacuated from Saigon. He had a couple of months of R & R before the CIA offer. Then all hell broke loose. You remember — all those investigations of illegal activities, clandestine operations, the stuff that committee dug up?"

"The Rockefeller Commission."

"I guess that was it. Anyway, Hagan was so enraged he almost quit the CIA. You had to know the guy. In Nam, he believed you should do your job. He was the same as all of us — he knew the whole damn Vietnam war was a botch, just like that bastard Robert McNamara admitted. You need to read his book. It came out a couple of months ago. But Brently's idea was do your job, right or wrong, do it well, and don't get your head in a knot. It was the same with that Rockefeller Report. He said the job of the CIA was to deal with the threats to American security abroad, not run secret wars. He was attracted to the FBI, until he discovered J. Edgar Hoover was collecting data on movie stars and poets and students. That pushed him toward the CIA—the lesser of two evils."

"So you're saying he would be appalled at the idea of our rigged phones."

"Furious! He'd go ballistic. He'd want to string up these guys by their balls."

"That's about how I feel, Alan."

"I don't blame you." Creighton's voice softened. "Darcy was… She was a gem, Broc, a real jewel. If these guys are doing stuff like that, well, hell, they deserve a firing squad."

"Okay, Alan, let's think about this a while." O'Neill took a deep breath, trying to keep his mind off Darcy. "We may need your friend Hagan, but don't call him yet. There are other options. Whoever these guys are, they're smart and they've got the deck stacked with high tech. Right now, they think I'm hiding out somewhere in Vermont. They don't know I know anything. The longer they believe that, the better chance I've got to penetrate—"

"Hell, Broc, you could get yourself killed."

"I've got a damn good reason to get myself killed!"

There was a pause on the line. "I'll tell you another way you could get yourself killed: if you don't get back in touch with that graduate student! Boy, she called here yesterday, and she was steamed! Seems you ran out on her."

"I didn't run out on her, Alan. She invited me to Vermont to talk. I was just visiting. It was time to leave before she got mixed up in this. Her car was riddled by gunfire. She almost caught a bullet."

"Well, I told Miss Washington I was sure you were thinking of her safety, but she wasn't having any of it. She said you have a death wish. 'If he gets shot,' she said, 'he'll damn well deserve it, and if he doesn't get shot before he gets back here' — wherever here is — 'I may shoot him myself!' I'm telling you, Broc, you have a wildcat on your hands."

"How did she get in touch?"

"On my house phone."

"Okay, from what I know, it's cell phones that are bugged, not house phones."

"So, our conversation probably was not picked up."

"That would be my guess." O'Neill checked his watch. It was 7:50 p.m. He had been up most of the previous night. "I'll tell you what, Alan. If she calls you again, tell her I'll get back with her in a couple of days. Tell her I'm okay and that I appreciate her concern."

O'Neill took a long hot shower, the spray beating on his head and neck. He could feel his muscles giving way, slowly relaxing under the relentless heat. Ten minutes later he crawled into bed and switched out the light, early enough to get a dozen hours of sleep. His thoughts roamed over Alan's conversation for a minute or two as sleep crept over him. The last thing he remembered wondering was what had happened to the wide-eyed innocent student in a soft green cotton dress who had told him a journal article he had written was the scariest thing she had ever read.

Chapter Thirteen

At 2:55 p.m. Monday afternoon O'Neill straightened his new tie, checked his suit jacket, and entered the Harrisburg Trade Building, a fifteen-story gray glass structure on the edge of downtown. GEO Corporation occupied the tenth floor and the five above it. Carrying a new briefcase, O'Neill left the elevator and began a slow circuit of the rectangle of halls laid out around the elevator shaft. A twenty-foot wall of glass opened into a company foyer crowded with banks of gigantic potted plants. The mandatory supermodel sat at the reception desk. The back wall was decorated with a U.S. flag on an earth-brown background along with gigantic framed portraits of Ronald Reagan, George Bush, and the Governor of Pennsylvania.

Reagan and Bush! O'Neill pondered. It was years since they had left office. There was some kind of statement there, he mused.

O'Neill had planned to go inside and ask directions, hoping to learn whether John Randolph was in. His task was simplified when he recognized Randolph as one of three well-suited executives standing in the foyer. He was clearly the center of attention and looked exactly like last year's photograph in the Harrisburg paper.

His presence was all Broc wished to verify, but during his four-second walk past the glass, he saw Randolph pull a cell phone from his pocket and do a half turn from the others to answer a call. O'Neill guessed it was his Worldwide Communications phone.

O'Neill completed the circuit to the elevator and headed to his car in a multi-level garage across the street — parked strategically so he could sit and see everyone entering or leaving the Harrisburg Trade Building. The time was 3:10 p.m. With luck he could meet John Randolph on neutral ground.

O'Neill examined the photocopied pictures and articles from the library. Before researching John Randolph and GEO Corporation, he had located a folder of fact sheets on another Harrisburg company, Brandeis

Electronics. It was over forty years old, founded by John Brandeis in 1953 and run by his son, John Brandeis II, from 1960 until 1988. Business had prospered in the fifties, then "leveled out in the sixties, as large electronics contracts flowed to the west coast." The wording surprised O'Neill until he recognized it as a dramatic prologue to what was to come next: the company had limped through the seventies; then, in the self-congratulatory rhetoric of ad pamphlets, "Brandeis Electronics had prospered under the direction of a nephew, Nathan Jamiessen, newly appointed to the helm of the family business, who immediately brought in thousands of new jobs and millions of new dollars to the capital of Pennsylvania."

In May 1990 Brandeis Electronics had gone public with a huge issue of stock. A month later, Jamiessen had signed a federal contract that, over the next quarter century, would be worth billions of dollars — specifically to design advanced electronic controls for missiles. Two months later, Saddam Hussein had invaded Kuwait. The President was rattling sabres by the end of the summer; when American missiles went screaming down Baghdad streets with pinpoint accuracy. The following January, Brandeis Electronics stocks went up eighty-five percent in ten days. By summer 1991, Brandeis had added six thousand employees.

Nathan Jamiessen was soon riding high, flush with the success he had achieved for a hitherto mediocre family business. He was now in his early fifties; his wife was a socialite in Harrisburg; he had two daughters and a son at various stages of college and graduate school. Jamiessen had recently been profiled in a fancy brochure that included numerous photographs of the family. Among several, there was one press photo showing him mixing with the local politicians at a 1994 political rally. The print identified them as the incumbent Republican Senators for the State of Pennsylvania, Republican Representatives for the fifth and seventh electoral districts, and two aspiring House members who had lost the last election but were still part of the inner circle of the GOP. The only important politician missing was the only Pennsylvania politician O'Neill could recall, the Mayor of Philadelphia, presumably because he was a Democrat.

O'Neill glanced through the sheaf of photocopies. Nathan Jamiessen was a clean-cut churchman, a sterling citizen, and a successful executive.

There were rumors he might eventually run for the U.S. Senate. He appeared squeaky clean. There was no reason why he might be under surveillance. Shoving the photocopies into his briefcase, O'Neill reasoned that it could take days to determine why someone had chosen to ruin Jamiessen's cell phone with static last November and then arrange to have a replacement supplied by Worldwide Communications.

John Randolph was another story, a heady mix of success and scandal fit for the tabloids. Employees from Randolph's building should be getting off work soon, but none had appeared yet, so O'Neill went back to the papers spread out on the seat of the car. He shuffled through a large packet of photocopied news articles that were stuck inside a glossy GEO brochure.

The glass doors of the Harrisburg Trade Building swung open at 3:37 p.m.; a wave of employees was coming out, all eager to get on the road and enjoy the summer weather while sipping gin and tonic on their back patios. Two minutes and fifty employees later, John Randolph appeared and crossed the road to the parking garage. O'Neill could not see which button he pushed on the elevator to the parking levels above, and it did not matter; the auto exit circuit would bring him past the spot where O'Neill was parked.

Four minutes later a new black Mercedes-Benz came around the corner, moved slowly past O'Neill's rented Tempo, and slowed further for the jam of cars moving through the gate. O'Neill backed out and followed, paid the six-dollar parking charge, and pulled out of the garage two car lengths behind Randolph into traffic moving west.

The Mercedes moved smoothly half a block ahead, signaling lane changes and turns, the habits of an organized executive. A few blocks along, Randolph made a turn and headed up onto the interstate, the logical route to his home in an upscale community across the Susquehanna River beyond West Fairview. O'Neill followed, letting Randolph gain distance, keeping several car lengths between his Tempo and the Mercedes.

GEO Corporation was a huge conglomerate that went back to a small tractor company around 1915. The company had done well all along, expanding into heavy machinery for strip mining in the twenties, and then into tank treads and heavy-duty power trains for military equipment during World War II. By the sixties it was providing landing gear for military transport planes and gear boxes for the largest helicopters used in Vietnam. The corporation had factories in half a dozen states, but its head office was in Harrisburg, and John Randolph was its Chief Executive Officer.

The previous year GEO Corporation had earned $1.1 billion on a gross of $5.8 billion, a stunning nineteen percent profit. Two years ago, John Randolph had collected a salary of $1.6 million; last year, $2.12 million. Among the news clippings were pictures of Randolph with his wife and children with a cluster of Harrisburg councilmen and prominent leaders of Harrisburg industry.

Then, ten months ago, someone had snapped Randolph's picture in front of the most luxurious private club in Lancaster, forty miles away. The blonde on his arm, an unidentified woman striking enough to star in movies, looked half his age. And now John Randolph was in the middle of one of the messiest divorce battles in Pennsylvania history.

The Mercedes was signaling; O'Neill followed it off the ramp; it made a long turn north and out of sight on the cross street. He followed at a safe distance, worried that he might lose sight, but as he came around the bend, he saw the car turn into a parking lot. As he cruised by, he saw Randolph carrying a sports bag into the Fairview Health Club.

O'Neill drove around the block, parked in a visitor's space, waited five minutes, and then checked in at the men's entrance desk. Randolph was not in sight. Within three minutes O'Neill had purchased a week's pass to the club on a special introductory offer and obtained a combination lock. The latest *Business Week, Sports Illustrated,* and *Penthouse* lay with two or three dozen other magazines; O'Neill stuck them under his arm. At the sports shop down the hall, he purchased a club T-shirt, shorts, swimming trunks, goggles, and new tennis shoes. He headed for the exercise rooms.

"Is there an easy way to program these machines?"

John Randolph turned his attention from the TV news, keeping the rhythm of his pace. "Skip the heartbeat controls, just set the speed and push the right-hand green button."

O'Neill worked with the controls, deliberately taking a good twenty seconds to get the treadmill working. Randolph looked away from the

TV twice, glancing at O'Neill then at the floor, and then they both settled into a brisk pace of 4.5 miles per hour. O'Neill had dropped his magazines on the floor between their machines with *Penthouse* on top.

Randolph was a couple of inches over six feet, well proportioned, and would weigh in, O'Neill guessed, at an even two hundred pounds. His attention was riveted on CNN, and O'Neill's was soon, too — a lengthy report on various economic effects now flowing from a rash of recent disasters, among them, Hurricane Bertha, which was petering out after damaging hundreds of homes from Puerto Rico to North Carolina, and a devastating earthquake in China that had left over a thousand people dead. Following that was a news byte from The White House with questions from reporters, half a dozen restating the same question in an effort to get President Clinton to slip up and provide a juicy headline. As usual, they were unsuccessful.

O'Neill calculated the probable time Randolph would stay with the machine, subtracting five to ten minutes he had been on it before O'Neill arrived. At 4:47 O'Neill brought his to a stop; standing with one foot on the tread and his towel over his shoulder, he watched the end of the report. Two minutes later, Randolph slowed his machine, stepped off, and dried his forehead. O'Neill picked up the magazines.

Randolph glanced again at O'Neill as he turned and Broc got ready to walk. "Are you new to the Club? Haven't seen you here before."

Broc nodded, then moved off ahead of Randolph, winding among the machines. As they passed a young woman on an exercise bike, O'Neill stooped to pick up her fallen towel and hung it on her machine; the woman smiled her thanks to both of them.

"Just moved here a couple of weeks ago from Missouri. But I miss swimming, so I figured the next thing was a club." O'Neill paused by the door to the swimming pool.

"Have you seen the other side?" Randolph asked, edging inside the door. "Weight room, racquetball, sauna."

Broc walked past him to a circular vinyl table by the pool and dropped his magazines. "Not yet, but I'll follow you over when you go." O'Neill fingered the goggles around his neck. "Are you interested? I thought I'd do a few laps."

Randolph shook his head and set his sports bag on a chair. "It's been a busy day. I've got a couple of calls to make." He touched O'Neill's magazines. "Mind if I—?"

"Go ahead," O'Neill, urged, adjusting the goggles. "By the way, I'm Jacob Wallace. Nice to meet you."

"John Randolph." He stuck his hand out and shook O'Neill's with the precise grip and correct contact time of the practiced business executive.

Following a quick change into his swimming trunks, O'Neill swam steady strokes for eight lengths of the pool before he stole a second on a turn to glance up. Randolph was reading *Business Week*. O'Neill swam for another six minutes before he paused briefly at the far end of the pool. Randolph was facing the other way, staring through the glass wall to the exercise room while he talked on his telephone, apparently watching three shapely young women who were all pedaling along, ignoring the TV. O'Neill swam another five lengths of the pool before he pulled himself out of the water.

Randolph was still on the phone. O'Neill signaled with a couple of arm motions as he walked past and Randolph nodded. Two minutes later he sat down with a dish of shelled peanuts and two cans of Heineken.

"So, what brings you all the way from Missouri?" Randolph asked as he shoved the phone back in his duffel bag.

"Needed to get away. A nasty divorce." O'Neill massaged his head with his towel as he invented an appropriate scenario. "The former Mrs. Wallace and I tried to manage things — we were partners in the same consulting firm — but it was clear one of us would have to go. We figured it would be easier for me to get started in a new place."

"At least you tried to manage things. That doesn't sound too nasty to me."

O'Neill threw his towel onto a chair and took a sip of beer. "I'm trying to give the bitch the benefit of the doubt by putting the best light on our post-marital battles."

"So it was like that—"

"Christ, John, I couldn't get away fast enough!"

Randolph studied O'Neill. He had blue eyes and hair only slightly graying at the temples. He was ruggedly good looking in the way Broc knew women would appreciate. "I've got one myself whom I'm trying to shed, but it isn't easy."

O'Neill nodded knowingly but secretly amused at Randolph's face saving. The gorgeous blonde in the photo suggested that Randolph's wife was shedding him while taking him for as many millions as her attorneys could leverage from his philandering.

"Damn little farm bitch," Randolph went on, "I should have known better than to get mixed up with a Hershey girl."

O'Neill glanced at him, signaling puzzlement.

"Jane worked at Hershey's Chocolates, but she's got Amish roots. The whole country east of here is full of what they call the 'Plain People' — that's what they call all those Pennsylvania Amish. I met her at a golf tournament in Hershey. Boy, could she handle the clubs, and she was anything but plain.

"But let me tell you, Wallace, the Amish claim to be above capitalism and all that good American stuff, but they're as capitalist as the rest of us. So Plain Jane from Hershey's Chocolates is doing everything she can to break me. The way she's got this thing worked out, she'll walk away with enough money to pay off her daddy's mortgage on fourteen hundred acres of Amish farmland, with enough left over for black hats and new buggies for the whole village. Shit! It burns me up. And on top of that, I think she's hired a suckhole private investigator."

O'Neill saw his chance. "Say, John, I saw you had a phone. I need to make a call to my brother. Could I borrow yours" — Randolph reached into his duffel bag — "unless it's one of those from Worldwide Communications?" O'Neill laughed as though he had cracked a joke.

"What's wrong with them?" Randolph set his cell phone on the table.

"Oh, didn't you hear? Maybe it was just a rumor out in Missouri, somebody's idea of a practical joke." O'Neill paused, flipped open the lid, planning to feign a call. He punched in the number for the national weather forecast, feeling Randolph's eyes on him as the voice at the other end of the line began talking. The voice was too faint for Randolph to hear. The weather girl promised a sunny week with no rain until the weekend. Fifteen seconds later, he closed the phone, shutting off any possibility of being overheard.

"He's not answering. I'll call him later," Broc said, handing the phone to Randolph. He waited as though he had forgotten the conversation.

"What's the practical joke?"

"Oh, yes! This guy told me that Worldwide Communications was the supplier for the simplest phones in the world to tap. If your wife's spying on you, one of these phones would be the easiest way."

Chapter Fourteen

"See, I've met this girl — really nice, the kind you can't stay away from." They had three cans of beer each on the table, but O'Neill hadn't downed more than an inch from any of them while Randolph was running on, his words beginning to slur. "I'll tell you, Wallace, it's bloody helpful to have a nice girl when your wife is giving you the shaft. I just keep her out of sight, at least away from any place my wife is likely to be. I mean, Plain Jane doesn't deserve to have a girlfriend who looks like Sandy in her face. Of course, you can't do anything in this bloody town without everybody knowing. So, she knows, she's figured it out."

John Randolph had forgotten the alarm O'Neill had momentarily set off over his telephone. He was swilling beer and beginning to ramble.

"She's sure I've got all kinds of secret bank accounts and money stashed away."

O'Neill nodded understanding, encouraging him to talk.

Randolph leaned forward and looked O'Neill in the eye. "First thing, you know what, Wallace? My lawyer starts asking me all this stuff about income. He says her attorneys want financial summaries. Next thing, I get this letter, a bloody audit notice from the IRS for tax year 1993. It's the third one. I was audited for '91 and '92. Anyway, we worked all that out: I went in and had the audit. They said I owed ninety-six thousand dollars in back taxes, but they were willing to negotiate. We settled up at fifty grand. Then the Department of Defense wants a review of the past ten years of contracts with my company; that's GEO. We make military hardware for tanks and planes. Investigations, subpoenas, you name it. Next thing, those suckholes at the IRS are sending notices again. Another tax audit, this one for '94!"

Randolph took another slug of Heineken, then slammed the can on the table. "It's been like this for months. Those suckholes at the DOD won't leave me alone! It's bloody criminal! You know what I told them, Wallace? I said, for God's sake, GEO Corporation is one of America's great saviors. I said if it weren't for GEO's power trains and tank treads, the whole damn American military would still be mired in mud in Vietnam. The bloody bastards don't appreciate us. Damn! GEO Corporation ought to be free of all this stuff; GEO shouldn't even have to pay any taxes!"

O'Neill could see the fury building. "Continual pressure! And you know what, Wallace?" He pounded his fist on the table. "The damn divorce attorneys and the bloody government, they're all in it together. You see a guy lurking in the shadows and you have no idea — No idea! — whether the bastard is a PI, an IRS agent, or a suckhole divorce attorney. And you know what, Wallace? It doesn't matter anyway because they're all criminals out to milk industry and the men who raised American business to be the best in the world."

They stood beside Randolph's Mercedes-Benz, an S500 2-door notchback worth around eighty thousand. Randolph had settled down; now he was checking his watch.

"Six thirty-five. She said she would be here at six thirty. You've got to meet this little girl, Wallace; you've got to meet her. Then you'll understand why the hell all this shit that Plain Jane is throwing at me is so criminal. If it weren't for Sandy, my life would be a bloody dump."

A car turned in from the street — low slung, fire red with a white top, a dazzling Mercury Mark VIII. O'Neill caught the flash of blonde hair through the windshield even before John Randolph had noticed. The car pulled up beside them. O'Neill's mind was in knots trying to contemplate the price tag. Darcy had longed for the Mercury Mark VIII, ignoring the forty-two thousand it would cost while she ran with her fantasies for a couple of hours. And then she had settled for Beemy at thirty-one five.

"Here she is, Wallace."

O'Neill watched as the leggy blonde in skin-tight white shorts and blouse got out of the car and walked up to Randolph, an eye-popping spectacle from her swinging ponytail to her white spiked heels. *Fuck-me shoes*, Darcy used to call them.

"Wallace, I'd like you to meet Sandy; she's the girl I was talking about." O'Neill recognized her as the unidentified woman in the news photo. O'Neill nodded as Sandy delivered a heavyweight knockout smile that would have sent Mike Tyson staggering to the locker room.

"Sweetheart, how've you been? How's everything?"

"Everything's fine, Randy, just fine. Except your Valentine present is ready for another oil and lube."

Randolph glanced at the Mercury, then at O'Neill. "Listen, Wallace, it's been nice to meet you. I guess I'll see you around the club. Maybe we can get together sometime. Maybe we can find you a girl and get together sometime."

At eight thirty Broc O'Neill picked up the phone in his motel room and dialed Jefferson State University. Seconds later his own voice came on — Broc O'Neill — and his greeting. Immediately, he punched in his code and waited for his messages. There was a brief pitch from a salesman at Aegean Park Press in California who wanted to talk to him about some new books in cryptanalysis. There was a message from the secretary of the History Department mentioning the first faculty meeting of the fall semester on September 18th at 9 a.m. Broc noted the date as the voice reminded him that last-minute changes for the following spring's schedule were due by August 8th; please call during office hours to request any changes.

O'Neill ignored the red tape; his schedule was predictable: one sophomore class in American history, 1865 to the present; one senior class on the politics of the Cold War; and a graduate seminar. If anything was changed, it would be the Cold War course, with Asian-American relations a likely alternate. The graduate seminar was the same one he had given three or four semesters ago when Christelle Washington had first enrolled.

Suddenly, her voice came on the line, loud enough to make him jerk the receiver away from his ear:

Professor Broc O'Neill! This is Christelle. Remember me? It's Sunday night and I want to know where you have gone! And why have you gone anywhere without telling me? And when are you going to phone and tell me what's going on? Your suitcase is taking up space in my closet. Where would you like me to ship it? Or just throw it in the trash? You've got some nerve sneaking out in the middle of the night!

There was a pause as though she was about to say more, and then a snappy "Good-bye," followed by a click as she hung up. O'Neill felt the beads of sweat forming on his forehead. Boy! Is she steamed! He was about to hang up when Christelle's voice came on again:

Broc... I'm sorry... I'm sorry for being so mad last night. It's just that I'm really worried. I don't know where you are; I don't know... whether you are even alive...

There was a long pause, a hesitant beginning or two, and then the sound of Christelle taking a big breath and forcefully expelling air.

Broc, I really, really want to hear from you. I can't do anything until I know. Please, Broc, please call me. I know what you're doing is dangerous, and I'm terrified. I don't want to find out in some obituary that you're dead. The number at the cabin is the same as before. Please, please call me.

O'Neill hung up the phone and sat for a long minute. Then he went to the mini-fridge and chose a Canada Dry. The prices were exorbitant, but he decided not to worry about the cost. He still had eighty-five thousand dollars in his luggage.

He sat down with photocopied pages from *Dun & Bradstreet* and flipped through to the summary on Kaiser Shipping Enterprises. Kaiser had warehouses in twenty-one states; the corporate office was in York, less than twenty miles south of Harrisburg. *The Million Dollar Directory* did not contain detailed information, just enough to indicate a massive shipping operation dedicated to inter-city and inter-state movement of entire companies. The company had a fleet of transport trucks and a line of ocean freighters. William Kaiser III was listed as president.

O'Neill could not concentrate. He kept hearing Christelle. Her voice was plaintive and she was genuinely concerned for his safety. That was why he left the way he did; she would have done her best to dissuade him from leaving, especially if she had had any idea of what he was up to. She would have insisted on coming, but he could not put her into any more danger.

Pondering the dull green of the TV screen across the room, he considered turning it on as he drank the Canada Dry then decided against it. He imagined he saw her through the glass sitting on the deck, her feet on a planter, the forest green tam on her head, auburn hair over her shoulders.

I can't do anything until I know. I don't want to find out in some obituary that you're dead. Please call—. Broc picked up the telephone and dialed the Vermont area code and then the number at the cabin. The phone rang twice; Christelle came on the line.

"Hi. I got your messages."

There was a sudden squeal, almost a shout of relief, and then Christelle was talking. "Oh, Dr. O'Neill! Broc! I am so glad you called. I have had an awful day."

"What's the trouble?" he asked in alarm.

"Just worrying. I've been worried sick. I've been so frightened." She paused to get her breath.

"I'm in Pennsylvania."

"I figured you might be. But what are you doing there?"

"Two people with phones like mine are here in Harrisburg."

"You've talked to them?"

"I talked to one of them, a guy who's president of GEO Corporation."

Broc heard shuffling of paper. "Is he this guy John Randolph on this list?"

"That's him. He's a high roller, loads of money, expensive car. I can't figure out why anyone would bother to set him up with a rigged cellular phone. He's got a fancy mistress, but half the rich guys in the country have them. Pretty old stuff."

"So, no clues?"

"He's a bit of a whacko. After a couple of beers, he goes into an anti-government tirade. Everybody is a suckhole. He's had a rough time with the IRS, and his company has been under scrutiny over defense contracts. This guy is pretty much off the wall."

"What about the other one?"

"Nathan Jamiessen — model citizen, the perfect family man, upright citizen. A good supporter of the community, the usual high visibility stuff these guys do. His company makes electronic guidance systems for missiles."

"But you didn't talk to him."

"It's not easy to get to these guys."

"So, you're going to quit and come back?"

"Not so fast. I've got some more I want to talk to—"

"Broc, this is really dangerous. I don't think it's worth the risk. Let's just throw away your telephone and forget all this."

"Christelle!"

There was dead silence from the other end of the connection.

"I'm sorry for shouting, but these guys, whoever they are, tried to kill me. Somebody out there killed my wife."

There was a long silence, and then he could hear her crying. O'Neill squeezed his temples, trying to drive away the knot of pain gathering in his forehead.

"Broc, I'm so sorry. I can't say how sorry I am. This is all so... so unfair. But you could get yourself killed, too, and what good would... would that be for... Darcy?"

His head was aching now. "I need a couple more days, I need to see a couple more of these guys. I just need to figure out why they've got rigged telephones."

"Okay. I guess I can live with that. I'll wait; carry on. But, Broc, can you make sure you call in a couple of days — say by Wednesday night?"

"Okay—"

"Promise!"

"I promise."

"Okay. So where are you going next?"

"Tomorrow I'm going to look up this guy down in York, big executive type, head of a shipping company. Wednesday, I'm going to do some research on this guy in Allentown, CEO of Pennsylvania Produce. He's agreed we could meet late afternoon or evening."

"So you could be ready to come back here Thursday."

"If everything goes as well as today, yes, I could be done."

"But you still have to call me, okay. Even if you're coming back the next day."

"Okay, Christelle. I really appreciate your concern. And I will call."

Chapter Fifteen

Susquehanna Valley
Tuesday, July 16

The Pennsylvania countryside southeast of York was a mixture of open farmland and forest with towns and sleepy villages every two or three miles: Red Lion, Keys, Brogueville, Kyleville. The land had been settled and cleared by pioneers nearly three hundred years ago under the leadership of William Penn. The people had prospered and laid a foundation for one of America's most powerful industrial states. Twenty minutes out of York, O'Neill found the turn onto a road that would lead into the valley of the Susquehanna River where William Kaiser's vacation cabin was located.

William Kaiser: Chief Executive Officer of Kaiser Shipping Enterprises. Owner of a Worldwide cell phone that had replaced an earlier Worldwide model bought five years ago. If the earlier model had the same capability, eavesdropping had been going on for a long time! Two hours ago, he had called William Kaiser from a public telephone; his secretary had suggested he call Kaiser at home. A housekeeper had given him a number at his waterfront retreat, where Kaiser and his wife were enjoying a week away from the office.

"My name is Wallace, Jacob Wallace. I'm with *Middle Colonies Enterprise*. It's a new publication featuring the accomplishments of the most prominent industrialists, especially those with deep roots in the original Middle Colonies."

"I don't think I've ever heard of it."

"That's because we're in the process of putting together the flagship issue. It's scheduled to appear early next year."

"So what's on your mind?"

"We've heard about Kaiser Shipping — especially its most recent acquisitions. It seems like a superb industry for a cover story."

William Kaiser gave O'Neill directions to Ubersicht — southeast on the Susquehanna River below the dam — and Mrs. Kaiser invited him for lunch. O'Neill glanced at his watch: 11:25. The road wound through the trees toward the river.

As he drove, O'Neill mulled over the previous two days: his research on Nathan Jamiessen of Brandeis Electronics and William Randolph of GEO Corporation. Both companies were big, successful, and rapidly expanding. But Jamiessen and Randolph were as different as night and day. O'Neill ransacked his brain, reviewing everything he had read, and ran through his bizarre meeting with Randolph and his sexpot mistress. Why would they be carrying a highly sophisticated cell phone from which their conversations could be plucked like so many ripe cherries?

Broc had two more opportunities to penetrate the mystery: William Kaiser this afternoon, then Walter P. Monahan this evening. Within the next two days, O'Neill was sure that he would encounter something — a minor fact, a casual remark, an obscure business connection, an innocuous bit of personal history — that would bring clarity to whatever pattern was so far very well hidden.

Finally, he was there. William Kaiser's summer home was built of logs, huge twelve-inch diameter timbers, which must have come from the Pacific Northwest. It was a sprawling mansion overlooking a vast expanse of the river, which flowed blue under the summer sky between dark green forested banks dotted with prestigious vacation homes. A carved sign by the graveled parking space read UBERSICHT. A white boat of luxury dimensions with a blue canvas top rested on a steep ramp that led from a boathouse to the water. Leaving his wife knitting under the shade of a huge canvas canopy, Kaiser came down the timber steps from his deck. He was heavy-browed with a distinctive Germanic ruggedness, a couple of inches under six feet, and overweight.

Ninety minutes later they had finished lunch, which was briskly prepared by a servant, a well-spoken African-American woman, who stayed around long enough to clear the table and fill a cooler with ice and Oktoberfest beer and then walked fifty yards down the river to another house.

"Wonderful woman, wonderful family. They've worked for the Kaisers for forty years," Betty Kaiser confided. "Her husband works in town. She looks after Ubersicht; it means 'Overlook', Mr. Wallace."

"When we bought it, the place looked like it had been overlooked for decades." Kaiser said, making a joke out of his wife's too obvious pride. "But we've brought it back." He motioned O'Neill to follow him.

In the south wing of the house, they entered a room dominated by eight floor-to-ceiling cabinets with glass doors. Kaiser touched a wall switch. O'Neill was taken aback; soft light in each of the cabinets flooded a gleaming arsenal of weapons. Two heavy infantry cannons stood against the far wall. O'Neill was drawn to the nearest cabinet, which contained five heavy glass shelves, each with three pistols. Kaiser brought out a key, opened the cabinet door, lifted out one of the guns, worked the action to demonstrate it was unloaded, and handed it to O'Neill. He could feel the pride of the owner of this impressive collection.

"There are several Lugers. This is one of the finest semi-automatics the Germans ever made. Eight shots, 7.65 mm Parabellum cartridges." Kaiser picked up another and aimed it toward the window. "This one takes the larger 9 mm Parabellum cartridge."

Kaiser placed the pistols carefully on the shelves and moved to the next cabinet. "You have to understand, Mr. Wallace: we Kaisers are of ancient German stock. Despite the unfortunate ideology that developed under Adolf Hitler's Nazi Party, we retain our pride in the technical achievements of the German people, which is well illustrated in their magnificent engines of war."

O'Neill gazed in awe at the firearms. "It's an intimidating arsenal," he observed, unable to respond to the individual weapons.

"That one" — Kaiser pointed to a deadly looking pistol — "is a Walther P 38, the principal German side arm used in World War II. That one, shaped like a rifle with an outer perforated barrel, is actually one of the earliest sub-machine guns, the Bergmann MP 18/1, used by the German army in World War I. Setting aside the time for snapping in cartridges, which feed into what's called a snail magazine, that weapon could fire four hundred rounds a minute. The weapon below it with the folding stock is an MP40 — the Germans called it a Schmeisser — capable of five hundred rounds per minute."

O'Neill scanned from weapon to weapon, astonished at the atmosphere of deadly force permeating the room. He was astonished, too, at the reverence toward these weapons, killing instruments of Hitler's forces. "This must be a very valuable collection."

"It's probably one of the most complete collections of German weaponry outside the war museums. But I've never had it appraised, Mr. Wallace. I don't exhibit them. Many of these were obtained decades ago when they became obsolete as newer models were introduced. Yes, I suppose they could be quite valuable. That thing" — he pointed at one of the heavy mounted guns against the far wall, which might have weighed several hundred pounds — "is the Panzerabwehrkanone, which the Germans introduced in 1936 — better known as a PAK 36. It's an anti-tank gun that shoots a 37 mm shell at a muzzle velocity of 2500 feet per second."

The figures meant nothing to O'Neill. "How does that compare with, let's say, your average 22 rifle?"

"About twice the speed, Mr. Wallace, but that is still not fast. The cannon beside it replaced it. It looks lighter, but it uses the Gerlich principle: a tapered bore, which increases the pressure on the shot as it travels down the barrel, combined with skirts on the cartridge, like arrow feathers that fold in as the barrel narrows. The bullet, a 28 mm projectile with a steel or tungsten core, has a muzzle velocity of over 4500 feet; that's well over three-quarters of a mile per second. Four times the speed of your 22 bullet. With that kind of speed, it had a very flat trajectory and was therefore the most accurate and deadly anti-tank gun of its day."

O'Neill gazed at the sinister weapon, then turned his attention to the final cabinet.

"Those, Mr. Wallace, are some of the brutal weapons Americans have had turned against them. These are all Japanese." O'Neill experienced a strange mixture of fascination and abhorrence. "The Arisaka Type 38 rifle, introduced in 1905; the Carbine version with folding stock used by paratroopers." He pointed to a gun mounted on a low tripod. "The Type 92 machine gun, which the Americans had to face on Iwo Jima and Okinawa."

O'Neill remembered the black-and-white documentary films of soldiers cut down as they stormed the beaches in the deadly campaigns of the Pacific war. He gazed around at the cabinets, which he guessed held close to a hundred weapons, all used by the enemies of the United States: Germany and Japan.

Japan! Why Japanese weapons? German pride in German weaponry was understandable, not unlike the fascination of American NRA members with old Colt handguns used on the American frontier.

"Well, let's get onto the river!" Kaiser directed, turning on his heel. "After all, the river is why the 'Overlook' is here; it's why we are here."

O'Neill followed Kaiser, who was carrying a cooler to the boat, a Sea Ray 250 Express Cruiser. They stepped onto the eight-foot swim platform, then into the rear deck. The motor at the boathouse set in motion a moveable pallet, which let the craft roll smoothly into the water. Kaiser lowered the props and turned the key; the inboard motor rumbled into life, backing them away from shore.

"It's a Chevrolet motor," Kaiser volunteered as he steered the boat around, "350 cubic inches."

O'Neill raised his eyebrows in apparent admiration as he slipped into the white vinyl seat by the flip-up table across from Kaiser. The windshield wrapped around in an angular taper that continued into the gunwales of the rear cockpit. The seats were enhanced by a vertical band of royal blue against a broader band of black; the molded dashboard displayed a line of eight dials. Through the half-open door, he could see down into the forward cabin with its miniature cook-top stove and molded counter, and beyond, the V-berth in the bow, the whole interior lit by three smoky skylights on the forward deck. The metal plate by the entrance rated the engine at 230 horsepower, delivered through a MerCruiser Bravo Two sterndrive. Weight: 4,200 pounds. Sleeping capacity: four.

Within minutes the cruiser was riding smoothly upstream toward the Holtwood Dam, the last man-made obstruction before the river dumped its water from half the state of Pennsylvania into Chesapeake Bay.

"We're very old Germanic stock, Wallace. The first Kaisers came out here to escape the narrow-minded bigotry of Northern Europe. You know, William Penn was a brilliant colonist. Legend has it our forebears were attracted by his Quaker beliefs and persuaded by his religious toleration."

"So, the Kaisers are Quakers—"

"Probably always will be."

They were having to shout to be heard. Kaiser wheeled the boat in a broad circle below the dam, then headed the bow downstream and cut the motor to trolling speed. O'Neill wondered how the traditional Quaker ideology of passivism squared with a collection of deadly war weaponry. As the boat settled down to an easy five miles per hour, Kaiser broke out two cans of beer so cold they were almost painful to hold.

"Kaiser Shipping was founded by my grandfather in 1914. He ran it until the fifties, then my father. I came to the helm nine years ago."

"I understand the company has gone international—"

"We've been fortunate, Mr. Wallace. In the early days we moved timber; later it was coal. Then, during the war, my father saw opportunities and took advantage." He glanced at O'Neill and then went on. "We concentrated on coastal shipping until about twenty years ago. Now we do big moving jobs on land — whole warehouses, factory assembly lines, corporate offices. Just before he retired, my father landed a government contract. Now we move tons for Washington — army hardware, records headed for storage, documents for presidential libraries — even emergency deliveries when the suppliers are overloaded — space shuttle parts, military hardware. We've got two transport planes entirely dedicated to serving bases in Alaska, but that is a minor contract. Kaiser Shipping has over two thousand eighteen-wheelers on the road."

Two thousand! O'Neill managed to conceal his astonishment. "That's all domestic shipping, things any journalist can find in half an hour. From what I've seen, less than half of Kaiser's work is domestic. What about the international stuff?"

Kaiser took a drink of beer. "We do some overseas work."

"I saw a reference to freighters—"

"Yes, we've got freighters."

"How many?"

"Seven in the Mediterranean." Kaiser stared off at the forest; O'Neill sensed he was feigning disinterest in his questions.

"Where else?"

"Be specific."

"In the Pacific."

"It's very difficult to say. A dozen, two dozen."

A dozen, two dozen! The answer itself told O'Neill that Kaiser wanted to avoid further questions about their international operations. Why?

But Kaiser went on: "Some of them sail around Singapore to the Indian Ocean. Would you count those?"

O'Neill shrugged. "So where is the home base?"

"I believe some are based in the Philippines."

I believe! His words were strange.

"And the rest?"

"Cyprus." The answer was abrupt; it seemed to say Enough! I don't like this line of questioning.

They were drifting past Ubersicht. O'Neill could see Betty Kaiser sitting on the deck in a white sundress. The house was stunning, an immense spread of stone foundation walls from the ground to the deck surmounted by heavy timbers and a red tiled roof. He estimated it at six-thousand square feet. The compound, which included the servant's house, boathouse, and two more homes half hidden in the forest, must occupy eight or ten acres. A pricey piece of real estate. With this much river frontage, it could be worth millions.

"Why so far abroad?"

"There are many places more favorable for doing business than the United States."

"But it's all American money, isn't it?"

"We send a lot of money to the islands, Mr. Wallace. Offshore banks. Most of it stays there, which means it's no longer American money."

And what it earns, O'Neill mused, is not taxable income.

O'Neill opened the second beer that Kaiser handed him. "It must have taken a while to build up a fleet of twenty or thirty ocean freighters. When did the company get into international shipping?"

Kaiser offered a cigarette to O'Neill, who declined, then lit up with an ornate gold lighter and moved a heavy metal ashtray closer on the console. It bore an engraved signature of Ronald Reagan; the date 1984, when Reagan was reelected; and the seal of the GOP. Kaiser leaned against the side of the boat and turned toward O'Neill while blowing smoke from the side of his mouth. "I think the international division is the least interesting aspect of Kaiser Shipping. And, unless I'm mistaken, the readers of your *Middle Colonies* magazine are going to have mainly domestic interests — indeed, specific regional interests."

O'Neill noted the skillful diversion. "Then let's pursue the regional angle. What year did the first Kaisers arrive in the Middle Colonies?"

"It was just a few years after William Penn's Charter. I believe the Wilhelm Kaiser family landed at Philadelphia in 1708. News of the Charter got all the way to Germany. It was the main reason they came out here. William Penn was their hero. He was almost like a god to them. And ever since then every Kaiser has had to memorize his words. My father stood over me — I remember: it was my tenth birthday — and made me learn the words. And he never let us forget them.

Because no people can be truly happy if abridged of the freedom of their profession and worship, I do hereby grant and declare that no person in this province or territory who shall confess and acknowledge one almighty God, shall be in any case molested because of his or their conscientious persuasion or practice, nor be compelled to maintain any religious worship contrary to his or their mind, or to do or suffer any other act or thing contrary to his or their religious persuasion.

Kaiser smiled. "It's hard to find finer words than those. You know, Mr. Wallace, when you come from a place of religious bigotry such as Europe once was, words like William Penn's are like a gospel."

It was all great speechmaking, O'Neill thought, but most of it sounded like an elaborate front, a deliberate ad campaign for the Kaisers, rehearsed so often that William Kaiser had come to believe it. The obvious contradiction was that Quakers were passivists. O'Neill was still trying to square Kaiser's praise for the Quakers with his arsenal of war weaponry.

A sleek speedboat heading upstream roared past, sending waves against the hull. Kaiser was obviously disgusted. "We're getting near the

Maryland border. There's a lot of traffic here from the Chesapeake. It's only a dozen or so miles downriver."

O'Neill finished his beer and set the can by the cooler. Looking toward the shore, he tried to sort out the contradictions. William Kaiser was a victim, too — the owner of a rigged Worldwide Communications cell phone. But why remained a mystery. O'Neill could see no pattern.

"You know, Mr. Wallace, they're always saying that the English Puritans founded this nation. But they've got it all wrong. The Puritans were the worst bunch of narrow-minded bigots this country has ever known. We've got religious freedom here, Wallace, today. Where do you think it came from? Not from the Puritans! The men who wrote the Constitution got it right here, from their own land, from Pennsylvania. It came from the man who founded the Quakers, William Penn."

O'Neill looked away, struck by the mixture of wisdom and ignorance. The ideal of religious freedom was, indeed, William Penn's legacy, but Penn was a skilled politician, not the founder of the Quakers. Adulation for the hero had led to mistaken mythology, as it always did. O'Neill willed himself not to correct Kaiser's history, meanwhile filing away the obvious: William Kaiser's stated beliefs and verbal reverence for the founder of Pennsylvania was so much bullshit. Where his true reverence resided was with his collection of World War II German weaponry. And... Japanese weaponry.

"Anyway, you can see we're deep into it here. The Kaisers are close to the heart of Pennsylvania. We're right in there with the Amish."

O'Neill looked down, if only to bring the rain of bullshit to an end. Apart from his Germanic pride, William Kaiser was transparent.

They ran at trolling speed for another quarter hour — to the Maryland border — and then Kaiser turned the boat and headed back upstream, the motor running at about one-half power at a steady fifteen miles an hour. Kaiser pointed out one house and property after another, naming their owners, describing their professional and business connections, commenting on what they did and who they knew.

When they were opposite Ubersicht, Kaiser hit the throttle and roared the cruiser upstream at full power. Kaiser was enthralled with power, O'Neill thought — 230 sterndrive horsepower, five hundred rounds-per-second power, 4500 feet-per-second power. Knockdown power. Penetrating power. German power. Japanese power. Within a couple of minutes, they were at the dam again and turning in a wide arc that sent four-foot waves across the river. Heading down river, the speedometer read 42 mph, but it felt to O'Neill like 75.

Chapter Sixteen

Rappahannock County, Virginia
Tuesday, July 16

The car — expensive, unmarked, with smoked rear windows — roared west on Interstate 65 out of Washington, taking the ramp to Highway 15 at Gainesville and continuing on toward Highway 211. John Orchard, judicial counsel from the Department of Justice, sat smoking in the back seat and watching the lights of urban Virginia roll by. An urgent message had come in earlier, shortly before noon. The whole Committee would need to be informed. Of necessity, Orchard had been on the phone most of the afternoon. Hastily, a meeting time was set for 9 p.m., time enough for various officers of the Committee to catch flights from New York, Atlanta, and Detroit.

Twenty minutes beyond Amissville the driver left the freeway and followed a two-way blacktop northwest. Two miles later, as they rounded a bend, Orchard checked the rearview mirror. The road behind was dark; they were not being followed. The driver turned right onto a gravel road marked with a brown and white historical marker sign: Rappahannock County Historical Museum. The car slowed a quarter mile along the road and veered at the first fork, marked "Maintenance and Deliveries." A hundred yards later the road opened into the south parking lot before the building, a one-story frame structure surrounded by a broad cement porch shaded by a heavy roof and surrounded by twenty yards of landscaped rock gardens. It was 8:28 when the car pulled to a stop. Thirty-two minutes early.

Orchard got out, walked round to the window by the driver, and spoke in a low voice. "I'll call, probably after eleven, certainly before midnight."

"I'll be within a quarter mile, Sir."

Orchard waited until the car had left, then walked to the delivery ramp, which ran sixty feet downhill to the basement level. He opened a door, making sure it was closed before he turned on the lights. He walked among crates and cabinets to a hall, followed it to the second door, let himself in with a second key, and switched on the lights. The windowless room had four doors, a twenty-four-foot conference table and two dozen upholstered chairs. Orchard lit up a cigarette, checked his watch, and sat down to wait. It was 8:36.

The museum upstairs had seemingly endless funds for purchase of artifacts. Its collection included pioneer furniture and clothes, metal ware from Virginia's colonial era, and a selection of diaries and letters written by the earliest settlers, all carefully arranged and displayed in glass cases. The building was surrounded with artfully laid out parking lots and ample greenery, which had the scarcely noticed effect, of making each approach to the grounds, invisible to the others. There were various entrances with stairs to the basement. The lower level was used for unpacking and restoring furniture, with one corner permanently locked and off limits to the daytime staff.

For the dedicated community ladies who managed the museum with Victorian propriety, the locked rooms were used, if used at all, only rarely. In fact, though none of them ever thought about it, these rooms had never been used since the building was dedicated some five years ago. The museum closed promptly at five thirty, Mondays to Saturdays, and all library personnel were required to be out of the building by six, thus allowing for its use for other purposes.

The Rappahannock County Museum was built with donated funds, the source of which had never been questioned; nor had the more puzzling aspects of the blueprints ever been noted during construction. The little ladies of the Rappahannock Historical Society went home every evening, proud of their work and the stunning collections that drew dozens of visitors every day. They were unaware of the more important but largely invisible functions of the facility.

Tonight, just after 7 p.m., the entire building had been electronically scanned.

At 8:38, the north door opened and Joseph Terrence came in, dropped off, Orchard knew, at the north parking lot. His driver, a trusted employee of the State Department, would be parked nearby on another access road. Terrence sat down, and they waited in silence for the others to arrive. At approximately two-minute intervals one of the doors opened and someone else came in, taking his place silently, waiting. None of them except Orchard knew how many would be there.

Certain of the participants knew others. As a member of the Justice Department, Orchard had high visibility, and Martin Atwater was known as the chief assistant to a prominent New England Senator. Colonel James Spiker, who had retired to his comfortable estate near Philadelphia just before Desert Storm, was known by three other military men. Wade Bracket, a senior officer in the CIA, was known to members from the FBI, but his precise position was not clear. William Masterson was always uncertain; tonight, he came in the east door at 8:58. Orchard recollected it was only the second or third time he had attended any of perhaps two dozen meetings in the past four years. Some regulars were present at every meeting, but Dwight Blakeney, a senior FBI chief from Indianapolis, had attended only once before and so was new to most of the others; and one participant was unknown to Orchard.

At 9:06, Judge Leopold Hudgeons entered from the west door and took his seat; at precisely 9:10, the unknown participant — a representative of the mysterious Veil — entered and sat at the far end of the table. All nine were present. Orchard lit another cigarette, stepped to a switch and turned on the exhaust fan, resumed his seat, and leaned forward.

"Gentlemen, I apologize for the short notice. I would always prefer at least three days' warning before convening a meeting of Lignum Operations. However, we've had word of a situation that needs immediate attention." He pulled a long drag on his cigarette and glanced around. "I believe our newest participant can explain. Please"— Orchard gestured toward the far end of the table — "introduce yourself—"

The new man leaned forward and introduced himself as Leonard Smith. "Gentlemen, a crack has opened up, a serious breach. Our sector leader has already reported this to Mr. Orchard. He has asked me to report this to the whole group. Our sense is that we need consensus on action to be taken."

Orchard pulled on his cigarette. As though by suggestion, Smith and Masterson pulled out packs. Smith struck a match. As Masterson's lighter flared, his heavy brows lowered, shielding his eyes from the sudden burst of smoke.

"A call came in late last night from one of our clients, one of our most important clients in Pennsylvania. The call was taped. May I?" He set the recorder on the table.

Orchard nodded.

"This call lasted twelve minutes. The brief segment you hear will be enough, I won't bore you with the choicer examples of invective. The first person you'll hear is John Randolph, Chief Executive Officer of GEO Corporation in Harrisburg. The calmer voice you'll hear is our man responding — or trying to respond." He pushed the play button.

"You damned sons of bitches! I ought to sue you guys all the way to hell. This crap has been going on for months and now I find out my bloody phone is tapped—"

"Mr. Randolph, I have no idea about your phone—"

"It's damn well tapped! That's how my suckhole wife is finding out all this stuff about me, and the bloody tax department. And you guys—"

"I don't think this has anything to do with us, Mr. Randolph. What gives you the idea your phone is tapped?"

"This guy told me. These phones are the easiest phones to tap. He told me—"

"And who was this guy?"

"A guy at my club. A guy from Missouri who just moved to town. I talked to him this afternoon—"

"Who was he, Mr. Randolph?"

"Who he was is none of your damn business! It's no more your business than anything I say on my bloody phone is your business!"

Leonard Smith clicked off the tape recorder. No one moved for several seconds. The tension in the room was electric. All eyes moved from the tape recorder to John Orchard.

"Sorry, John," Colonel James Spiker half apologized, "but is this the same John Randolph who's in that big divorce case that's been all over the papers?"

Smith nodded, then spoke: "The timing is most unfortunate. Randolph's been shouting at his attorneys for weeks that his wife's got a PI tailing him and trying to dig up dirt for the divorce, so he's suspicious of everything and everybody. Apparently, she's been hitting him pretty hard. The guy is near the breaking point. Now it appears that our surveillance has become entangled with his paranoia."

"He's been cooperative for the past seven years, hasn't he?" Orchard asked.

"Until six months ago," Smith confirmed, "when we began to put pressure on him."

"Why? Why the pressure?"

"He got stubborn. We asked for an increase in his payment and he resisted. Then he decided he didn't want to pay anything."

"Pressure. Is that what he's talking about — that stuff about the tax department?"

Smith nodded.

"Damn it!" Colonel Spiker banged the flat of his hand on the table. "We need to put pressure on people, always have, always will. But all of you should know that the worst way to put pressure on anybody is through the IRS! Executives like Randolph have too much to hide — unreported income, inflated expense accounts, deductions on vacation homes. They're all paranoid when the IRS comes after them." Spiker paused, regaining his composure. "How bad is it? I mean, what has the IRS done?"

"Company audits for 1991, '92, '93, and '94 is in the pipeline—"

"Christ! No wonder the guy is cracking up! Getting the IRS into it is absolutely the wrong kind of coercion! It's harassment. Anyone can see that!"

The senator's assistant from New England, Martin Atwater, leaned forward and eyed Spiker across the table. "Colonel, some of us thought a certain warehouse fire in Atlanta was, shall we say, too much coercion."

Spiker was furious. His neck turned red and the color spread to his face. After a minute he spoke, barely containing his rage: "The biggest monthly deposit we've had, the biggest we've ever had, was $6.3 million. May I remind you that it came from my sector — from the owner of that warehouse! When you can show me results like that by sending out the IRS auditors—"

"Gentlemen!" Orchard butted his cigarette. "We've got far more serious things to argue than who has the best system of extortion. We've got a dangerous client who is furious, who's talking lawsuits, who's threatening to go to the papers."

"What can he prove?"

"Nothing, but that's not the point. We can't take a chance on him even suggesting anything, especially about tapped telephones. We've got over four thousand out there. They are the best spying gadget anybody ever designed; we don't have a backup. If the secret of the phones is exposed, our whole operation could be shut down."

"What about this guy Randolph met — the guy at his club?"

Orchard spoke: "We had someone check it out. He was a walk-in. He bought a week's pass yesterday just after Randolph signed in. A guy by the name of Jacob Wallace from Missouri." Orchard turned to a participant who had not spoken. "Could you fill us in on this Wallace?"

The dusty blonde dressed in Levi shirt and jeans spoke slowly. "The computers ran all afternoon. There are about forty Jacob Wallaces nationwide. We had them check Sector Eight very carefully. All three Jacob Wallaces from Missouri were in Missouri yesterday."

"So, what do you conclude?"

"We've got a maverick," Martin Atwater concluded, "a 'Jacob Wallace' who doesn't exist."

"Maybe," Orchard suggested, tapping another cigarette onto the table, "maybe this guy's comment about the telephones was offhand, a throw-away remark? It's got to the point where bugged telephones are pretty much an urban legend."

"I'd think that — if we could get a positive ID on him. The cameras in the club were down all afternoon, so we don't know what he looks like." Smith pulled out another cigarette. "He's just come out of nowhere.

And even if it were offhand, he's got Randolph coming off the walls. Right now, he is our worst liability."

John Orchard listened, watching the participants, his eyes sweeping all of them, taking in expressions, the position of hands, movements of fingers. His instincts — responses trained through years of studying human behavior under stress — told him a committee consensus was near. "Does this mean" — Orchard paused, trying to read face after face — "does this mean termination?"

"Let's vote a little later. It's urgent that we investigate the Jefferson State case."

Orchard was reluctant to open up the topic until Dwight Blakeney spoke. "I agree; it's urgent. As a starter, let me report on Professor Broc O'Neill's publication. It called for Senate hearings on domestic intelligence operations. The journal has just over two thousand eight hundred subscriptions, two thousand four hundred to libraries. We managed to have almost every issue disappear. We've picked up the other hundred plus from private subscribers by burglarizing offices and homes. And three hundred or so overrun copies disappeared on their way to storage—"

"So, O'Neill's article has been buried. But what about him?"

Blakeney turned, annoyed at the interruption. "We don't know much. Just over a week ago, we had an interceptor in Vermont ready to take out O'Neill. Then we lost him—"

Judge Leopold Hudgeons was agitated as he spoke. "With the entire resources of the FBI at your disposal, Blakeney, you just don't lose someone."

"It would be nice, Your Honor, if we had the entire resources of the FBI at our disposal. Unfortunately, it's problematic using a federal agency for clandestine operations beyond the purview of the agency itself—"

"I don't recall you mentioning such limitations before this, Blakeney. On the contrary, you've been touting your resources as the kingpin in this whole operation—"

"We lost him, Leo!" Blakeney shouted, furious. "We got one quick radio communication from the agents that some broad had picked O'Neill up at the Burlington airport, and they were tailing them—"

"Agents?"

"Two friendly Bureau guys from local operations in Rutland. Next thing, their car had gone off a mountain road and they were frying in the wreck."

"Can't your other local-operations guys follow up?"

"The pickup was reported at the airport, not the make. O'Neill and the broad disappeared."

"So, who is she?"

"We tracked O'Neill's call to the Fletcher Library in Burlington. The librarian remembered the call. She said the caller asked for his daughter, Miss O'Neill. She had been sitting reading all day. We've checked. O'Neill doesn't have a daughter."

"Any other information about her?"

"According to the librarian, 'nice girl with auburn hair'. She didn't check anything out. We've no idea what she was reading. She carried in her own books.

"Shit! So, we've got absolutely nothing!"

"I think I said that at the beginning, Leo."

"So, this guy vanished after his wife's funeral in Indiana; then he surfaces five weeks later in Vermont with a daughter who doesn't exist, and now he's disappeared again!"

"We've got a little more, though it's too late to do us any good." Dwight Blakeney had everyone's attention. "We've picked up a bank transfer: $300,000 wired from Jefferson to Michigan, a bank in Battle Creek, on July 2nd—"

"But you didn't pick it up in time to intercept him at the bank."

Blakeney shook his head. "Even if we'd been there, we would have missed him. Evidently, he went into the Battle Creek branch the day before the transfer and left orders. As soon as the $300,000 came in, the manager immediately wired it on — to the Lansing branch. We checked it out. O'Neill was fifty miles away waiting in the bank in Lansing when the money came in — with a new account ready. He deposited $210,000 and took $90,000 with him. The bank had been forewarned. They had the cash on hand."

"Blakeney, stop covering your ass!" Hudgeons slapped the tabletop. "Give us the facts, not some cock-and-bull story about a master sleuth. He's a history prof, isn't he? An egghead academic?"

"He's a historian, Leo." Blakeney was seething over yet another interruption from the Judge. "Special field of expertise, the history of American intelligence. He's written a string of articles and two books displaying more knowledge of American intelligence than anybody in your damned Federal Court can hope to know in a lifetime! Evidently, he knows how to use what he knows."

Infuriated, Judge Leo Hudgeons glared at Blakeney.

"What about his flight into Burlington?" Colonel Spiker asked.

Dwight Blakeney turned away from the Judge toward the Colonel. "He flew from Grand Rapids under his own name, connections in Cleveland and Newark. He bought the ticket just before takeoff—"

"With cash, of course. He had $90,000 with him."

"With cash! So, you see what we're up against. He's not making any credit card purchases. No paper trail. As long as he moves quickly, he can stay out of reach."

"By my count," Orchard began to summarize, "his call to this broad in Burlington was the fourth time he used the phone — after a month's silence. He disappeared with his wife's car, but we never picked up even a single sighting, not a clue. We have no idea where he was all that time. For all we know, he was chasing butterflies in Monterey or contemplating frogs in the Okefenokee Swamp. No calls. We figured he had ditched the phone. The call to Vermont caught us by surprise—"

"Still, we managed to have these guys at the airport in time."

"They were supposed to terminate O'Neill."

"Their weapon was recovered, John — a Skorpion vz. 61 machine pistol that holds a twenty-round clip. There were eight rounds left. Our man apparently fired a dozen rounds before the car ran off the road. Presumably, O'Neill was the target."

"But no body. The bastard leads a charmed life. Well, there's nothing to do but wait. But he's on the run; he's bound to make a mistake."

"But," Smith observed, "it's doubtful the mistake will be another phone call that can be traced. We don't know what happened on that

146

mountain in Vermont, but twelve rounds were fired from an automatic weapon. O'Neill is bound to figure things out. Two of his cell phone calls have led to close encounters of a near-death kind."

"What's your point, Leonard?"

"My point, gentlemen, is that we now have three people who know about the phones: John Randolph, Jacob Wallace, and Broc O'Neill. That calls for immediate action." He looked directly at Orchard. "You suggested termination a few minutes ago. Have you contacted the Admiral? Veil?"

Orchard nodded. "They're all informed. Even Ironwood is aware of this. He sanctioned tonight's meeting. But how we handle this is up to us. I'll inform the Admiral and Veil in the morning." He addressed Wade Bracket, the officer from the CIA. "I suggest you decide on your options and have a procedure in place within twenty-four hours. Obviously, we can take out Randolph by then. Meanwhile, we've got to find Broc O'Neill."

"Isn't this internal, 'domestic' as they say over on the Hill, a matter for the FBI?"

Orchard glanced from Bracket to Blakeney. He felt a wave of tension, a decades-old territorial instinct — something he knew it was necessary to restrain. "Let me remind you, Sir, we are operating under the auspices of Lignum Operations, not the Joint Chiefs of Staff. So far, we've managed to avoid pissing on posts. I'd like to continue the tradition."

Wade Bracket nodded and began speaking without a flinch. "Of course, we've got more than Professor Broc O'Neill and John Randolph to deal with. We've also got this maverick Jacob Wallace somewhere in Pennsylvania—"

"Damn!" The outburst drew everyone's eyes to Leonard Smith who was looking around the table, his forehead deeply etched. "Has it occurred to anyone else that these two guys may be the same guy? That Jacob Wallace might be Broc O'Neill?" Smith paused for a few seconds. "And if so, what is he doing in Pennsylvania? And why was he talking to John Randolph?"

Chapter Seventeen

Allentown, Pennsylvania
Wednesday, July 17, evening

Broc finished a club sandwich and salad, spent an hour reading *The Philadelphia Inquirer*, then went out to the truck-stop parking lot. He guessed there were thirty vehicles on the ten-acre lot, and at least a dozen eighteen-wheelers with engines running as their drivers ate dinner inside or browsed around the gadget shop. He pulled his rented Tempo up to a gas pump, checked the oil, brake fluid, and coolant. Everything was in order. He paid for the gas and checked his watch: 9:28 p.m.

O'Neill pulled onto Interstate 22, drove east toward Allentown, exited at Cedar Crest Boulevard, and then headed along back routes he had checked out earlier in the day. The downtown was quiet. Streetlights marked out the sidewalks with splashes of light.

He saw the flash of an explosion—

No! He refused to relive the agony. He tried to relax, fighting the tension, struggling against the anger washing over him again — a rage that made him want to lash out at the world, the fury driving him to find those who had cut out a hole in the middle of his life — to find them and destroy them.

At nine that morning, O'Neill had checked out of his motel in Harrisburg, paid cash, driven the eighty miles to Allentown, and headed to the Chamber of Commerce. His goal was to meet Walter P. Monahan: President of Pennsylvania Produce.

O'Neill had spent an hour searching local records. In the *Allentown Morning Call* he found a reference to a mid-June Pennsylvania Produce warehouse fire in Atlanta. Articles from the June 17th, 18th, and 19th in *The Atlanta Constitution* reported the conflagration had occurred late on a Sunday night. Estimated losses were $6 million. The June 18th article had pictures and an interview with Walter P. Monahan, President of

Pennsylvania Produce, whose main offices were in Allentown. Among a dozen quotations from the interview were allegations of arson. A week later another article ruled out arson. Allegedly, it was faulty wiring.

But why did Monahan have a rigged telephone? O'Neill screwed up his forehead in frustration. He was no further ahead than he had been three days ago. For most of the afternoon he had mulled over his earlier meeting with William Kaiser. The man was a fanatic about his German ancestry and about weaponry from the two world wars. He was also a prideful egotist: his avowed reverence for the Quakers and William Penn was tissue thin. O'Neill wondered what kind of insecurity William Kaiser was trying to hide.

Still, despite Kaiser's fabricated self-importance, O'Neill had come up empty. It just didn't make sense: so far, he could see no pattern.

O'Neill turned right and headed into the old residential district of Allentown. The houses resembled old New York brownstones: tall and narrow, all brick in construction, with three steps up to ornate doors. He drove slowly down the street and then decided to drive around the neighborhood, circling several blocks until he had memorized the layout of the streets.

Walter Monahan was head of a family business that stretched back to the early part of the century. Family lore, however, had added a level of legend to the corporate history. In the colonial period, 1740 to be precise, one John S. Monahan had staked out six hundred acres in Pennsylvania and laid foundations for the family's rise to fortune. The farm had been passed down through seven generations. In the late nineteenth century, three Monahans in one generation and five in the next had managed to acquire farmsteads totaling, by the turn of the century, over 40,000 acres, with plots dotting much of Lehigh and Northampton Counties.

The development of a shipping station on Monahan land in 1902 had brought a brief period of remarkable family cooperation in the collection and bulk shipment of grain to the coast and overseas. Then, in 1906, nine Monahans had joined their lands under the corporate ownership of Pennsylvania Produce.

Through the early years of the twentieth century, the company had operated as a grain-producing business with thousands of acres of prime farmland in full operation. Following World War I, it had aggressively added shipping stations and grain warehouses, managing to hang on through the devastating depression years. After World War II, the company had expanded westward, continuing to build the business by a combination of good planning, lucky purchases, and hard work. And now Pennsylvania Produce owned trucks and grain depots all across the country, with more than ninety thousand acres of industrial farms in the Midwest, including cattle feedlots in Texas and Oklahoma and dairy operations in Michigan and Wisconsin.

Monahan himself was an austere man. Eschewing the trend of modern corporations ensconcing themselves in glass high-rises downtown, Monahan chose a ninety-year-old brick house, modernized for his executive quarters and office staff of three. The larger bureaucracy necessary for an agricultural operation of this size was now located in a three-story office building somewhere outside Chicago. In his renovated Allentown house, Walter P. Monahan himself was largely invisible.

O'Neill drove past for the second time. A lighted neon sign projected from the building over the front stoop with plain red letters: PENNSYLVANIA PRODUCE, INCORPORATED 1906. The old fire escape was intact at the front corner of the building, which measured not more than twenty-five feet in width. The front wall of the second story had been redesigned to incorporate two windows, with a door onto a three-foot balcony with a wrought-iron railing. The second story was clearly where the main offices were located.

O'Neill turned at the second corner and parked two blocks north. He put his briefcase into the trunk with his luggage, locked up the car, and walked briskly to Pennsylvania Produce. He checked his watch as he rang the bell. It was 10:10; he was five minutes early.

A voice came from a small speaker above the bell. O'Neill identified himself and was invited in. The lock buzzed and he pushed open a door that served as entrance to the darkened ground floor and levels above. The stairs were steep. They came up in a long hall six feet wide that ran thirty feet along the side of the building, with four doors along one side. Light issued from the open door nearest the front of the building.

O'Neill stood in the doorway for a minute. The office, perhaps eighteen feet wide from the hall to the far side of the building, ran from

150

the front windows some thirty feet. The long wall was covered with numerous framed black-and-white farm photographs, some he guessed dating to the beginning of the century. Most included a barn or grain elevator or truck bearing the Monahan logo in the background; the foregrounds were filled with farmers holding various awards or families, including children, lined up for group pictures. The pride of family and business success was everywhere.

O'Neill saw the shadow behind the frosted window to an adjacent room, the second one back from the front of the building, and heard a voice — apparently, the final seconds of a telephone call — and then Walter Monahan came through the door and walked around to shake O'Neill's hand. He was around six feet tall, slim, with middling brown hair and blue eyes. O'Neill knew he was fifty-six, and he was impressed; Monahan looked more like forty.

"I'm glad you called, Mr. Sanderson, but sorry you don't have more time. My wife had already scheduled a club meeting; otherwise, we'd have invited you for dinner."

O'Neill held up his hands. "My thanks for the thought, but" — he glanced around — "the company environment seems better."

"Here; have a seat." O'Neill sat across the desk and Walter Monahan sat down. "You're a journalist; is that right?"

O'Neill nodded. "With a particular interest in federal policy on agriculture—"

"Past or present?"

"Actually, both. It's all interesting," O'Neill said. "There are few agricultural corporations spanning the entire twentieth century. My sense is that Pennsylvania Produce would have a long-term perspective."

Monahan got up and walked to the far end of his office, opened up a door of his credenza, and drew out a gray-covered book. "We've got a couple dozen of these left; you can take this," he offered, handing the book across the desk to O'Neill. "It was an in-house project written by my nephew two summers ago."

O'Neill read the title, stamped into the cover in gold: *Pennsylvania Produce: A Corporate History*. He flipped through the book, a substantial work of two hundred fifty pages with a modest insert of photographs, primarily of company installations.

"I'll give you my own perspective, Mr. Sanderson," Monahan began, taking a seat again. "Pennsylvania Produce began in the farming business but moved into storage and shipping in the twenties. Whether that was well-planned or simply fortuitous is difficult to know; neither my grandfather nor his father kept planning notes. In my view, that shift was all that saved the company because that was when American agriculture entered its modern-day crisis."

O'Neill waited, his attention squarely on Monahan.

"In the early twenties the idea of controlling surplus farm produce was first suggested. That led to the tariff system, which propped up grain prices overseas. Few people today are aware, for instance, that almost the whole overseas market for grain was kept afloat by credits to the consuming nations — millions of dollars in loans that were never repaid."

"I would surmise, then, Mr. Monahan, that you have little good to say about New Deal farm relief programs—"

Monahan nodded vigorously. "You're quite right! Take the Agricultural Adjustment Act signed in FDR's first year in office. In theory, it was good. But what did it lead to? Subsidies to cut production that benefited big owners who cut the acreage of their renters and sharecroppers while keeping their own lands in full production. Who administered it? Rich whites. Who were the sharecroppers who lost out? The Poor. New immigrants. In the South, mostly Blacks; in the Southwest, Hispanics. Almost every farm subsidy since the New Deal has favored the wealthy. This is 1996, but our economics is medieval. Take last year's 'Freedom to Farm' bill! Now there's a sinister title for federal legislation! I always thought our Bill of Rights would include freedom to farm, but I don't believe such rights mandate that the government should throw good money after bad to continue a doomed and disappearing way of life. Maybe we should subsidize Amish farmers who use horse-drawn plows or covered-wagon vacations on the old Oregon Trail so the romance of pioneering in Early America will not be lost!

"Mr. Sanderson," he went on, "farming is the only segment of the economy, short of government spending, where full capitalism — the law of supply and demand — is eroded by government intervention." Monahan leaned back, crossed his legs, and tapped a pencil on his shoe.

O'Neill closed the book and leaned forward. "Of course, the supporters of government subsidies have always held they were necessary to preserve the family farm—"

"It's a romantic ideal. The trouble is, subsidies aren't really preserving the family farm. Their numbers have steadily declined; their income has continued to drop. Over eighty-five percent of farmers in the U.S. earn under $40,000 a year. Meanwhile, the top five percent — mostly owners of huge agribusiness operations — own eighty percent of the land, make millions in profit. And they collect the lion's share of subsidies.

"Do you realize that we're running close to two and a quarter billion in annual subsidies to the grain-feed industry — $340 million to subsidize rice, $680 million to subsidize cotton. And the absurdity goes on, with increases every year."

"Why do you suppose it has continued so long?"

"From Roosevelt through the nineties we had well over half a century of Democratic control of Congress. Farm subsidies are one of their sacred cows. So now farm subsidies are regarded as entitlements, and the Republican-dominated Congress in the nineties doesn't know how to back out. Now it's been renewed—"

Monahan banged his desk, his eyes blazing. "Listen, there's more to this absurdity — guaranteed agricultural loans to farmers who have already defaulted! That adds up to another seven or eight billion dollars over six years, loaned at four percentage points lower than loans to credit-worthy farmers! And, if that isn't enough, American farmers have been bailed out by disaster relief so often that they will no longer buy insurance. I buy insurance, you buy insurance, but why should farmers buy it? They don't need it. Uncle Sam will save them. So now the government is subsidizing crop insurance! It's a particularly abhorrent form of welfare to Americans who are not poor. They're land rich—"

O'Neill wrestled with everything Monahan said. He tried to ignore the annoying fact that much of what Monahan was saying about farm subsidies made good sense, though it conflicted with his own standard liberal views. But he wasn't here to debate American politics; he had a more important objective. Somewhere in Monahan's politics might be a clue to his rigged telephone.

"Where does Pennsylvania Produce fit into this?"

Monahan leaned forward with his elbows on his desk. His eyes were steady, his voice now level and controlled. "By the end of the thirties, we had reduced agricultural production to forty percent of our business. Today, it is only four percent."

"But you've got thousands of acres in production."

Monahan nodded. "Thirty thousand acres sounds like a lot compared to the old family farm, but it's tokenism for Pennsylvania Produce. A substantial portion of that acreage is given over to storage facilities, equipment sheds, maintenance garages. We've got many more trucks than cattle."

"And the agricultural lands?"

"In terms of our ideals, our belief in the American market as the final determiner of pricing and profit — our capitalist ideology if you will — our hearts are in the shipping. I would gladly shear away the entire agricultural side of the company. Hanging onto farming operations is almost a matter of sentimentality now. It is required to maintain the image of the legendary Monahans. 'The Farming Pioneers of America' as they call us. It's a motto that endures.

"The truth is that more than half of our thirty thousand acres are given over to recreation — hiking and camping wilderness for Boy Scouts — or the tourist business, dude ranches, places where families can see mock-up pioneer villages with displays of ancient tractors and early agricultural methods. Public image enterprises that do not generate or qualify for a dime of subsidies. In fact, in keeping with our opposition to government support of business, we take no agricultural subsidies. We haven't for over sixty years."

O'Neill studied Monahan, then thumbed through the book. "I think I need to do some more research. I gather this summarizes what you've been saying."

"And a good deal more, Mr. Sanderson. If there's anything you need to know not in that history, why not call again? I'd be glad to fill you in, even get a luncheon together with some of the senior executives."

O'Neill pulled out his notebook and flipped through. "Okay, I've got your office phone number here—"

"Feel free to call me at home," Monahan added, passing across a business card.

O'Neill glanced at it and spoke while he copied the home number into the notebook. "I guess you don't spend all your time here? You must be on the road a lot. Do you have a cell phone?"

"I leave it at our cottage in the mountains. No one has the number; no one calls me on it; it's for emergencies only, and I haven't used it for months, maybe a couple of years."

"You don't carry it with you? So, I can't reach you away from the office?"

There was a distinct pause while O'Neill wrote. He looked up; Monahan was staring at him, his eyes ice cold.

Monahan got slowly to his feet and leaned his fists on his desk. "Why don't you guys get the hell out of my life?"

O'Neill was stunned. "I'm sorry, I don't understand—"

"They warned someone might come nosing around, asking questions about my phone service."

An alarm went off in O'Neill's head. Monahan shook with anger. "Damn you to hell, all of you!" he shouted. He snarled, his face twisted in fury. "You've set fire to a six-million-dollar warehouse. Isn't that enough?" His voice had risen to a roar. "I'm not going to put up with this! It's extortion!"

O'Neill saw the rage in his eyes and sensed the Chief Executive Officer had gone over some kind of edge. Monahan pounded the desk and then, with fists clenched, he moved around the side of his desk and his face colored in rage. Then Monahan reached toward the open drawer.

Behind him O'Neill heard a crash of shattering glass. He turned, startled, as shards splintered across the floor. Through the jagged opening of the smashed window, he saw the muzzle of a gun. The voice came out of the darkness from the balcony.

"Don't move another inch, Mr. Monahan!"

A hand came out of the darkness, reached into the room and turned the knob of the door; it swung back, and Christelle Washington walked in with a gun pointing at Walter Monahan.

Chapter Eighteen

Christelle was dressed in pale denim blue jeans and jacket. O'Neill stared as she walked slowly across the room, her eyes unwavering, looking past him at Monahan, the gun pointed at his chest.

"Step back from the desk, Mr. Monahan."

O'Neill turned. Monahan's hand was frozen in mid-air as though he might yet reach into the drawer. The gunshot was deafening. Monahan staggered backwards in terror against the credenza as a shattered picture two feet to his left crashed to the floor.

"Don't even consider hesitating again," Christelle ordered, her gun steady as a rock.

"You'll never get away with this," Monahan blurted out, his eyes a confusion of terror and hatred. "They'll get you, Sanderson; it won't be long now—"

O'Neill was around the desk before he knew he had moved. "Who? Who will get us?" He had Monahan by the throat. "Who?"

Monahan's face was contorted in panic, his lips squeezed together. O'Neill drove a fist into his midsection, doubling him over and driving him to the ground. "Who, Monahan? Who's behind this?"

Monahan glared up at O'Neill, eyes like ice. O'Neill brought back his fist ready to drive his face into the floor.

"Just a minute. Hold him!" Christelle bent over Monahan, put the muzzle of the gun to his lips, and gave a quick jab, forcing the barrel between his teeth. "Mr. Sanderson just asked you a question. "Monahan's eyes were bugging out of his head as he sputtered and heaved in fear. "When you're ready to tell us, I'll remove it." She pressed the gun to the back of his throat until he gagged.

Terrified, Monahan let out a guttural cry. His eyes revealed 'yes,' he would talk. Christelle slowly removed the gun.

"I don't know who, only a name." His eyes were round as they darted from O'Neill to the gun. "He... he phones... He... he is called... the Colonel."

Christelle moved the gun a little closer. "So help me God! That's all I know!"

Christelle stood up, and O'Neill hauled Monahan to his feet, leaving him gasping against his credenza. She reached into the drawer and lifted out the gun, a black-barreled weapon with a heavy handle. "This is nice," Christelle said, handing it to Broc, "a Browning automatic." She jabbed her gun at Monahan. "Where's the ammunition?" He looked at her stupidly. "The bullets, where are they?"

"In the next drawer."

O'Neill pulled open the drawer while Christelle kept her weapon pointed. The box held fifty rounds of 9 mm shells. He dropped it in the side pocket of his jacket and shoved the Browning in his belt.

"You won't get away with this," Monahan declared in a low voice. "They know you're here. They're on their way now."

O'Neill tore down the block and across the street three yards behind Christelle. *They know you're here.* Damn it! Monahan was in the back office when I came in! He must have called someone to say I was here! *They're on their way now!* They dashed around the corner at full sprint and he saw Christelle's Grand Am facing them. There was no fumbling of keys; she had them ready. In seconds she had the doors open and they were inside.

"Get down!" Broc shouted as the headlights came around a corner two blocks behind them. Seconds later a black car roared past, wheeled around the corner, and screeched to a stop just out of sight — presumably in front of the Pennsylvania Produce building. They heard the car doors slam.

Christelle turned the key and seconds later was backing up the street and around the corner. She put the car in forward and headed off at right angles, then braked to a jolting stop and opened her door. "Broc, get around here! You drive!"

"What the hell! You're doing fine."

157

"No, you drive!"

Broc got behind the wheel as Christelle slammed the door.

"Drive to the next corner, Broc, take a left, and another left." Broc looked at her as though she was crazy. "You drive; I'll do the rest!"

Whatever the rest was, he wasn't sure.

Christelle moved and got onto her knees on the seat facing the side of the car, her feet braced against the console. Broc drove slowly around the corner onto the street in front of Pennsylvania Produce. Christelle rolled down her window.

"Down the middle of the road, Broc," she directed, "ten miles an hour."

Christelle held the 45 with both hands and braced herself. The black car that had roared past them a minute earlier was parked a yard from the curb, engine running. Rear window, driver inside, don't want to kill anyone, aim to the right. She pulled the trigger and the back window turned into a spider web of radiating lines. The windshield would be blown out, too.

Rear tire. She aimed carefully and pulled the trigger.

A movement by the door of the building caught her attention. Debris is as dangerous as bullets, a piece of wisdom from her instructor at the firing range. She aimed at the neon sign and pulled the trigger as someone came out of the door. The sign exploded, sending a shower of glass across the front of the building. He dived back into the doorway.

They were nearly abreast of the car now. Don't want to kill anyone, just spread fear. As they passed the driver, she caught terrified eyes and saw the driver duck out of sight as she fired across the front seat, taking out both windows. She swung the gun. Got to disable it. She aimed at the grill and fired into the radiator. Sparks flew from metal biting into metal. Almost unconsciously, she had been counting: one shot in Monahan's office, and now five more. The ammunition clip was empty.

Above, in the lighted window, she caught a glimpse of Walter Monahan, and then Broc hit the gas. The car lurched forward and squealed around the corner.

"My God, that car is shot to pieces!"

"Too bad this doesn't hold more bullets! I'd have given them the works." She glanced at Broc, who was genuinely startled, then pointed the empty gun toward the windshield and pulled the trigger another half dozen times. "I didn't appreciate those guys putting bullet holes in my car! That will teach them something, and fixing that Lincoln will cost them more than twenty-eight hundred dollars!"

Broc glanced at her as she craned her neck to look out the back window. He made another right and then a left, braking to a stop beside his Tempo. Christelle jumped out and ran around her car as Broc shoved his key in the door. "Where will I meet you?"

"Highway 33 to Scranton. Hertz Rental, first exit past MacDonald's."

Christelle followed the Ford Tempo as Broc headed uptown. She felt her insides jump; a dozen blocks ahead high-beam headlights lurched onto the street toward them. The Tempo signal went on and Broc turned right. Christelle touched her signal and drove the next half block at twenty with her stomach in her mouth, watching the car speeding toward them. Terrified, resisting every urge to hit the gas, she turned the corner, her car under perfect control. Broc was moving steadily ahead. She held her breath and watched her rearview mirror. Seconds later the dark sedan screamed by. She let out her breath as Broc's Tempo surged ahead and around another corner, and she tramped the Grand Am.

Broc turned another corner, and another, zigzagging away. Christelle followed, her tires screaming, watching her rear-view mirror. Nothing. No one following. Within three minutes they were on the Lehigh Valley Thruway heading east.

She gripped the wheel. Her ears were ringing from the gunfire; her heart was pounding like a jackhammer. She could feel the tightness across her back. It had been a difficult scramble onto the fire escape, and her last three shots were at the wrong angle. That Colt had a lot of kick, and a 45 — that was a lot of lead. If she stood the wrong way, it would knock her flat on her fanny.

Christelle relaxed her grip and rotated her shoulders, then pulled them up toward her ears several times until she felt more relaxed. After a few minutes she contemplated the gun on the seat, then slowly slid it off onto the floor, edging it under her seat with her foot. Then she focused her eyes on the taillights of the Tempo ahead.

In the darkness she imagined she saw his eyes. They moved restlessly about, then came to rest on hers.

That's it! That's the last time, Broc O'Neill! You are not getting out of my sight again.

Christelle came across the Hertz Rental parking lot with a plastic bag from the farmers' market. "Here" — she tossed the keys to him — "you drive. You did a great job last time."

Broc wheeled the Grand Am onto the street. He had filled the Tempo with gas, parked and locked it, and dropped the keys in the Hertz mail slot wrapped in a note to send any refund to Dillon Shaver in Belleville, Ontario — the address on his borrowed passport. Within five minutes Broc and Christelle were out on Interstate 81 heading north to Binghamton, New York. It was ten minutes after midnight. The radio was playing softly, a late-night hour of soft jazz, as they drove on in the darkness.

The whole evening was overwhelming — a landslide of emotions, a river of adrenalin. It was too much to take in. O'Neill felt physically alert but emotionally exhausted.

It was a full ten minutes before she spoke. "You like my car?"

He caught a glimpse of light shine on her face from oncoming headlights. Her nose had a little curve that he hadn't noticed before; it made her look young and innocent. It was hard to reconcile her soft voice and smile with the wild-eyed ferocity he had seen little more than an hour ago.

"It's a little battle scarred," she reminded him, "but Robb fixed it up real nice."

He felt her hand touch his. He took the section of orange she had been peeling in the dark and bit into it, crushing it into juice and swallowing it down.

"I know you can't see it at night, but it has nice upholstery, nice colors."

Broc had ridden in it once before, from the airport to the cabin, but he had been in too much turmoil to notice anything. Now he pushed himself into the padded seat and felt the wraparound backrest against his sides. It felt luxurious and comfortable. The dials glowed rose-red through the steering wheel. "I love it, Christelle, I love your car, especially the new paint job."

He caught her smile in the glow from the dashboard, and they drove along for another quarter hour, eating oranges in the dark and listening to the music.

"I guess it was pretty easy finding Pennsylvania Produce," Broc surmised.

"It was a surprise. The nerve center of the company is in Chicago. Monahan seems pretty private with his office in an old Allentown brownstone. But it wasn't hard finding the address. The hard part was climbing from the fire escape to that balcony. They aren't connected."

"How much of the conversation did you catch?"

"Just the end. You'll have to fill me in."

"These were the craziest three days. All the guys I saw are nutcakes. The worst was John Randolph, president of GEO."

"Isn't he the guy with the divorce?"

"You mean it's news all the way to Vermont?"

"I stopped for a snack this afternoon. There was an article in the local newspaper. Mostly, it was about his wife. She's suing for millions and millions of dollars."

"Did it say anything about his girlfriend?"

"Not that I saw. Did you meet a girlfriend?"

"I can hardly believe he's kept her out of the papers. Sandy. She's driving a Mark VIII, which she called his Valentine's gift. He's completely whacko over her. Looks like his time with her is just one long emergency."

"So his wife is jealous."

"If you saw Sandy, you'd know why. She could be a supermodel. His wife, on the other hand, is a colorless Amish woman. Randolph calls her 'Plain Jane'. He met her at a Hershey Chocolate golf tournament. But she's swinging a much bigger club these days."

"You didn't have any difficulty meeting him?"

"He's a political type. He was going to run for office before this divorce thing consumed his life. You just stand beside those guys and pretty soon they're talking, then glad-handing, and soon they're telling their life stories."

"Have you learned anything from all these interviews?"

"Pretty well nothing. I think we've run into a dead end."

Talk had started on the radio. Christelle fiddled with the dial for a few minutes and finally tuned in on a Binghamton station playing Country & Western music. "You like this stuff?"

"It's okay. But I can do without Loretta Lynn."

Christelle laughed. "I guess we agree. I can do without all the lonely girls and cowboys remembering sad times. I think I'll exercise my option as owner of the car to find something else." She played with the dial another minute, found nothing, and shut it off. He heard her rustling in the dark, then felt her hand on his. He accepted what she offered, a clump of seedless grapes.

"What did you mean by that, Broc? That Randolph's girlfriend was just one long emergency?"

O'Neill felt a sudden wave of memories sweep over him. He watched the distant tail lights of a truck ahead and the long beams of headlights in the distance. He glanced at Christelle. He could feel her eyes.

"It was something Darcy used to say." Hesitating, he looked out the side window; the night was clear; the stars were out by the thousands. "She had this way of talking. When we were together, alone, you know, after an evening date. When we got home, she... she would say... 'I think this is an emergency situation'. Sometimes she would say, 'Is this a real emergency, or just a red alert?' or 'I've been having an emergency all afternoon. It can't wait another minute; we have to fix it.'"

Christelle sat quietly for a moment, staring ahead. "You really loved her, didn't you?"

O'Neill felt himself choking up. He drew a deep breath and sat for a minute trying to regain control. "It's the things she said that are the hardest to forget."

He felt Christelle's hand on his again. She gave it a little squeeze and then pushed more grapes into his palm.

"I wish Geoff had said things like that."

She spoke quietly; she was leaning back against the headrest. "I was married for a while in California. But it was so unmemorable."

"I didn't know."

"I don't talk about it much; I hardly ever think about it. We were so mismatched. I met him at college; we got married our last year. He was a computer programmer. He had this amazing technical mind, but we lived in different worlds. After graduation I worked for this little institute for political analysis in San Jose. I loved it, but I got peanuts, and Geoff thought I was crazy for wasting my education. This was seven years ago or so. I was just a child and, you know, so naive and idealistic, and he was such a whiz. He used to sit for hours and plan out software in his head.

"I guess what finished us was when I started working for the Democratic campaign for the Senate. It was a wonderful six months, a real high for a baby Democrat like me, and we won, and by that time our marriage was finished."

"Was it a nasty ending?"

"It was as uneventful as it had been for the whole two years — colorless at the beginning, gray at the end. We parted friends, shook hands and went our separate ways. He packed his shirts and computer; I packed my books. He got a big position in Phoenix. I guess he's making a lot of money now. I went back to school for my master's. Finished that up in a couple of years and then came to Jefferson State." She paused and took a deep breath. "Pretty dull life, huh? Actually, I've had more excitement in the past week than in the whole rest of my life put together."

"It's excitement that could get us killed." Broc paused for a minute and checked the time. It was 1:05 a.m. "How far is it to the cabin?"

"Most of the night."

"Then, Miss Washington, I suggest you crawl in the back seat and catch some sleep. You drove all day; I'm wide awake." He signaled and drove onto an exit ramp. "We need gas. One fill-up here ought to get us there. I think we ought to get back to Vermont ASAP, get this car out of sight, and then figure out what to do next."

Chapter Nineteen

Broc swore under his breath. He had the maximum number of windows open that his Microsoft program would allow, and it still wasn't enough. There was just too much data. Silently, he cursed as he struggled to navigate the tangle of screens, trying to access information he thought he had seen a quarter hour ago. Brandeis Electronics had made a substantial donation, $4 million, to the Anatran Foundation back in December, $4 million in March, another $4 million in June. Must be a quarterly donation. O'Neill was sure he had seen something else about Anatran within the last hour, but he could not remember where.

"Are you interested in food?" Christelle asked from behind the kitchen counter.

"As soon as I figure this out." He clicked back to another screen, then another — lists of public-service organizations in Philadelphia, Harrisburg, and Pottstown.

Then he caught the aroma of cinnamon under his nose. Christelle was standing beside him with a bowl of steaming apple cobbler. "Is this breakfast?"

"You've already slept most of the day away, missed breakfast and lunch. And you've almost missed the first two courses of dinner. This is your last call — for dessert."

His eyes followed her as she carried the cobbler back to the kitchen. She was wearing a tan sundress with big brown and yellow sunflowers, and a white apron. Broc pushed back his chair and followed her to the table.

"I had almost given up," she teased, setting a plate of steak, baked potato, and glazed carrots in front of him. "But now I know how to get your attention."

Broc gazed at the table. She had set out woven bamboo place mats, big wooden salt-and-pepper shakers, and a basket of rye bread. He could smell the spices in the gravy. "You sure do know how to whip up a meal."

"It's easy with an older sister to pave the way." Christelle held up a battered paperback copy of the *I Hate to Cook Book*. "Joyce has built a twenty-five-year marriage on this. The only thing it doesn't include is how to get a professor away from his research."

"It's the quality of service that did it," he rationalized, watching her bringing a bottle of wine. "Also, I like the waitress uniform."

She set down the bottle and curtsied. "Thank you, Sir. That's what we had to say at Benningan's when customers said nice things."

"I'm sorry for holding up supper. It's just that I've found hundreds of people with cell phones like mine. But I can't figure out why. They all seem like good honest Americans. Some are a little skitzy or fanatical, but I can't see any reason anyone would want to violate their personal privacy. I keep feeling this whole thing is going to come clear as soon as I download the next file."

Christelle looked at him, tentatively. "You don't have to explain. I understand."

"I'm sorry, I should know better. Darcy made me read *Men Are from Mars, Women Are from Venus*. I just forgot there's nothing more important when a woman is serving up a home-cooked meal. You've been feeding me like a king. I'll try to come next time when I'm called."

Her eyes sparkled as she passed the wine bottle, brought two tall wine glasses and sour cream to the table, and sat down, watching as he twisted the corkscrew. He poured a half inch into her glass, held it up as she breathed in the aroma, and poured the glass to the brim. Her eyes moved from her glass to his hands, and then to his eyes.

"If it weren't for a gang of vicious murderers out hunting for us, this would be a nice vacation." He watched her over his wine glass as they drank. "Actually, it's a nice vacation even though a gang of vicious murderers is hunting us." He cut off a piece of meat and took a bite. "I have to say, Christelle, the cooking is every bit as good as the service."

She smiled her thanks. "It's all in the wrist."

"Just like shooting that gun," he recalled, digging into his baked potato.

"It's the aftershock that's all in the wrist," she added, rotating her hand and wrinkling her forehead. "That Colt is too big for me. If you don't mind, before I do any more shooting, I'd like to trade the 45 for Mr. Monahan's Browning. It fires 9 mm shells."

"Before you do any more shooting! I don't think we should let you outside with a gun — or a car. You use these like weapons of war! It's too dangerous for bystanders."

"You mean too dangerous for us, Broc O'Neill! By my count, last night was the fourth time you were nearly killed. You weren't armed. Someone would have transformed you into a corpse, if not Monahan, then those thugs who nearly caught us." Broc caught her eyes on his, knowing how right her instincts had been.

"Anyway, I've booked us tomorrow morning down at the shooting range."

Broc stopped eating.

"Like I say, you get the Colt 45; it's got too much kick for me; I get the Browning. Why are you acting like that? Haven't you ever fired a gun?"

Broc picked up his wine glass. "Once, in a fit of rage."

Surprised, Christelle shared her lately found wisdom: "Hal — he's my shooting instructor — he says that's a very bad time to fire a gun. Most murders happen that way. Did you kill someone?"

"Just a raccoon. He was dumping my garbage."

"Hal will have you shooting like a pro in three days."

"I'm not sure I want to shoot like a pro in three days. I come from a long line of liberal pacifists who think the Second Amendment should be repealed and the entire membership of the National Rifle Association thrown in jail for abusing the First Amendment with their inflammatory rhetoric."

"It's surprising how fast your views change when you get shot at."

"That's true, but you weren't shot at; it was your car."

"It's the same thing! My car is me. I am my car! Anyway, until all the bad guys are dead, I think we need to be armed."

"We?" asked Broc.

"That's right! I think we need to go after these guys like Bonnie and Clyde, and if one of us gets killed, the other one should make sure to kill the killer."

Two months ago, she was a studious doctoral student in political science. He had misgivings as he thought about the violent world he had dragged her into. *If one of us gets killed, the other one should kill the killer—* "This is very dangerous," he said in a low voice. "Wouldn't you sooner stay home and bake?"

Christelle set down her knife and fork. "It was very dangerous for Darcy, and she never even knew it. No warning. No advice to exercise caution. But I know it's a very dangerous world. And Darcy was my friend. I want revenge for her death as much as you do. Yes, there are a lot of things I would sooner do, and one of them is stay home and bake, and maybe when this is over, I will stay home and bake. But whoever is behind all this murdered a beautiful person, and… and ended… and broke a beautiful thing, and people can't just sit back and let that happen."

Walter Monahan was angry when he reached for his gun as though O'Neill was an enemy probing into his private life. The query about his phone had spooked him. Obviously, he was on edge about something, but it didn't come up in their conversation.

O'Neill scrolled through the Brandeis Electronics website for the third time. It was a sterling organization with soaring profits from government contracts and a spotless reputation for quality in electronics. Jamiessen and his wife were the celebrities in Harrisburg. They had boosted the local economy with thousands of new jobs. They donated money to big charities and several foundations O'Neill had never heard of.

He glanced over to the couch in front of the fireplace. Christelle was curled with a blanket and a book she had been skimming for her dissertation, a treatment of the Iran-Contra scandal. Reagan had neatly sashayed out of the guilty box on that one.

O'Neill clicked to another screen, then undid the last five and tried a new route into the maze of Pennsylvania financial summaries. Kaiser Shipping had been a steady supporter of the arts, three Quaker museums, and the Goethe Institute of Pennsylvania. O'Neill screwed up his forehead at the inconsistency. William Kaiser seemed more interested in

German weapons than the arts! But the company was also tied into various foundations. In February it had made a gift of $3 million to a new Holocaust Museum in Philadelphia.

None of it made sense. Why the hell would anyone want to eavesdrop on Nathan Jamiessen, Walter Monahan, William Brandeis, or William Kaiser?

O'Neill spent another thirty minutes scanning financials for corporations in Philadelphia, searching those whose CEOs were clients of Worldwide Communications. The numbers were a maze. Many were contained in chamber-of-commerce data sheets designed to boost the image of the city — never entirely reliable, always self-serving. O'Neill surfed back to the city of York, where he found more figures on Kaiser Shipping.

Kaiser had donated money in regular amounts to the Metropolitan Museum, the Quaker Preservation Foundation, and the Anatran Foundation. O'Neill had doubted Kaiser's gushing enthusiasm for William Penn, but his dedication to Quakerism was backed up with substantial financial support.

Of course, huge amounts of money flowing to charitable causes was not surprising. The whole economy was booming; it had been for years, riding the wave of new technology startups. Ted Turner, Bill Gates, Warren Buffet — they were all making news with charitable donations. Jamiessen, Kaiser, Monahan, and the rest of them were small fish in this immense ocean of American wealth, but the benevolent spirit of the billionaires appeared to be trickling down to the mere multi-millionaires.

Christelle had just gone through a box of books under the coffee table and was flopping about on the couch, piling cushions under her head, and rearranging her blanket. Her book on the Iran-Contra scandal was on the table. She had switched to a novel.

O'Neill thumbed through *Pennsylvania Produce: A Corporate History*, found a page of statistics, and went back to the screen. Forty minutes later, he had verified the existence of several theme parks and tourist farms in the Midwest. Walter Monahan summaries were accurate. Pennsylvania Produce collected no agricultural subsidies and turned hundreds of thousands of dollars back to charitable causes every year. The biggest donation was a $6.3 million gift in June to Texas Lands

Preservation, a local version of the national Nature Conservancy, and this had been written up in the *San Antonio Express-News* on June 23, with a picture of Monahan presenting the check against a backdrop poster of The Riverwalk. The article included a pledge of a further $10 million during the next biennium.

Thumbing through the thirty or forty sheets of printout, O'Neill pushed his chair away from the computer. It was after midnight. He stretched and stood up. Christelle was asleep, her novel on her stomach: Sue Miller's *The Good Mother*. He walked across the carpet as quietly as he could to the sliding door to the deck.

"Where are you going?" Christelle was sitting up, her eyes round.

"I need some fresh air; I haven't been outside all day." Christelle's face remained expressionless, as though half asleep. "I'll be up half the night. Why don't you go to bed?"

She swung her feet onto the floor. "I'm not going to sleep while you're still up. You might sneak off again."

O'Neill crossed the room, knelt on the carpet, and faced her across the coffee table. "This is silly, Christelle. I promise: I won't sneak off."

She looked at him for a minute and then jumped up. "I'll make some coffee!"

O'Neill followed her around to the kitchenette and got out mugs. She scooped coffee into the top of the machine, filled it with water, and then raked her fingers through her hair.

"Well, what have you found out?"

"That I'm the pauper among Worldwide Communications clients. The salaries of the three I interviewed range from seven hundred fifty thousand dollars to more than two million."

"What else?"

"That if you're poor like me, you get a bugged phone, they track you and do their best to kill you off. If you're rich like these guys, you get a bugged phone and they keep you alive."

"Correction: If you're smart and have a PhD, you write dangerous articles that make them come after you! You know what, Broc? I don't think it was your reporting on that early draft of NSCID No. 9 that got them upset. It's too far back to be of much concern whether it disagrees or matches the final NSCID No. 9. I think it's what you wrote at the end of your article — that you had other materials you intended to publish in a follow-up article, along with recommendations for congressional control of the National Security Agency. That seems pretty innocuous, no more threatening than all those congressional investigations into the CIA back in the seventies. On the other hand, from the standpoint of the NSA people, with their paranoia and obsession with keeping everything secret, your recommendations sound like... maybe like academic terrorism."

"Wow, that's a new one!"

She was leaning on the counter, still in her flowered sundress, waiting for the coffee to perk. "Pretty clever, huh?"

Academic terrorism—

"Look at it this way," Christelle continued. "We think of adolescents with guns as terrifying. We have a way to deal with them, some of them. If we can catch them at the toy gun stage, we put them in Boy Scouts. If they're hung up on real guns, get them to boot camp or into the military. Now, consider the intellectuals in universities. Sedentary warriors. No one knows what to do with them. Governments have always been frightened of them. The Soviets used to lock them up or send them to some camp in Siberia. Hoover kept FBI files on them. More enlightened governments co-opt them. That's what President Kennedy did. You know, 'the best and the brightest' — he brought all the smart ones into the inner circle of advisors. Or like you said the intelligence community did with all those whiz kids at Yale — got them into breaking secret codes, gave them a piece of the action.

"But these guys in the intelligence community are just as frightened of intellects running loose as we are of Middle East terrorists and suicide bombers. They worry about professors like you digging things up, calling for Senate investigations, endangering their power, regulating their operations, threatening their livelihood. I'm sure they regard your publishing that article as an academic drive-by shooting."

"Except that our academic freedom, our right to conduct inquiry and our freedom of speech are all protected by the Bill of Rights. First Amendment."

"And their right to run around with guns is protected by the Second Amendment, which — even though you'd like to see it repealed — is also in the Bill of Rights."

O'Neill was fascinated by what she said; it took him by surprise. The coffee was ready. "You know, Christelle," he said with amusement, "you're just as frightening when you talk as when you drive or shoot a gun. It terrifies me to think of you adding a PhD to this arsenal of ideas. I'm not sure Jefferson State University should add its imprimatur to such deadly thoughts."

"I'm no scarier than you publishing in *American Documentary History*." She poured the coffee and flashed a smile. "Maybe you should open the refrigerator." He opened it. "There's some apple cobbler."

He brought it out and set it on the counter. "More of this! I thought we finished it at dinner."

"I made doubles." She put it in the microwave and pushed the one-minute button. "I figure I need lots of this to distract you from dangerous deeds and to keep you around as my third reader."

Broc shut off the computer. "It's after two in the morning, Christelle. I'm not ready to sleep, but I'm going to bed so you will go to bed, too."

She pulled out the box of paperbacks and rummaged for a minute. "There's a good light in your room. Try a novel. Here's some that men like to read."

Broc took the books and said goodnight. "You aren't going to lock me in, are you?"

"If you come out and walk around, I might think you are a burglar."

"So you'll just shoot me—"

Broc sat in bed reading *The Pelican Brief*. It was new, a best seller a couple of years ago. Everything went well through the first chapter — a tense political scene set in Washington, DC — but Broc was stopped cold on page seventeen when Darby Shaw walked into Thomas Callahan's constitutional law class. He flipped back to her description: "an attractive young woman in tight washed jeans and cotton sweater." *Darby...* *Darby... Darcy*— That was about all he could take of Darby Shaw.

He set the book aside and reached for The *Parsifal Mosaic*. It began with someone called Michael Havelock watching Jenna, a beautiful woman he loved, being chased and then mowed down by gunfire on the Costa Brava, a lonely moonlit beach on the coast of Spain. By the time he got to page 5, Jenna was dead and Broc was in a cold sweat.

He sat for several minutes trying to unwind, and then crept softly to the door, opened it, and walked quietly down the hall. The stove light was on, casting a dim glow across the counter. O'Neill hunted through the cupboard and found a tin of cocoa, then turned on the stove. He got the milk out and mixed the powder while the kettle came to a boil.

As he finished pouring, he heard a noise. Christelle was standing watching him from the doorway. "Don't shoot! I'm just making something to put me to sleep."

She smiled as she walked back down the hall.

Chapter Twenty

Christelle stood at the counter as Hal studied his computer screen. She had fired a lot of ammunition and still felt warm and flushed even though she had taken a shower. She had taken time to dry her hair, which tended to tangle and curl when wet. Hal picked up Walter Monahan's gun and checked the numbers stamped into the barrel, then typed them into the computer.

"It's a Browning. I guess you figured that out, Miss Washington. The Hi-Power model, one of the finest handguns ever made." He looked up as the computer did its search. "You did pretty well this morning. How did you like shooting it?"

"I see what you mean. A 9 mm gun is a lot easier to handle, and I like that it holds thirteen cartridges." She glanced through the glass at Broc, who was sitting in the lounge with a coffee reading the newspaper. "He used the 45, his first time. I wonder whether it made his arm ache."

"Actually, Miss Washington, I started your friend off with a 22 like we did with you. He's emptied the 45 only once, six shots." Hal typed some more numbers into the computer and waited for the information to come up. "This Browning is the No. 2 Mk1 version made in Canada for the British military. It's the standard weapon for the SAS — the Special Air Service. The serial number says it was manufactured in the 1950s." He picked it up and worked the mechanism. "Hardly used, as good as the day it was issued. Probably the fifty rounds you fired this morning were more than it had ever fired before. There's no way to figure who it was issued to—"

"How did it get to Pennsylvania?" Christelle asked.

"No way of knowing. And it's not even worth trying to figure out. Handguns move invisibly. The registration paperwork's a hassle, so nobody bothers. A few years back there was talk of registering guns in Canada, so every Canadian with a second home in the U.S. has been smuggling them across the border, burying them in luggage. Guns like this migrate all over the world. This one's never been registered in the U.S."

"What about shells fired from it? Can they be traced?"

"Only if someone has the bullet and the gun, but the bullet has to be intact, probably embedded in something soft. Even then, it's not easy to match bullets to guns, and impossible if hollow points are used. The best 9 mm bullets — the Winchester Silvertip or Eldorado Starfire, both high-velocity hollow points — blossom on impact and become so distorted that matching them to a specific gun can't be done."

"Blossom? I'm sorry, Hal, I'm just an innocent student. This is all new to me."

Hal talked, his hands moving. "With handguns, it's all about killing, or at least disabling, someone. You need to know this so you know what gun and ammo to use. First, you find a long-barreled weapon capable of a high muzzle velocity. That insures deep penetration. There are guns with a muzzle velocity as low as 650 feet per second. With this barrel, this baby gives you up to 1150! Of course, the most powerful firearm will put a bullet right through and out the other side."

Christelle shuddered.

"Next you choose the heaviest load — the weightiest bullet you can use — because the combination of the weight and velocity creates an impact, like a punch by a heavyweight boxer. A high-velocity, heavy-load 45 cartridge, for instance, will knock a man off his feet, like a punch from Mohammad Ali. On a smaller cartridge, like a 9 mm, which won't go all the way through, what you want is a deep crush cavity — the actual tissue contacted, crushed, and destroyed by the bullet as it penetrates. The crush cavity from a solid bullet may be deep, but it's only the width of a pencil. Unless it hits something vital, it usually does little damage, and it's reparable. Dig out the bullet and pump 'im with antibiotics. A man hit with two or three solid 22 bullets that don't reach vital parts may still be mobile and lead an assailant on a pretty good chase.

"Now, what makes the difference in the effectiveness of smaller 22 and the 9 mm bullet is blossoming — the way the bullet expands on impact, usually to about double its original width, which means it produces a crush cavity about four times as big. It won't penetrate as far, but it does a fierce amount of damage."

Hal was animated now; his eyes were big and his hands were moving as he unwound on his favorite topic. Christelle felt her hands beginning to tremble. Her stomach was rolling over.

"You get that blossoming from hollow points. When a bullet like the Starfire or Golden Sabre hits, it creates a nice neat little hole, but as soon as it hits denser tissue — right under the skin — the point of the bullet 'blossoms' into a kind of jagged rose, which tears as it penetrates the flesh. Here you have to talk about something else, the stretch cavity, which is the whole area around the path of the bullet that's damaged — stressed, ruptured, or torn."

Christelle's lips were dry. She felt the nausea rising.

"A good hollow point creates a massive damage cavity. Of course, it's under the surface where you can't see it, but a good damage cavity mushrooms out under the skin — maybe to the size of an orange. Of course, if this occurs in a vital organ, it's pretty much bye-bye for the victim, but even in non-vital areas like arms and legs, the damage cavity is so extensive that it will disable the victim."

He smiled at her, ecstatic with his information. "It's all about what's called wound ballistics."

Christelle fumbled with her purse. Her hands were shaking, her stomach sick. She was relieved when she felt Broc's hand on her arm. "You finished, ready to go?"

She nodded weakly, feeling numb, then startled. His face was ashen. She picked up the Browning and shoved it in her duffel bag. "What's the matter, Broc?"

He walked out of the building, leading her briskly to the car. They sat in the front seat and he showed her the newspaper, today's issue of the *Burlington Free Press*. The article did little more than state the facts in two six-inch columns of print.

"My God!" Stunned, Christelle looked up at him.

"I think we should drive down to Middlebury for brunch. It's a university town. There's bound to be a good news stand."

They sat side by side in the restaurant booth with the front page of yesterday's *Philadelphia Inquirer*. The headline glared at them — two lines of two-inch print: "BRUTAL SLAYINGS ROCK PENNSYLVANIA." Below, in bold half-inch capitals: "A NIGHT OF

VIOLENCE: SLAUGHTER OF THREE EMINENT CITIZENS LEAVES THE STATE REELING." The stories ran down the page side by side. They read the one on the left together:

ALLENTOWN, PA — The quiet city of Allentown is going through the worst shock of recent history from last night's brutal slaying of two prominent Pennsylvania citizens.

Shortly after 11:00 p.m. last night, police were summoned downtown only to discover that the main office of Allentown's most prestigious corporation, Pennsylvania Produce, was the scene of a violent shooting. Dead are Walter P. Monahan, 56, President of the century-old family-owned company, and Colonel James Spiker, 77, veteran of World War II, Korea, and Vietnam.

Mr. Monahan and Colonel Spiker were apparently talking on the front doorstep of Pennsylvania Produce when they were cut down by a blizzard of gunfire. Police have recovered more than two hundred shells from the street where Colonel Spiker's private auto was virtually destroyed by heavy-caliber bullets.

Christelle turned to Broc with wide eyes. "More than two hundred shells! I fired only six. And Walter Monahan was not at the door. He was upstairs. I saw him at the window!"

The photograph showed the black Lincoln parked at the curb, its windows blasted away, a puddle of radiator fluid under the front bumper. An inset showed the door of the building riddled with bullet holes, and two more inserts showed recent photos of Walter Monahan and Colonel Spiker.

Colonel Spiker, who has kept regular office hours since his retirement in 1989, apparently drove alone from Philadelphia to Allentown late Wednesday night. His date book listed an appointment with Walter Monahan. His secretary said the meeting had been arranged "a day or two ago."

"Drove alone!" Broc ran his hand through his hair and faced Christelle, who was wide-eyed with astonishment. "There was someone

176

else in the car, and someone else in the doorway when you were shooting. He wasn't alone!"

Monahan's son spoke with investigators, noting that "the loss to Pennsylvania Produce is incalculable," especially following the $6 million loss of their Atlanta warehouse last month. But who was responsible is not known. Police are investigating.

Broc leaned back, stunned. It was a vicious crime with no evidence of who or why. Christelle was reading the second article. "Broc, this one is about John Randolph and his sexpot girlfriend?"

O'Neill stared at the photograph of the home. Probably worth six-to-eight million. Inserts showed John Randolph and the blonde he recognized as "Sandy."

"Listen to this, Broc—

HARRISBURG, PA — Prominent businessman John Randolph, Chief Executive Officer of GEO Enterprises, and Sandra Drake, his alleged mistress, were found last night shot to death in his Harrisburg home. Police were called to the scene by volleys of gunfire to discover the most brutal slaying in Harrisburg's history. The couple were alone at Randolph's home and were apparently surprised by the slayer.

Police are holding Jane Randolph, his estranged wife without bail, pending further investigation and ballistic tests. Police recovered her husband's gun from the trunk of her car."

"Randolph never had Sandy anywhere near his home." Broc turned to Christelle. "He made sure he kept her out of sight. They must have been caught and forced to his home, then murdered. It's a frame up to simulate a crime of passion."

The shooting has shaken the nearby community of Lancaster to its roots. Mrs. Randolph, the former Jane Kranner, was born and reared in this quiet Amish community. The story of their meeting at a Hershey Chocolate Golf Tournament is local legend. Her closest school friend said this was 'impossible to believe. Jane Kranner was a mild-mannered woman in the gentle lifestyle of the Amish.'

Jane Randolph's prominence in the Harrisburg community was equally well known, as was his wife's pending divorce and lawsuit against her husband, said to be worth $20 million. Court filings indicate infidelity as the motive.

They studied the pictures until the waitress arrived, shoving the paper aside to make room for their food. Broc moved to the other side of the table and looked down at his clam chowder. Christelle stared limply at him across the table, not even acknowledging her spinach salad.

"I think the rules have changed, Broc. It's not just little people like us in danger. The rich and powerful are getting knocked off, too."

"Maybe it's just a coincidence—"

"You told Randolph his phone might be rigged."

That was it! He was drunk and the remark went right past, but later he would have remembered and repeated the rumor. Maybe he was overheard in a tirade to Sandy. That could be why she was murdered, too.

O'Neill looked again at the newspaper. "That might explain why Randolph was murdered, but Monahan said his phone was at his cabin. He rarely used it!"

"But somebody knew you were at his office. They were coming after you."

O'Neill paused, thinking. They had told him someone might come nosing around about phone service. "Monahan must have received advanced warning."

The memory came back. "Monahan was on the phone when I arrived! It was a trap! But once they told Monahan this was about phones, they had to get rid of him. That was probably Colonel Spiker's mission."

Christelle mused a minute. "And he would have got away with it."

"Right, until you shot up Spiker's car. A simple plan backfired. That created an embarrassing situation."

"Why, Broc? He could have just reported vandalism to the police."

O'Neill held a spoonful of soup, letting it cool. "Pennsylvania Produce was the scene of a crime. If Spiker had lived, the police would have wanted to know everything and why he was there. They couldn't risk him exposed to a police interrogation." Broc swallowed the soup and spooned up more, then paused. "Whatever this phone eavesdropping is all about, these guys will do anything to conceal it."

"But the Colonel," Christelle posited, "wasn't he one of them?"

O'Neill nodded.

"So, he was eliminated by his partners in crime, whoever they are."

O'Neill felt the hair on his arms tingling. He set down his spoon. "We know we saw one other person in that car, and there may have been another one inside the building with Spiker when you began shooting. After we left, I'd guess the two of them waited until Monahan had come downstairs and Spiker was with him at the door, then opened up and killed them both."

"There could have been others. We saw a second car—"

Of course. "Two hundred shells! It was like a military operation!"

Christelle's salad was only half eaten. She was sitting with her hands under the table, her shoulders drooping. The color had drained from her face. "You seem really beaten up."

"Broc, I'm scared." Her lips were trembling.

"I thought we were going to wade into this like Bonnie and Clyde."

Big tears were forming along the bottom of her eyes. "That was before all this. Now people are getting assassinated. And if we do one thing wrong, if we make one mistake, we'll be murdered, too."

She pulled a Kleenex from her purse and wiped her eyes.

"Just tell me one thing we can do, Broc. We can't use credit cards. We can't write checks. We can't go anywhere we're known, and if we go anywhere else, we can't use our own names. We can't call any of our friends. We can't go back to Indiana. You can't investigate any more people on the list. They'll get killed; you'll get killed; I'll get killed. We'll die in some back alley. They'll set it up to look like I murdered you or you murdered me. One day we'll be plastered all over the papers; the next day it will be over. Nobody will know who we are. We won't be good for anything except forensic research. They'll stick us in the nearest body farm. Nobody will know what happened to us, why, who did it — nothing."

The waitress was standing by the table. "Would you like anything else?"

Broc looked at Christelle. She didn't seem to hear. "Coffee, and I'm sure the lady would like one, too."

The waitress moved away. Broc reached across the table and took her hand. She gazed at him for a few seconds, then managed a half-hearted smile. She squeezed his hand in return, and then stood up. "I'll be back in a few minutes," she said, heading off to the ladies' room.

Broc's mind was churning. Christelle was right. They were in severe danger. They could sit tight and hole up in the cabin for the rest of the summer. Except, how long were they safe there? His landing in Burlington was a clue to his whereabouts. The car that ran off the road was another clue. Combing the area might be next. He and Christelle couldn't wander in malls or safely shop for groceries. They might be seen. Vermont was no longer a safe haven.

Maybe they should go back to his place in the Wisconsin wilderness. But how? Fly? He had gotten away with that once, but it wouldn't work again — not from any airport within a hundred miles. Driving was a risk. They could run into a dragnet.

And even if they could figure out how to get back to Wisconsin, what would that accomplish? They couldn't stay there forever. And whoever they were — whoever was eavesdropping and killing people — had to be located and stopped. Innocent people were dying. Vicious killings were disguised as random violence or lover's revenge. Whoever was behind this was willing to murder their own for some bigger goal.

How could life become so tangled in a world of such beauty? Looking out toward the pine-clad mountains and struggling to make sense of things, Broc tried to form a plan. Something evil was at large, but it was hidden in fog. One thing was clear, though. They could not flee and hide. They had to search, find, and somehow stop it.

Bloody extortion— Those were Monahan's words. Somehow all this had to do with money, very large amounts of money. Somebody was spying on the rich, and the rich did not know how it was happening. If they found out, they were dead within hours. It was power on the loose with all the resources of big money, intelligence, technology. This was the worst thing that could happen: a Washington underground, a shadow government. It was clear that they would go to any length to avoid being found out.

The waitress brought coffee, and Christelle, seeming much better, came back to the table. She looked at him, her face expressionless, as she tore open a bag of sugar. They sat in silence for a few minutes before O'Neill spoke.

"We can't go back, Christelle. We've got to go ahead. And we have to stay alive."

"That would be nice. Definitely," Christelle agreed. "It would be a good idea to stay alive." She gazed at him, pulling back the corners of her mouth in a half smile that didn't quite work.

"Let's go back to the cabin. I think I know what to do next."

Chapter Twenty-one

Yellowstone National Park
Wyoming

Alan Creighton had just finished packing his pipe on the back deck of the cabin when his wife set down a Coors. "I guess you'd like this after that walk. I'm going to have a nap."

"Thanks, Annie; you go ahead. I think I'll just rest here a while."

Annie went inside and Creighton leaned back, tamped down the tobacco, and lit it, blowing smoke until he was sure it was lit. He took a mouthful of beer and savored the sting as the alcohol worked on his tongue, always a little tender from two bowls smoked every day. He gazed at the bulk of Mount Sheridan and farther south the blue lines where the Grand Tetons were barely visible forty miles away. Annie had booked this cabin months ago — a good thing, given limited accommodations at Yellowstone in July. Now they were nearing the end of their week. Checkout was at noon tomorrow.

Creighton checked the date on his watch. July 25, more than a week since Broc O'Neill had called him from Harrisburg, Pennsylvania. A week since the stories of violent murders in Pennsylvania had hit the papers. He had picked up *The New York Times* at Rapid City. Sitting in a restaurant, he and Annie were riveted by the stories. That afternoon he had hardly been able to focus on the presidents carved on Mount Rushmore. During the drive across Wyoming, he had scarcely noticed the Bighorn Mountains until the car had overheated.

Sensing a disaster, Creighton wanted to turn around and go home, but Annie bucked him up and they drove on to Yellowstone and their reservations. There would be plenty of time later, she declared, to find out what had happened. For a week he had wondered whether Broc O'Neill had made it back alive to Christelle's cabin in Vermont.

Creighton eyed his telephone. Annie had little patience with his calls to the university for his voice mail during vacation. He had to do it on the sly. He glanced at the window. The curtains were closed; Annie would be asleep. He picked up the phone and dialed his office at Southern Illinois University. His Worldwide phone was bugged, he knew, but Broc had advised that he continue to use it for innocuous routine calls. As soon as he heard his name, he punched in his code and then listened as three days of messages came over the line. The last message caught his attention:

"Dr. Creighton, this is Susan, your secretary in the History Department. I'm sorry to bother you during vacation, but I thought you'd like to know. I just got a message from computing. That data you requested on labor unions has come in. You can download it any time. Thanks. Have a happy vacation at Yellowstone. See you in September." Click.

Creighton was thoroughly puzzled. He had not requested data on labor unions. No one at Southern Illinois University knew where he and Annie had gone on vacation. And there was no secretary called Susan in the History Department.

But the voice! Creighton pushed the code for replay and listened again. This time, he was sure. The voice of "Susan" was the voice of Broc O'Neill's doctoral student, Christelle Washington. He had talked to her by telephone twice; there was no doubt. The message was a careful cover story to protect this channel of communication.

Creighton went around the cabin to his car and got out his laptop, then moved his lawn chair to the shade of the back deck of the cabin. Within minutes the screen lit up. But he couldn't rely on battery alone. He plugged in the converter, then hit the icon for Rapid Link Wireless, which allowed use of the Internet anywhere within fifty feet of his cabin. Within a minute he was connected to Southern Illinois University; in a few more seconds, he had punched in his username and password and was connected to his personal webspace.

Christelle Washington. He had told Broc he would be in Yellowstone at the end of the month. Her message told him Broc had sent something to the SIU mainframe.

So Broc had escaped the brutality in Pennsylvania that was somehow tied to his investigation of Worldwide cell phones. Broc and his student were working as a team.

Creighton read the screen in amazement. The SIU mainframe contained an enormous file that probably would add up to two hundred fifty pages of single-spaced print. He rummaged in his computer case, found a new diskette, shoved it into his machine, then typed instructions. Several minutes later, the job was done: the whole monster file had been downloaded.

Creighton scrolled to the beginning and began to read — four pages from Broc.

July 19th. Alan — I'm sending all this to you for safekeeping. You've probably heard about the murders in Pennsylvania. These were the result of my investigations. For obvious reasons, Christelle and I are going to avoid communication of any kind for at least a couple of weeks, so don't be alarmed that you don't get any calls. We're okay, for now. To keep it that way, we're going to stick to mainframe-to-mainframe data transfer. If you hear nothing from us within three weeks, assume we have been caught, and use this information as you see fit.

This is a printout of over four thousand customers of Worldwide Communications, all with HPE phones bugged like yours and mine. These are arranged as I found them, in sixteen "sectors," which correspond to areas around the country. Each sector is a kind of "territory" monitored by a person or team, though for what purpose I have no idea.

Researching the whole list would take months, so I have included only three sectors in the attachment below — the one I've been investigating and two from your region. The other thirteen have been mailed in hard copy to your office. It'll take months to go through all that.

On the list of Eastern Pennsylvania customers, you'll find John Randolph and Walter Monahan, both now dead. You can put two and two together — my meddling stirred up a hornets' nest. (Incidentally, from first-hand experience, I advise no visiting, questioning, or contact with any of these customers — not if you prefer to stay alive.)

The list of Missouri customers, executives and companies in your state, may be familiar. I suggest examining public-access information — what these guys do, what their companies do. All of them are victims of phone monitoring. None of them knows this. The reasons are not at all clear, but somehow all of them are victims.

Creighton picked up his Coors. It was getting warm. He dumped it on the grass, went inside to the refrigerator, opened another can, and went back to his laptop.

What follows is what I've been able to dig up on sixty-two World-wide customers in Pennsylvania, New York, and Massachusetts. It's a random selection chosen from hundreds (see pp. 5 to 84). If there's a pattern here, it's not obvious. They're all big — nationals and multinationals with a world-wide reach and net worth like some of the smaller nations of the world.

What do you make of the following? On pages 85 to 110, you'll find summaries of government contracts held by these companies. Some of these are for hardware, some for services. Building contracts, military supplies, shipping, equipment, printing, automobiles — everything down to fencing on air bases and runway paving. All in all, contracts worth $118 billion over the next five years — from just sixty-two companies. Assuming proportional contracts for the other four thousand + customers, we've got one hell of a lot of government connections represented.

Then there's the stuff on pages 111 to 164. A lot of it doesn't make much sense. It's staggering, Alan. These same sixty-two companies have disbursed over $800 million in donations in the last six months, in amounts ranging from $280,000 to $6.3 million.

Creighton gulped his beer. Donations — from huge corporations? There were a lot of donations these days, but very few companies donated money in those amounts. After all, the very idea of charity was like welfare — decidedly against the grain.

American corporations were all in a high-profit mode, modernizing plants to speed production, expanding within rigid parameters commensurate with growing markets, plowing funds into computer hardware, advanced software, complex websites. They were doing everything to cut expenses, closing facilities to cut duplication of operations, keeping themselves lean and efficient. They opposed every form of government regulation, negative on taxes, opposed to anything that might slow the flow of cash from income to profit, with investment in research strictly curtailed by what conservative stockholders would tolerate. A certain amount of public-image charity would be allowed, but nothing like these amounts.

Of course, there were always a few super-rich and largely independent moguls, Ted Turners and Warren Buffets, who liked to break into headlines with big donations for fighting river blindness in Asia or making prosthetic limbs for maimed children in Beirut — projects with a triple whammy: huge publicity, big tax deductions, and prayers of thanks from weepy little ladies in small towns across the Midwest.

What do you make of the list on page 165? Of these sixty-two companies, twenty-eight made donations totaling $135 million dollars to a nature conservatory outfit called Texas Lands Preservation. I can understand Pennsylvania Produce having some interest in Texas land — they've got pretty big agricultural interests there — but a donation of $6.3 million is a bunch of money! And how do you explain a Massachusetts auto-frame fabricator donating an even three million every quarter? And what's the motive for a New York clothier donating to a foundation in California?

Forty companies on the list made donations to Anatran — a shadowy foundation I cannot trace except for bank transfers to a mysterious group called Lignum Operations. It's not a U.S. registered company. The transfer numbers suggest offshore banks.

186

Every time you try to trace this money, you end up in a morass of untraceable transactions — at least untraceable with the limited resources of a home computer. The whole thing is a web with a bunch of black holes.

Creighton sat back and lit his pipe. Then he scrolled through to the Missouri companies. Good God! What a list! He recognized most of them. Huge conglomerates in St. Louis, Springfield, Columbia, Cape Girardeau, Kansas City. Trucking and agribusiness, manufacturing, engineering, builders, mortgage companies, munitions.

Munitions. He recognized the company where his old buddy from Nam worked: "Haze," they called him — John Hazelton, Comptroller for Independent Machine Parts. What a euphemism! "Independent machine parts" meant bullets and bombs — everything from pellets for air rifles up to giant daisy-cutters so big they would hardly fit in anything but a specially modified bomber.

Victims. The reasons were not at all clear, but somehow all of them are victims— Victims of what? Surveillance, for one thing. All of them had a president, chief executive officer, comptroller who was under surveillance for reasons unknown.

Creighton scrolled back to Broc's letter and read the last two paragraphs. It seemed reasonably certain that Christelle Washington's computer account at Jefferson State University was secure; he and Christelle had been using it as the gateway into the maze of corporate records. O'Neill was less certain about his voice mail; he had advised Creighton against leaving messages. But if Creighton wished to communicate, a "document" loaded into the Jefferson State University mainframe would be in his hands within twenty-four hours. At the end of the message, he found the codes — the precise instructions for accessing Christelle's account.

Creighton went back to the car and got his briefcase. Before he and Annie had left for Yellowstone, Creighton had taken his cellular phone to a friend in St. Louis, an engineer with the best electronics qualifications in the city. Within a few hours he had figured out the phone: its extra rapid-frequency alternation transmission. The were made and assembled in the Philippines and Malaysia.

Creighton swore under his breath. Hi-tech American equipment made in the Philippines and assembled in Malaysia! He remembered peering into his first computer, an Apple IIe purchased in St. Louis in the 1980s and was shocked to discover the words across the bottom of the vinyl case: MADE IN MALAYSIA. Pretty soon the U.S. could lose all its technical know-how as third-world nations mobilized their work forces to make what Americans wanted. One day we would need to launch an air strike against somebody, Pakistan or maybe Indonesia, and discover our planes were using computer components made in Pakistan or Indonesia.

Creighton cleared the screen and typed out a brief note on his off-the-cuff observations and then followed O'Neill's instructions. In ten minutes, the information was in Christelle's webspace at JSU.

He shut off the computer and went back to the deck. The cell phone manufactured by Hai Phong Electronics was still sitting on the rail. It was time to make some calls, but not from this phone! They would have to wait. Tomorrow he and Annie would check out, and if Annie's preferences in the past were any indication, she would want to be back home as soon as possible. It was an easy two-day drive from Yellowstone Park to Clayton, Missouri. They would be home by late afternoon Monday.

Chapter Twenty-two

Dillon Shaver saw the car parked near his house as he came around the corner. He pulled into his driveway, and walked casually out to his mailbox, a rural style on a post at the curb. He pulled out a handful of mail. Recognizing a letter from his mother on top, he was about to tear it open when he sensed two men approaching. Both wore blue business suits and power ties; they flashed FBI badges as he turned.

"Mr. Shaver?" The larger of the two men spoke.

"That's me. What can I do for you?"

"If you don't mind, Mr. Shaver, we're trying to track down some stolen property. Perhaps you could help us. Where do you work?"

"Bell Communications—"

"Have you been in town the past couple of weeks?"

"I'm a working man, you know how it is, eh? My vacation doesn't start until week after next. But... uh... answering questions about me is not helping to track stolen property. What's this all about?"

"I wonder if you could show us your identification."

Shaver was annoyed at their brusqueness, but he decided to swallow it as he pulled out his wallet. He glanced at his license for a second. "Nope, it hasn't expired." He handed it to the shorter of the two.

The FBI agent examined the license issued by the State of Vermont. "You know a guy called Jacob Wallace?"

He shook his head. "Not anybody I remember. Who is he?"

"What about Broc O'Neill?"

"I think I'd remember a guy with a name like that. My high school track coach was called O'Neill."

"Do you have a passport?"

"Don't have one. I'm not an American citizen. I'm a legal resident with a green card." Shaver pulled the cards from his wallet, then handed over his Resident Alien Card. "Two more years to go before I can apply. I'm still a citizen of Canada—"

"Then, you must have a Canadian passport."

"Sure do," he confirmed, spinning on his heel and heading to his car, a late model Cavalier. The agents followed. He pulled out his key, opened the door on the passenger's side, and reached for the glove compartment. "I keep them here: Canadian driver's license and passport." He pulled out a wad of maps, gas receipts, and insurance identification papers, sorting them onto the front seat of the car. When he was finished, he picked up the two thickest maps and ruffled the edges. "Damn! They're gone! License, passport! They're gone!"

"How long have they been gone, Mr. Shaver?"

"Hell! I have no idea! I thought they were here. Last time I used them was, let's see, last Christmas. Me an' my wife went up home to Canada. Always use the Canadian license in Canada. I keep it and the passport in the car so I know where they'll be." Shaver ruffled the pages of his owner's manual, then leaned into the car and shuffled through the glove compartment.

"Where are you from in Canada, Mr. Shaver?"

"Belleville, Belleville, Ontario. Not far: you can make it up there from here in about three and a half, maybe four hours."

"Actually, Mr. Shaver, we know your license and passport are missing. They were used by somebody else."

"What the hell! I must have left the car unlocked. Who the hell was it?"

"We're not sure who. They used your name and Canadian address and paid cash. Have you received any mail from Pennsylvania lately?"

"I don't know anyone in Pennsylvania. Never even been there."

"What about today's mail?"

Shaver sorted the pile from the top of his car. Junk mail, one credit card bill, and the letter from his mother. "Just this." He tore off the end and pulled out the letter, four handwritten sheets. Inside was a commercial check from Hertz Car Rental in the amount of $34.16 made out to Dillon Shaver. His mother's Belleville address, the address of record on his Canadian license, was typed at the lower left. A note clipped to the check from his mother said, "I thought you'd want this; every penny counts."

Shaver looked at the check and then at the FBI agents. "Damn! What kind of trouble am I in?"

"I don't think you're in any, Mr. Shaver. Somebody rented a Hertz car with your license and passport, paid cash, left a deposit, and turned the car in early. The refund was sent to your Canadian address. I'd say go ahead and cash it. You're the only person we've heard of who made a profit from being a victim of a crime."

Dillon Shaver waited until 9 p.m., then drove downtown to buy a carton of cigarettes. He gave the cashier an additional four dollars and asked for change in quarters. Near the drug center, there were pay telephones. Shaver had committed the number to memory; he dialed and waited while the connection was made.

Broc O'Neill had figured out that someone was monitoring several thousand cellular telephones. Shaver was sure that powerful government agencies were involved: they were the only ones with equipment powerful and sophisticated enough to monitor and then unscramble the transmissions. But now this, a sudden new wrinkle: the FBI!

Someone picked up the receiver in Clayton, Missouri. "Hello—"

"Is this Alan Creighton?"

"Speaking—"

"This is Dillon Shaver. We have a mutual friend who is staying out of sight. I've got some new information for you to pass on. They've tracked O'Neill's ID."

Washington, DC

John Orchard looked at his watch as the phone rang. It was 10:10 p.m. Reaching for the phone, he glanced at his wife, who was watching the news.

"John, this is Blakeney—"

"I'm sorry, you must have a wrong number," Orchard answered, waiting for the click before he hung up the phone. He waited five minutes and then said goodnight to his wife as she headed off down the hall to the bedroom. Downstairs in his study, he picked up the phone and dialed.

"Blakeney here," came the curt answer.

"Sorry for the delay, I hope it wasn't urgent."

"Just a report on the last twenty-four hours. We've had a couple of guys working on this. They came up with something, a motel rental in Harrisburg from July 14th to 16th — rented under the name of Dillon Shaver. He came out of nowhere, rented a car in Scranton on the 14th, turned it in on the 17th, then disappeared."

"Any connection with 'Jacob Wallace'?"

"The car Wallace was driving the day he met Randolph was a Ford Tempo. That's what Dillon Shaver rented. But he's not Dillon Shaver, either. The real Dillon Shaver is a Canadian, a resident alien living in Waterbury, Vermont. We've talked to him. His story seems okay. He was in Vermont between the 13th and 17th. In fact, he hasn't been out of Vermont since Christmas. We've got credit-card statements to prove it. But his Canadian passport and driver's license are missing from his car, and he has no idea how long they've been gone."

"So 'Jacob Wallace' is some guy using Dillon Shaver's stolen documents—"

"It's better than that. We fed Shaver's name to Veil. He's got access to commercial records worldwide. Someone using Dillon Shaver's ID made a purchase about twenty minutes ago, so it looks like we've located 'Jacob Wallace.' And our hunch was right: 'Jacob Wallace' is also Professor Broc O'Neill."

"Well, damn it! We should have him in hand any minute, shouldn't we?"

"It's not quite as simple as that, John."

Orchard looked at the scattered lights across the Potomac River, and the patch of darkness where the main buildings stood. It appeared as though everyone was sleeping, but it was an illusion. There were receptors and feelers everywhere, all connected, all linked together in an all-seeing, all-hearing web, all running back into that darkness across the river: the headquarters of the CIA. "Where is he, Blakeney?"

"Southeast Asia."

Seeing nothing, too astonished to move, Orchard stood at his window. It was several seconds before he spoke. "I don't understand, Blakeney. How could he get out of the country?"

Orchard heard the long exhale in his ear; he knew Blakeney had lit up a cigarette. "He flew from Washington."

"Washington! Right under our damn noses!"

Orchard heard another breathy sound of air, and then Blakeney was speaking. "After a purchase in the name of Dillon Shaver showed up at the Washington airport, we checked every flight. O'Neill flew from Washington National Airport on July 22nd under his own name."

"Under his own name! I am beginning to lose confidence in American intelligence."

"John, we've been monitoring O'Neill's accounts, but the tickets were bought back in May by O'Neill's wife on her credit card a week before she died. They must have had a vacation in mind. She had insurance on all her cards: automatic payoff in case of death. The transactions slipped through."

"So, O'Neill's been sitting with two tickets in his and his wife's names for the last ten weeks and you guys didn't find out until after he's split! Shit! What about his wife's ticket?"

"He got a refund, an automatic insurance refund, so he flew by himself. Washington to L.A., L.A. to Singapore."

"So how long is it going to be till you pick him up?"

"It could be a while. You can't waltz into Singapore and take prisoners."

"Hell — it's just a bloody dot on the map."

"Well, you get into that little dot and your life is in their hands. I spent a year there — I know! You get caught doing anything shady, you're in more trouble than you can imagine. You get caught with drugs, it's the death penalty. And there's no right to bear arms."

"Unbelievable! Haven't they discovered civilization? Don't they have a Bill of Rights?"

"And if you overstay your visa by one bloody hour, you go to jail. Write a joke in a restroom stall, get caught, and you get caned. Remember that kid who spray painted cars? John, if you want to go and bring

O'Neill back, you go right ahead. Not me! Those places don't operate like we do. There's no plea bargaining, deferred adjudication, probation, community service, or walking away from capital crime if you can pay for a hot-shot lawyer. They don't use juries that get hung and let you walk. You get waylaid in Singapore and you're behind bars for good.

"You get caught bringing in a handgun, that's presumptive evidence of intent to rob or kill. Undertake subversive political activity or join a criminal organization, you go directly to prison. And if you get the death sentence, you get it! They don't mess around for decades with endless appeals. The American Embassy guys get the hell down to your jail cell, deliver your messages to Mom, and hand you forms to make out a will.

"Nothing anybody says or does here will make a bloody bit of difference. You'll still die by firing squad. Ask them why and they say there's no way they're going to allow American-style crime — juvenile vandalism, street gangs, drug trafficking — to get a foothold in Singapore. So, all the President's soldiers and all the President's men aren't going to set you free again."

"Hell, Blakeney — they're not going to mess with CIA guys."

"The hell they aren't! They've seen the CIA mess around with secret wars in Laos and clandestine operations in Indonesia. If they caught a CIA guy on Singapore turf, he'd be lucky to see the light of day before the next decade."

Orchard sat down. Dimly, he knew Blakeney was right. He had done secret service work in Asia. But it infuriated Orchard that a Midwest history professor could evade the greatest intelligence network ever assembled on Earth.

"Dwight, it looks like this thing is out of FBI hands." There was a silence on the phone; Orchard knew Blakeney was steaming. "Let me get on with this. We'll try something else."

Orchard hung up and then dialed another number. Within a minute he had Wade Bracket from the Office of Special Operations, CIA, on the line. Briefly, he recounted his conversation with Blakeney.

"Blakeney is right about Singapore. But there's another hitch. O'Neill may not be back in the U.S. for a while. A lot of people disappear into Southeast Asia. It's a pretty easy place to live. Good food, lots to see. All you have to do is make sure you don't break the law. If it were me, given the way we've made hell of his life, I'd be somewhere else for good. Maybe Singapore would be the place."

Orchard squeezed the bridge of his nose, thinking about the fury that would come down from his committee superiors once they heard of this development. "Okay, okay. Do you have a way to tail him in Singapore, just keep track of him?"

"Cautiously, yes."

"And wait for him to go where he can be nabbed?"

"Probably, yes," Bracket agreed conditionally. "Unofficially, of course. But we're talking about manpower, resources in that part of the world. It might be better to monitor the airlines and wait. Get him as soon as he steps back onto American soil, if he ever does. If he doesn't — if he stays there — he's pretty well out of the picture."

"I don't think we can let him go. But as long as we're making progress, I can hold off reporting to the Admiral, and Ironwood. See if you can set up something." Orchard heard the sound of Bracket exhaling again. "By the way, you said you knew where he was. How exact is that?"

"By my watch, John, it's exactly 10:41 in the evening. In Singapore, it's 11:41 in the morning. Broc O'Neill has just boarded a plane in the Singapore airport. In four minutes, it will take off — for the Philippines."

"What in the hell is he doing?"

"Don't know, but we think someone is flying with him."

"Think?"

"Well, he made a restaurant purchase in the airport, meals for two. He used a credit card for the first time in three months. My guess is he's with a female, maybe on the vacation his wife planned."

"What about the tickets his wife bought?"

"A round trip to Singapore for two, return date flexible. But it didn't include a side trip to the Philippines. Looks like that is his own idea."

"Think about it, Wade; he was picked up at the Burlington airport by some broad, and before he died, Walter Monahan said he saw a woman running off with O'Neill in Allentown, the one that shot up Spiker's car."

"What's your point?"

"Other countries have extradition laws for suspected criminals. Monahan and Spiker are dead. We've got two sterling American citizens

195

six feet under, and who's to say O'Neill's broad wasn't the one who put them there with O'Neill as an accomplice?"

"Except O'Neill flew alone to Singapore. We don't know who's with him on the way to the Philippines. He may have picked up a local broad."

"Possibly, but we don't know for sure that he flew alone."

There were a few seconds of silence on the other end of the line, and then Bracket spoke: "Well, tailing him is an interesting angle, one worth pursuing. O'Neill may not be so far out of reach."

"I'd say he's within reach if your guys can get near them and pull it off."

Orchard listened to the sound of Wade Bracket exhaling into the phone. Then he asked, "What about this broad who may be with him?"

"We can't be sure," Wade paused, "but a ticket was bought within seconds from the same cashier by someone called Christelle Washington. Singapore is such an international city — she could be a local, a tourist, or even an expatriate stationed there. No way to tell."

"Okay, Wade, check her out."

Chapter Twenty-three

Christelle sat with her face against the window as the plane picked up speed and soared free of the runway. She glanced at her ticket: Changi International Airport. The foreign words were hard to remember. She wondered which was correct, 'chan-gee' or 'chan-jee,' and wondered which language it was. But she had heard the ticket girl say something more like 'chan-dee.' That didn't seem to match the spelling, but neither did a lot of words in English. She would have to listen more carefully. What must be right is the way the Chinese pronounced it. There were Chinese all over Singapore, and Malays, too, and there were two Chinese and two Malay stewardesses helping them as they boarded — pretty girls with big brown eyes and beautiful uniforms made of colorful batik.

The plane climbed. Tall glass towers and office buildings made up the Singapore skyline, gleaming under the tropical sun. She had never dreamed it would be like this in Asia. She and Broc had spent most of their mornings wandering up and down Orchard Street, the main downtown thoroughfare; feasting on the scenery; watching the people. The street seemed so broad, with a roadway in the middle and wide brick walkways on each side, with shade trees and flowers and enclosed malls like Lucky Plaza and Orchard Towers and Tanglin Shopping Center. It was a good thing they were flying back to Singapore later; there was lots more to explore, including that crazy 'Texas' store with boots and cowboy hats in the window. Broc had said he thought women looked good in cowboy hats and boots.

The plane banked, circling toward their route to the Philippines. Straining to see, Christelle pressed her forehead to the window. The harbor was crowded; there were big tankers and freighters anchored offshore, hundreds of them dotting the water for miles. Their travel book listed Singapore as the second busiest harbor in the world after Rotterdam.

Christelle gazed off at the receding islands south of Singapore, hundreds upon hundreds of them: big ones with steep hills all covered with jungle and smaller ones that lay like green jewels on the water surrounded by a pale green halo, which she had read were coral reefs. She tried to imagine the endless dots in the ocean. The Indonesian archipelago: fourteen thousand islands spreading for thousands of miles along the Equator, most of them deserted like magical places in a book of fairy tales, and her travel book said the Philippines had seven thousand islands.

In a few minutes they were flying over the South China Sea; when she looked straight down, she could see the perfect shadow of their plane racing across the waves. They would be back in Singapore in a few days, and that excited her, but she was excited about the Philippines, too. Both were places she had never dreamed she would ever see.

They had driven from Vermont at night, parked her Grand Am in long-term airport parking, stashed the guns and car keys in a safety deposit box, and flown from Washington to L.A., then nonstop to Singapore, a flight that had taken hours and hours, with their day seeming to stretch forever, and then the night seeming to last forever, too. Somewhere in the Pacific they had crossed the date line and a whole day just disappeared — poof! — and they landed a whole day later. Broc checked them into adjacent rooms at the Hyatt Regency on Scott Street, but once they slept off jet lag, they spent every waking moment together.

Saturday morning, they went to the Botanical Garden, to be sure they didn't miss it, and found themselves in the middle of five wedding parties with brown-eyed, dark-haired brides in white dresses and flower girls posing on the lawns while everyone ran around talking all at once in Chinese.

In the afternoon they taxied out to the Van Kleef Aquarium, and that was it! Christelle couldn't tear herself away from gazing at all the fish: the pamphlet said there were 4,500 different kinds in the South China Sea. They weren't all here, but there were hundreds of varieties of every size and color. They stood at some of the windows for ten or fifteen minutes, amazed at the brilliant colors and schools with thousands of fish moving together and quickly turning as though by some invisible signal.

Finally, Broc went on ahead, and when he came back, she was watching clown fish scooting in and out of waving coral flowers. He had found a crash SCUBA course starting Monday, four afternoons in a Singapore pool, with open-water dives at Tioman Island to complete their certification. Tioman Island was somewhere off the coast of Malaysia to the north. After gazing at beautiful fish for an hour, Christelle thought SCUBA diving in a tropical sea sounded like the most exotic thing she had ever heard of, and half an hour later they were signed up. The pool classes started Monday; the open-water dives could be scheduled any time during the next six weeks.

In the evenings they wandered. One night in Little India; another in the old part of the city near Raffles Hotel, where they ordered the legendary Singapore Sling for which the hotel was famous; and still another on Sentosa Island, sampling exotic dishes like nasi *padang*, *satay* and *kon loh mee*, and fruits like mangosteen, and papaya with fresh lemon juice squeezed on top.

Broc watched the jungle rolling by. The plane had been following the northeast-running coast of Borneo for hundreds of miles. Now in the distance an immense mountain loomed up in the clouds. O'Neill checked his map: Mount Kinabalu: the highest peak in Southeast Asia.

A Chinese stewardess came by and handed him two cups of juice. Christelle turned and, looking past him, thanked her with a smile. She took a cup, murmured approval and thanks, and went back to her window. Broc looked out at the mountains. He caught the faint aroma of Christelle's perfume; it made him focus for a few seconds on her hair, which cascaded in glossy curls with the light of the window coming through along the edges. He admired her blouse, a soft silk garment in green that set off the color of her eyes. Her skirt, a sheath that ended just above her knees, was patterned with dark green leaves and white blossoms of frangipani.

O'Neill felt a twinge of guilt. Six weeks ago, Christelle was an innocent graduate student; now she was caught up in a deadly dragnet. They were reasonably safe now, though Broc could not stop looking over his shoulder. They had escaped from the U.S. through sheer chutzpah, flying on separate tickets, hers bought with her own credit card. They had made a successful getaway.

But had they? Her identity might still be a mystery, but someone may well have picked up Broc's name on the flight records by now. If not, it was just a matter of time until something came up on a computer screen in front of hostile eyes. A message from Alan Creighton had warned Broc that Dillon Shaver's ID had been compromised. He had no choice but to travel under his own name. Moreover, both he and Christelle could be in severe legal danger if caught using false ID in Southeast Asia. Balancing risks, they had decided to use their own passports.

Christelle turned toward him again, gesturing toward the distant green horizon. "What does the map say it is?"

He flattened the map and pointed to the long island called Palawan. "I guess that's the beginning of the Philippines."

Christelle drank another mouthful of juice and laid her head back against the headrest. After a minute she rolled her face toward him and spoke in a low voice. "What's the name of the place we're going to see?"

"It's an industrial center near Manila called Caloocan City. The company's called Teleconic Manufacturing. According to Alan Creighton, the phone chips are made there."

Christelle went back to her window.

Once in Singapore, it had been difficult to think about the situation back in the U.S. For several days, O'Neill let it all go and enjoyed wandering in Singapore with Christelle, thinking of other things. It was the first time he had begun to feel anything other than numbness and rage — the first time in ten weeks that he experienced hours, whole half days, when he did not think of Darcy. The SCUBA course helped; the sound of his own bubbles overcame the dark memories. The absurdly awkward visage everyone had as they spent their first hours submerged was entertaining. Christelle bore no resemblance to the wide-eyed models in the magazines peering through their masks, enticing everyone to "Come Swim with Me." Taking the advice of her instructor, she wore her oldest denims and an oversized Singapore tee-shirt as protection against sunburn and the chafing of straps and tubes.

Five days after their arrival, wary of the standard 220-volt electricity, O'Neill hooked up a 220/110 converter; he wondered whether his laptop would explode when he plugged it in. But everything worked fine. Within a few minutes he found a new file in Christelle's student account in the JSU mainframe. According the Creighton, most components of the Worldwide phones were made in Taiwan and Thailand, except for the doctored chips, which were made by Teleconic Manufacturing in the Philippines. Assembly occurred at Hai Phong Electronics in Penang, a manufacturing center off the West Coast of Malaysia. Altogether, four manufacturers were involved, but Teleconic and Hai Phong provided the specific components behind the eavesdropping feature.

Darcy's tickets suggested an escape to Singapore, and Alan Creighton's discoveries added the Philippines to their itinerary. Pursuing the doctored cell phones to their source was the only safe thing they could do. Getting out of the country was the best way to escape detection, at least for a time. Of course, it could be fruitless, a time waster, but it gave them an excuse to relax for a while, and they might learn something.

How safe they would be was unknown, but O'Neill guessed they had several days' jump on their pursuers.

After a quarter hour pouring over a travel book, Christelle suggested the Manila Hotel because it offered "elegant, historic, colonial-style accommodations." It was near Rizal Park and the ancient Spanish walled city of Intramuros, and it offered a discount in the off-season, June to September. By five in the afternoon, they had registered for a three-room suite facing Manila Bay. Christelle was subdued from the drive in from the airport. While their taxi waited at stoplights, dozens of tiny Filipino children had mobbed their car, shouting "Americano! Money! Money! Please, Americano, money!" Christelle was ready to empty her change purse, but the driver would not roll down the windows.

"Ten million people in Manila, and they're so poor!" she exclaimed sadly, as they sipped mai tais in the hotel bar. Christelle had her travel book open. "It says here that a quarter of the population live in shantyvilles, and there's one place called Tondo where nearly two hundred thousand people are crowded, more than ten to a hut, in less than two square kilometers." She stared across the table at Broc. "Wasn't this once an American colony? How did we leave behind such a mess?"

"We gave them independence before they were ready. Manila was half destroyed in World War II; 1946 was just too soon. We should have worked up a mini-Marshall Plan. But we could hardly resist when they chose our day for their independence. July the Fourth. That tells you how friendly the separation was."

"I guess if we hadn't done it in a friendly way, there could have been a war."

He nodded. "Judging by insurgency against the Dutch in Indonesia, bloodshed against the French in Indochina, and terrorism in British Malaya, yes. We'd have risked a war of independence here within a few years."

Christelle tried not to gawk. The hotel was palatial. The restaurant and bar were opulent. So were the vast foyer, stairways, auditoriums, and hundreds of rooms. There were massive wooden columns, thick rugs and gilded decorations everywhere. She went back to her travel book. "It says here teachers make the equivalent of eighty-five U.S. dollars per month. How much are we paying for our suite?"

"Three hundred sixty a night."

Christelle closed the book and shoved it in her purse. "It's sinful. That driver should have let us give those children some money. There should be some kind of government relief program."

"All academics think that way. We're victims of Democratic ideology."

"What other way is there to think?"

"Well, there's the old trickle-down idea. It's been questioned in the U.S. and it's always ambiguous, but there are some ways it works in places like this. There are dozens of hotels like this in Manila, probably a total of twenty thousand rooms. With vacationers like us, that's a lot of foreign money coming in. Hotels may have majority foreign ownership, but the employment opportunities for locals are enormous. Add in bars, restaurants, entertainment, taxis, and you've got millions pouring into Filipino hands."

"And I suppose this company we're checking out fits into all this. Worldwide Communications is buying telephones with chips made here by the locals."

O'Neill nodded.

"But what about the argument that overseas companies take jobs from Americans? You know, outsourcing."

"On an individual case, yes. You can point to workers laid off in Massachusetts or California, and you can point to factories in Mexico or Taiwan that get contracts. But on a collective count, the argument is not so clear — U.S. unemployment is at a record low for the last thirty years. Service industries catering to the wealthy in America have blossomed, and a service person here, like our Filipino waiter, is not taking a job away from an American."

Christelle listened, thoughtful, focused, feeling the persuasive strength of his words.

"What's happening in the U.S.," he went on, "is that many low-skill jobs are going overseas while U.S. management and technology positions requiring advanced training are increasing. The overall effect is low level jobs replaced by new patterns of employment that require an associate's degree. In general terms, the American worker is employed very high on the economic food chain."

Christelle regarded him for a minute. "That's not a political view, is it?"

"Occasionally, you get an election candidate trying to make it political, like Ross Perot, who's railing about American jobs going to Mexico. Conservative thinking tends toward protection of one's own nation and economy. But in a global economy, that's hard to achieve. Especially because U.S. tax law often encourages overseas operations."

"Encourages? Where?"

"Puerto Rico, for one. It's an American protectorate with tax breaks for foreign-owned manufacturing companies. There are dozens of U.S. firms, Microsoft for instance, that use Puerto Rican labor to generate high profits that are virtually tax free. It's a beautiful place, and it spreads wealth from American business across the Puerto Rican working class."

Christelle pushed the sections of orange down below the ice in her mai tai and stirred before taking a drink. "Nothing is simple; there's always another side to consider."

"I think that's the point of your dissertation."

"Yes, some of these things belong in my dissertation."

"A lot of things belong in your dissertation! Double-agenda politics is great for analyzing things otherwise befuddling. Your biggest problem is limiting the topic."

Christelle stirred her drink again. "My biggest problem is finding time to begin."

"Well, I guess when you're running for your life, you have to set priorities."

Christelle appeared amused by his macabre sense of humor.

"If we get caught, you won't have to write a dissertation—"

"And you won't have to read it! I guess that will simplify our lives, but I'd prefer free choice rather than premature burial to decide my fate."

She watched him pull his mouth back at the corners as he half smiled at her. He really could be funny when he wasn't thinking about Darcy. She felt enormously well protected — the ingrained response, she supposed, to a competent, powerful male presence. Broc was very intelligent; otherwise, he would have been dead within a week of Darcy's funeral. But behind the ever-working mind lay a powerful strength, the result, she thought, of trekking in the wilds, running rapids, and chopping wood at his cabin somewhere up in Wisconsin. She wanted to be with him as they faced the dangers ahead.

He had dressed in a dark tan jacket, and slacks, a nicely fitted summer suit custom made in forty-eight hours by Chinese tailors in Singapore. The dark brown tie went with his chestnut hair and eyes; the thin gold tie clip provided the perfect touch of elegance.

Her eyes took in the breadth of his shoulders. His hair — sometimes she wanted to reach out and run her fingers through it and hold his head against her breast. Then she realized he was looking at her, and she dropped her eyes as the rising warmth flushed her skin.

When she had regained her composure, she asked, "What's your idea with Teleconic?"

"First, I want to hook up to the mainframe at JSU to see whether we can get a little more information from Alan Creighton. That'll take a couple of hours; we could do it tonight. Then we ought to have a look at Teleconic. But I think when is up to you. This is also supposed to be a vacation."

Christelle riffled the pages of her travel book. "Well, as much as I'm dying to run around and see everything, maybe we should visit Teleconic first and get it done with." She paused a second, then leaned forward. "Broc, look at those waitresses. What do you think?"

He gazed at them. "Is this a trick question? They're beautiful."

"I know that!" She poked his hand with her finger. "I mean their dresses."

"I hadn't noticed their dresses."

"Broc O'Neill! You ought to be ashamed!"

"See, it was a trick question. But since you ask, their dresses are beautiful, too."

"That's what I was hoping. The first thing I want to do is buy a dress like that."

Chapter Twenty-four

City of Caloocan
Manila, Philippines

They watched the jeepney pull away with its remaining eight passengers, honking, bells ringing. "Bye, bye," the Filipinos shouted — an old lady with a chicken in a cage, two dark-eyed mothers, and five cute little brown-eyed children. Their arms were sticking out all over, waving.

Christelle was nearly hysterical with laughter. "I saw a picture in the travel book, but I didn't believe they were real."

The jeepney was a jeep — lengthened, chromed, polished, and decorated with bells, horns, antennas, and three iron stallions in place of a hood ornament. The sides were painted with gaudy pictures; plastic streamers flew from all the antennas; and an icon of the Virgin Mary hung from the rear-view mirror.

Christelle went on: "It says in my book the number of stallions on the hood tells you how many mistresses the driver has." They watched the jeepney lurch off around a corner, amazed at the happy children in the middle of one of the poorest cities in the world. "They started making those from American jeeps left behind after World War II." She paused a minute. "Do you think he really has three mistresses?"

"I doubt it. He'd need low maintenance girls to afford three."

"You should be an economist," Christelle advised.

"Anyway," Broc went on, "I think stallions on jeepneys have now become status symbols. Three mistresses would be a recipe for bankruptcy." Christelle glanced at him. "There's no such thing as a low-maintenance mistress," he added. "In the U.S. they want an expensive car on Valentine's Day."

"I would have imagined more practical benefits," Christelle smirked. "Like free graduate school tuition."

"If that's what you want, the recognized institution is the 'sugar daddy'. But working in one of those high-tip bars on the weekends, say like Hooters, could be pretty lucrative."

Christelle wrinkled her nose. "Neither of these is to my taste. I'm going to hope that Daddy keeps paying my tuition."

The driver had dropped them several miles north of the Pasig River on a busy street in Caloocan City, an area of crowded homes, small businesses, and factories. They started to walk. Wherever there was open space — in alleyways, against fences, beside factories, over drainage ditches — there were shanties built of scrap wood, cardboard, and corrugated tin. They walked along, mingling with the mid-day crowds, passing hawkers selling food and little knots of bare-footed children watching them with big brown eyes.

A smiling Filipino beckoned them into an open-air eatery where they sat down and studied the map.

"I think we're very near." Broc thought within two blocks. "Too bad the streets aren't named."

The waiter stood beside them; his face crinkled as he smiled. "Ah! Americanos. My name Ho Say." Broc thought José but the waiter said Ho Say. "We have excellent food for Americanos. You like to order?" O'Neill sensed this man might be the owner.

"All those wonderful smells have made us hungry," Broc admitted to Ho Say, whose eyes were scarcely above the level of his. "But we'll need your help."

"Ah! The best! Balut. You like balut! Also, maybe beer? Beer very good with balut. American beer? Maybe Filipino beer?"

Broc deferred to Christelle, who raised her eyebrows and puffed her cheeks. "Why not? Yes." She smiled at the owner. "Balut, we'd like that! And Filipino beer."

"Smart Americano lady!" He winked at Broc, then rushed away.

"What on Earth is balut?" Broc asked.

"I have no idea. I guess it will be a surprise."

The Filipino was back in less than a minute with two bottles of ice-cold beer and a dish with two large eggs. "Ah! Balut, you like balut!"

"Excuse me," Broc said, "we're looking for a place, a business, called Teleconic. We think it's near here."

"Ah! Teleconic!" He turned and pointed across the intersection. "There, Teleconic! You know someone at Teleconic?"

The aging corrugated steel building was plastered with posters. "No, we just wondered—"

"Miguel!" Ho Say stood up and waved to someone at another table. "Americanos. *Dito lang!*"

A man dressed in a tan business suit jumped up, grabbed his beer and rushed over. Broc glanced at Christelle. What do we do now?

"Miguel, Americanos ask about Teleconic." He turned to Broc and Christelle. "Miguel Tong long-time friend. Better him call Tong, Tong Miguel. We grow up on same street. Tong eat meal here. He main boss at Teleconic."

"Supervisor," the man corrected, sticking out his hand as he sat down. "Ah! Ho Say" He turned to his friend. "They have balut! You bring me balut too, also beer."

Tong turned to O'Neill. He had an ageless appearance. He could have been forty, fifty, or seventy. As he smiled, his eyes closed to slits.

"So you are from China?" Broc guessed.

"Many generation ago, one hundred, two hundred year, Tong family come to Manila long before Americanos."

Overseas Chinese. Fifty million of them, Broc remembered. Powerful clans in all the Chinatowns of the world, a vast diaspora. There were no more powerful people on Earth than the overseas Chinese who called themselves 'Sons of the Yellow Emperor'.

"So, you would like to learn about Teleconic?"

"We're researchers, economists," Broc said, his mind racing for the right story. "As you know, the Philippines were once very dependent on the U.S."

"Ah! My father use to say crazy — crazy for Filipinos go independent so soon. Filipinos in big trouble for many year."

"That's what we thought. We are trying to find out about Filipino business today. How much is foreign owned?"

"Ah! Filipino business coming better and better. We build more industry, more business. Use much foreign capital but keep industry in Filipino hands. Like Teleconic."

"Tell us about Teleconic?"

"Not good business till 1985, much better business now. We need some modern facility. New contracts. Six year ago we make two big contracts, three year ago, five more. Now Teleconic is full busy, lots of work."

Tong reached for his egg, then leaned like a conspirator toward O'Neill. "You know balut?" He broke a tiny hole in the end and turned the egg over. Nothing leaked out. "Good! Well cook. He cracked it open. "Balut is boil duck egg. See, open; cannot eat if not open!"

O'Neill and Christelle did what Tong had done. Nothing came out of the hole, so they cracked the shell open. There on their plates were two ready-to-hatch ducklings, surrounded by what was left of the white of the egg, still steaming. Broc and Christelle looked at each other, then watched Tong as he popped his in his mouth. O'Neill peered at his again. The duckling's beak and downy feathers were visible in the transparent albumen of the egg.

O'Neill picked his up and began to talk to distract himself. "What kinds of contracts do you have? What does your company do?"

"Make electronic chip, chip to regulate carburetor, chip for refrigerators. Things like that. Computer chip, telephone chip."

"It must be a very good business," O'Neill suggested, popping the duckling in his mouth. He glanced at Christelle as Tong began to talk, and chewed like fury.

"Ah! Wonderful business! And now new contracts with China."

"What are your biggest contracts?" O'Neill asked as soon as the duckling had slid down his throat. He thought Christelle was getting ready to pop hers. "Any American contracts?"

Tong shook his head. "Teleconic circuits in appliances, calculators sold to U.S., but Teleconic never make these things. Only make chips. Clients assemble them. Main contracts with Taiwan, Malaysia."

Christelle had managed to get her duckling in her mouth, chew it, and swallow it in about three seconds. She followed it with a good slug of beer and O'Neill did the same.

"That was good," O'Neill said. "I've never had balut."

"Ah! Is a great delicacy." Tong leaned forward again. "You know, balut is say to bring strength to man." He winked at Christelle. "Young lady, know what I mean?" His face broadened in a knowing smile.

"When young man want to call on young lady, you know what I mean, when young man want lots of strength, lots of power, much big, to persuade young lady, he eat balut." Tong picked up his beer. "Then young man chase down balut with lots of beer!" Ho Say lay back in his chair, laughing and slapping his knees, then leaned forward and urged O'Neill, "You young man; you have another!"

O'Neill glanced at Christelle, who was looking at her hands. "I think one will be enough," he assured, winking. "You know, Miguel, it's just a little too early in the day."

Tong nodded understanding.

"Miguel, you said Teleconic uses foreign money."

"Ah! Yes, American money. Three year ago, Teleconic in big trouble. Then Americanos come in, buy seventy-five percent interest. Rest stay in Filipino hand."

Miguel Tong stood up. "Come; perhaps you like to see, have a tour?"

O'Neill stood up, delighted at his sudden good fortune. He reached in his pocket and pulled out a handful of pesos.

"Ah! No!" Tong objected, "Balut and beer on me!" He counted out the pesos too fast for O'Neill to follow and piled them on the table, signaling Ho Say he was leaving, and pointing to the table. "Come; I show you Teleconic."

"Who are the Americans who bought the company?" O'Neill asked as they crossed the street.

"They name Lignum Operations. Their president do everything. He come here every six month, man call Terrence, Joseph Terrence."

Lignum Operations. O'Neill scrambled through the wad of papers from his suitcase. He sorted them into piles on the carpet in their hotel suite. Lignum… Lignum…

"Christelle! Lignum Operations is where all the money is disappearing. Donations from those companies in the States to Anatran, then those bank transfers we found from Anatran to Lignum. Here it is: Lignum Operations."

"My golly!" She skimmed the page Broc showed her, part of a mass of data he had sent to Alan Creighton. "And I'll bet there are similar transfers from Texas Land Preservation, and all those other foundations and things to Lignum."

"There's obviously a pretty big financial investment by Lignum in Teleconic and a substantial investment in that assembly factory in Malaysia, but these don't account for hundreds of millions collected from thousands of American companies. The big question is what is Lignum Operations? And where is all that money going?"

Christelle stood up and rubbed the back of her knees, which were stiff from kneeling on the floor. "Another big question is, who on Earth is Joe Terrence?"

"The name is awfully familiar. I've heard it; it's on the tip of my tongue; I just can't think who he is. He's well known, but not quite in the limelight."

O'Neill unfolded his legs and lay back on the carpet. It had been one hell of an interesting afternoon. Miguel Tong had toured them through the entire plant, from the loading platforms all the way to the research and prototype labs. There were numerous assembly rooms where dozens of Filipino girls worked with special magnifiers, and high-tech centers where advanced machinery stamped out the miniature circuit boards.

The most astonishing part, however, was that he, Broc O'Neill, had talked his way into this tour with the principal Filipino owner, who was so uninformed about his own chips that he harbored no suspicion. His American partners — Joe Terrence and Lignum Operations — essentially left the running of Teleconic to Tong, who knew only what he needed to know to fill orders to Taiwan, Thailand, Malaysia, and half a dozen other Pacific-rim nations. Indeed, it was probable that the full power of Teleconic's chips was simply not obvious in this Philippine facility. Likely, it would become obvious only as chips were stacked and linked together with other components at Hai Phong Electronics in Penang.

Christelle was mixing drinks at the bar. She was dressed in her favorite uniform, a white cotton blouse, pale green earrings, and faded denims. She wore them well, he thought, as she turned to cross the room and stooped to hand him a gin and tonic.

"Unless you know tricks I don't, you're going to have to sit up to enjoy that."

O'Neill rolled onto his side, leaned on his elbow, and set the drink on the floor.

Christelle hunted in her handbag and pulled out a pencil and the map, which she spread on the coffee table. She worked over it for a minute. "There, I've marked Teleconic Manufacturing, and the balut café, if that's what you call a place like that." She shivered as she recalled swallowing the duckling. "We've got the street names now, so it should be easy to find again."

"You're pretty good at sketching," O'Neill observed, sitting up and taking a mouthful of his drink. My, she did mix them well! "How well do you remember the interior? I mean, can you remember the layout well enough to draw up a rough floor plan?"

"I can try, sure." She fished in her handbag and pulled out the half dozen sheets of paper. "What I'd like to know, Broc, is what are you going to do with these? What good is a list of Teleconic employees and their addresses, all two hundred and sixty-eight of them?"

"I'm not sure. Maybe we'll throw the list away, but not yet. We've got one hell of a lot of information to gather; I don't want to part with any of it until we've figured it out."

Christelle gathered up the papers, arranged all the page numbers in order, then added her map to the top of the pile. Watching O'Neill, she sat back and stirred her drink. "Okay, we've finished our assignment. So we can begin sightseeing tonight. Have you got any ideas?"

"I heard somebody say all the best restaurants are in the big hotels. I think we ought to take a taxi to the Shangri La."

Christelle looked at her watch. "That will take, say, three hours, four if the service is really slow. What then? There ought to be some good entertainment."

"I specifically rule out all those dance-hostess places downtown."

Christelle sat up, her eyes wide. "A male ruling out a strip club! Should I call a doctor?"

"It's not for me; it's for you." O'Neill took another drink while Christelle stared at him. "I think those places are a bad influence. You've got to write your dissertation."

"What on Earth! Writing a dissertation is not my only purpose in life!"

"You mean you're going to take up another career on the side?"

"Broc O'Neill! That's not what I mean! I just mean how on Earth are stripper places going to be a bad influence on me?"

"When you discover you can't go back to Jefferson State University, or even the U.S., that you have to hide out in Asia from the bad guys, you're going to need something else to do. As the only advisor in a position to counsel you, I think it's my duty to make sure you pick a healthy occupation."

"Well, I don't plan to become a dance hostess — or a Hooter Girl! But one must keep on learning. Who knows, I might be able to pick up a few pointers."

Chapter Twenty-five

U.S. Military Cemetery
Manila, Philippines

Broc and Christelle moved slowly from one stone tablet to the next. The memorial, a series of polished stone walls standing on a low hill, stood at the heart of the military cemetery near Forbes Park, the most lavish section of Manila. The columns of names, arranged by places of origin, were engraved in alcoves, an astonishing procession of men who had given their lives throughout the Pacific more than half a century ago. Halfway around, O'Neill stopped and walked slowly toward the edge of the grass. Christelle followed and stood by his side.

He gazed at the rows of white crosses arranged in giant circles, hundreds upon hundreds of them stretching away in every direction until the crosses seemed like rows of white dots in the distance. He was shaking, unable to contemplate the cost of seventeen thousand Americans who had died before he was born for reasons whole generations of Americans had already forgotten.

"My God! It's beyond belief," Christelle exclaimed.

"It's beyond belief because this is only one cemetery for World War II dead. My Uncle Edward died in Europe. He was twenty-four." He stared at the endless crosses. "I guess he's buried in one of the American cemeteries just like this on the coast of France. Thousands of men who died in the Normandy invasion."

He could see the dampness along Christelle's eyelids as she spoke: "We just... just have to believe that they... that all these men... died for something good, for something... important. We just have to believe these were as important as the deaths of soldiers hunting down Adolf Hitler."

O'Neill felt the sudden rage in his chest, a fury that he could hardly contain. He realized Christelle saw it, too. Beyond his control, his hands

214

slowly clenched into fists. His mind raged over unnecessary deaths. Darcy. It was a minute before he could spit out the words. "A lot of these men, maybe most of them, did not have to die!"

"Broc, how can you say that?" Christelle appeared puzzled by his words. "They had to die to stop the Japanese, to save the world from… from aggression, from a nation bent on conquering everyone and taking it all for themselves."

"That's what we're supposed to believe. That's what all these crosses say. And I suppose a lot of people who come and stand here couldn't face it any other way. But it's only part of the story. People don't always die for good causes, for something important. Often, they die because of the arrogance, the stupidity, the unmitigated egotism of those who have power."

"The Japanese?"

"No! Not the Japanese! General Douglas MacArthur!"

Christelle could tell he was about to explode as they rode the elevator, floor by floor, to the top of the Manila Hotel. Broc's face was a mask of fury. Afraid to speak, she had sat beside him in the taxi on the way back to their hotel.

The elevator stopped. They followed the bellboy down the hall.

"Very beautiful penthouse! Most beautiful view of Manila Bay. You like to move to this suite, the General Douglas MacArthur Suite?" The boy turned to them as he inserted the key in the door. "We have no reservations for this suite for several days. You talk to the manager. Only two thousand six hundred U.S. dollars a night."

They walked into a well-appointed foyer. Christelle was awed by the spacious quarters, the opulent furnishings, the art, the fine carpeting splashed with sunlight from the sun dropping in the west. "Two thousand six hundred dollars a night!" She stared at the bellboy, then at Broc. "Are you thinking of changing our reservations?"

"Could you leave us for a little while?" Broc requested of the bellboy. "We won't disturb anything. We'll pull the door closed when we leave."

The bellboy bowed slightly. "Of course, of course. Take your time. And come to the front desk if you would like to take this suite for the rest of your stay."

Christelle watched him walk slowly to the westward facing window. "Broc, I know we're on vacation and you've got thousands in your wallet. But this would not be a very good way to—"

"Christelle, I wouldn't stay in this suite if they paid me a million dollars!"

She stared at him, trying to fathom his meaning, the rage in his voice. He led her down the hall and around a bend. He stopped dead, surprised and disbelieving, before a huge oil painting of Douglas MacArthur.

"There he is, the bastard! This suite, the penthouse suite of the Manila Hotel, is not just an advertising ploy. It was the command headquarters of the most self-centered bastard ever to serve America."

Christelle gazed at the painting and the familiar face, still one of the most well known in the U.S. "This is a luxury suite. How was it a military command headquarters?"

"Because Douglas MacArthur was an egotistical, arrogant fraud."

Christelle remembered his photograph from her college history text. "I thought he was called the 'American Caesar'."

"The original Caesar won his reputation leading his men into battle, risking his life. This so-called 'American Caesar' spent little time on the battlefield. He made decisions that cost American lives, here, in this luxurious penthouse overlooking Manila Bay! Hundreds, maybe thousands, of Americans, men out there under those white crosses, men we are supposed to believe died for a noble cause."

Saying nothing, Christelle watched him as he paced.

"General Douglas MacArthur. What a bastard! He was a man of unmitigated arrogance. He should have been removed. It was corruption in Washington that allowed him to remain in command. He was shabby, petty, headstrong, and cowardly. His only skill was framing glowing words of self-aggrandizement. And if we admit to the facts, he was responsible for the darkest day in American military history."

Christelle sank, watching him, into the coolness of a huge leather chair.

"Why did the U.S. enter the War?" O'Neill quizzed, drilling her like an undergraduate.

"Pearl Harbor."

"Why did we drop the atomic bomb?"

"A lot of reasons, but one was revenge for Pearl Harbor."

O'Neill nodded. "To this day, Americans have focused on Pearl Harbor as the great outrage, the final travesty, as though we lost more there than anywhere else. Roosevelt called December 7th, 1941, 'a day that will live in infamy', quote unquote. But the real day of infamy came the next day, December 8th, when the Japanese wiped out half of the American air power based here in the Philippines."

O'Neill turned slowly, eyeing the spacious dimensions of the suite. Christelle could see the fury in his eyes.

"It happened right here, right in this room! MacArthur received the news of Pearl Harbor within an hour. And then, what happened?"

Christelle watched him, fascinated with what she was hearing.

"You have to picture it, Christelle. The Japanese were voracious. Several hours north of here, they had established an immense air force on Formosa; it's called Taiwan today. And when they struck Pearl Harbor, they already had their destroyers in the South China Sea ready to invade British Malaya.

"There was one air force that could have stopped them, and it was here. Japan wanted the wealth of Southeast Asia. We had the power to stop them. Clark Field was the base for the greatest concentration of air power outside the United States, all under the command of General Douglas MacArthur, who was nicely housed in this luxurious suite overlooking the harbor. I really wonder whether Roosevelt and Truman ever knew the opulence MacArthur arranged for himself."

"So, what happened?"

"MacArthur's standing orders were to prevent a Japanese invasion. This meant a preemptive strike against Japanese airfields on Formosa. But when the news of Pearl Harbor reached MacArthur the morning of December 8th, he did nothing! No deployment of aircraft, no strike on Japanese airfields. Nothing!"

O'Neill strode across the room and stood by the window. His outrage was clear. He seemed ready to explode. Christelle was appalled and mystified at what she heard.

"Nine hours later, the Japanese air force struck. It wiped out Clark Field. Our planes were lined up like a row of sitting ducks. They never got off the ground." O'Neill spun on his heel, his face a mask of fury.

"We lost over fifty P-40 fighters and twelve of the most advanced planes in existence: B-17 heavy bombers, the greatest military planes the world had ever seen, the 'Flying Fortresses'. It was a loss equal to anything at Pearl Harbor."

"You mean, all that was lost," Christelle tried to understand, "because of MacArthur?"

He nodded, his fists still clenched in anger. "Oh, of course, MacArthur denied it, covered it up. Records of what happened and what was said — here, in this room — conveniently disappeared. The bastard issued his usual self-serving reports. He said that the forces in the Philippines were inadequate, that the Americans at Clark Field fought bravely against overwhelming odds. He said Clark Field was another Pearl Harbor; we had been caught in another sneak attack."

"But wasn't he... didn't he ever have to explain? Wasn't there an investigation?"

"Not one. The government conducted eight separate investigations of Pearl Harbor, but not one of this disaster. Yet what happened at Clark Field was the real day of infamy. Two thousand men died at Pearl Harbor. But over the next few weeks, how many of those seventeen thousand out there under those white crosses died because of Douglas MacArthur's dereliction of duty? The Japanese swept through Southeast Asia like a tidal wave. Within weeks the Philippines was overrun, the American forces went down in defeat, and the Filipino people endured the worst atrocities of the Pacific war."

"I cannot believe it, Broc. How did it happen? Why?"

O'Neill spun around. "Corruption! Everybody thinks American government was squeaky clean before Watergate. Everyone thinks Vietnam was the first dirty war and Robert McNamara the first wartime traitor. No! There were thousands in World War II who died because of corrupt leaders. The first traitors were Douglas MacArthur and those in

Washington who protected him. And it's worth saying, since you and I tend to blame the worst on Republicans. Democrats occupied the White House from 1932 until 1952, right through World War II. Plenty of questionable stuff happened then."

"Like what?"

"Well, for instance, the Supreme Court kept undoing FDR's New Deal orders, so he tried to pack the court from six to nine to get a majority of Democratic judges. That may be the most audacious exercise of power ever tried!"

"I have never heard of that, but obviously he didn't get his way."

"It's a good thing. It was a really drastic way to solve a problem, like dropping an atomic bomb to end a war."

"So, MacArthur was tolerated despite questionable military decisions? But why would he expose American armaments to invasion?"

"MacArthur had cozied up to President Quezon; he had cut a deal. By the 1940s, the Philippines wanted independence from the U.S. They wanted neutrality; they wanted to get out from between Japan and the U.S. Douglas MacArthur made it happen."

"You mean… what? MacArthur never got the planes off the ground? You mean he allowed the Japanese to invade?"

"Exactly, to honor a deal with Quezon. Quezon wanted to end American military presence in the Philippines; he wanted to work toward neutrality. What better way than to cripple American defenses, to destroy American power in Southeast Asia?"

"But what a cost! Why would MacArthur go along with it?"

"For the same reason people always become corrupt."

Puzzled, Christelle gazed at him.

"How much do you think half a million in 1942 would be in today's dollars?"

"My God!" Christelle stared at him. "Twenty times that much. Maybe ten million."

"Would that be enough?"

"Broc, you don't mean MacArthur was paid?"

"It's all on record. Three weeks after the disaster at Clark Field, President Quezon issued a secret executive order that paid $640,000 in U.S. dollars to General Douglas MacArthur and his staff, $500,000 of which went to MacArthur himself for exemplary service in the Philippines. The bank records have been found."

Christelle recognized the travesty. "And so, hundreds, maybe thousands of Americans died who did not need to die."

"We'll never know how many died from this atrocity. But it's a reminder. There are dangers from outside and dangers from within." He stood at the window, his face splashed with the fiery red of the lowering sun. "People die, ordinary people, like these poor Filipinos, like our soldiers, like you and me, while some in high places earn fame. Their names go down in history, and sometimes they become very rich; yet the shiny surface of things hides a hellish darkness."

There are dangers from within — a terrible realization. There were dangers from within their own government today, and decades ago. Greed and corruption were always there, the subterranean evil of history.

Broc turned; he wandered back to a couch and sat down, his whole body wracked in agony. She saw the pain rising up again, enclosing him, walling him into a prison of grief — pain and grief mixed with anger and fury.

She tried to imagine the terrible shock of that moment when his whole life was blown apart. She sat by his side and touched his hand. "It's Darcy, isn't it?"

Broc raised his head; she saw the pain in his eyes. She wondered whether he could ever get past the shock and pain of that terrible moment.

"Darcy was one of those people," she said, "one of us. And she's gone, and somehow there are people out there who have gained something — power, position, wealth — something we don't understand, and we have to go on and stop this from happening again."

There were no more words for him to say, but she knew he was glad she was there.

A short taxi ride had taken them across town to another five-star hotel. Broc and Christelle gazed at the photographs: huge black-and-white enlargements of scenes from Asian history with a focus on the Philippines. The exhibition included mounted pictures, artifacts on loan from various Pacific Rim museums. Capsule accounts of major WW II campaigns filled the foyer of the Shangri La Hotel. Advertisements for the exhibit, "The Heritage of the Philippines," were posted all over Manila.

They had been wending their way through the maze of mounted enlargements for several minutes when Christelle pointed toward the nearest of the indoor shops. "They have those pretty Filipino dresses we saw. Do you mind?" She glanced at her watch. "They're open for only another hour."

It was the first time Broc had focused on her since they had arrived at the exhibit.

"It's okay. You stay. I know this war stuff is interesting, but it's just so depressing."

O'Neill watched her crossing the carpet. She looked so innocent, so pristine and wholesome, too young to be burdened with the tragic history of corruption and wars before she was born. He turned back to the exhibition. It was unique: it included photos and artifacts that might never be seen beyond the Philippines. For a historian, seeing all this was the opportunity of a lifetime.

I SHALL RETURN

Below the words was a cluster of photos of General Douglas MacArthur taken early in 1942 during the final days of the American defense of the Philippines. O'Neill gazed at the man, the Pacific general whose career had soared through World War II and the occupation of Japan. Forced out of the Philippines under the relentless attack of the Japanese, he had promised to return. The display suggested that MacArthur had shouted the words to thousands of cheering Filipinos, or perhaps flung them in the faces of invading Japanese. In reality, he had escaped to Australia when he said, "I came through and I shall return." It was one of the most pompous sentences ever uttered, and soldiers who stayed behind in the trenches knew it.

I am going to have a shit, a soldier said. *I shall return—*

I HAVE RETURNED.

The 1944 photo showed MacArthur wading ashore on a beach, eyes hidden under dark glasses. Everything was there: the imperious overblown ego, the dauntless military bearing, the heroic bravado that had found its way to the front pages of a thousand newspapers around the world. But MacArthur had waded ashore five times; his "return" was photographed five times; and the picture copied worldwide was MacArthur's choice of the image that best showed off his narcissistic view of himself.

What a great shit that was, the soldier said. *I have returned—*

Eventually, the great man had fallen. His self-serving rhetoric had overshot his pay grade and enraged President Truman. He had been recalled, fired, and driven into the oblivion he deserved.

O'Neill stood before the photographs, subdued by the descriptions of Japanese atrocities, not only here but across the Pacific. Pictures of dead soldiers in New Guinea half buried in sand as waves washed over their bodies, the sword of a Japanese executioner about to decapitate a blindfolded prisoner, trenches on Okinawa filled with bodies of the dead and the terrified eyes of those still alive who had to fight on. The flag being raised on Iwo Jima and the huge mushroom of destruction over Hiroshima.

The final section of pictures was captioned 'Manila and Manila Bay'. The ruin was staggering. Mile upon mile of city covered with smoke, buildings burning, battle-torn streets, people weeping over the dead, children wandering alone, ragged, crying.

Across the foyer O'Neill saw Christelle waving for him to come.

"What do you think?" she asked, holding out her arms. The dress was black at the back to the waist; the front was embroidered in a pattern of linked triangles of blue and green. The skirt was decorated with the same linked pattern of slightly larger triangles. She spun around as he watched; he caught a flash of her legs as the skirt flared.

"And look at these earrings!" She walked up to him and stood a foot away, her eyes glittering. The earrings were cloisonné, a pattern of green and blue against gold that brought out the lights in her eyes.

"There's no doubt about it, Christelle; it's just right for you." He pulled out his wallet.

"Hey! This is my gift to me," she objected, backing away.

"It *was* your gift to you, but I remember from last year: your birthday is coming up in about a week. So, the whole outfit, including a purse and shoes to match, is on me."

Christelle looked at him, then at the pretty Filipina saleswoman, who lifted her shoulders and smiled at him. "He's a very nice man."

Christelle kissed him on the cheek. "You're a very nice man, but now it'll take at least another half hour to pick out the purse and shoes. You better go back to your pictures."

O'Neill walked slowly back across the foyer. Dresses. They always say look at the dress, and then they spin around and you can't help seeing their legs, and women's legs look better that way than any other. It really isn't the dress you're noticing. He remembered Darcy had once said that to him when she showed off her latest outfit.

It's not about dresses at all, Professor; it's about the goodies inside— she explained. *But we're married—* he had said. *The disposition of the goodies has already been decided. From now on they're free. Why do we have to keep spending money on dresses Because men are so stupid—* she said. *They're easily distracted, their attention wanders. So, wives have to keep wrapping the goodies in new dresses—*

Darcy. He felt the sudden pain of remembering.

O'Neill turned back to the photos, pictures of the destruction across Manila Bay. The harbor was dark with smoke. In the gray sky, Japanese planes were flying low over the ships, dropping bombs. O'Neill felt the weight of the past, the wanton destruction, the senseless losses that sent the best men of a whole generation down to the garbage dump of history.

He saw her walking across the pavement. A blinding white flash, and everything he had ever loved and lived for was suddenly gone—

O'Neill struggled against the pain, feeling as though he would fall. He stood, feet planted on the floor, struggling to get beyond the pain, willing himself beyond the past. He moved on, focusing again on a new display of photographs. More enlargements of planes bombing ships. Across Manila Bay the hulks were burning, hundreds upon hundreds of watercraft of every size. Exploding, burning, sinking.

He gazed for several minutes, trying to fathom the sea littered with so many burning ships. Then, as he stared at the huge photos of the destruction, he saw something. A strange feeling swept through his body as he struggled to comprehend.

"Broc! Broc! What's the matter?" Christelle was standing by his side. She was back in her white cotton blouse and denims with a big shopping bag. "Are you okay?"

O'Neill squeezed the bridge of his nose. "Christelle. What do you see?"

"Ships, burning. Lots of them. Lots of ships burning. Why?"

He pointed at one. "There, the flag, look at the flag."

"It's an American flag. Why?"

"Look at the words, the words on the ship."

She stepped closer to the picture.

"The letters are very small. I think it says *Die Macht Amerika*. That's strange, a German name on an American ship."

"Below the name; look below the name."

Christelle leaned closer. She stared at the words, which were smaller, hardly visible: *Kaiser Shipping*.

Chapter Twenty-six

They sat at the table in the Manila corporate registry office. Christelle thumbed through a fat record book. O'Neill ran his finger down the numerous columns of the register.

"How many so far?"

"I'm up to seven."

Seven freighters destroyed in and around the Philippines, seven freighters owned by Kaiser Shipping, all caught in the bombing raids by American planes during World War II.

Kaiser Shipping was bought by my grandfather in 1928. My father saw opportunities during the war—

"Eight," Christelle added, jotting the name of the ship on her list.

When did the company get into international shipping—?

He remembered the evasion, the way Kaiser had reached for an ashtray and lit a cigarette. He hadn't wanted to say when Kaiser was established in the Pacific.

I think the international division is the least interesting aspect of Kaiser Shipping— But O'Neill had learned a little: Kaiser had a base for its ships in the Philippines.

O'Neill straightened up and spoke as Christelle continued scanning the record book. "It doesn't make sense. William Kaiser led me to believe the company got into shipping in the Pacific after the war. But it's clear that Kaiser Shipping was already solidly engaged in this region during the war. How many bombed Kaiser ships have you found?"

"Three more, that makes eleven." Christelle looked up and stretched her arms. "I had no idea. This book is a sort of national inventory of Filipino losses during the war. It's got sections on the harbors, railroads, factories, bridges. The devastation is incredible." She turned a page and glanced casually at it while Broc sat up and rotated his shoulders.

"It's very strange," he mused. "Eleven freighters destroyed in 1942. Why was Kaiser so evasive about the company's contribution to the war?

He's so damnably patriotic. You'd expect him to tout the heroic sacrifices the company made during the Japanese invasion of Manila."

"Two things, Broc." Christelle had her finger on the page. "First thing, here's a block of... let's see, two, four, six, eight, ten. Oh, my golly! Thirteen more Kaiser ships destroyed. That makes twenty-four. It's a miracle the company even survived! Second thing, we're not talking about 1942 and we're not talking about the Japanese invasion of Manila. These records cover losses in 1944."

O'Neill straightened up, following her finger to the handwritten date at the top of the page.

"Not one Kaiser ship was lost in 1942. These are 1944 shipping losses."

O'Neill ran his fingers through his hair. "American ships bombed in 1942 would have been destroyed by Japanese planes from Formosa. But ships lost in 1944 must have been destroyed during the American return to the Philippines. It doesn't make sense."

"What doesn't make sense?" Christelle queried.

He flipped over another page in the big record book. "Those Kaiser ships in the photograph had clear American markings. It's an American company. They were flying American flags. But they were bombed by American planes. They must have been deliberately targeted."

He ran his finger down the page. Endless columns of corporations, every company formed in the Philippines, every branch office established on Philippine soil.

There it was. "Got it! 'Kaiser Shipping, branch office, established in 1934. That's way before the war began. Initial funding, twenty million dollars.' My God, that's a fortune! Ships listed under initial registering: thirty-eight!"

"And here's another block of nine sunk in 1944," Christelle said. "That adds up to thirty-three. You know, it looks like nearly the whole Kaiser Shipping fleet went down."

"Talk about friendly fire! That's one hell of a lot of American freighters to get caught and destroyed accidentally by American bombs."

"Maybe it wasn't accidental."

Maybe it wasn't accidental—

"Well," Christelle went on, "what if they were carrying freight the Americans wanted to destroy?"

O'Neill had a sudden knot in his stomach, a strange realization that was still too deep for words. Kaiser. The ancient roots of the family were in Germany. The memory of William Kaiser in his private arsenal loomed up. *There are several Lugers. This is one of the finest semi-automatics ever made—* German weapons. A whole room, a home museum of weapons, cabinets of weapons. Machine guns on wheels. *That one is a Walther P 38, the principal German side arm used in World War II. That one is the PAK36, an anti-tank gun that shoots a 37 mm shell at a velocity of 2500 feet per second. Probably the most complete collection of weaponry outside the war museums—* German weapons.

But there were also Japanese weapons! *The Arisaka Type 38 rifle. The Type 32 machine gun, which the Americans had to face on Iwo Jima and Okinawa—* William Kaiser had an unusual interest in Japanese weaponry.

"Christelle, it's weapons! These Kaiser freighters were carrying weapons, guns, ammunition."

"But why would we blow them up?"

"They were American ships. Suppose they were carrying weapons to the Japanese! Weapons or technology sold to an enemy. Greed overriding patriotism. It's happened before. But even if the weapons were Italian or French or Turkish or whatever, American freighters were assisting the Japanese."

"Shipping weapons for the enemy! Oh, my God! That's treason!"

"That's a nice legal word, but there really isn't any way of describing anything so despicable. And somehow, the American military must have discovered it. That's why Kaiser's freighters were bombed."

Christelle gathered her hair and flipped it back over her shoulders. "Of course," she continued, "bugging Kaiser's telephone would hardly be necessary. If anyone today ever found out about this — that Kaiser transported material for the Japanese during the war — they would have a nifty piece of treason to work with. Extortion would be a snap."

Damn! "That's it! Christelle, I think you've hit it! It all finally makes sense! Worldwide Communications gets a rigged telephone into anybody's hands they can manage. Then they just listen and wait.

Mostly, they just uncover dirty little secrets like John Randolph's sexy blonde mistress. That's useful information for extortion. But with Kaiser, they struck it rich. Can you imagine if weapons transported for the Japanese ever made the papers! A company, worth billions would be dead in the water. The company is a model for extortion."

Christelle wrinkled her nose and made a face. "It's such a nasty way to get money. If it were me, I would take a kinder approach. I would give out favors."

"That's because you're a woman. Women have always been good at getting things that way."

She gave him a dirty look.

"Well, I don't mean it in any nasty sense. It's just that, hell, I think you've hit it again! Favors!" He went on excitedly. "Whoever is running this is very well placed. CIA, NSA. Dillon Shaver was questioned by the FBI. These are high-level mavericks, the kind who control vast resources, entire agencies. Well-placed government people. What kind of favors could people like that offer?"

"I don't know, Broc. I guess anything that would benefit the company. Chocolates wouldn't quite do it. Big bribes might."

"What about government contracts?"

"Well, some of those guys you went to see were tied into government contracts."

"In spades! Kaiser Shipping transports government goods and moves government offices. Brandeis Electronics makes missile guidance systems. GEO makes every tank tread and landing gear used by the U.S. military."

"So, if these guys are getting favors in the form of government contracts, why the harassment? Why would the IRS audit Randolph?"

O'Neill thought for a minute. "People are very different. Some guys would see the benefit of a big contract and play the game, figuring a donation of a few hundred thousand, or even a few million, was worth it. But Randolph was putting up a lot of resistance. So, somebody arranged for IRS audits."

"Everybody is afraid of the IRS. That would soften any of these guys who were cheating on their taxes. You know, claiming losses or padding deductions."

"That was Randolph. He had to write out big settlement checks to the IRS. But the more we talk, the more I'm convinced the phones are peripheral."

"You mean these phones have kept us chasing shadows for a month?"

"Maybe. Bugged phones provide extortion talking points. But that won't always work. Monahan never carried his phone; he left it at his vacation cottage. He was absolutely clean. No secrets to hide. No leverage for blackmail. But Pennsylvania Produce was enormously wealthy with money to spare. Whoever is behind this needed another way to get him to cooperate. That Penn Produce warehouse fire in Atlanta might be it. They declared it wasn't arson, but I have my doubts. A six-million-dollar fire would be a pretty good persuader.

"Whoever is behind this is smart. Nobody found out about Kaiser carrying weaponry to the Japanese in 1944 by listening to telephone conversations fifty years later. That required some pretty astute digging. The real point is extortion, and the phones are just one way to discover the pressure point for extortion. The real issue is the money, the money trail."

"Darn! So the telephones aren't the center of things. That means we don't need to go to Penang. I was really looking forward to that."

"Well, in my opinion, we should still go to Penang. We've found out an owner for Teleconic Manufacturing. That's a lead we need to pursue. We'll find out more in Penang from seeing Hai Phong Electronics. There aren't many obvious points of attack. These companies are definitely weak spots."

Christelle stood up and closed the registry book. "We've discovered some other things, too. We've got the names of people in their ranks. Colonel Spiker. We can explore him, and Joe Terrence, and Lignum Operations. We've got lots to do."

"What do you think? Tomorrow?" Broc was downing the last mouthful of a rum and Coke Christelle had mixed as soon as they got to their suite. "I guess we need to fly back to Singapore, see what else we can dig out of the computers, and get on to Penang."

"I guess," she conceded, a little sadly. She walked to the window, pulled back the curtains, and gazed out at Manila Bay, dotted with ships. "Five days here. It's not quite long enough. I'd really like to see those amazing terraced mountains up in the north, in Luzon. But we don't have time; we'll just have to see them another time."

"Okay, that's a good plan." He set the glass on the bar and headed for the door. "I'll arrange a flight back to Singapore with that travel agent by the front desk."

Christelle walked slowly into her bedroom. She felt hot and sticky; it was time for a shower. She sat on the edge of the bed and pulled off her denims.

We don't have time; we'll just have to see them another time— Then she realized what she had said. And what he had said.

Okay, that's a good plan—

Chapter Twenty-seven

Singapore
Friday, August 9

Christelle set the book down: a collection of stories called *The Shadow of a Shadow of a Dream, Love Stories of Singapore*, by Catherine Lim, a lively lady who seemed to be Singapore's celebrity writer. She had read several of the stories on the flight back from Manila; they were a nice relief from the glitzy novels by Danielle Steel in all the airports. She picked up the other paperbacks. *O Singapore! Stories in Celebration* could wait; she'd take that one back to the States to read later. The other one, *They Do Return*, was a collection of ghost stories. That would be fun to read in bed tonight.

It was 6 p.m. Christelle flipped on the TV International news with the volume low: Broc was working in his bedroom on his laptop. It was a slow day in the States. The first segment was on the latest blockbuster movie, which had been on the market for little more than a month. *Independence Day* had already grossed over $300 million. Trailers showed a lot of mayhem and over-the-top patriotic hype. Not her idea of entertainment.

Sports were next. The Summer Olympics had been running while she and Broc were in the Philippines. The American women's gymnastics team — now the "Magnificent Seven" — had won gold for the first time. The heroine was Kerri Strug, whose astonishing second vault after injuring her foot on the first, won the victory for the U.S. team. The video of Kerri being carried to the bench by her coach had catapulted her to fame: America's latest sweetheart.

Christelle was about to turn off the TV at six thirty when a political analysis began. Senator Richard Robbins, a Republican from somewhere in the Southern states, was sounding off during an interview.

Senator Robbins: "The fact is that Democrats repeatedly set up straw men at the expense of the Republican Party. But all the alarmist talk we've been hearing about continuing cuts in the budget and economy by Republicans is just so much political hay. Our President is a Democrat" —

Broc walked into the room with today's *International Herald Tribune* in his hand. "Look at this guy, Senator Robbins," Christelle motioned, pointing at the TV. "He's the one making political hay!" Broc sat down at the end of the couch.

Senator Robbins: "The fact is that social programs have not been ruthlessly slashed as Democrats in Congress have been worrying about for more than a decade. With few exceptions, programs put in place during the half-century of Democratic control have been honored. Who would want to mess with Social Security? We've cut out some fat and trimmed where trimming was needed, but sectors of American society in need are being served as well under a Republican Congress as they were under the Democrats. In fact, it's arguable that the underclass is being helped today better than it ever was under Democrats like FDR, Kennedy, or Johnson — certainly better than under Carter when interest rates went through the roof. And the general population, the working people, have more opportunities now while Republicans control Congress."

"Those darn Republicans are really good at spin," Christelle said. "They point to increased dollars spent in all the social programs, but they don't mention the increased number of people below the poverty line who need the dollars. Or, darn it, the declining value of the dollars!"

Jim Braxton: "Thank you, Mr. Senator. Let us turn now to economic analyst Dr. Jonas Reynolds, Chair of the Economics Forecasting Symposium in San Jose, California. Dr. Reynolds, you heard what Senator Robbins just said. Do you have any comments?"

"This will be good," Christelle said. "I've followed this guy since I was an undergraduate. I heard him speak. He visited our campus once. His analyses are always right on the money!"

Dr. Reynolds: "Here at EFS we've been looking for several weeks at allocations in sectors of society usually deemed as problem areas. We've been much encouraged by the state of the economy. Our figures appear to verify what Senator Robbins is saying."

"What on Earth!" Christelle turned to O'Neill, her eyes round with disbelief. "How can he say that?" Broc sat forward on the edge of the couch.

Jim Braxton: "Dr. Reynolds, a Democratic Senator has charged that the decline in the rate of increase of tax dollars spent for social programs means funding is not keeping up with inflation, which amounts to a decline of benefits."

Dr. Reynolds: "That's been the persistent Democratic claim. But our analyses indicate that this is somewhat exaggerated. Let me give you a few examples because the American public has been misled by uninformed rhetoric, and the taxpayers really need to know the facts. Late last month — TVI, in fact, reported this — a massive expansion of low-income housing loans was approved, funds that will directly affect the well-being of approximately four hundred sixty-five thousand below-poverty-line families in thirty different cities. It's worth doing the math on that; close to two million low-income Americans will be affected. Or, to cite another important case — you can read it in last Sunday's *Post* — single mothers are benefiting from new funding at far higher levels than they ever were under the Democrats."

Jim Braxton: "Dr. Reynolds, what is the political affiliation of the Economics Forecasting Symposium?"

Dr. Reynolds: "The EFS is entirely non-partisan. It was set up by the economics departments of twelve cooperating universities. In fact, I am not a registered member of either political party, and I do not know the political preferences of any members, many of whom I've been working with for a dozen years. But I must go on to say, the figures we're seeing are rather surprising. Given the historic position of the Republican Party, almost always in the direction of trimming social programs, these huge increases are indeed against what any of us would expect."

"What do you think, Broc? Is this guy for real?"
"It's surprising, but I've read the reports of EFS for several years. Their research is always impeccable." Broc pointed to the *International Herald Tribune*. "I was going to mention it earlier. There was an article this morning on what they're saying."

Jim Braxton: "Let me turn now to Dr. Allison Cooper, who chairs the Charity Services Coalition based in Baltimore. Dr. Cooper, as I understand, your organization, CSC, funnels charity money, which is usually backed by matching federal dollars to needy organizations."

Dr. Cooper: "That is correct, Sir."

Jim Braxton: "There's been a lot of talk lately of the role played by the rich. As we all know, the highest income Americans give a lot of money away. There's been some speculation that a lot of that money is finding its way to the kinds of needy sectors Dr. Reynolds mentioned."

Dr. Cooper: "It's an interesting speculation, but I would have to say it's just not realistic. It's true, the very wealthy in this country, people who show up for instance in the Forbes 400, do support charitable causes, often with amounts in the tens of millions. But there are two observations worth making. One is that the super-wealthy are rarely sympathetic with low-income housing projects or assistance to single mothers, programs like that. Typically, they regard those kinds of programs as a drain on the government we would be better off without. Their money usually goes to support high-tech medical research, or museum expansion. The arts, culture, TV documentaries. They also like high visibility. Housing developments don't provide the publicity they want.

The second thing is that all the donations of the wealthy in this nation would have little impact on the huge social ills that have been developing for the past two or three decades. You might as well try to move the sand on Fire Island beaches with a child's plastic pail and shovel."

Jim Braxton: "Then, Dr. Cooper, what do you think is happening?"

Dr. Cooper: "I'd have to agree with both Senator Robbins and Dr. Reynolds. We are seeing some surprising expansions in the social welfare sector. They are surprising because they do not match the political ideology of the Republican Party. Moreover, the trend began when the Republicans started to make gains in Congress in the election of 1990. These extensions of social funding mean, I think, that the alarmist rhetoric of the Democrats is largely unjustified."

Broc stood up. "I hate to interrupt this wonderful program, Christelle. I know looking out for the poor is your thing. And I wish I knew more about economics so I could know what to think. But" — he looked at his watch — "it's nearly seven and we haven't eaten."

Christelle turned off the TV and walked over to their tenth-floor window. "See down there." Broc looked at the street. "I read about it in the lobby. It's the 'Rasa Singapura Food Center'. It's spilling right out onto the sidewalk, with hawker stalls of Chinese food, Malay food, and stuff from all over: Thailand, Indonesia. I'd like to eat some local food instead of the stuff they serve in these fancy hotel restaurants."

Sitting across the little table, O'Neill watched Christelle, whose eyes were darting everywhere, taking in the rows of lamp-lit hawker stalls and candlelit tables. The night air was a perfect temperature. "What's your fancy tonight?"

"I'm going to try some Indian food, but I can't resist that *satay*. I think I'm going to have two sticks: chicken and peanut sauce. Just smell it! What about you?"

"You go, Christelle. I haven't decided what I want. I'll hold our table. And when that hawker comes around, do you want beer?"

"Sure do. I'd like a bottle of that local brew, Anchor beer." She smiled and headed off toward the Indian food stall.

O'Neill looked around at the tables and hawker stalls that locals set up every evening at dusk. The Rasa Singapura Food Center spread over half an acre of sidewalk where Tanglin Road met Napier and Grange. The towering bulk of their hotel, the Marco Polo, stood across Grange; the British High Commission and the Burmese Embassy stood on facing corners. The British influence was evident: 'Burma,' the British colonial name, had not yet been replaced by the new yet more historic name, 'Myanmar,' authorized by the revolutionary leaders. Food smells were a medley of ethnic variety. The place seemed an intersection of Asian nations with the Singapore Handicraft Center and Cultural Theater only a few yards away.

O'Neill ordered two bottles of Anchor beer, then poured half of his into the glass. He watched Christelle, who was moving among the Malay hawker stalls. Flames darted up into the darkness from the braziers. The place was getting crowded; nearly every table was taken. Three quarters of the diners were Chinese; the rest were a mixture of Malays, Indians, Australians, Brits, Japanese, and a smattering of others whose origins O'Neill could only guess.

Christelle was back, her eyes glittering in the candlelight. He recognized most of what she had from their evening wandering in Little India: *dal*, a kind of porridge made with lentils; *masala dosai*, curried vegetables; and bean-flour *papads* with chutney sauce, all of it spread on a huge banana leaf she had balanced on her palms. On top of it all, lay two sticks of Malay *satay*. She sat down as she set her banana leaf on the table, glancing from one delicacy to another, then up at a crowd of noisy

Chinese passing their table, then at Broc. "Aren't you going to get anything? The *satay* is wonderful."

Broc twisted the top off her Anchor beer and slowly poured her glass half full. Peering at him over the edge of the glass, she drank, puffing her cheeks in satisfaction as she set the glass on the table.

"Last night, I had Malay food; tonight, I'm going to have Chinese, pure Chinese. I'm not going to confuse my taste buds by mixing in *satay*."

Christelle wrinkled her nose at him as he got up and headed for a Cantonese food stall.

"I had no idea," Christelle said as Broc sat down, "that people over here would even care about news from the U.S. But they get CNN news everywhere, and *Time* magazine and *Newsweek* and yesterday's sports scores. How do they get anyone to watch?"

"Hollywood, Fifth Avenue, Disney World, the Hamptons, American movies. The U.S. is everybody's fantasy land."

Christelle pushed her chicken off the stick onto her leaf, then dipped one into the peanut sauce. "If you ask me, this is fantasy land!" She glanced at him as she popped the sauce-covered meat into her mouth. "Why is American cooking so dull?"

"At the risk of sounding patronizing," O'Neill remarked, digging into a pile of strange-looking vegetables, "I did not find your cooking dull."

"You just wait! First thing when I get back, I'm going to get a big spice rack and load it up with all this stuff they put on their food here. And tomorrow I'm going to buy an Asian cookbook. You won't believe the storm I'll cook up."

"While you're writing your dissertation?"

Christelle wrinkled her nose at him again. "Just in case my dissertation is a flop, I'll need some other skill to bribe my advisors."

They ate in silence for a few minutes, listening to the sounds of Chinese and Malay as people ordered and chatted. O'Neill guessed there were eighty tables and thirty different hawker stalls.

237

"What did that article say? The one in the *International Herald Tribune?*"

"It was talking about the confusion among Washington Republicans. Same as what we saw on TV, a big surge in social spending. The Republicans are saying it's because of an entrenched Democratic bureaucracy that has more control than Congress over the budget. There's some truth to that. Government bureaucrats are career people. They serve through one administration after another. They develop their own culture. They tend to do things the way they have always done things. It's why presidents get so frustrated. Tradition holds back reform. Since the Republican sweep in 1994, there's been agitation for tough program-slashing bills to get it all under control, like Newt Gingrich's 'Contract with America'."

"That's all we need! Don't they care about the poor?"

"It doesn't matter whether they do or don't. We've got a Democratic president. Clinton won't sign any program-slashing bills. But I don't think it will come to that."

"Well, it's a pretty ambitious bunch of Republicans in office now."

"True, but they're divided. There's this other faction. Every time the Democrats complain, young Republicans in the House sound off. They use the sudden surge of program expansion to prove that they are not the bad guys Democrats think. They want to take credit even though it's against their ideology. It's predictable behavior. It's ludicrous, a division within the party over why the charity sector is flush."

"Well, one way or another," Christelle said, gazing at the lights, "it suits me that the country may not be going down the tubes."

"It was supposed to. Everybody expected a crisis with Republicans controlling both House and Senate. It hasn't happened, but it may. The party that should be in control is in disarray. The national debt accumulated by years of Democratic programs is still soaring while Republicans, bicker. It's politics subverting governance."

"I may be a political science major "but 'politics' is a different animal. It's not 'science', so there's a lot I don't understand. You've been looking at all these big companies. All this money disappearing and funny stuff going on in spending, all kinds of improvements. Republicans don't know whether to stomp it or cheer."

Broc sat back in his chair, motionless. He watched Christelle scooping vegetables on her fork. Their understanding of economics was superficial, but one didn't have to read *Economics for Dummies* to see that something strange was going on.

"You look crazy; what's the matter?" Christelle fixed her eyes on him.

"You know, something has just dawned on me. Walter Monahan spent most of our interview complaining about New Deal agricultural subsidies. He was a Republican spouting pure Republican economics. His family despised farm subsidies. They were so much against Democratic redistribution of wealth that they moved Pennsylvania Produce almost entirely out of productive agriculture."

"I don't see the point."

"Then there's Jamiessen and Brandeis Electronics. There are all kinds of photos of him at Republican campaign rallies. And Randolph. I got a look at GEO. There was a picture of Tom Ridge. He was the governor of Pennsylvania, a Republican."

"And they always have a picture of the president in those places, don't they? Just like in the post office."

"They had one, yes, but not Bill Clinton. It was Ronald Reagan. It's like a nationwide club all sporting the same symbols. Thousands of high-powered executives making regular donations to mysterious companies like Lignum Operations. And every damn one of them is a Republican!"

Christelle took a slow drink of her beer. "Every one of them except you."

"Yes, and I'm unhappy with both the company and the consequences."

Chapter Twenty-eight

The whole intersection was filling up, swollen with Singaporeans out enjoying the town on a Friday night. There were conversations in half a dozen languages; nearly every table in the Rasa Singapura Food Center was taken. Three Chinese youths with guitars were singing American folk songs to the customers. Taxis were stopping at the curb to let people out and take others away. The air was filled with the mingled smells of spiced meat and curry.

O'Neill finished eating. He watched Christelle finish her spiced vegetables and dip her last piece of chicken in the sauce. Her eyes darted here and there as the sounds of conversation and music swelled.

Broc leaned forward, elbows on the table. "Christelle." She looked up, startled. His eyes locked onto hers. "I'm going to find us some dessert. While I'm wandering would be a safe time to look around. But don't let on you know we're being watched."

"Watched?"

"Watched and followed," he affirmed. She kept her eyes on his, unmoving. "I had this funny feeling in the airport yesterday. Then last night down on Orchard Street I saw two guys across the street when we came out of the restaurant. One of them was in the lobby this morning when I bought the *Tribune*."

Christelle stared at him, her eyes wide open, her lips parted as though she wanted to say something, but she was speechless.

"Right now, there's a guy, he's Chinese, standing in the doorway of our hotel. There are two guys, probably American, at a table about thirty feet to your right. And there's another Chinese guy across the street. I wouldn't trust my life with any of them."

"Oh boy!" She leaned forward on her elbows. "This is scary. What are we going to do?"

He wanted to reach out and put his hand over hers to reassure her, but he resisted. The time wasn't right; they needed clear heads. There was barely room on the tiny table for their empty glasses and elbows; Christelle's face was about a foot away, her big eyes looking into his, waiting for instructions. They must look like newlyweds.

"I think we should go ahead with our plans, maybe with a few changes, and not make it easy for these guys to figure out what's going on."

"So, Penang?"

O'Neill nodded. "I called this afternoon. It turns out we can do those certification dives from a SCUBA shop at Penang the day after tomorrow."

"But, didn't you book our hotel here for several more days?"

"Three more days, until Monday, and you can bet these guys watching us know it. But suppose we catch a flight out of here early, say tomorrow afternoon?"

"Won't they just follow us?"

"Yes, and that gives us the advantage. If you don't know you're being followed, then you're followed. Once you know, you can evade. Suppose we get up very early and send our luggage to the airport on the hotel van. We can catch up with our stuff later on. Then we can lead these guys on a boring traipse around town."

"That sounds really nice. I'd like another day of shopping."

"Then that's what you can do. Shop." O'Neill chuckled. "If there's anything that will drive a spy, nuts, it's following a woman while she shops. We'll go our separate ways. I'll tour some really dull places. After three or four hours of parading around in crowds, these guys will be fed up and off guard. It won't be hard for us to find the right moment and get rid of them. Separate taxis to the airport. We'll meet in the airport bar around four. Flight to Kuala Lumpur at five, stay overnight there, catch a flight Sunday to Penang. My guess is these guys will still be watching the elevators here until Monday while we're SCUBA diving in the Strait of Malacca."

"What about Hai Phong Electronics?"

"We need at least one day without these guys on our tail. Suppose we book into a Penang hotel Sunday, say for three nights, Sunday, Monday, Tuesday on my credit card, and go on our dives Sunday afternoon. When we get back on shore, we'll take a taxi to a different hotel. If anyone has tracked us to Penang, they will be watching the wrong hotel. We'll have a day to see what we want, including HPE, without anybody watching."

Christelle sat back. "This is going to be fun."

By ten thirty Saturday morning, Christelle had ambled from the Marco Polo Hotel to Scott Street, with meandering expeditions through the Tanglin Shopping Center and Orchard Towers. Broc was right: the same two Chinese men were following. She was annoyed but decided to make it easy for them to follow until she was ready to disappear.

She spent a quarter hour moving slowly through the expensive racks of clothing at the Shaw Center, then ambled leisurely across to the Dynasty Hotel, where she sat for another twenty minutes enjoying a morning coffee and reading the *Singapore Straits Times*. It was difficult to dwell on the past in these surroundings; the deadly dangers back in the States seemed unreal. Her trailing Chinese, who were now lurking by the tobacco store, resembled amusing cutouts from a cartoon.

The hotel architecture was spectacular and so was the city, a kind of Paris of the East. The excitement of their planned escape had caught her imagination. That seemed to be the way with Broc, too. She could still see him sitting across from her, his deep brown eyes holding hers, planning their getaway. He was focused now. It was days since she had seen that strange emptiness in his eyes, the grieving loneliness of learning to live without Darcy. It had passed after he raged up and down a penthouse suite in the Manila Hotel. Somehow, he had fitted the grief and pain and Darcy's death into the larger tragedy of war, where thousands die for no good cause, where history litters the Earth with graveyards of people who have died so that others can somehow go on living. His whole attention was now focused to a fine point. He saw a way, a road to follow that would transcend his personal loss. She knew that he was mending, that the running was nearly over. Broc O'Neill was ready to turn and fight and lash out like a vicious jungle beast.

Christelle felt a sudden rush, as though someone had shot her full of adrenaline. She knew where it came from, remembering the beautiful exhilaration when she aimed that big Colt 45 in front of Pennsylvania

Produce and fired away, not content until every shell in the clip had been blasted at the enemy. It was good the guns were locked up in Washington; otherwise, she would be tempted to blast these stupid little Chinese spies into oblivion. She felt a little guilty for such thoughts until she remembered that somebody who had hired them had almost killed her and Broc.

She knew what it was: the danger of the chase, planning the getaway, the excitement of being with Broc while they figured things out. They were getting closer now. Once they investigated Hai Phong Electronics, she knew Broc would figure out what to do next. That was what she liked about him. He had thoughts and plans and goals, and always a way to get things done. And once he decided to get something done, it would be done in a flash.

Christelle glanced at her watch as she stood up: 11:15 a.m. Lucky Plaza was next door. She did a circuit of the ground floor, making sure her trackers were with her, then caught the elevator to Venus Queen Ladies' Wear. She hadn't bought a swimsuit; she hadn't even put one on — for three summers. Vermont water was too cold even in August for a Southern California girl. But here all the hotels had lovely swimming pools, and they might be here for a while.

Inside the store, she found an issue of *Asia Swim*. It was like *American Swimwear*, except the Asian models had beautiful coppery skin and long black hair.

"You need American swimsuit, Miss," the salesgirl stated. "Big girl, too big to fit Asia swimsuit."

Christelle hadn't thought of herself as "big"; all the health charts said her one hundred twenty-four pounds was pretty good for a height of five seven. But she guessed that was not what the salesgirl meant, for she towered over the petite Chinese beauty by a good six inches. Her brain clicked: ninety-eight pounds.

"It's okay," the girl added — her name plate said Susie Ling — reaching under the counter and pulling out the latest issue of *Swimwear USA*. "This is what you need. I'm sure there will be something you like."

Christelle flipped through the pages of eye-popping American beauties. "These are all made by Venus Swimwear. That's an American company; it says it's in Florida."

"That's right, Miss; we carry every kind of Venus Swimwear. You pick out what you like. The change room is behind the palm tree."

Christelle went through the samples, amazed at the colors and the overwhelming number of styles. She spent a good fifteen minutes picking out a dozen suits.

It didn't take long to reject three of the suits, just by trying on the tops. The "Jasmine Vine" and "Lite Bright" patterns were too busy. The "Pink Floral" had a nice sedate look about it and even gave her breasts a little bit of a rounded sexy shape. But when she spread the bottoms, she realized most of the bottom was missing. The thong would leave her whole behind right out in plain view. Shoving the "Pink Floral" suit back in the bag, Christelle wondered what girl would have the nerve to wear that! Maybe Madonna.

She paused for a minute with the "Jungle Fever," a spotted leopard pattern. She checked the bottom; yes, there was a back end, a big triangle of nice shiny material covered with leopard spots. She giggled to herself; the only thing missing was a tail. It was a pretty sexy suit. She might come back to it.

When she put on the "Green Bamboo," she knew this was it. She should have known from the start; green always worked for her. This one, a bikini model with shoulder straps, was green and yellow like bamboo leaves, with fine lines of black, all in material with a sheen like the jungle leaves in the hotel lobby. Hurriedly, she slipped off her denims and tried on the bottom. The bows at the sides matched the bow in the middle of the top, sort of sweet-like and innocent, but it sure was skimpy! She stood back from the mirror and inspected herself all over. She ran her fingers over her hips and hooked her thumbs under the edges, pulling the back of the bikini out over her bottom, then turned around, peering over her shoulder at the mirror.

Whoo-oo!

Then she noticed there was something else in the plastic bag, a wrap of the same green bamboo material. She pulled it out and tied it around her waist. Now that was cute! A neat little skirt. All you had to do was make sure you kept the skirt on until you got in the water before anybody saw.

There was one more; she might as well try it on. It was the only one-piece she had picked out, a nice-looking suit called "Black Shimmer." After a little wriggling to get into it, oh my, how nice it looked. It really covered everything pretty well, except the whole center from neck to well below the navel was a sheer mesh that somehow made everything look even better than bare skin. The bottom covered a little more of her behind, but the high cut at the sides left her hips bare. Not that she had bad hips; they curved out rather nicely, and so did her behind, maybe a little nicer than her breasts, though every one of these suits made her look okay in that department, too. She paused to contemplate. She turned this way and that, pulling the material down here, out there, over this and that. One piece, two piece; somehow, every Venus swimsuit gave the impression of being barely there. This one had a wrap, too, a flowing sheer black net, which covered her bare hips but somehow made the high cut even more daring.

She examined her reflection for a good three or four minutes. Then she checked price tags. Each of the suits ran about $180 in Singapore dollars. That meant about half that in U.S. money. Yes, she had to get this one, too, especially because it made her feel pretty good about herself. She slipped the suit off and, wondering about the beaches at Penang, pulled on her denims. You really shouldn't wear suits like this if anyone was looking. Not even Broc.

Outside the store the crowds were building up. The loudspeakers were pounding out a song with the thump and tone of a hit-parade song by Cher, except it was in Chinese. The Chinese men were still following her. As she came out of the store, she glimpsed them through the rail on the next floor down sitting at a table drinking coffee.

She ambled along the balcony looking in the windows. A couple of minutes later, she stopped dead in her tracks. There it was: The Texas Store. The Chinese mannequin wore a black vest and jeans with a silver belt buckle, a white cowboy hat, and silver six-guns at his hips. The female Chinese mannequin matched: hat and guns and all, except she was wearing white short-shorts and high black boots with silver studs.

I think women look good in boots and cowboy hats— Broc's opinion settled it.

Christelle glanced at her watch. It was twelve forty-five. She had at least an hour before she had to think about getting rid of those stupid Chinese spies. Why not? It would be fun to look around at western wear. She had never been to Texas.

An hour later she came out of The Texas Store with another big shopping bag. It was big but not heavy and that was handy. It made her appear much more weighted down than she was. She rode down the escalator and sauntered across the crowded main floor, which had now reached the pitch of a Barnum Circus. There were mothers with their children, wandering crowds of teenagers, people everywhere. She had seen nothing of her pursuers, but she sensed they were somewhere nearby.

Outside, she walked slowly back toward the hotel, a good twenty-minute walk away. At the corner of Scott, she entered the tunnel, crossed to the other side of Orchard, and continued west, turning in at the Far Eastern Shopping Center. They were with her again, seventy-five yards behind, looking as fed up with the job as she had intended. Near the entrance she paused at the store window. Out on the sidewalk one Chinese tail was lighting a cigarette for the other.

Christelle walked four steps, ambled leisurely around the corner into the center of the mall, clutched her shopping bags, and dashed diagonally toward the east door, dodging children and shoppers. It couldn't have been more ten seconds before she was out the side door onto Angullia Park, a one-way street running away from Orchard Road. A taxi at the curb stood with door open. Christelle slipped into the back seat, pushing her bags ahead of her, and pulled the door closed. She guessed her shadowers were barely entering the north door of the mall.

"I'd like to go to the airport."

Chapter Twenty-nine

National University of Singapore

Broc had spent an hour and a half in the library of what he knew was the preeminent university in Southeast Asia, not searching for anything in particular, just seeing what the place was like. NUS was interesting. The language of instruction was English, the result, he now understood, of the British establishing Oxford-like centers of learning in all their colonies.

The library towered on the side of a hill, a single rambling structure set among tall tropical trees. Its hillside setting reminded him of the University of California campus at Santa Cruz. Like everything Singaporean, the grounds were immaculately tended and the students, virtually all Chinese, appeared dedicated, scholarly, intent on whatever they were doing. It was Saturday afternoon, but the library was full of students.

O'Neill came down three flights of stairs from the library entrance on the top floor and moved toward the concrete rail where masses of foliage stood between him and the parking lot another level down. There they were. His two tails, the same ones he had seen in the Rasa Singapura Food Center, were loitering at the corner of the parking lot close to the taxi drop-off and pickup. That was a problem and a challenge: how to leave without them following.

O'Neill had spotted them outside the Marco Polo Hotel when he left at 9 a.m. He had made it easy, catching a cab where they could catch one, too, and watched them poke through shops down in the old historic district. For two hours he led them from The National Museum and Art Gallery to the National Library, then to the National Archives, picking up pamphlets and information sheets along the way. Then he stepped up his pace, crossing the Singapore River on foot and following the west bank down to Raffles Place, where he found himself a place to have lunch, skim the headlines, and gaze out at Marina Bay. Finally, at twelve thirty, he caught a cab and directed the driver to take him out to the university.

His followers were bored. If they didn't stop smoking cigarettes, they would soon drop dead from lung cancer. O'Neill studied his campus map, then glanced toward his pursuers again. One of the Americans said a few words to the other and headed off down Kent Ridge Crescent at a good pace toward the lower entrance to the Faculty of Arts and Social Sciences complex. The other loitered on the grass in the shade of the trees. If both of them wandered off, the problem would be solved, but that was unlikely.

A Toyota Cressida pulled into the lot and backed into a space three or four cars away. O'Neill watched the smart-looking Chinese youth get out; he was dressed in dark slacks and light summer jacket and carried a book and notebook. He walked around the car, straightening his tie on the way and opened the door. A very attractive Chinese girl got out. She was dressed in a dark skirt and white blouse. The girl paused as she stood up and met his eyes, making herself available while the door of the car was still open. His arm went round her waist. He kissed her on the forehead, then gently moved her notebook from her hand to the top of the car. Her eyes swept furtively around the parking lot, missed Broc's stalker staked out in the shade of the trees, and then her arms were around his neck and they were kissing, one of those passionate nuzzling kisses you could see a dozen times a day on the Jefferson State University campus.

O'Neill watched them. The young man's hands, hidden from the street by the car door, drifted below her waist until they cupped her bottom, pulling her hard against him. The kissing went on, perhaps a little more fervently than before. The stolen intimacy in a public place told O'Neill they probably weren't sleeping together, but it was a virtual certainty that it wouldn't be long before they found a way.

After another minute they let each other go, and the young man closed the car door. Retrieving their books, they walked hand in hand across the parking lot toward the outdoor café below where O'Neill stood. He watched them cross the shaded brick, shouting greetings to friends, and climbing the stairs on their way to the library. He was clean

248

cut and good looking; he looked professional, a man on his way up. She was pretty, generously endowed, with round eyes and a rich mane of hair fanning across her back. They might have been about twenty or twenty-one.

As they came onto the second level, O'Neill stepped forward and introduced himself. "I'm wondering whether you would be willing to assist me," he said. "I'm an American university professor visiting NUS." He held out his hand. "Broc O'Neill."

"Would you like us to show you around?" the girl volunteered. My name is Susan Wu. This is my friend John, John Chen."

"You're students here? What year?"

"We're finished third year; we'll both graduate next June. Could we show you around?"

"Thank you, I've already wandered all around. But I have a favor to ask. Please tell me if you don't have time. I don't want to interfere with your studies." He glanced at the book and notebook in Susan Wu's hand. "It's just that I've got a bit of a problem."

"You won't be interfering, Sir," John Chen clarified. He glanced at Susan, his eyes wavering for an instant. "The books are — they're just for show." He glanced at Susan again, and she looked from him back to Broc, trying to appear innocent. Her hand came up and touched her hair and O'Neill caught the flash of sunlight on a diamond ring.

Engaged. "What are your plans after graduation?"

"Well, we're both in health sciences. We're not sure if we can afford it, but we'd like to come to your country to study."

"Both to the same city, the same university?" O'Neill asked, pulling out his wallet and searching for his business card.

Susan seemed a little flustered, but Chen spoke up right away. "We're going to be married after we graduate. Next July. So, I guess, yes, to the same university."

O'Neill passed his business card. "Jefferson State University might not be the right place for study in the health sciences, but I know people in a dozen or so universities. When you're ready, please contact me. I may be able to help."

Susan Wu beamed, a wide smile. She had beautiful dark eyes, very full lips and a classical bearing. O'Neill could understand how John Chen would have difficulty not stealing every kiss he could manage.

He motioned them to the edge of the balcony. "Look through the leaves. See that guy in the blue pants."

"He looks like an American," John Chen guessed.

"He is American. Not only that, but he is some sort of agent, a spy." John and Susan seemed a little startled. "Am I right," O'Neill went on, "that Singaporean laws are not very tolerant of foreign spies?"

"It's not just the laws!" Chen said, his eyes showing a touch of anger. "Ever since that trouble in Indonesia — it was before I was born, but we've all heard about it — ever since then, we are very suspicious of your American CIA spies."

"I'm not sure that they are CIA," O'Neill admitted, "but they're just as bad."

"What would you like us to do?" Susan Wu asked, eager to help.

"I'd like you to stay here and watch, maybe for the next ten or fifteen minutes. There are two of them. Come down when you see me wave."

O'Neill cut across the café, found a path through greenery at the far end, crossed the street, and circled behind the grove of trees. He came through on a bed of fine pine needles, stopping while he was still out of sight. His American tail stood facing the other way, twelve feet away, leisurely standing with his hands in his pockets.

O'Neill hit him full force in the small of the back, knocking the wind from his lungs and sending him sprawling on the grass. Before he could move, O'Neill had him in a painful hammerlock, his knee on the man's back. The American gasped in pain. There was no holster in his armpit, but O'Neill felt the lump on his leg above his shoe. In two seconds, he had the handgun in his hands. A Glock 17, mostly plastic, a smuggler's delight. In another second, he had found the American's wallet.

O'Neill stood up. "I see your name is Stewart Smith," he said, examining his Singaporean driver's license. "American, with a Virginia driver's license, too. Stewart, I'd like you to roll over on your back very slowly. I've got your Glock. I'm sure I don't need to detail the mess to the face a 9 mm shell will make."

Painfully, the American rolled over. O'Neill stood six feet away, out of reach of arms and legs. Smith squinted, blinded by the sun.

"Ah! I recognize you now!" O'Neill said. "Camp Peary, maybe 1980s but could have been anytime. I was there every couple of summers."

"It was 1984."

"Gotcha! I've never been there, but if you have, you're CIA. Let's see, what have we got here? Ah, ha! Business card! Tanglin Corporation. That tells me a lot. Okay, Stewart Smith, you roll over."

The man on the ground hesitated. O'Neill was on top of him, the gun barrel pressed against his cheek, hard. The man cringed away, gasping. "Be thankful for the pain," O'Neill growled. "It means you're still alive. But I don't have a bloody drop of patience. A bullet might not kill you, but you know what it will do to your face. Roll over."

In half a minute he had pulled off Smith's necktie and tied his hands behind his back. With his own necktie, Broc tied his feet. Then he lifted Smith's jacket and tore out the back of his shirt, wadded it in a ball, and stuffed it into his mouth.

"I don't appreciate CIA goons following me all over Singapore when I'm on vacation," O'Neill said, rolling him down the grass to the pavement and under the first car. The American's eyes showed a good dose of terror as Broc pointed the Glock under the car and jammed the barrel against his face. "I see your friend coming back, but one sound from you and you get the first bullet."

O'Neill waited in the trees. The second American walked across the grass to the parking lot and gazed around, obviously wondering where his partner had gone, then stood with his hands on his hips and looked up at the massive building on the hill.

"Don't move or you're dead, just like Stewart Smith," O'Neill growled, the Glock shoved against the man's spine. The American froze. "Now, walk in a slow half circle back to the grass by the trees."

O'Neill followed, then forced the man down on the grass and had his gun and wallet within seconds, the gun shoved in his belt. "John. Now isn't this a coincidence! John Wayne. I'd say you've got a few things to learn to live up to your namesake."

O'Neill whipped off Wayne's necktie and bound his hands behind his back. Then he stood up and waved in the direction of the NUS Library.

"John Wayne, Maryland driver's license. Singapore driver's license. Employed at Raffles Hotel, home of a great drink, the Singapore Sling. Well, we have class, haven't we?"

"What the hell do you want?" Wayne snarled, his eyes blazing anger.

"We'll see in just a minute."

Susan Wu and her fiancé were coming across the parking lot at a run.

"Mr. Chen," O'Neill directed, "I would like you to back your car up here and open the trunk." Chen went to the car and within half a minute had backed it up to the edge of the pavement.

"Stand up, Wayne," O'Neill ordered, the Glock pointed at his chest. "That's right, slow and easy. Now, walk over to that car and climb in the trunk."

Wayne stopped at the car and O'Neill was on him in an instant, the gun against his neck behind his ear. "You want to survive this? Don't even dream of hesitating!" Wayne climbed into the trunk awkwardly, having difficulty balancing with his hands tied. "Now, move over. The Japanese don't make big cars, and we've got to pack two of you in there."

In another minute, O'Neill had Stewart Smith out from under the car, and had rolled him the remaining eight feet to Chen's car. O'Neill stuck the Glock in his belt. "Give me a hand, Chen."

Together they dumped Smith into the trunk on top of Wayne, who cursed furiously. O'Neill yanked up Stewart's coat, tore away another chunk of shirt and stuffed it in Wayne's mouth. "You need to learn that Singaporeans are very cultured people, much more than you, and not used to such fowl talk."

The two Americans squirmed together, shifting furiously in the confined space.

"Mr. Chen," O'Neill said, gazing down at the prisoners. "These men are both Americans, both working for the CIA. O'Neill stared down at them. "They have what's called 'commercial cover'. They've been placed as spies in Singaporean companies without diplomatic immunity, so they are subject to Singaporean law. They are carrying guns, which should land them in jail for a long time. Mr. Chen" — O'Neill watched the prisoners' eyes — "are you willing to drive these men to the Tanglin Police Station? It's just up the street from the Marco Polo Hotel."

The Chinese student stared down at them, a sneer on his face. "It would give me a great deal of pleasure!"

O'Neill pulled their guns from his belt, released the clip of cartridges from each and put them in his pocket and tossed the empty guns in with the gagged prisoners. "Mind your fingers," he cautioned, and slammed down the lid of the trunk.

He motioned John Chen and Susan Wu away from the car, out of earshot. "Those guys are having the biggest scare of their lives. They think they are going to a Singaporean jail where bamboo slivers will be driven under their fingernails for the next twenty years." O'Neill got out his map of Singapore and unfolded it. He ran his fingers along the scattered roads and numerous waterways along the north coast. "Where's the loneliest place on the island?"

Chen's finger came down in an instant.

"That's not lonely," Susan blurted. Broc looked at her. "Well, it's not!" She looked from O'Neill to John Chen. Her skin seemed to have colored a little.

John Chen smiled. "That road is where everybody goes, you know, Sir, for car parking." He glanced at his watch. "It's very lonely now. But by nine tonight, Saturday night, it will be very busy."

Lover's Lane. Perfect. "Well, it's afternoon; it hasn't heated up yet. Would you be willing to drive these guys out there now and dump them out as far away as you can get?"

John and Susan both nodded vigorously. O'Neill pulled out his wallet and counted out sixty Singaporean dollars, enough for a couple of tanks of gas, and then some.

"No, no, we do this as a favor. Please," Chen entreated. "Let us do this as a favor; favors are much more the Chinese way."

O'Neill put the money back in his wallet. "All right, but only if you'll let me do you a favor." They nodded again. O'Neill turned to

Susan Wu. "How long do you... How long were you planning to be at the library?"

"Until closing time, nine thirty tonight. My parents expect me home by ten."

"And tomorrow?"

"Same thing, John and I come to campus on weekends, from early in the day until closing time." She looked a little embarrassed. "I have a big family. It's very difficult, very hard to have any time — together." She looked from John to O'Neill, her soft brown eyes looking innocent.

O'Neill glanced at his watch. "It's three now. You should be back from dumping these jerks by five. Then I'd like you to go down to the Marco Polo Hotel." He pulled out the key. "Room 1062."

John and Susan stared at him blankly.

"This is my favor." He dropped the key in John's jacket pocket. "You can use the room this evening and all day tomorrow. It's reserved in my name until Monday noon. You can eat in any of the hotel restaurants, two, three meals a day, however long you're there. Just bill it to Room 1062. They'll charge it to my credit card. Have whatever you want; think of it as an unlimited expense account. Bouquets of frangipani for Susan in the morning, sandwiches delivered at noon, wine with dinner, whatever you want."

John Chen and Susan Wu stood speechless, astonished.

"I'm going to catch a cab for the airport. I'm flying out of Singapore in a couple of hours." He stuck out his hand and shook John's hand, then Susan's. "And, thank you; you've really helped."

O'Neill waved as he walked down the grass. Within a minute he was in the back seat of a taxi." I'd like you to take me out to Changi Airport."

Chen and Susan Wu were standing by their car, still in mild shock. They waved as the taxi pulled away. They were a handsome pair, absolutely beautiful. Blood pumping, hormones raging. Local kids with no place to go, no way to be alone, suddenly shacked up in a world-class five-star hotel. They would have fun. Right now, he guessed they were wondering whether they had died and gone to heaven, or were just dreaming.

Chapter Thirty

St. Louis, Missouri
Thursday, August 11

It was 5:30 p.m. when Alan Creighton, having spent several hours reading newspapers from New York and L.A., came out of the main library at Washington University. Broc O'Neill was right: there had been a lot of expensive new research programs and projects funded the past few weeks. A few hours had yielded a pile of photocopies sufficient to fill his briefcase to bursting.

Broc was right, too, on the sudden availability of funds for massive social programs. It did not square with the general mood of the country during the Republican-dominated Congress of the current government. On Sunday morning Creighton had caught highlights from Jim Braxton interviews on TVI that seemed on par with O'Neill's findings, but just how was still a puzzle.

It had been weeks since Creighton had downloaded O'Neill's 250-page file. That was on July 19th. O'Neill had said he would be out of touch for a while and hinted darkly that Creighton might not hear from him again. For the next three weeks, Creighton had tapped into Christelle Washington's JSU account twice a day, but by late last week, he had begun to despair that both Christelle and Broc had been caught. Creighton hadn't wanted to think about it, not after the violent murders in Pennsylvania.

Creighton turned his Mercury west on Ladue Road for the two-mile run to his home in Clayton. The temperature was still hovering around 100 degrees, the usual unbearable heat that burned over St. Louis every August. He would have stayed at home if it hadn't been for the short communication that had appeared in the JSU mainframe Saturday afternoon. Oddly enough, it was dated six hours in the future, one of the conundrums of Malaysian time twelve hours ahead of Central Standard

Time in the U.S. Broc had sent it on Saturday night, August 9th, from The PJ Hilton Hotel. Creighton had to get out his atlas to find Petaling Jaya, a small city in Peninsular Malaysia south of Kuala Lumpur, just minutes from the main airport.

It took but a paragraph, however, for everything to come clear. Broc would be flying into Penang the next morning and would communicate again as soon as he had scouted out Hai Phong Electronics. He had already been to Manila and found Teleconic Manufacturing, met the local supervisor, toured the factory, and uncovered the crucial connection. One of Teleconic's American owners was Joseph Terrence of Lignum Operations.

Creighton had felt the hair on his neck bristle when he researched Joe Terrence, an employee in the State Department. O'Neill's research had stirred up deep government people inside the Beltway. Prominent people were dead. And now, just two days ago, half a world away, O'Neill had jumped two Americans tailing him in Singapore: field officers from the CIA.

Creighton worried about Broc. He was highly intelligent, but a little reckless. They had met one summer in Idaho on a river-running expedition where O'Neill was determined to ride life on the whitecaps. O'Neill was a nineteen-year-old undergraduate river guide earning summer money; Creighton was a tourist, twenty years older, late in completing his doctoral work after years of post-high-school service in Vietnam.

Broc O'Neill was known by every river guide on the Middle Fork of the Salmon River as the most outrageously daring river runner anyone had seen in a kayak, and when he steered his craft through a fifty-foot maelstrom that, if not quite vertical, damn near seemed like it was, Creighton decided that no insurance company could responsibly hold a policy on his life.

What the hell was Broc O'Neill doing jumping CIA agents in Singapore?

That was what Creighton expected Brently Hagan to say.

What Hagan asked was, "What the hell are CIA agents doing tailing Broc O'Neill in Singapore?" Creighton always forgot the depth of Hagan's condemnation of the CIA record: covert operations in a dozen countries, attempted assassinations, clandestine wars, secret files on innocent Americans.

"Those bastards!" Brently shouted over the phone. "And what the hell is Special Operations doing with agents in Singapore, anyway? We pulled out of Southeast Asia in 1973!"

"I think we were chased out," Creighton corrected, recalling the fall of Saigon. Viet Cong firing at American helicopters trying to get airborne. He wondered whether the American government had learned from its mistake: interfering in a culture it really did not understand.

Brently Hagan, an explosives expert and Officer-in-Charge of Creighton's Vietnam platoon, spoke about the Directorate of Operations with unmitigated invective. He worked in a different division of the CIA, the Directorate of Science and Technology, specifically the Office of Development and Engineering. The rivalry between more than thirty different offices, and even more between the four main directorates, was intense, confrontational, often outright hostile. Hagan and his colleagues in engineering regarded the entire Directorate of Operations as well to the right of the KGB.

Creighton had outlined what he knew to Hagan on Saturday night.

"Blast all of them!" Hagan's voice verged on fury as it did even during normal conversations. "O'Neill must have stirred up a wicked brew to have CIA officers tailing him overseas. I'd say he's in pretty serious trouble. Look, Alan, I can't find out anything until after the weekend; I'll get back to you Monday night. Is this phone line clean?"

"It's my renter's phone from the garage apartment. I've had the number changed just to be sure. It's an unlisted number under a fake name."

"Okay, carry on and let's hope this O'Neill friend of yours survives a few more hours. By the way, you said he had a girlfriend."

"Not exactly. She's a grad student who somehow got mixed up in this. She was with O'Neill three weeks ago in Vermont. Somebody nearly got both of them with a machine-gun. She was helping him while they were in the country, but he hasn't mentioned her since. Given the danger, the foolhardiness of what he's up to, we should hope he sent her back to her library carrel before he flew to Singapore."

Creighton stopped by the liquor store and picked up a dozen Coors. Twenty minutes later he turned into his driveway and drove his car into the welcome shade of the garage. He heard the phone ringing and saw Annie answer it as he came into the kitchen.

"It's Brent, Brent Hagan from Washington." Annie handed him the phone.

That was fast. Hagan must have got right to the problem and have something to report.

"This is a tough nut to crack," Hagan said." Not only is Special Ops sneaky about everything, but they resist inquiries. They don't like questions, they don't share information, and they have their own computer network."

"So, we're locked out?"

"Not entirely," Hagan reported. "I've got friends in the Directorate of Administration. I've talked to a friend in the Office of Personnel. There are three commercial cover officers in Singapore, and O'Neill ran into two of them. These guys, Stewart Smith and John Wayne, were placed in Singapore by the Directorate of Operations, but their main contacts are with Intelligence, specifically Counter Narcotics. Singapore is neutral ground within a few hours of the main drug routes in Thailand."

"Narcotics! What the hell is the connection? O'Neill is not—"

"There's no connection, Alan, and that tells us something. An authorized CIA operation would utilize new officers inserted for that purpose. Special Ops would not risk blowing the cover of established narcotics officers for a temporary project. These guys were hired to tail O'Neil, but it's not their line of work. That's why he caught them off guard so easily."

"So, you're saying this was not a CIA operation."

"Right. Whoever put them on O'Neill's case could be in the CIA, but not necessarily. Somebody needed a bit of amateur surveillance over the weekend. Smith and Wayne were contacted and used, hired as temps, because they were there and willing to take on the job for some extra cash. But your friend O'Neill is pretty savvy."

"Very savvy! He's managed to stay alive against pretty severe odds, and maybe now he's home free."

"No, I think he's in considerable danger. These guys he neutralized will report what happened. Whoever's tracked them to Southeast Asia has substantial resources. I'd guess they'll step up their efforts, hire better help, or send in some of their own troops. O'Neill may not have such good luck again."

"So things are going to get worse rather than better."

There was a minute of silence before Hagan spoke. "Why is O'Neill in Asia?"

Creighton ran through a brief history of Worldwide telephones, including O'Neill's success in the Philippines. He was now headed for Hai Phong Electronics in Malaysia. "All this fitted in with vacation plans his wife made before she died. He had plane tickets to Southeast Asia. It was convenient to use them and then to do a little sleuthing on the side."

"Alan, how much does O'Neill know about us — our unit in Vietnam?"

Creighton began to draw wild river waves on his doodle pad. Details of more than a dozen missions swept across his mind: vicious raids, violent explosions, lethal killings with never a failure — the classified dossier of a Navy SEAL team in war. "I gave him a rundown last month. No specific details, just a little of what we did. We didn't have time to talk, but he has a rough idea."

"Okay, have you kept track of our guys? I mean, what about Matthews?"

"I had a Christmas card from him last year. He's still in Singapore. But O'Neill's in Malaysia. We couldn't persuade him to go back there, not for a while."

"It doesn't matter. Matthews' only love was the platoon. He would lay down his life for any one of us. And anyone who is our friend is his friend. If Matthews hears about this, he will make sure he meets O'Neill. He travels all over the region."

Creighton crumpled the top page of his notepad." Getting in touch with Matthews may not help O'Neill deal with these guys, whoever they are."

"That's true, Alan, but Matthews might help him deal with Teleconic and Hai Phong. O'Neill may be running for his life, but he's managed to penetrate this monster. He's found a weak spot in the system.

Remember, our team was expert at hitting the enemy at its most vulnerable point — in its soft underbelly."

Creighton leaned back in his chair, his eyes on the massive pile of greenery beyond the deck in his back yard. His mind went back...

March 1969. Vietnam— Stars splashed overhead, a vast blackness on either side of the boat, a state-of-the-art aluminum-hull insertion craft edging upstream at 6 mph. Night on the Cua Lon River, the main waterway into the Ca Mau peninsula, a vast tangle of mangroves at the southwestern tip of the Mekong Delta. Creighton stood in the darkness at the rail watching the jungle, sensing Brent Hagan and Wally Matthews beside him. Hagan was the Officer-in-Charge, Matthews was the Second-in-Charge, the OIC and 2IC. There were eleven others on the SEAL Team Assault Boat, acronym STAB, a fourteen-man platoon whose specialty was deep penetration into enemy territory against overwhelming odds followed by a silent getaway, almost always by water. Their survival record surpassed every other military unit in Southeast Asia. No Navy SEAL in their platoon, wounded or dead, had ever been left on enemy soil.

Alan had met Hagan, Matthews, and three others in the platoon at Camp Peary during the deadliest twenty-five weeks of his life, the six-month training common to the Underwater Demolition Teams, the UDT, and the Sea/Air/Land Teams, the Navy SEALs. Three kids out of high school searching for adventure, they had found themselves undergoing the most grueling physical training known to modern man. Before they were done, they could run a marathon, swim in the open ocean for over five miles, and work continuously, night and day, under fire and in constant danger, surviving on no more than three hours of sleep a night for a week, broken into fifteen-minute catnaps while lying in mud, floating on water, or lodged in the fork of a tree.

And now they found themselves sneaking upstream on a muddy river in a jungle in Southeast Asia, part of the American Brown-water Navy. Richard Nixon had been inaugurated two months ago and had ordered B-52 bombing raids into Cambodia to flush out an estimated forty thousand Viet Cong along the Vietnam border. Part of the strategy was SEAL penetration of the southern and western shores of the Mekong Delta to locate and destroy Viet Cong strongholds in the most impenetrable jungle in the region.

Creighton remembered every man in the platoon. On mission after mission, nineteen in a stretch of four months, they had inserted themselves deep into enemy territory, drifted silently ashore with blackened faces, scouted out enemy strongholds, placed and wired their explosives in the dark, then melted away into the leech-infested swamplands.

They had never failed. In six months, their platoon had destroyed over two hundred Vietcong buildings in sixteen secret strongholds, blown up an estimated thirty tons of ammunition, and left an untold number of VC dead to rot in the jungle. The two masters were Brently Hagan and Wally Matthews, men with such steady hands and nerves they could wire up explosives within five yards of a sleeping guard, strategists with such practiced eyes that they knew precisely where to place a charge to inflict maximum destruction.

After the Fall of Saigon, Hagan had come home and procured himself an education paid for by the CIA, who wanted him for advanced demolition planning in the Directorate of Science and Technology. Easily derided by anti-war protesters, Hagan, like Creighton and other veterans who had served in Vietnam, soon discovered that he was better off hiding his past. Wally was another story. Disabled in 1972 with a minor shrapnel wound, he had been given a well-earned month of R&R from which he had never returned. In fact, he had disappeared for over twenty years. Then, three years ago, a postcard had reached Creighton, and after he replied, a long letter.

In Thailand, Matthews had learned that both his parents had died, his brother-in-law and bitch of a sister had sold his parents' things and moved to parts unknown, and his wife in Oklahoma now had two kids by a live-in boyfriend. Angered, furious, in shock, Matthews had disappeared, melted away into Southeast Asia as though this were his final Navy SEAL mission. For months he had wandered, losing himself in brothels and bars, until somehow, he had landed in the staid tropical world of Peninsular Malaysia, the only country, he said, that had successfully fended off a communist insurgency to become an independent nation.

There he had met a young Malay woman with whom he had fallen deeply in love. He was reluctant to convert to the Muslim religion, and she had sided with him in his decision, forsaking the demands of her family. Together, they had headed to Singapore to begin a new life, where they had now lived for nearly twenty years. Matthews had never been back to the U.S. As far as Creighton knew, he was the only one from the platoon whom Wally Matthews had ever contacted.

Creighton faced toward their garden for a long time while daylight waned, his mind wandering in the strange darkness of the past, struggling to make sense of the paths fate chooses for men.

Annie was cutting up carrots for supper. He glanced at his watch: 7:15 p.m. Twelve hours difference: it was morning in Southeast Asia.

Creighton picked up his telephone and dialed the operator. "I need assistance with a call. Could you connect me to Information in Singapore?"

Chapter Thirty-one

Maryland
Thursday, August 11

Just beyond the southeast boundary of the District of Columbia, not far from Andrews Air Force Base, John Orchard pulled his car into the mall parking lot, which was filled almost to overflowing. A huge crowd was pouring from the eighteen-screen theater and milling past the line of people buying tickets for the next showing of the summer box-office hit, Sean Connery in *The Rock*. The pounding rhythm of rap music filled the air as a pickup on risers cruised between the cars, all speakers blaring. It was 9:05 p.m.

Orchard walked toward the supermarket. Inside, he wheeled a shopping cart, walked slowly down the aisle, stopped in front of the magazines, then headed toward the meat counters in the back corner of the store. The refrigerated glass containers were half empty, the choicest plastic-wrapped cuts of beef and pork already gone. The meat cutters had gone off duty an hour earlier.

Two women, occupied with shopping lists and animated talk ambled off toward the dairy section. Leaving his buggy, Orchard headed toward the double aluminum doors and slipped into the refrigerated meat delivery room. Walking past shipping crates and cutting tables, he headed to the second floor. Past a pile of empty cardboard boxes, he fitted his key into a door marked 'Storage', and went in. Joe Terrence, Richard Swentz, and Martin Atwater were already seated at the table. The room had a water cooler, a refrigerator, a TV, and a VCR. It was used by those in charge of Sector Four.

Terrence looked sullen. Manning stood at the window. Stinson was nursing a Coke; it was his first appearance at a meeting for more than a year. Over the next half hour, sixteen more arrived, including four from

Sparsum Operations. It was the first joint meeting of SO with Lignum Operations since their founding meeting almost six years ago.

Thirty minutes into the meeting, tempers had risen to a boil. Leopold Hudgeons had already sounded off. That had started it. Orchard fumed. Terrence had uncharacteristically blown his stack. Blakeney sat smugly; Orchard assumed this was because his primary role in the pursuit of Broc O'Neill had been usurped by Wade Bracket who was now in the hot seat. Manning, who smoked at a rate that exceeded his reputed intelligence, lit up another of his infernal cigarettes. Hudgeons cursed and hit the switch behind him, turning on the ventilation fan.

Finally, Judge Hudgeons got fed up and turned to Craig Ramer, one of the four from Sparsum Operations. "The gist of the matter, as everyone seems to agree, is that there's been a flood of cash, a damn tidal wave, and it's been noticed."

Ramer's eyes blazed at Hudgeons, then at Orchard, the moderator to whom everyone else reported. "But Lignum has faltered the past few months. Cash outlays of this kind require commitments for continued funding. Lignum has been moving with the speed of a turtle with a hernia. In recent months, the accounts have barely shown sufficient balances—"

"Let's cut the crap!" Orchard was as furious as the rest of the Lignum people. "Too much overspending! Two billion in disbursals in four weeks! Not even the American economy can absorb that kind of money without obvious repercussions. Don't you guys have a budget?"

"As I recall," the black-haired senatorial assistant said, clearly straining to keep his voice level, "our founding meeting was six years ago. Three years passed before anything happened. While Lignum Operations has been snail pacing, demand has been building. Sparsum Operations is under pressure—"

Orchard sat forward, glaring. "Anybody dissatisfied with the situation ought to be thankful there is a Sparsum Operations. Sorry, Ramer, you'll just have to live with it."

"Sparsum was formed to meet legitimate needs."

Martin Atwater sat forward, clearly agitated. "None of those legitimate needs will ever get met without some sensible precautions." He stared down the table at Craig Ramer. "Presence at these meetings, which, admittedly, you were not expected to attend, would have apprised you of a long list of obstacles. Lignum is, unfortunately, in charge of the most unpredictable sector of Ironwood. There have been some unfortunate leaks, some real loose cannon. Now, after three years of success, we're seeing our own incompetence undermining overall plans and goals."

"I think incompetence is a little strong, Martin."

"Sorry, but those of us inside the Loop have a different perspective. I sit up there on the Hill and listen, hour after bloody hour, day after bloody day. You have no idea of the furor that's been raging. Maybe you should read the papers. They're full of it, and it's been all over TV. Everybody on the Hill is confused. Shit! Rumors are flying—maybe some bloody bureaucrat is secretly diverting funds earmarked for the military, or infrastructure repair, or the war on drugs. If this thing opens up a Senate investigation—"

"Okay, okay!" Ramer held up his palms. "I get the message. What the hell do you want me to do?"

"Slow down!" Joe Terrence broke in. "Ease into this thing. No more commitments till the situation cools. Avoid any promises we might not be able to keep. And, damn it all, if Sparsum is going to disburse funds, find a way to keep it out of the papers! Hell, there's a reason Lignum has taken so long with collections. Need I remind you we're sailing a fragile ship in a typhoon. It might be sensible for Sparsum to realize the same thing. If one unit fails, the whole of Ironwood goes down the tubes."

The north door to the basement meeting room opened. Everyone turned. All expected participants had arrived by nine thirty; it was now ten fifteen. The dark-haired, slightly obese man was a stranger.

"You can all relax," Orchard remarked. "This is Shane Webster. He's unknown to members of Lignum and Sparsum, but he's been a part of Ironwood from the beginning. I've invited him to see whether we can deal with the current emergency. Shane, have a seat."

"Okay, but I've brought a couple of guys. They're downstairs filling shopping carts. I think we're going to need them."

"Mind if we break for coffee?" Orchard suggested. "Go ahead, Shane; bring them up. "There was an audible breath of relief, which required no reply. Within seconds they had all pushed back their chairs.

"Gentleman," Orchard began, stirring his coffee. "Mr. Webster is from CIA, Special Ops. A couple of weeks ago, we passed a problem on to him, thinking it would go away. Unfortunately, it has not. Rather than continue along the same lines, we thought it would be best to have the entire group working on this." Orchard looked around. Faces were attentive, interested. The two additions to the group were in their twenties, rugged, blocky, sleeves torn out of their shirts. They resembled California weightlifters. The bigger of the two had a shock of reddish-orange hair; the other had a prominent scar down one cheek.

"Perhaps you'd like to fill us in, Shane."

Webster shifted and set down his coffee. "This concerns Professor Broc O'Neill." Tension rose around the table. "We spotted O'Neill when he flew into Singapore from Manila. That was last Thursday. Two days later, we think sometime Saturday, we lost him."

"Excuse me." Hudgeons stared at Webster. "You think sometime Saturday?"

"That's what I said. We think. O'Neill and his student were under surveillance Saturday morning but weren't seen Saturday night or Sunday. We thought they were holed up in their suite at the Marco Polo Hotel. We had a twenty-four-hour watch on every exit. Checkout time was Monday noon. The hotel records show them charging room service for every meal, and their account was cleared Monday at 11:38 a.m., but they were not seen leaving the hotel. Saturday afternoon O'Neill disarmed our tails and had them dumped out on a country road. We think he and this broad disappeared later that afternoon."

"So what about the charges to his account?"

"No idea. Maybe he phoned room service remotely and had meals sent up. We don't have anyone there to check at the hotel desk."

"So we lost him, maybe Saturday night, and haven't seen them for two days." Hudgeons set down his coffee and turned back to Webster. "How could a history prof get a jump on them? What the hell kind of agents is the CIA turning out these days?"

The newest additions to the group turned their eyes on Hudgeons, their cold fury clear to everyone.

"As good as always," Webster confirmed, "for the job they have to do. That's why Orchard and I decided we would lay this out to everyone.

The CIA has only a few overseas officers, and Ironwood is a domestic organization. When it comes to surveillance in Asia, we have to make do with what we have. What we have is three officers under commercial cover in Singapore. They were inexperienced, so they got tripped up. We don't have the resources for serious surveillance, and this O'Neill is smarter than any of us suspected."

"So, he's in Singapore?"

"That was our assumption when we got wind of this. Check out time was noon Monday; that was midnight Sunday here. We learned of it this morning. Nothing turned up on the airlines, but we couldn't check all of them. We suspect he got out of Singapore on the Malaysian airlines, MAS. They've got touchy protections on their records, so we couldn't get into their flight lists. It wasn't until late this afternoon that something showed up, a hotel booking."

"Where?"

"Penang, Malaysia."

"Penang!" The outburst came simultaneously from at least three members of Lignum. The tension escalated. Orchard felt very cold, then very clammy. The realization struck him like a rolling boulder. O'Neill had arranged two side trips from Singapore, to Manila and Penang. The odds against coincidence were too great: O'Neill's flight to Manila must have had something to do with Teleconic; his flight to Penang was probably a fishing expedition aimed at Hai Phong Electronics.

Half a dozen others in the room had made the same connection.

"Shane! Am I right? There was no surveillance on O'Neill in Manila?"

Webster nodded.

"So, we don't actually know how he spent his time. And there's no surveillance on him in Penang."

"That's the reason I'm here, John. We don't have the manpower. All we know is he checked into a Penang hotel Sunday night." Webster glanced at his watch. "Right now, it's 10:42 Tuesday morning in Malaysia, and they're still there."

"What they've been up to since Saturday is just guesswork."

Webster smiled. "We've got reports from our officers in Singapore. From what they saw, O'Neill and the bitch with him act like they're pretty buddy-buddy. Incidentally, we identified her a few days ago. She's a graduate student from California attending Jefferson State University. We've got her picture. She's a zinger."

Trying to think, Orchard drummed his pencil on the table. It was remotely possible their side trips were coincidence. But could they afford to take a chance? Maybe they could. Maybe it was stupid to think that Broc O'Neill was interested in anything other than staying out of danger and playing with his graduate student in expensive hotels.

"Gentlemen," Hudgeons waded in. "Let's think this through. O'Neill knows too much. He's called for congressional investigation of the intelligence community. I think it's time to get serious. Forget the surveillance; get on with the task."

"I think most of us are agreed," Atwater injected. "We came to that conclusion a month ago when O'Neill was nosing around in Pennsylvania. But it's August; the fall semester at his university will start in September. Why not wait until he steps back on American soil?"

Judge Hudgeons objected: "If we could be sure he would return. But he's got $700,000 in his account in Jefferson, $210,000 in Michigan. He took $90,000 with him in cash. There's another million somewhere from his wife's life insurance policy. He's financially independent. He could travel all over the planet for the next decade. He's had some brushes with death. The U.S. is not a healthy environment. It's likely he'll stay away for a while. I think we'll have to take him out while he's over there."

"If he stays out of the U.S., who cares? It could be several months. Permanently gone would be ideal. Why not take up this matter when he returns?"

Dwight Blakeney sat forward. "I am of the same opinion. Out of the country, he's no danger. But my perspective is a little different. Why not make sure he stays permanently out of the country?"

Orchard looked at the FBI officer, and so did everyone else. Blakeney lifted a briefcase to the table and brought out a videotape. "Here's something you ought to see."

Blakeney slipped the tape into the VCR.

The screen showed a static view of a nondescript sidewalk and street. "This is an entrance surveillance tape from the night of July 17th," Blakeney announced. "It's been in the possession of the FBI since the night Walter Monahan and Colonel Spiker were killed. Let me fast forward."

The tape whirred for a minute. "Here, watch. In about five seconds."

Unexpectedly, two figures appeared running away from the camera, a tall male in a dark suit, a female in denims: slim, athletic, hair flying, the litheness of her flanks viscerally obvious as the streetlights fell across her racing body. "Broc O'Neill and his student," Blakeney said.

'Zinger' was right, Orchard thought.

The group watched; the seconds ticked by. A car lurched into view, came to a screeching halt, and the doors flew open. Colonel Spiker got out and walked toward the camera, then disappeared at the bottom of the screen.

"Okay, there's nothing on this for the next fifty-seven seconds." Blakeney pushed the fast forward and stopped it almost immediately. "Looks like about five more seconds."

They watched as a dark sports car moved slowly across the screen. A handgun was sticking out the window, the woman's face lit up by streetlights. In the four seconds while the car crossed the screen, they saw her squeeze off three shots, including one that blew the curbside windows of Spiker's car across the sidewalk toward the camera.

"The photo lab has enhanced this tape," Blakeney said. "You'll see a still in about five seconds."

The image was clear, with superb definition: the image of a woman aiming a gun. The two-handed grip was right; she looked professional.

"So," Orchard concluded, "the FBI has got the proof that she fired on Pennsylvania Produce."

"It's pretty damning evidence, except that no one in the FBI knows who she is."

Of course. The members of Ironwood knew because of their own investigations. But for the officers of the FBI, the face of the woman was one out of perhaps ten million women in America somewhere in their twenties.

Blakeney pushed rewind and turned on the lights. "My view, gentlemen, is that we focus on Miss Washington. She's committed a crime. The FBI can prosecute. If we get her, we'll accomplish our other objectives. Let me introduce two colleagues from the Office of

Operations, Covert Action division." He gestured toward the two muscle-bound visitors who looked like thugs from Chicago's lower East Side. "Troller and Senelik." They nodded in turn, and Blakeney continued. "They've been called in on a dozen kidnappings, enemy infiltrators in the military, terrorists on aircraft in flight."

"I apologize for interrupting, Dwight," Orchard said. "I'm sure your colleagues can lay their hands on Washington. But how will prosecuting her accomplish the other objectives?"

Blakeney stood by the table, smiling. "It's not prosecuting her that will do it, John. That's the final step. But given the law today, we might not even make a murder rap stick. That doesn't matter. We'll accomplish what we want in the first step."

Everyone waited, watching Blakeney, listening.

"O'Neill will be neutralized the moment Ms. Washington is seized — if it's done over there, and if O'Neill is left stranded so he can't get back."

"O'Neill is not that easy to—"

"O'Neill lost his wife less than three months ago! We've inquired about his marriage. They were happy, successful, well qualified professionals on their way up. She was pregnant when she died. What would that do to a man?" No one moved to answer.

"It's likely that O'Neill went under. He disappeared without a trace for over a month. What will he do if another woman is yanked away?"

No one uttered a word.

"She's a student, probably an accidental partner. He'll see another loss as his fault. He'll be incapacitated, drowning in guilt, suicidal. He could crack up. One thing is certain: we'll be able to forget about him."

No one spoke. Orchard could tell that everyone was thinking the same thing. There are things that can be done to a person much more devastating than death.

"Of course," Blakeney continued, "extracting Ms Washington and leaving O'Neill there is the simplest plan, but it's not the only one. If O'Neill gets in the way, he won't ever get to miss the bitch. Termination in Asia would be the ultimate solution. Done the right way, there'd be no investigation. He would just disappear."

Orchard looked from Troller to Senelik. Their faces were expressionless. They stared back at Orchard, their eyes never wavering. This was good. Inevitably, Broc O'Neill would get in the way, and these thugs would put him away for good.

Chapter Thirty-two

Penang, Malaysia
Friday, August 12

Broc finished drying his hair, then went to the mini-fridge and found two cans of tonic water. He and Christelle still had half a bottle of gin, and she had bought fresh limes at the hawker stall across the street from the Oriental Hotel.

He heard the shower go off as he moved to the coffee table in the common area of their suite. He turned on the laptop. Two minutes later, he had the file booted up — a hefty collection of data that Alan Creighton had loaded into the JSU mainframe overnight. He read Alan's e-mail again. Certain sentences leapt off the screen.

Have you checked the dates on Walter Monahan? The fire at the Pennsylvania Produce was on a Sunday. Monahan was in Atlanta to survey the damage on Tuesday and Wednesday. He flew directly to San Antonio later in the week. The Pennsylvania Produce donation of $6.3 million to Texas Land Preservation was handed over Friday. You think there's a connection?

O'Neill went to the refrigerator, got out cheese and crackers, and proceeded to slice off half a dozen squares that fit the crackers exactly. Christelle had bought a jar of dill pickles. Thinking about what Alan had written, he sliced one up and chewed on the cracker. It was difficult to fathom the level of charitable benevolence — $6.3 million — following so closely after the warehouse fire, unless...

Of course, there was a connection! There were dozens of ways to extract money. Bribery and coercion were most common, but arson was a particularly deadly persuader. And it would take something deadly, for the Monahan whom O'Neill had met was opposed to the whole agricultural subsidy program that had been bailing farmers out of debt for the past half century. He had seemed pretty tight fisted, not a man likely to donate money voluntarily to anything — certainly not $6.3 million.

O'Neill and Christelle had spent the day touring the sights around Penang: the Buddhist Temple of Paradise and the weird Snake Temple, where scores of vipers, hypnotized by the sweet smell of incense, coiled on altars and candle sticks and stone Buddhas. The brilliant reds and golds of altars and urns were dazzling — signs, perhaps, of the association of everything in Chinese religion with good luck and wealth.

Rides around George Town in trishaws had taken them past an incredible array of markets and stalls until they were hot and exhausted, and ready to retreat to the air-conditioned comfort of their hotel suite.

Christelle walked out of the bedroom with a towel. She was back in her denims, wearing a blue cotton blouse tied at her waist with bows. She came over to the bar, took a cracker with cheese, and popped a dill pickle in her mouth as Broc surveyed her hair.

"What's it called?"

"It's a budget spiral perm, which thousands of women would die for," she explained. "My hair does this when it gets wet." She rubbed her head a couple of times with the towel, which didn't seem to do more than rearrange a multitude of tiny curls. "Too bad it doesn't suit me. One of these costs $150 back in the States. They spray stuff on it to make it last a month or so. Mine falls out as soon as my hair dries. And anyway, I think brunettes wear it better."

"Sort of like Jane Seymour in *The Scarlet Pimpernel*," O'Neill compared admiringly, taking the towel and motioning her to sit on the couch.

"I wish!" she said, with a quick glance at him.

She didn't have to wish much, he thought, as she sat down. Nevertheless, he had better not name any more movie stars. Jane Seymour might intimidate any woman! Broc moved behind Christelle and proceeded to dry her head.

"Eye tpott 'f dyenn a hare drayr."

Broc stopped. "What did you say?"

Christelle lifted the towel away from her face. "I thought of buying a hair dryer. But I guess with this 220 power, it wouldn't work back in the States."

"It might with that 220/110 converter." He went back to work, gathering her hair in bunches and rolling it between folds of the towel. After two or three minutes, he went back to her head and gave it another long vigorous massage with the towel.

"Dhatt peylles leelee buud."

He stopped and she pulled the towel off her head. "I'm sorry — I mean that feels really good." She rummaged in her purse and brought out a comb and brush.

Broc handed her the plate of cheese and crackers, then glanced at his watch. "It's seven thirty, morning in the States. I think I'm going to give Alan Creighton a call; there are some things in that file that came through this morning that need clarification."

Christelle was combing her hair. "Go ahead; these snacks will hold us for a couple of hours. But let's go out later, down that street with all those hawker stalls."

"Jalan Penang. I looked it up. It's close enough to walk to—"

"That's it!" Christelle was already excited. "The travel book says they have wonderful *satay*."

"I might have known!" Broc picked up the phone. He dialed the international code, waited a few seconds, and then dialed the area code for St. Louis and Creighton's 'clean' telephone line.

Christelle's hair was nearly dry. The tiny spirals had been smoothed out; big wavy curls tumbling over her shoulders and halfway down her back. She grinned at him over her shoulder. "I'm going to try on some new clothes," she said, heading for her bedroom.

O'Neill lifted Christelle's handbag from the side table to the floor, uncovering the new certificates documenting that they were now each an 'Open Water Diver' trained by the Professional Association of Diving Instructors — PADI.

Alan Creighton answered: "Thank God you're still alive, Broc, but what about those tails?"

"We shook them in Singapore. We're in Penang now and haven't seen a sign of anyone. But just to be sure, we've given anyone who might be tailing us a bit of a run-around — paid cash and changed hotels twice. Anyway, what have you found out?"

"I followed your advice, Broc. Tracing all those donations seemed like a dead end until I started looking at banks. It turns out there are four where all the money is going: in New York, Washington, Houston, and L.A. The names on the accounts are all just assumed names, which anybody can register for twenty-five or thirty dollars. The owners could be researched, but assumed names are established at the state level. Somebody would actually have to go to the registry offices."

O'Neill made a guess. "What do you want to bet that even the owners behind the assumed names are also fake?"

"If what's happening is illegal, it's a certainty. But, here's the interesting part, Broc. These accounts are emptied out almost as soon as deposits are made. And all the funds are going to the same place." Broc waited, silent. "An account in the Cayman Islands owned by Lignum Operations. Hundreds of millions of dollars every month."

"Then what?"

"Then we've got a problem. The Cayman Islands is a notorious tax haven. They keep information on customers private."

"But don't we have tax treaties with these Caribbean banks? Aren't owners of accounts reported to the IRS?

"It's my understanding they are. But I phoned a colleague over on the campus, a guy in the law department. Companies that set up accounts in those places can often evade reporting; it depends on how ownership is set up. A tiering of assumed names, limited liability companies, and corporate shells makes it almost impossible to discover owners. The Cayman Islands banks are as tight as Swiss banks."

O'Neill gazed out at the blue of the Strait of Malacca, visible between two other hotels. The sun was low in the western sky. "We've found one owner of Lignum: Joseph Terrence. Have you checked him out?"

"As far as I can see, he's clean. He works for the State Department. Despite what you learned — that he gets to Southeast Asia fairly regularly — there's no record of any trips to the Philippines. In fact, Terrence hasn't been out of Washington in the last five years."

"So we've got some pretty shrewd overseas travel going on. I never would have learned even his name if I hadn't run into this guy in Manila."

"Broc, what exactly did you find in Manila?"

"We saw Teleconic. I've got a map of its location, a roll of photographs, and a sketch of the layout. Also, a map of George Town, the city in Penang where we're staying, and photos of Hai Phong Electronics." O'Neill reached down, pushing aside a novel and a pair of sunglasses, and dug into Christelle's big handbag. He pulled out the cell phone. "We brought my Worldwide phone for comparison. Christelle spotted an identical model in a mobile-phone outlet here. We checked out what the store carried — forty or fifty different computer products. We talked with the owner for an hour or so. Obviously, he's not on the inside, but he filled out the picture. Hai Phong supplies phones locally, ordinary phones we think, nothing with those dirty little chips. But Hai Phong also makes half a dozen different computer modems, several phone answering machines, and three heavy-duty fax machines. Most of these are high-priced, business-quality machines. And most are shipped to the U.S."

O'Neill heard Creighton's low whistle over the phone twelve thousand miles away but as clearly as though he was in the next room. "All these could be connected. Good God, Broc, what do you think the odds are that —?"

"I think Hai Phong Electronics assembles a lot more than Worldwide telephones. It appears like there's a massive network of illegal surveillance developing. Our cell phones are just the tip of the iceberg."

Creighton was silent for a minute, perhaps as stunned as he and Christelle had been when they left the phone distributor this morning. "Okay," Creighton began, "I've talked with Brent Hagan. He's my Vietnam platoon officer. He's checked the records. There are a few CIA officers in Malaysia, but they're all under commercial cover, and all of them are in Kuala Lumpur. After the way you roughed up those guys in Singapore, it's not likely these guys will put any amateur tails on you. And if you keep moving and paying cash, you'll stay out of reach."

"And where would you suggest we keep moving to?"

"Hagan came up with one. I have no idea where it is. Have you ever heard of Tioman Island?"

"Sure have. In fact, Christelle and I changed plans when we came to Penang. We were scheduled to do SCUBA dives there for certification. But we finished them here instead. Four open water dives in the Strait of Malacca."

"Hmm. Must be nice! Well, I suggest you put Tioman back on your list. If you stay in Penang too long, they may catch up. Get out of there within a day or two. And there's someone you need to meet. I've talked to him. He'll be at Tioman Island on Saturday."

Broc stood behind the bar, cut more slices of cheese, poured a jigger of gin over ice in two glasses, and topped them with tonic water. He looked up as Christelle came out of her bedroom to the bar, her bare thighs moving beneath a tiny skirt. *Oh my*— She pulled up a bar stool facing him, picked up the knife, and cut two slices from the lemon, catching his eye as she squeezed them into the drinks.

She was wearing a chestnut brown cowboy hat that set off the rich fall of her auburn hair around her face. Her lips had a moist shine from a touch of lip gloss. A gold necklace followed the V-neckline of her white blouse; the water-green jadestone hung against her skin where the soft swelling of her bosom began. Her tawny doeskin vest wanted to be touched.

"Where are we?" Broc asked, looking at her hat. "Is this Dodge City? What's going on? Where's the rodeo?"

"You like it?" Christelle smiled and pulled the brim of her hat a little lower, seeming as pleased with herself as a cat full of cream. "I went to that Texas store in Singapore."

She sipped her gin and tonic and watched him, her eyes unmoving over the rim of her glass. *My, oh my*— Broc's eyes drifted from her eyes to the gold ring with its matching jadestone, then to the embroidered edge of her vest, then to the glossy cascade of hair over her shoulders. "Does it come with Annie Oakley pistols?"

Christelle stood up. A brass belt buckle with a relief engraving of Colt revolvers showed between the panels of her vest. She walked around the suite.

"Only imaginary ones." She drew her hands from make-believe holsters and pointed her forefingers, shooting at unseen enemies, making little gun sounds through her teeth as she walked toward the window. O'Neill felt the blood pulsing in his neck. The dark brown doeskin of her skirt rode on her hips as she moved, the soft edge swinging against the curve of her behind. She was wearing pale suede boots laced with dark rawhide to her calves.

She turned at the window, elegant in every movement. She had good legs — very fine legs. *Oh, my goodness*— She aimed her imaginary pistols across the room and fired away at the lamps and vases, enough to empty both guns. "What a rush that was in Allentown," she crowed, walking back to the bar, "firing off a whole magazine from that 45 — as though you had just one minute to live and you had to empty the gun or you would die."

Her doeskin vest and skirt were sensuous. Her earrings caught the color of her eyes. He wanted to reach out and touch her hair.

Christelle held his eyes as she walked around the bar and stood beside him, gently lifting his drink from his hand and setting it on the counter. She held his gaze for a few seconds, then moved closer until her forehead touched his chest. He felt the softness of her hair against his neck. Blood hammered in his temples.

He heard the soft sound as she whispered. "I think... Broc, I think this is an emergency situation... and I think... we have to fix it... real fast."

Things fell to the floor like windblown leaves — hat, boots, vest, his shirt, her skirt, his shorts, her blouse — everything but her earrings with their jade-green stones. She rushed onto the bed and fell back on the pillows, his hands in her hair, gasping as he rushed into her. Her softness drew him in, setting off fires, and they were rushing — like runners pounding together down a racetrack.

Their bodies ran out of control, consumed with the gathering storm. He caught and covered her mouth with his, his breath taken away as she held him — pulling him into her life and being, her legs winding round him, their bodies locked in a trembling rhythm like waves crashing somewhere on a beach.

Chapter Thirty-three

They lay gasping for breath. O'Neill felt as though he had come through a maelstrom, like taking a kayak through some impossible roaring rapids on a western river. Still trembling, she gripped him, her soft breasts heaving against his chest. For several long minutes they clung to each other, until their breath came back, and Christelle crowded even more tightly against him, her hair spilling onto his chest. He held her to him as though he was holding his own heartbeat, lost in her warmth and her lips against his neck.

It was a long time before they moved. Christelle slowly sat up on the edge of the bed holding his hand, the fingers of both of her hands twined through his. Her misted eyes moved over his face.

"I guess we broke some sort of record," he said. "A one-minute mile."

She rolled back onto the bed and covered his body with hers, flooding his face with her kisses. After a minute she pushed herself up and met his eyes. "I'm an impossible romantic. There's only ever one first time. The only way to do it is a way you'll never forget." She rolled off onto the bed and sat up again.

She was right: he would never forget.

"I guess I took a chance." She almost apologized. "Maybe it was too soon."

O'Neill smiled at her. "The time was right. Considering our situation, it couldn't be better. Next week would be too late."

She smiled. He watched her walk to the window and pull the sheer curtains across the setting sun. Her hair glowed; she moved like a nymph out of a dream, a princess from a children's book. She went to the kitchen. He could hear her gathering things from the refrigerator. She came back with a tray piled with snacks and their half-finished drinks.

"What about that *satay* down on Jalan Penang?" he wondered.

"It's moved down to Number Two on the priority list," she said, setting down the tray. Her eyes moved over his face, from his chin to his hair, then back and forth between his eyes. "We've got more important ways to spend our time tonight."

There were grapes on the tray, cheese and crackers, dill pickles, peanut cookies, chocolate bars, two containers of lemon yogurt, and apples rolling off onto the bed.

"You've got funny tastes," he said, scanning the feast.

Her cheeks spread in a big grin. She picked up a paring knife and started to peel an apple.

Unable to resist, he leaned over and kissed her breasts, one nipple and then the other.

"Whoo-oo!" She shivered. "You'll make them stand right up on end!"

"It's a good way to get even."

She leaned forward and kissed him on the lips, a long lingering kiss with plenty of feeling, ratcheting his pulse up a few beats. Then she sat back. "You've got all night to get even. But if we don't fuel up beforehand, we'll die of exhaustion before morning." She handed him a big chunk of apple and took one for herself.

They sat propped against the pillows, one lamp on in the gathering darkness, her head on his shoulder, finishing their gin and tonics. O'Neill set his glass down on the night table and pulled her to him, holding her face against the palm of his hand. The curves of her long legs were all softness, molding themselves to his. He ran his fingers through her hair, sensing the delicate aroma of her perfume, feeling her, absorbing her, tasting the fine softness of her forehead against his lips, not believing he could have done without her like this for a month.

"What did Alan say?"

"He's changed our plans. We're going to Tioman Island after all."

Christelle drew back and gazed into his eyes, her eyes wide with surprise and excitement. "What's at Tioman?"

"There's nothing at Tioman; that's the point. Creighton says we need to keep ahead of the bad guys. He says there aren't any bad guys there. Just people who want to do nothing."

Christelle leaned her head on his shoulder again. "I read about it. The Chinese used to stop there, hundreds of years ago. It was on their trade routes. They've found all these treasures — whole bunches of vases and pottery. And then there used to be pirate hideouts. And now there is only one hotel, and these little villages down the coast. Can you imagine? Staying on a little island like that, all surrounded by a tropical sea, with palm trees and banana plants, and nothing to do all day but fish and walk on the sand. Maybe we could just move there."

"What about your dissertation? I doubt that Tioman Island has a library."

Christelle sat up. "And you know what else? There's this little pool in the rocks, way on the other side of the island. Remember that movie, *South Pacific*? They filmed some of it there. Remember the pool where all those lovely Polynesian girls went bathing? They filmed it on Tioman Island."

"So maybe we'll take a lovely American girl there so she can bathe in the same pool and forget about the dissertation."

Christelle pushed herself back against Broc's chest. "It sounds so romantic. And we can go diving there, too. The book says there's lots of coral. And I can wear my new bathing suit."

"What new bathing suit?"

"I bought a bathing suit in Singapore. Actually two."

"Why didn't you wear one yesterday, and Sunday? We did four dives."

"One is sheer, see through. The other is a bikini, sort of... a little skimpy."

"So you bought them but haven't worn them?"

"I tried them on yesterday."

"Do you think you got your money's worth?"

"A girl buys a lot of things she doesn't get to wear much. Take all my nice cowgirl things — they weren't on for five minutes! But I think I got my money's worth."

282

"That was way too long. I wouldn't give them two minutes next time."

They stayed in their suite at the Oriental Hotel until noon Wednesday, venturing out in the afternoon to see the Butterfly Farm and the Penang Bird Park, then spending the last hours before sunset roaming the shore near Batu Feringhi, where a row of world-class hotels lined the white-sand beaches on the Strait of Malacca. They watched the fiery sunset from the beachside bar of the Casuarina Hotel, then caught a taxi to George Town for an evening of wandering on Jalan Penang and a feast of chicken *satay* with peanut sauce, an Indian salad with bean sprouts called *pasembor*, shredded cucumber and prawns, and *roti canai*, a wheat-flour bread made with milk and eggs.

Thursday morning, they caught a taxi to the Penang airport and boarded an MAS flight to Kuala Lumpur, forty minutes down the coast. The plane, a modern American-made model, glided easily over vast palm oil and rubber plantations, then circled past the stunning glass towers of Kuala Lumpur, and headed toward a landing at Subang International Airport at Petaling Jaya.

"It sure is a world class city," Christelle affirmed. "I had no idea how beautiful these Asian cities are."

"Apparently, there are plans for things even more spectacular, buildings taller than anything else in the world."

"The States used to have all the highest buildings," she said. The Empire State Building, Sears Tower. What's happening to us?"

"I don't think anything is happening to us. It's not an interesting game. They're getting too high. Safety is an issue. Remember that bomb that went off in the parking garage a few years ago?"

"In the basement of the World Trade Center?"

"Think what would have happened if it had been better placed, or maybe bigger. It was good that the building stood the shock. Big buildings in Kuala Lumpur or Mumbai or Tokyo bring instant status. But in the States, they are targets, too hard to protect. We're better off letting other cities outdo us with their skyscrapers."

At the airport, Christelle bought a book of Malaysian hawker recipes and a paperback, a collection of Somerset Maugham stories set in old-time British Malaya, and they had a fruit salad in the airport cafeteria. Ninety minutes later, they boarded a plane for the flight west across Peninsular Malaysia — a two-prop aircraft that whined as it carried its twenty passengers to 10,000 feet, then bumped and tossed through the constant winds over the green jungled mountains, a vast rain forest. Christelle gazed at the hills. Her travel book said the jungles had remained unchanged for one hundred twenty-five million years.

"There are elephants down there," she motioned, staring out the window, "and tigers and big pythons. And it says here"— she pointed to a picture of black-skinned natives with curly black hair, all clad in breech cloths — "there are people in these mountains who still live off the land and hunt with blowguns and poisoned darts."

"We're in enough trouble dodging bullets," Broc reminded her.

"It says they're very friendly. They're called… let's see, *Orang asli*, which means 'original people'."

They looked at the pictures together until the plane dropped unexpectedly, giving their breakfasts a bounce. For a few minutes, the plane seemed to follow the course of a huge muddy waterway winding through unbroken jungle — the Pahang River, according to their map — and then they were crossing a beach that stretched off to the north and south as far as they could see. Twenty minutes later the plane broke through a bank of clouds, and they were staring at an unbelievably beautiful island with white sand beaches and mounded emerald hills.

Their plane headed toward a hill that rose hundreds of feet above the ocean, then banked sharply to the right just above the coconut palms.

"Broc, where's the airport?"

The plane dropped between the trees. A minute later it touched down on a runway, a two-lane dirt road through the palms. As they rolled to a stop a hundred feet short of the jungle, they looked at each other, not quite believing what had just happened. The 'airport' was a single building behind a wire gate the size of a three-room house. This was, Broc thought, an island at the end of the world.

Six Malay boys loaded the luggage onto carts, which disappeared over a hilly red-clay road, while the passengers boarded sampans for the ride to the hotel. Half an hour later, they had checked into the Tioman Island Resort, clusters of dark brown wooden, steep-roofed cabins linked by roofed decks stretching off among the trees.

They fell onto the cool bed together; they held each other for a long time, enjoying the breezes sweeping off the ocean through the open windows. Then they got up and put on bathing suits.

"I see what you mean about the bikini." Broc eyed her across the bed. Christelle put her hands on her hips and pulled back the corners of her mouth, waiting for an explanation. "I can't tell which is better — what it hides, which is not much, or what it reveals, which is a whole lot. But it sure does make you look good in all the right places."

"Watch this," she demonstrated, wrapping the sash around her hips, tying a knot at her waist, and turning around in a slow circle.

"There is no doubt about it," Broc ventured, walking around the bed and smoothing out a long tail of her hair. "It's another one of those things designed to come off almost as soon as you put it on."

She moved against him, tilting back her head and inviting him to kiss her. They stood together for another minute, and then he felt her fingers pushing through the hair on his chest, stroking his skin.

"You're pretty nice yourself," she intimated, rubbing her palms down his back and hooking her thumbs under the elastic waistband of his bathing suit. "There's lots more than girls' bikinis designed to come off almost as soon as you put them on."

They walked along the sand hand in hand, staring out at the blue-green water of the South China Sea, watching the wheeling seabirds and listening to the cries of kingfishers in the trees. Broc felt a wonderful calm descending.

"What would you like to do tomorrow?" Christelle asked.

Broc pointed at the high green mound a hundred yards off the beach. "The map in the lobby calls it Renggis Island. I heard someone say it's surrounded by coral. Let's rent tanks and do our first dive." Christelle smiled her approval. "And then let's hire a boat to take us 'round the island. That pool where they filmed the girls in *South Pacific* is near a place called Juara Village. There's a trail across the island, but it's a four-

285

mile hike each way, and it goes over this big hill. I think I'd sooner go around by boat."

They ate at a little table in the open-air restaurant, just above the beach. Christelle felt warm all over, rosy from less than an hour on the sand under the afternoon sun. Waiting for their meal to come, they sipped white wine. She gazed at the fiery red ball dropping toward the horizon, then at Broc. He was watching her. She reached out and he held her hand, and she felt good, very good, inside. She admired his dark eyes and hair, happy to be near him, scarcely believing they were in this place, and wanting nothing more than always to be near him.

They ate by candlelight while watching the glow of the sun disappearing over the horizon and the darkness settling over the sea until there was nothing beyond the beach but the distant stars. A little later, lights lit up the palm trees and the sound of music filled the air.

They left two hours after sunset, ambling across the dark sand to the wooden steps, following the dim-lit deck away from the lights on the beach. Their cabin was cool. When they switched out the lights, they could see a patch of stars through the trees and, to the west, the white light of the rising moon.

They lay in the darkness, his body covering hers. She held his head to her cheek, feeling his lips following the edge of her hair, luxuriating in his warm presence, feeling his hands moving over her skin.

"Broc," she confessed between sighs, "I know this... this girl. I think she's... I think she has... something wrong with her—"

He lay still for a few seconds.

"She... she has... a crush on her teacher."

He kissed her. "I know her," he paused. "There's nothing wrong with her. It's him. It's her teacher. He's fallen hopelessly in love with her."

Then everything broke up inside, leaving her helpless, in pieces, unable to do anything but hold him as her heart ran out of control.

Chapter Thirty-four

O'Neill spent over an hour trying to arrange for a boat to take them SCUBA diving the next morning. But Sunday was the busiest day at the resort; all the dive boats had been pre-booked by tourists before they landed at Tioman. However, the tour guide managed to make special arrangements for Monday. A local Malay boy would bring his fishing boat from the village just down the coast at 9 a.m. In the meantime, they might have to be content with snorkeling around Renggis Island.

O'Neill walked out to the beach carrying icy cans of Coke wrapped in newspaper. Christelle sat reading her paperback in the shade of a palm tree. She was wearing her green-and-yellow bikini and staying out of the glare of the tropical sun. He sat on the wooden chaise lounge, snapped open a Coke, and handed it to her.

Christelle smiled her thanks and held up her book. "This is the neatest story, Broc, by Somerset Maugham. It's called "The Book Bag." It starts out where we were in Penang. Apparently, Maugham traveled all through Borneo and Malaysia back in the twenties when they were still British colonies. Anyway, he carried this big bag full of all kinds of books — old classics, mysteries, poetry, anything."

"Books are heavy things to cart around on vacation. Especially hardbacks."

"Listen to what he carried:

There were books that you had always wanted to read, but in the hurry of life at home had never found time to. There were books to read at sea... books for bad weather... books chosen solely for their length, which you took with you when... you had to travel light...

"I like that. Somerset Maugham had the right idea—"

"Are you imitating him?" Broc asked, peeking in the top of Christelle's handbag. He pulled out a handful of novels. "You're well on your way to your own library; here—"

"And I had the idea before I read this story. Anyway, it may look like a library, but it's not all books. Your cell phone's still underneath."

"You don't have time for stories. You should be reading for your dissertation."

Christelle furrowed her forehead at him. "What a slave driver! Anyway, I have been reading for my dissertation." She pulled the *International Tribune* from under her behind and thumbed through. "This is a report on a press conference held by a bunch of senators last week in Washington."

"Let me remind you," O'Neill interrupted, "that your dissertation is on 'double-agenda' politics. The first rule is you must stick to the topic."

"Well listen to this." She ran her finger down the news column. "Here it is: It's a quote from Senator Hallenburg":

It is of little concern to the Republican Party whether the old Democratic social programs remain in place a while longer, as they seem to be this season. Let the Democrats enjoy the policies that have been their banner and strength for the past sixty years.

"What do you think that means, Broc?"

"He's probably mumbling to his nearest aide, 'If we could just get our back-bench Republicans off their butts and agree on something, we could get rid of all this stupid waste'."

"Maybe, and that's the point, but he's saying something else, too."

"How do you read it?"

"It's a 'double-agenda' message. On the face of it, he's sounding benevolent, praising the opposition. But his hidden message is, 'Look, people, the Democrats are still wasting money. Throw your weight with the GOP. We know how to save billions of dollars in tax money.' It's rhetoric for the next election, which is only three months away!"

"Most of what we've been hearing is election rhetoric," Broc added. He was impressed at how carefully she was sorting the news.

She stretched out her long legs, decidedly elegant in the dappled sunlight. "See! I am reading for my dissertation, and I'll bet there isn't another American girl sitting on an island in the tropics doing anything more than reading beach books." Christelle laid her head back and adjusted her sunglasses as though she had said the last word on the topic.

Double-agenda politics— She was right, except that policies and programs in Washington were confused and confusing. There were layers under layers; you couldn't be sure what was mask and what was real. But for a moment he didn't care.

"I admit," Christelle promised, "I'll have to start reading books and articles in *Congressional Quarterly* as soon as I get back. But this is vacation, so I'm confining myself to a file of newspaper clippings."

O'Neill had noticed holes in the editorial page of the papers ever since they arrived in Singapore. "I think you're on the right track." Pausing and looking at her, he knew her eyes were attentive behind the sunglasses. "But there's one problem with this dissertation," he began with as straight a face as he could. "I may have to recuse myself as third reader."

Her forehead knotted. "Why is that?"

"It's all a matter of impartiality. In order to authenticate the validity of the research, the readers of a dissertation must be mentally, intellectually, ethically, morally, and spiritually free of encumbrances, especially those that might involve a special attachment to the topic, evidence, methodology, argument, procedures, or conclusion—"

"You forgot emotional attachment to the student."

O'Neill squeezed his lips together and gazed out to sea. He saw a dot on the horizon to the south, a darker blue than the seawater, with a white haze behind it. "I was about to mention that. It says in the dissertation advisor's rule book that the readers of a dissertation should never form, have, contemplate, imagine, or dream of any special attachment to the student."

"There isn't any dissertation advisor's rule book."

She was right on that, too. "It's a big problem," he feigned worry. "It's going to be difficult to say anything if you turn in stuff that is really stupid. I guess the only safe thing would be to get another reader—"

"I have another idea, Professor Doctoral Dissertation Third Reader. I'll do my best not to turn in any stupid stuff. You say nothing if I do. And we'll just keep working on all the other stuff." She leaned forward and planted a long, wet kiss on his lips.

"What other stuff?"

"The good stuff. The interesting stuff. Emotional attachment to the student."

The huge watercraft, an immense blue hovercraft at least forty feet wide and a hundred long, arrived at the resort from the south. The sea spray rose around it like morning mist. The cabin was lined with dozens of round windows. Gigantic white letters identified it as the *Singapore Seabird*. They watched it turn out beyond Renggis Island, the entire hull riding clear of the waves, its forward thrust provided by huge twin propellers. The craft slowed, edging over the last two hundred yards of shallow water to the concrete dock. The propellers whined down, and the fiberglass craft settled into the water.

Within seconds there was a flurry of activity on board, and then a long line of tourists began to disembark on a runway that had dropped to the dock. A few minutes later, little Malay village boys ran onto the craft and were soon hauling suitcases to the shore. Other boys arrived with carts; they went to work loading luggage while Singaporean tourists threaded their way along the beach toward the hotel while gazing around at the beach and the sea and the trees. They all seemed to be wearing white clothes and sunhats, and they all seemed a little overweight, the way one got, Broc supposed, when one was old enough and wealthy enough to vacation in places like this. They had brought altogether too much luggage.

"I guess that's him," O'Neill motioned as an authoritative figure appeared on deck. Christelle shoved her newspaper in her book bag as they walked toward the dock. They met him at the runway — a rugged American of about fifty-five — tanned, muscular, fit, with a short black beard and blue eyes the color of the ocean.

He surveyed them a minute. "You must be Broc O'Neill and Christelle Washington. Welcome aboard the *Singapore Seabird*. I'm the Captain, Wallace Matthews — Wally, if you please."

He led them across the deck to the cabin and then into the lounge, which was decorated in white and royal blue. They sat, cooled by the breezes blowing off the South China Sea. Wally Matthews wore immaculately creased white trousers, a white jacket trimmed in blue, and a black and gold sea captain's hat.

"So, you're a friend of Alan Creighton!" Matthews gazed at O'Neill. "He was one of the explosives men in my platoon. If you could have seen him crawling through those bloody Mekong swamps in Nam, you would never have guessed that he would become a professor of history! Tell me, what kind of a man is he today?"

"He's probably the foremost historian of American high-tech weaponry. I've read his books, his articles. He's the best in his field."

"And Brently Hagan, our Officer-in-Charge? Creighton tells me he's in the CIA!" Matthews shook his head in wonderment. "I was out of contact for years; I'm in contact with only Creighton and one other guy. I've talked with Alan three times this week, in fact, for a whole hour this morning before we left Singapore."

Someone walked in, a slim Malay woman in a batik dress. She was carrying a tray with drinks and a plate of sandwiches. "I'd like you to meet Rozita, my wife," Matthews said.

O'Neill stood, and shook the hand that was offered. She leveled a winning smile toward Christelle as they exchanged greetings. Rozita had broad cheeks and coppery skin; her black hair fell in what looked like the latest American style of elegant taste. Two young men dressed in casual shirts and white shorts appeared behind her.

"And my sons, Kareem and Samir."

They greeted him in perfect English. One of them turned to his mother and spoke in rapid Malay. She answered and then excused herself in English, nodding to Broc and Christelle in turn. The boys stood like military men at ease, young men in their twenties with a blend of Rozita's coppery coloring and Wallace's powerful Caucasian jaw and cheekbones. They bowed and left when he signaled with a nod, revealing a remarkable respect and honor for their father.

"Twins," he confirmed. "Classes are not in session at the moment. Next month they'll be seniors at university in Singapore."

"The National University? It's an impressive institution,"

Matthews nodded. "I heard from Creighton… that you had a little escapade on the campus. Those rotten bloody CIA bastards! Of course, there are good ones, like Hagan, and then there are the rotten ones. They've wreaked havoc through these parts, all the way back to their covert actions in Laos in the sixties, and Vietnam. I would sure like to see Langley cleaned out."

"You seem to have a lot of interest in the U.S.," Broc observed. "How often do you go back?"

Matthews leaned forward and picked up one of the drinks. O'Neill and Christelle took theirs and sipped. *Seven-Up.* "I'm one of the lost ones, Broc. I've never been back. When your family betrays you, when your fiancée shacks up for six years while you're fighting a war, you don't want ever to see them again." He sat back in his chair. "I've been out here ever since. Rozita came at the right time. She… she saved my life. We've built a life together. I've worked hard, the American way, and now I own this boat. We make trips from Singapore out to the islands: Bangka to the south, but mostly around the Malaysian coast. Tioman, Pangkor, sometimes as far up as Langkawi. It's good work; we lead a good life. Two, sometimes three trips a week, except this week. We're on vacation."

"You're staying?"

Matthews nodded. "For ten days. This batch of tourists is prepared to stay that long. So it's free time for us till we load them all up and return." He pointed out the window toward the rear of the hovercraft. A white fiberglass powerboat with an in-hull cabin rested on a wooden cradle on the rear deck; the numbering on the side told O'Neill it was 24.5 feet in length.

"We'll launch tomorrow morning, boat around to the other side of the island, and drop anchor. We're all snorkelers, divers. My sons like to camp and hike. There's a freshwater stream, good fishing, wild fruit, sand beaches. If you haven't already discovered it, this place is a paradise on Earth."

Matthews chose a sandwich and offered the plate to Christelle.

"What did Creighton have to say this morning — for a whole hour?"

"He's filled me in on everything, Broc. I haven't been in the States since we did our SEAL training in the sixties, but I've kept up, read every news magazine, followed elections, enough to see the trends. Since Nixon and Watergate, it's been one long lousy slide downhill. The stupidity is appalling — Ford pardoning Nixon, Carter's abortive Tehran rescue, people electing a Hollywood actor, Bush ending Desert Storm before taking out Saddam Hussein. And then there are the really stupid ones who spoil a promising political career — Ted Kennedy and Chappaquiddick, and Gary Hart was a frontrunner candidate until his dalliance with Donna Rice. As far as I can see, the last couple of decades have been just one long story of stupidity. With every election, you build your hopes, and then, within months, it starts all over. It affects everything: Congress, the Administration, both parties."

"So you wouldn't give Reagan credit for bringing down the Soviet Union?"

"Partly... maybe... some, but it was going downhill for years. Somehow, the U.S. has managed to have both guns and butter. America prospers on war, but the U.S.S.R. deprived its people of butter trying to keep up with American guns."

Broc nodded, noting how astutely Matthews had sorted and filtered twenty years of news from the other side of the world. *Stupidity*— An interesting summary, too, Broc thought. Wally saw stupidity where he saw corruption. Interesting, too, that Wally allotted stupidity about equally to Democrats and Republicans.

"Anyway, we clearly have another round of stupidity to deal with." Matthews reached for a briefcase, pulled out a sheaf of paper, and continued talking. "I took notes. Creighton outlined some things to pass on." He leaned forward and, gazing at his ballpoint scrawls, put the papers on the coffee table. "First of all, it's wonderful when you get a name. Creighton says you identified a guy called Joseph Terrence. Alan and Brent cooked up a ruse. They used Hagan's lines in the CIA and got a court order. They put a tap on Terrence's phone a couple of days ago. Then they decided to pull up his phone records for the last six months. As soon as they thought of that, they thought of someone else, some guy called James Spiker, a colonel. Have you heard of him?"

"He was assassinated by his fellow thugs."

"Jesus! Well, Hagan worked out the court order to have Spiker's phone records pulled, too. It will take a few days, but Creighton is working full time on this. They should start getting results pretty soon." Matthews looked up. "I don't understand all the details yet. How does it sound to you?"

O'Neill could feel the adrenaline pumping. Things were beginning to move. His hands curled slowly into fists; his eyes connected with Matthews'. "I think I'm beginning to understand you guys," Broc empathized. "Creighton told me about the way he used to feel when the team had strung a line of explosives and made a getaway. How it felt as you waited for a whole Viet Cong stronghold to blow sky high. I think that's how I feel."

Matthews gazed at Broc, his blue eyes steady. "Creighton told me… he said you were one of us, just born too late for Nam. He said you would have done well there. That's the way it was. We worked best when the odds of survival were at their worst. And we always came through. Everyone in our platoon came through."

"Alan had a reunion two or three years ago. He said you were the only one who didn't come."

"I just wasn't ready. Sure, we were good; we did our job; we never failed. But the whole thing — the stupidity of the Vietnam War — eats away at me, and I didn't want to lay that on the rest of the platoon. What does doing well in a war mean if the whole thing was a mistake? That's how I've felt all these years."

"They've got a name for it now — post-traumatic stress."

"Yes, I've heard. But it's more. It's more than emotional. It's cognitive. It's a disruption of your entire life, a flattening of moral standards, an assault on reason."

"If you had come, you would have discovered something about the guys in your platoon: Hagan, Creighton, the rest. They've all asked the same thing. We've all asked the same thing, even people like me who were just kids when it was going on. Vietnam was a big black hole in our history. Everything fell in. All kinds of people fell in; some of them have never climbed out."

Matthews nodded. "There was another guy in our platoon," Matthews mused, "that Creighton never found. But he and I got in touch just a few weeks ago. Willy Rand: he's in Hawaii. He says one day he's going to come out here and see Southeast Asia again, maybe even go back to visit Nam. He's the same way: wondering what it was all about, wondering whether anything he did in four years of duty made any difference."

They sat for a few minutes, silently, struggling with a past that O'Neill could not contemplate but Wally Matthews had lived through. Finally, Christelle spoke. "Did Alan have anything else to say? Did he have any ideas where we could go next?"

"He didn't know," Matthews said. "All he said was that he thought you were in danger wherever you went. And it isn't going to let up. I think you know that. But, for the moment, I think you might be in the best place right here. The end of the world, but it's the best end. Hell — half the world would die to come here if they could see it. I hope *National Geographic* never does a documentary on this place."

Broc gazed off through the windows at the white sand beaches, the palm trees waving in the wind, the rising hills. Off to the northwest he could see Tulai Island, where they were going to dive next week. In the sky he watched an image like a distant bird that soon took shape as an airplane.

Matthews followed his gaze. "See that. A Cessna. Guys learn to fly in those, the Cessna 152, little put-puts that can barely fly 120 with a tailwind. That one is the Cessna 172, a four-seater, the bottom-line luxury plane of the moderately rich. I haven't been on a plane since the war. They're fast and convenient, but I prefer a boat."

They watched the tiny aircraft circle slowly toward the hidden runway a half mile up the coast, and then it disappeared among the palm trees.

"Here's what I think," Matthews theorized, pulling his focus back from the sky. "You've found out two names and now their phone records are being pulled. That's the thin edge of the wedge. Those records will spit out more names. If you're lucky, most of the membership will be known in a couple of weeks. That will open all kinds of doors."

"After the past month, I hope Alan and especially Brent can take over the footwork, at least for a while. Brent has got research resources Alan and I just don't have with laptops." Broc glanced at Christelle. "And we've had altogether too many near-death experiences."

"Well, I think you should just park here for a while. Out here you're in paradise." Matthews looked at Christelle, and Broc could see the admiration in his eyes. "You've got everything a man could possibly want, right here. I wouldn't throw it all away. My stateside platoon buddies can work this out. They've benefitted from what you've discovered. You've got your life to protect. Let them take over."

O'Neill looked at Matthews for a long minute, thinking, measuring what the man had said. *I prefer a boat*— O'Neill looked around. His Malay wife was standing at the rail and gazing at the hills. *You've got your life to protect*— O'Neill felt the pull, the lure of the place, the possibility of escape. He glanced at Christelle, who sat watching him, knowing that whatever he decided, she would be with him. He stared toward the beach at Tioman Island for another long moment before he spoke.

"There are losses," O'Neill went on, "travesties, violations so great, that you cannot let them go. You've got to go after them; you've got to run them to the ground. There's no other way. Somehow, you've got to make something decent come out of the losses. You've got to do it, even if you know you may not survive."

He looked again at Christelle. She understood.

Matthews looked him in the eyes, and Broc knew that he, too, understood.

After a minute, Matthews spoke: "Creighton said you had something to show me."

O'Neill glanced toward Christelle again, and she reached for her handbag, digging out paperback books, her comb and brush. Finally, she brought out sheets of folded paper and handed them to Broc.

Matthews sat forward and watched as O'Neill flattened them on the table: Christelle's sketch of the Teleconic factory in the Philippines and another of Hai Phong Electronics in Penang.

Chapter Thirty-five

Christelle and O'Neill made three trips into the water, dragging their SCUBA gear from the beach and throwing it into the wooden fishing boat. Then they climbed aboard and sat on a pile of ropes and lifejackets in the shade of the cabin while their Malay boatman backed away from shore. The deck was littered with fishing gear, as well as their goggles, fins, air tanks, weight belts, regulators, even diving knives in vinyl sheaths. At the equipment rental desk Christelle had picked out a Buoyancy Control Device, an inflatable air vest known as a BCD, with green trim to match her bathing suit. O'Neill had accepted plain black.

Other boats were launching: fifty-foot commercial dive boats with a dozen tourists aboard, which motored away from shore toward Tulai Island, five miles off the northern tip of Tioman. As their slower boat put-putted away from shore, O'Neill gazed at the huge *Singapore Seabird* at the dock. Wally Matthews and his beautiful Rozita had stayed on board the hovercraft an extra day, entertaining Broc and Christelle through the long hot Sunday afternoon, telling stories of Vietnam and the exploits of their platoon of Navy SEALs. There was no mention of Darcy, but he knew that Creighton had filled him in. There was nothing he could say, nothing O'Neill would have wanted him to say. A military man was not one to pour on sympathy, but he understood revenge, and he understood that Christelle Washington was like his Rozita: the woman who stood between Broc O'Neill and the sinkhole of loss and despair.

They were beautiful people, and by the end of the day O'Neill had no doubt that Matthews' decision to stay in Asia was the best thing that could have happened in his once-shattered life. He understood Alan Creighton better, too, the man he had met years later on the Salmon River, realizing now that his long years of silence on his years in Vietnam masked an emptiness that Creighton preferred to leave behind. It was the same with all of them, a generation of men who had fought in Vietnam but felt they had accomplished nothing.

O'Neill watched the *Singapore Seabird* half a mile away. Matthews and his sons had hoisted their speedboat over the stern; Rozita was lowering coolers and duffle bags. When everything was aboard, she climbed over the rail and dropped to the speedboat deck. She must be in her late forties, but she was as trim and athletic as a woman twenty years younger. Within seconds they had the boat untied, started up the motor, and headed away from shore, outdistancing everything else in the water. They watched it until it was little more than a speck heading south along the Tioman coast to a quiet beach and camping spot on the other side of the island. What a place for a vacation!

Momentarily, O'Neill wondered whether his choice was right: pursuit and revenge. There was another world out here, a world Wally Matthews had found and chosen away from everything O'Neill despised about America: the endless corruption that had infected nearly every federal administration of the past three decades. Matthews seemed to accept it a little better by calling it stupidity. It was a temptation to stay, simply to disappear and make for himself, and now Christelle, a new life somewhere in this vast tropical paradise. A temptation, yes, but he had to reject it.

Pulau Tulai was an uninhabited island of bays and rocky shores perhaps two miles long, ringed by coral reefs. By the time they got there, several other dive boats were in place. There were a few snorkelers already near the beach, but most of the boats were servicing divers on the coral reefs two or three hundred yards offshore. He gazed at a party of recent arrivals from Singapore in the nearest boat: overweight, out of shape, unable to get their tanks on without help. They would make a big splash getting in and would need to be hauled out at the end of their dives. These Malay boys running the boats must get fed up with overweight tourists needing help.

O'Neill and Christelle worked as efficiently as they could for new divers, putting on equipment, adjusting each other's weight belts, then checking their regulators. They had already done this four times — four open-water dives in the Strait of Malacca completed requirements for their open-water certification. But the South China Sea was much clearer.

Viewing it over the side of the boat brought a surprise. Shells were visible on the sunlit bottom twenty feet below.

Air pressure in their tanks sat at 3,000 pounds per square inch, enough for more than an hour underwater. The Malay boatmen dropped anchor off a rocky promontory; a minute later, Broc and Christelle, tumbled backward off the side of the boat and entered the magical world under the sea. The water was comfortable, like a mildly heated swimming pool.

They were anchored on the edge of a coral bank that ran out from the shore and then dropped off to the bottom, sixty feet below, about the official limit of their PADI certification. The coral, waving leaves and fronds in a dozen colors, was alive with darting fish. Christelle drifted down, one hand on the anchor rope, her eyes on her depth gauge, and Broc matched her descent, until they were thirty feet below the surface, and then they began a slow exploration, floating over great slabs of white and green coral, drifting through an unbelievable world of color, silent except for the sound of air as they breathed. Bubbles rose slowly to the surface.

They stayed within sight of the anchor rope for a time, until they had their bearings and a sense of how the embankment ran, and then they swam slowly along at a depth of thirty-five feet, following the line where coral ended and the sandy bottom began. The sun lit up the water, casting the shadows of waves at the surface on the golden sand. Swarms of tiny fish drifted by, thousands of them in schools, all moving the same direction, then instantly changing course. O'Neill could see by the way Christelle drifted and watched it all that she, too, was entranced.

There were other divers. They came into view fifty or sixty feet away in pairs, following their own silent path of exploration. The bottom sloped down. It was strewn with boulders and things that had once fallen from boats: an occasional bottle all covered in waving green seaweed, or a loose piece of cable where a tangled anchor had been cut loose. They drifted down, gliding over the sunlit sand, poking among the sea bottom debris, picking up shells.

O'Neill watched his pressure. At 1500 pounds they turned and headed back, swimming silently, enjoying the unbelievable peace of the depths. Above, the dappled surface of the water shone like crystal lit by the late-morning sun. They had been down fifty-five minutes when they saw the anchor rope. Slowly, lifted by tiny blasts of air into their vests, they drifted upward through the crystalline water, surrounded by thousands of fish, following the anchor rope toward the black shadow of the boat above. Broc checked his remaining air; his pressure sat at 250 pounds per square inch, Christelle's at 400.

"That was unbelievable!" she shouted as soon as she had her mask off.

The Malay boatmen hauled their tanks aboard, and they climbed out into the sun.

It was an incommunicable beauty, an experience beyond words to describe. O'Neill understood how divers could go back again and again, how they never tired of the silence and the coral and the teeming sea life.

Christelle got out the vinyl sack packed by the resort, a special 'dive lunch' of sandwiches, with an orange drink and cookies. They sat in deck chairs and gazed at the beach of Tulai Island. It was all wild and untouched: wide sand beaches, then a wall of green, then jungled hills. It was a new world, Broc thought, a world before any of the tangles people had added; it was still simple and pure. It had the aura of a place where one might want to escape.

After eating, they entered the dive in their log books, calculated the residual nitrogen in their blood, and then stretched out and snoozed in the shade. After a while, Christelle pulled out a paperback, and O'Neill gazed at the seabirds circling in the sky.

They waited the required two and a half hours before their next dive. The boatman hauled up the anchor and motored slowly along the edge of coral, accustomed to the routine. There were tourist dive boats anchored every two or three hundred yards. Some were leaving, others arriving for afternoon dives and, perhaps for a few adventurers, night dives after sunset.

They drifted down, twenty feet from the coral embankment, into a boulder-strewn seascape fifty feet below the surface. The water was a little darker, but still well lit, and the temperature was cooler by perhaps two or three degrees. The crumbling wreck of a fishing boat attracted them; drifting slowly over its deck, they watched the fish darting through crevices and cracks in the rotten hull. Close to the bottom, Broc reached out and touched Christelle's arm, pointing. A piece of what looked like rock on the bottom had moved. A lionfish, one of the deadliest of undersea creatures, with a bite so painful it could send a diver into uncontrollable convulsions and almost immediate death. Broc signaled another couple, probably honeymooners, and pointed at the lionfish, warning them of the danger.

Shadows passed overhead. They hung motionless, watching the steel-gray bodies of barracuda gliding by like torpedoes. They drifted into a maze of boulders, snaking through the passageways, swimming different ways around obstacles, then meeting on the other side. A patch of sand opened up; a fishing net lay on the bottom, one corner tangled on a rock. A few feet away, an anchor rested on the bottom, the thin white line rising vertically to the surface. A cloud of sunfish surrounded him; they darted away when he waved his arms. He turned to find Christelle.

He swam back toward the boulders. Christelle — where was she?

Somewhere above, he sensed something. He searched. Above the anchor rope he could see the shadow of their Malay fishing boat, nearby a much larger shadow, maybe a forty-footer. Then he recognized the color of her suit. Christelle was fifty feet up, struggling, two divers holding her by her arms, rising to the surface. O'Neill pushed away from the bottom.

A diver came at him around a boulder and grabbed him by the arm. O'Neill pulled away, amazed at the firmness of the grip. He knocked the hand away just as another diver came into view. Instinctively, he knew he was prey.

He kicked, heading away, then felt a hand grasping his ankle. He turned in the water, and lashed out with his free foot, catching the diver on the shoulder, but the grip did not loosen. He felt a sudden surge of fear. The second diver was following fifteen feet away. Rage took over. Broc pulled his leg in and rolled, and with both hands he ripped off the face mask of the diver. Immediately, his attacker let go, momentarily disabled by seawater in his eyes. Salt water fifty feet down — that would be painful. It would be several seconds before he could get his mask on and clear it of water.

The second diver was on him. O'Neill brought his knee up, catching him on the side of the head, and thrashed away; but the assailant followed. O'Neill turned, ferocious. They were after him; they had taken Christelle. He grabbed at the mask and missed, grabbed and missed again. Then he grabbed the diver's regulator and gave it a heave, yanking it out of his assailant's mouth.

In the seconds of sudden confusion, O'Neill went for his mask again, this time yanking it from his assailant's head. Without clear vision and air, he would be disabled and desperate. O'Neill caught sight of the man's face and a huge scar as he drifted against the anchor rope, struggling to put on his mask

O'Neill turned. The first diver was drifting, bubbles coming out all around his mask as he struggled to recover his vision and tried to expel air. In seconds, he would be on the attack again. O'Neill reached for his knife and struck toward him, slashing out at his regulator, severing the breathing tube. His mouthpiece useless, the diver made one more attack. O'Neill kicked away, and then turned on him, catching him by surprise as he yanked his mask away again, dropping his knife. He caught a flash of bright red hair and sudden desperation.

The other diver was clinging with one hand to the anchor rope but having trouble adjusting his mask, clearly blinded by the salt water. O'Neill darted toward him, grabbed the anchor rope above his head, and looped it around the diver's neck. Confusion gave him his chance; he yanked off the face mask again, this time letting it sink to the bottom.

O'Neill felt the other diver's hand on him again, but he was swimming blindly now. O'Neill jabbed at his eyes. The pain made a flood of bubbles appear from his mouth. He pitched, slowly rotating backward. O'Neill grabbed his fin and tilted him back, noticing again what he had seen minutes before — a rock on the bottom that moved — and drove his attacker toward the bottom. And then he saw what happens when someone is stung by a lionfish. It was a horrifying sight.

O'Neill spotted his knife on the bottom, retrieved it, and headed up. The diver with the scar was gasping, drowning, and struggling with the anchor rope around his neck. O'Neill circled and cut the rope above his head, stuck the knife back in its sheath, and tied a hitch in the rope, then two more, anchoring Scarface permanently to the bottom. Then, inflating his vest, he thrust toward the surface.

He broke surface fifty feet from the boat. Christelle was on the deck of a bigger boat, in the hands of two captors. Her things were being passed from their fishing boat to the larger dive boat. He noticed the pistols come around, and immediately he went down, hearing the strange smack of bullets on the water inches from his head.

Holy blazes! He expelled air and floated down to fifteen feet. He sensed something wrong: his air flow was weak. He checked his pressure gauge: 300 pounds. He could not stay under more than another two or three minutes, five at most. There was nowhere to go, nowhere to hide, no escape that would not end with a bullet in his head.

He expelled more air and headed back down. A minute later he found the bodies. He checked the air on the anchored Scarface: 2700 pounds. Quickly, he undid the air vest, sliding it free of the lifeless arms. Momentarily, it snagged on Scarface's watch; O'Neill yanked it free. He transferred the regulator to his own mouth, undid his own BCD, and struggled into the new one. The air came fresh with full pressure, enough air for forty minutes.

O'Neill noted the watch, an expensive model, and undid the strap. The back was engraved with a name: John L. Senelik. A pouch at Scarface's waist yielded a key to the resort; O'Neill shoved it and the watch into the pocket of his bathing suit. The body of Redhead was lying on the bottom, drifting, thirty feet away. O'Neill swam down and undid the pouch at his waist. Inside, he found a plastic PADI identification card. Robert Troller.

Bodies. Bodies that could be identified.

O'Neill undid the BCD from Redhead and pulled off his diving gear, weight belt and fins, stripping him clean. With the knife, he slashed his midsection open, then his throat. He swam back and removed the anchor rope from Scarface's neck, stripped him of weight belt and fins, and slashed him open.

Blood clouded the water. Sometime in the next few minutes this would be a very dangerous place; O'Neill would prefer to be somewhere else. He looked up; the two boats were still there, dark shadows sixty feet above. Slowly, he ascended toward their smaller boat until he found the dangling anchor rope. He followed it up, keeping in the shadow of the hull, and cut it free six feet under the surface. Then he descended and swam slowly toward the larger boat where Christelle had been dragged aboard.

He came in under the hull, where his bubbles would rise and spread, breaking the surface imperceptibly. The craft was large, at least forty feet long, with a metal structure around and below the propeller to protect it from rocks and coral. He worked quickly, tying one end of the rope to the metalwork with half a dozen hitches, then descended to the bottom end of the rope, forty feet down. He tied a large loop, and then another, fashioning a rappelling harness, and then slipped his legs through and adjusted himself until he was comfortable. And then he settled down to wait.

Consciously, he slowed his breathing, relaxing, sitting motionless. The men in the boat would wait. It would take time, but when his assailants did not surface, they would assume the worst. From the pressure gauge on Christelle's tank, they would know he was out of air. They might assume he had been injured by their bullets. They would wait another quarter hour, perhaps thirty minutes; it was doubtful whether anyone would dive down to investigate, not with two men already in the water. O'Neill checked his watch, astonished to discover that he had been under water for an hour and twenty minutes. The pressure on Scarface's confiscated tank showed 2000 pounds, enough for another thirty minutes.

O'Neill felt his insides go cold. Twenty feet below, he saw a dark shape moving, an immense blunt-nosed beast. Shark! Drawn by the smell of blood. He watched it swim off and circle. It raced in, and he could sense by the sudden murkiness below that it had struck. Frozen, holding his breath, hanging motionless, he waited. Suddenly, he saw it again, and now there were two dark shapes. There was a sudden fierce commotion below, and then he saw one of the shapes tearing toward the surface, the mutilated body of one of his assailants in its huge jaws. He watched it break the surface, almost as though to taunt those who might be watching.

As he tried to imagine the shock on board the boat above, he heard the sound of the motor. The propeller spun to life; the boat was starting to move, and O'Neill felt himself dragged on an angle toward the surface.

Chapter Thirty-six

O'Neill twisted the anchor rope around his forearm, shoved his mask against his face, and flattened out. The boat dragged him in the churning wake of the motor forty feet behind, out of sight five feet below the surface. He felt the speed build up until the pressure of the rope on his arms and legs seemed unbearable. He estimated: five miles, twenty miles an hour. He had to hold on for fifteen minutes.

Christelle... They had Christelle. He had to hang on or they would take Christelle.

He was aching, exhausted, near the breaking point, almost fainting, about to give up when he felt the boat slow. The bottom, a litter of broken coral and rocks, was visible ten feet below. He was safe from laceration as long as the hull of the boat was safe; the local pilots were ever watchful. The speed dropped; the sea bottom was no more than four feet below. O'Neill drew his knife and cut himself loose.

He drifted, watching the trailing anchor rope move away. Submerged, he began to swim, painfully, fighting exhaustion, his legs feeling useless from loss of circulation. His air pressure was 800 pounds, enough for another ten minutes. Gradually, the movement came back to his limbs, and he swam toward shore, feeling the urgency of something he could not contemplate.

Christelle...

Cautiously, he raised his eyes above the water. He was two hundred yards from the beach of the Tioman Island Resort. The boat had landed. Two men had Christelle, still in her bathing suit, carrying her handbag; they were leading her toward the beach. She seemed to be stumbling along, as much from emotional shock as physical fatigue. O'Neill ducked beneath the surface and headed toward the other dock. He had to keep out of sight. It took him several minutes — his air pressure had dropped to 450 pounds — before he hauled himself onto the sand in the shade of a pier and ripped off Scarface's SCUBA gear.

The adrenaline was pumping now, reviving him, as he dashed onto the open beach. There was no one in sight. They must have taken her to the lodge. Damn them! There were hundreds of cabins, and they were armed; he couldn't just go and start banging on doors!

Then he saw her. The motorized cart was rolling up the red-dirt trail, four hundred yards away, with Christelle seated tightly between two men. As O'Neill watched, the cart reached the top of the low rise and disappeared over the hill. O'Neill ran, heated, yet feeling his blood running cold. He broke into a sprint, tearing along the beach toward the road, then up the hill, avoiding stones whenever he could. His lungs were bursting as he tore over the top of the hill.

Two hundred yards away, the plane was loading up, the engine running. A Malay youth tossed a suitcase in the luggage door; a man climbed into the rear seat. O'Neill dashed down the road, catching a glimpse of Christelle's auburn hair in the cockpit; and then the plane was rolling toward the end of the runway for the turn and takeoff. His impulse was to dash. He could possibly have reached the runway ahead of the plane, but only to be sliced up by the propeller and run down. Watching, feeling the rage surging through his body, he stepped into the shadow of a big jungle plant where he would be hidden from the air.

It was the Cessna 172 they had seen landing two days ago. There were four people in the cockpit, three men and Christelle. The engine whined up to full power at the end of the runway, and then the plane roared away. Thirty seconds later, it was in the sky, barely clearing the tops of the palm trees, leaving O'Neill standing stunned in the shadows. Half blind with anger, flooded with fury, he watched it. He saw it tilting, slowly banking away from the island, and then it headed off into the blinding-blue afternoon sky to the northwest. In seconds, it was a mere dot in the sky.

The dot seemed to swell into a huge white splash against the sky. And then it seemed to explode with a soundless white fire, blinding, like a whole world coming to an end — a shocking flashback. O'Neill shook himself free of the memory in time to see the distant dot once more before it disappeared.

Christelle — where are they taking you?

O'Neill tore back down the road and ran to their cabin. The door was ajar; he burst in. There was nothing but his empty suitcases lying open. Christelle's suitcases were gone. He tore open the drawers. Empty. He ripped open the closet door. Empty. There was nothing, not a shirt, not a pair of pants. His things were gone. Trying to think, he sat down on the bed.

He ran to the hotel lobby. Somewhere the plane had to land. He asked the clerk for a number for the Malaysian police, then asked for the phone.

"We will have to charge it, Mr—"

On impulse O'Neill blurted, "Senelik, John Senelik," and pulled the key from his pocket. The number 65 was stamped into the stainless steel.

"Thank you, Mr. Senelik," the clerk said, reaching for the key." But your account has already been closed. Do you have a credit card?"

"Unfortunately, everything's packed. But I have a friend, Broc O'Neill, Room 147. Perhaps we could put it on his account."

The clerk turned to his screen and punched in the room number. "Sorry, Mr. O'Neill checked out several hours ago. I apologize, Mr. Senelik, but we will need an account number. Perhaps, you could open a suitcase and locate your cards."

Furious, O'Neill tore out of the lobby. Back in his room, he looked around. *Several hours ago!* They had closed out his account while he and Christelle were diving then come after them. His clothes were gone; his wallet, his money, and his return plane ticket were gone. He scoured the suitcase, checked the pockets. There was nothing left except a single brass key in the back pocket, the key to their storage locker in Washington. He crawled under the bed and hauled out three shoes: his white jogging shoes and one of his brown dress shoes — nothing else. Stunned, he sat on the bed. He had been left behind; not only that, he had been stripped of every accoutrement of civilization. He was on an island in the South China Sea with no way to leave.

Slowly, only half aware of what he was doing, he pulled the shoelace from the dress shoe and tied it in a loop, fastened the brass key to it with a slip knot and put it around his neck. Then he put on the jogging shoes and walked out, dazed as he made his way along the wooden walkway toward the front of the resort. He checked his watch; it was 3:30 p.m.

He stood at the steps to the beach trying to grasp what had happened. Christelle was in the air being taken somewhere — God only knows where! — and he was helpless to follow. He would never see her again. He stared out at the water, the brilliant blue sky, the mound of Renggis Island, the *Singapore Seabird* moored at the dock. Paradise had vanished.

O'Neill tore up the beach. The *Singapore Seabird* — Wally Matthews. It was fifteen miles to the other side of the island by boat, shorter on the trail to Juara Village. The trail began between the lodge and the airport at Terek Village. Within minutes he had found it. He tore through the village past startled Malays and sprinted up the dark trail that wound among huge jungle trees, twisting and turning up steep hillsides on a rugged four-mile route to the far side of the island.

O'Neill raced, driven by the specter of a plane carrying Christelle away, terrified that she might be gone forever. The first section of the trail was steep, switchback after switchback, taking him within a mile to the summit of the trail; the marker indicated an elevation of 1200 feet. He paused for a minute, winded, gasping for air, gazing back at the blue sea below, the high summit of Bukit Parang Panjang off to his left, and the sweep of the South China Sea ahead. He waited until the burning in his lungs had settled, then tore off, running at breakneck speed, making good time on the steady downhill course. The trail wound through trees, around high outcrops, over streams. Then he recognized the pool in the rock that he and Christelle had admired three days ago.

The last quarter mile of the trail was familiar, wide and well-worn from the hundreds of tourists who came to see the famous pool where a scene in *South Pacific* had been filmed. Two minutes later, he was on the beach. There it was: Wally Matthews' speedboat, well down the beach, anchored offshore.

Fighting to save time racing down the sand, O'Neill was fighting the fatigue of running four miles over the island. Leaving the shoes on to save his feet from coral lacerations, he dashed into the water. Then he began swimming with the shoes around his neck, laces tied together. It was only two hundred yards, an easy swim, but the past two hours had taken their toll. The last fifty yards was agony. He struggled against exhaustion, fighting to stay alive for Christelle. He had to follow Christelle.

There were no signs of life on the boat, and O'Neill had neither the wind to shout nor the strength to climb aboard. Finally, clinging to the rear ladder, he hammered on the hull with his shoes and waited, hoping there was someone on the boat with the strength to haul him on board.

"O'Neill! What in bloody thunder are you doing here?"

Wally Matthews and his sons hauled him on board. O'Neill collapsed, gasping on the rear deck. They carried him to the cabin and laid him out of the bed. My, how good that felt. Rozita had a cold container of orange juice at his lips; he looked at her coppery skin and deep brown eyes as he drank, gasping between mouthfuls. Then, slowly, his wind came back.

Struggling against exhaustion, O'Neill got out his story, fragments and pieces yanked from the afternoon. Suddenly, Matthews was gone. In seconds the engines had started, and O'Neill felt the surge of the powerboat turning and accelerating.

"Kareem, that Cessna is probably out of KL," he heard Matthews, shout to his son. "Head for Kuantan; that's where it will touch down."

Matthews was back in the cabin, bracing himself against the pounding of the hull against the waves. O'Neill could feel the boat gaining speed. Matthews dialed and waited, gazing at Broc. "Operator, can you connect me with the control operator at Kuantan airport?"

A minute later, Matthews was talking in Malay to someone on the phone. Broc heard 'Cessna' several times. Rozita tilted more orange juice into his mouth.

"Broc, what time will it land? When did it take off?"

Time… damnation! What time? "It was three thirty last time I looked, at the resort. I guess it took off about three fifteen."

"How many passengers?"

"Four, and suitcases."

"Okay, it was fully loaded. They wouldn't try a direct flight to KL without refueling. They would have to land in Kuantan."

"Where's that?"

"On the coast, ninety miles from here."

Matthews was speaking into the telephone in rapid Malay.

He covered the receiver and spoke to O'Neill. "It landed at 4:22, refueled, then took off about an hour ago headed for KL." They glanced at their watches: five thirty. "It's still in the air; it will be landing within the next thirty minutes, probably at Subang International."

Matthews hung up and immediately began dialing again. Broc felt a sinking feeling. Christelle was already hundreds of miles away.

"Hello... Peter... Hey, Pete! This is Wally, Wally Matthews. We've got a little bit of an emergency here. Wonder if you could help. You got time tonight? Could you take a little stint over to Selangor? That's right... Fast! It's an emergency."

O'Neill caught the sound of meat sizzling and the smell of steak. Rozita was standing at the cooktop while balancing with one hand against the bumping of the hull and working the spatula with the other. He watched her take out a spice bottle and sprinkle the meat.

"Okay, Pete, we're off the north shore of Tioman, speed about thirty knots. We'll be at Kuantan in about two hours, forty minutes. Can you meet us? Good, and Pete, can you come up with a set of clothes, you know, shirt, trousers? American size?"

The conversation went on for another minute, and then Matthews hung up.

"Pete's a buddy of mine who services the *Singapore Seabird* whenever we're in Kuantan. He's got a flying license. You want a fast ride over the mountains of Malaysia? He's got a Piper PA46 Malibu: single-engine prop, cruises to 230 miles per hour at 20,000 feet. Pete can get it overnight. He'll have it ready and waiting. He'll get you across Malaysia in an hour." He consulted his watch. You should be at Subang Airport by nine tonight."

O'Neill did not have the geography clear, not yet. That Cessna was landing about now. "Where can they take her from Subang?"

"Nowhere, Broc. The airport guy at Kuantan said it was a KL-based Cessna, probably a rental. Whatever they do, it probably won't be in that plane, and it probably won't be until morning."

O'Neill sat at the table as Rozita served up a slab of peppered steak, potatoes with gravy, and carrots. "Rozita knows how to make an American meal," Matthews asserted with pride. "She learned that a long time ago. It looks like your tropical vacation is over. You need to be re-Americanized ASAP."

O'Neill was feeling a whole lot better. The meal revived him, and soon he was up in the cockpit with Kareem. The speedboat was planing along at a ferocious rate. Off to the left, the pale blue-gray of the Malaysian mountains rose in the distance. He glanced at his watch; it was 7:10 p.m. He calculated; it would be 7:10 a.m. CST in the U.S.

O'Neill went back in the cabin. "Wally, what's the capacity of that telephone?"

"The best. Where do you want to call?"

Chapter Thirty-seven

Langley, Virginia
August 19
8:35 a.m. EST

Brently Hagan was three hundred yards from the main gate into the CIA parking lot at Langley when his cell phone rang.

"Brent, this is Alan. I figured you'd be on the road. Is it possible to reach you once you get to your office?"

"It's not very easy, Alan, what's going on?"

"Then pull over and listen. This is important."

Hagan wheeled his car into a gas station, the last one before the main gates, and put it in park. It was a good thing he was early for work.

"It's Broc O'Neill, and he's in trouble!"

"Hell, where is he now?"

"He's on Wally Matthews' boat in the South China Sea."

"My God...! So they connected!"

"It's a bloody good thing, Brent. He's been cut off, stranded. Everything stolen: clothes, wallet, money, credit cards, air tickets, everything. And his graduate student, Christelle Washington, has been abducted."

Hagan felt a sudden dampness under his shirt. It was mid-August in Washington, another sweltering day on the way.

"You have any ideas, Alan?"

"Not many, but I just talked to him. O'Neill's fired up, he's angry, he's furious, and he's ready. If we can get him back on the trail, he's going to tear these guys apart. He needs information and he needs help."

Brent understood immediately. "So... any kind of support we can come up with."

"Right. If he gets that, he'll want to handle the details himself. First off, Christelle's abductors probably landed at Subang International

Airport a few minutes ago. Likely, she'll be transferred to another plane. What do you think you can find out?"

"You never did give me easy problems, Alan."

"Second, two guys tried to do O'Neill in. He's got a plastic PADI identification card under the name of Robert Troller and a watch engraved with the name J. L. Senelik. Also, a hotel key for the Tioman Island Resort, Room 55. Both his attackers were Caucasians, presumably American, though Broc says they didn't survive long enough to ask."

"Jesus, what happened?"

"They were playing on a coral reef. Sharks got them. O'Neill says their bodies may never show up."

"Your friend moves fast. Everywhere he goes, he stirs things up. Any idea what his next move is going to be?"

"Wally will get him to Kuantan; that's a town on the east coast of Malaysia. And he's arranged a flight to Subang. O'Neill will be there in a little over three hours. But he'll be stranded after that."

It was a hunch. But it was worth following. As soon as he was in his office, Hagan booted up his computer and started surfing through the 'public' network, files available to any employee in Langley or any regional office in the U.S. Within minutes, the names had come up: Robert Troller and John Lee Senelik were CIA officers, aged twenty-six and twenty-eight, in the Directorate of Operations, both with five years of experience, mostly in street work in Baltimore. What on Earth were they doing? What had O'Neill said? "Playing on a coral reef"? Hagan searched their personnel records. Neither had any credentials for work at sea — nothing more than elementary diving certification years ago. They were little better than amateurs, like the two who had tailed O'Neill in Singapore. It was no surprise that O'Neill got the best of them.

Hotel reservations on Tioman Island might be useful, but he could find out more from airline records. Hagan started pulling up flights into Kuala Lumpur during the last ten days, letting the computer search. Three minutes later he had it: Robert Troller and John Lee Senelik had flown into KL on Wednesday on a Pan Am flight from Washington, with connections in L.A. and Hong Kong.

313

Hagan scanned the passenger list, recognizing only Troller and Senelik. Within three minutes the computer had cross checked the passenger list with personnel records, over twenty-five thousand CIA employees around the world. Another name came up: Wade Bracket. What was his connection? Maybe FBI. He remembered Dillon Shaver had been questioned by the FBI. Within seconds the computer had completed a cross check with Bureau personnel. Nothing. Creighton's account of the surveillance network linked to Worldwide telephones led Hagan to the National Security Agency, which maintained duplicate personnel files in the offices of the Department of Defense. He spent another ten minutes, but it was worth it: Bullseye! Two other passengers on the same Pan Am flight into Malaysia were employees of the NSA.

At 9:55, Hagan stopped for a break, got himself a coffee, and read his mail. At 10:20 he went back to the screen.

The five passengers matched what Creighton and O'Neill had described. After Troller and Senelik were eaten by sharks — whatever that meant — three men had abducted Christelle Washington. In a few minutes, Hagan punched his way into the airlines' reservation network. Troller and Senelik had arrived in Malaysia on Wednesday the fourteenth. There were only three hotels close to the airport. The names came up within minutes. They had stayed at the P.J. Hilton Hotel on the fourteenth and fifteenth, then checked out, probably to fly to Tioman Island. The NSA men, John Bradshaw and Steven McClosky, had stayed in an adjacent suite with Wade Bracket until Saturday the seventeenth; presumably they were the three who had flown into Tioman Island in the four-seater Cessna later in the day.

Suddenly, Hagan saw it happen before his eyes. The computers were still on search mode when the names popped onto the screen: Mere seconds ago, Steve McClosky had used his VISA card to reserve a three-bedroom suite at the P.J. Hilton. Suite No. 614. Occupants, four: Steve McClosky, John Bradshaw, Wade Bracket, and Christelle Washington. Time: 9:35 p.m. Monday the 19th. Hagan confirmed with his watch: 10:36 a.m. Eastern Standard Time was eleven hours different from Malaysian time; Christelle Washington's abductors had checked in less than a minute ago!

Hagan picked up his phone, punched in his PIN to have the call billed to his home, and dialed Alan Creighton in Missouri.

"Al, where's O'Neill now?"

"I'd guess Matthews dropped him off at Kuantan a while ago. By now he's on a flight across Malaysia."

"Okay, I know this much: five guys out of Washington — three CIA, two NSA — flew into Malaysia last week. Two CIA officers were wasted in the South China Sea. The others have just checked into a hotel in Petaling Jaya. They've got Christelle. I've got the hotel and suite number."

"Okay, Brent, let's get the information to O'Neill—"

"Hold on, Al. What on Earth can he do?"

Creighton was silent.

"He can't do a damn thing. He can't take on three guys. He's not armed, and if he were, he'd be in deep trouble in Malaysia. With their NSA credentials, they would outmaneuver O'Neill; he'd end up in jail."

"Listen, Brent, you've got to understand," Creighton urged. "O'Neill sounded really broken up on the phone. I think he's fallen for this woman."

"I understand. But you've agreed: he's angry, furious. That's not a good mix for sensible thinking. In fact, it's a recipe for disaster. Like driving under the influence. If he knows where they are, he'll try to handle this himself. There's got to be another way. When will O'Neill get into Subang Airport?"

"About ten thirty at night for him, maybe an hour from now."

"Then I suggest you get your friendly travel agent in Clayton to punch in a reservation for him at the hotel closest to the airport, but absolutely not the P.J. Hilton! He's bound to call you again. Tell him what you've done, tell him to get some sleep, tell him we know Christelle is still in Malaysia, and remind him that we will be working on this all day — while he's asleep. Just don't tell him where she is. If you do, he'll get himself killed."

Hagan stared at the Hilton hotel reservations, which indicated a one-night stay. Christelle's abductors had to get her out of Malaysia, but how could they do it? Hagan leaned back in his chair and sipped his coffee. They couldn't take her aboard a commercial airliner and expect her to remain a quiet captive for a fifteen-hour flight. But obviously, they could get her where they wanted her. The CIA had proved they could move equipment and soldiers undetected; they had sponsored secret arms shipments to Nicaragua in the 1980s. Moving Christelle to Washington was small potatoes for the CIA, but it would undoubtedly be a covert operation.

Hagan sat up and surfed through various screens on his computer until he was into the files of the Office of Logistics, part of the Directory of Administration. Logistics was in charge of the immense network of dummy companies, secret shipping channels, clandestine flights, obscure links throughout the world, which allowed the CIA to accomplish any task, almost always undetected. Basic to the network were up-to-date files on standard transportation worldwide.

The Subang International Airport was the hub of Malaysian transportation. The Malaysian Airline Service, MAS, linked up with every major city on the Pacific rim. Hagan scanned the roster, a list of scheduled arrivals and departures over a typical week along with actual times, flights canceled or added, and unscheduled traffic. There were planes landing every few minutes, not only MAS flights but also landings by Singapore Air, Japan Air, British Airways, Air India, and several American airlines. The flights in were routine, regular, on time. The whole complex was a model of modern efficiency. There was nothing strange going on, and only one plane had landed that Hagan could not identify. The records showed it was still there.

Hagan picked up his phone, looked up a number, and called Bill Henk at the NSA. "Sorry to bother you, Bill, but I'm trying to get into flight records. Our Office of Intelligence is a little touchy."

"What do you need, Brent?"

"Three days ago, Saturday, August 17, 11:04 a.m., a plane landed at Subang International Airport. Designation and origin unknown. What can you tell me?"

"As much as you want to know. You want to hang on?"

Two minutes later, Henk was back on the line. "Okay, Brent, we've got it. What do you want to know?"

"Flight plans."

"None have been filed. And I'll tell you something else, Brent, none are likely. We picked it up from Big Bird, the stationary satellite over Borneo. It's an unscheduled flight, part of a clandestine network. It's just a guess what their mission is."

Hagan stared at his screen, shocked at how far the network spread, astonished at the power of a few corrupt officers scattered through the most powerful intelligence agencies in the world.

"I've got a favor to ask, Bill. We've got something nasty going on, some bad apples over here at Langley, but it looks like there are some in the NSA, too."

"Serious?"

"Bloody serious. Extortion. Money laundering, billions of dollars. All kinds of illegal stuff. And now innocent lives are in jeopardy. We're in the middle of a nasty one now. An American woman has been kidnapped. We need to track it all."

"Brent, did you ever wonder how we managed before we had all this stuff: radar, satellites, data banks, and computers?"

"I wonder whether it's all worth it. Corruption is getting more sophisticated every day. I'm not sure we're keeping up."

Ten minutes later Brent Hagan hung up. It was nearly noon. Things were beginning to move, but they were getting tight. Thinking, he tapped a pencil:

O'Neill's fired up, he's angry, he's furious, and he's ready. If we can get him back on the trail, he's got what it takes to tear these guys apart. He needs information — and he needs help—

Hagan reached for the phone and dialed Operative Support one floor down. His instructions were rapid fire: contact the major clothing chains in Jefferson, Indiana; find out who made Broc's last suit, get his measurements, and order up a complete wardrobe in his preferred colors. Jacket, slacks, shirts, ties, socks, shoes. Air Express to Washington within twenty-four hours. Sooner if possible. Hagan indicated delivery at his home address.

Hagan mused for another minute, then typed an e-mail to his favorite secretary, Kay Brennan. He knew her computer was always on; it would signal the arrival of the message. He waited three minutes for her to read it, then phoned her at the CIA printing center tucked away in the basement of the new building. Printing center — a euphemism for Fabrication Office.

"What's the timing on rapid turnaround?" he asked.

"Analyzing this request, Brent, I'd say you want a driver's license. We can have it within two hours. Matching Social Security card, three hours. Passport the same, three hours."

"It's all replacement stuff. Use Broc O'Neill's address in Jefferson, Indiana."

"Come on, Love, give me a challenge."

"Okay, after you've finished replacements, here's a second order: we need two detection-proof ID packages, the best we can provide, one keyed to an existing post office box in Eagle River, Wisconsin, the other an apartment address in Kalamazoo, Michigan." Hagan glanced at his notes and read the addresses and zip codes Creighton had sent. "We may have to redo this in a few weeks if there are any address changes, so this may be temporary."

"Okay, Love, can you send down the clearance papers?"

"There are no clearance papers, Kay, there cannot be any clearance papers. We've got 'an inside malfunction' with this one"— code words for hostile observers within the CIA. "This has to be kept off the screens. But you've got my personal guarantee. This is legit."

"Your personal guarantee was pretty good last night, Brent. The restaurant, the dancing, the whole evening." Kay Brennan had a particularly tantalizing way of saying things. She went on: "What's the personal guarantee on this one?"

"The patience to wait. This O'Neill thing has mushroomed into an around-the-clock operation. It could be this way for several days. I have to stay on task."

"Besides patience?"

"A dozen roses, Love. When you get them, be assured we've scheduled a rerun of last night within twenty-four hours."

"Sounds wonderful," she purred into the phone. "What's for encore?"

"If they survive, I want us to meet this guy, O'Neill, and his graduate student. I promise you, from what's already happened, it will be the most interesting evening in a long, long time."

"Okay, you've got it. What do you need on these? Short-term, or lifetime detection proof? You know, what we call the max-package?"

"Give me the details."

"Driver's licenses — in this case two — one for the Michigan and one for Wisconsin, Social Security cards, double passports, bank accounts, discount memberships, credit cards, etc., etc., with deep-cover documents spanning the past twenty years in place within three days — or we can make it lifetime, all the way back to birth records."

"Jesus! I'd be better off with that than what I've got. Make it lifetime."

"You get your clearance papers, Love, and I'll set you up better than you are."

"How soon will these be ready?"

"We've got a five-hour turnaround on the max-package. It's twelve thirty now. For you, Love, we'll do it in four hours, forty-five. It'll be on your desk by five this afternoon. The deep-cover stuff within twenty-four hours. Is there anything else?"

"I don't know. What else is there?"

"Bio Alteration."

"Don't the new ID packages do that?"

"Not quite. The max-packages provide a new identity, but the old person remains unchanged in the records. Bio Alteration works on that. It changes the subject's original identity."

"How extensive are the changes?"

"Well, there's a Bio Enhancement version that fabricates details. Some facts disappear from the record. Others are added. Birth records are altered. Someone who was never in the military acquires a record, maybe even a Purple Heart. The original person pretty much disappears."

"My God, who thought up all this stuff?"

"Who knows? The Bio Enhancement is pretty amazing, but it's rarely used. I remember only one in my eight years in this job."

"Well, let's try it out. How soon?"

"It should be done in a week. And, of course, once any of these are complete, all internal evidence on the computers is scrubbed. They call it invisible fabrication."

"Jeez, Kay, you deserve a hundred red roses, but you'll have to issue me a max-package before I can afford them."

Hagan hung up the phone and stared out the window, seeing nothing. His mind was on Kay Brennan's pale blue eyes, honey-blonde hair, and long legs. He was glad they had had their own personal bash at her apartment last night; it might be a while before the next one.

He needs our help —

Hagan checked his watch. He had one more phone call to make, and he needed to do it now. The head office of the SAS, the British Special Air Service, would be closed now. It was dinner time in London, but Walker Cannington could be reached at home, and if not, he would hear any message left on his phone within two hours.

Chapter Thirty-eight

Subang International Airport
Petaling Jaya, Malaysia
Wednesday, August 21
8:15 a.m.

O'Neill sat by the window of the observation deck. His clothes, an odd assortment provided by his pilot the night before, included a light brown trench coat, light hat, and dark glasses, enough to screen his identity from casual travelers. He held a newspaper, turning and refolding it every few minutes, attempting to hide his real purpose: watching everything in the terminal. Every so often, he glanced across the open foyer at the steady stream of pedestrians of all nationalities. Another plane took off every six or eight minutes.

O'Neill had spent a restless night agonizing over Christelle and able to console himself in his hotel room, only because he knew she was alive. The objective of her captors was clearly to abduct her but not to kill her.

A news item on the airport TV— 'Shark Attack at Tioman Island' — caught his attention. He walked forward to hear above the airport noise. No one paid any more attention than they had to the last fifteen minutes of news. He listened to the summary:

Fishing boats ferrying divers to and from Pulau Tulai, a favorite SCUBA diving site five miles from Tioman Island, have reported two deaths. Witnesses report that sharks surfaced trailing human remains. The resort managers' report that this is the first shark attack at Tioman in forty years, but this has done little to allay the fears of alarmed vacationers, who are cutting vacations short. This incident is fueling fears that tourist revenues will be sharply reduced over the next few weeks.

The missing divers have been identified from the SCUBA equipment rented at the Tioman Dive Shop. Missing and presumed dead are Robert Troller, twenty-eight, of Bethesda, Maryland, and Dr. Broc O'Neill of Jefferson, Indiana, age unknown, who were vacationing at the Tioman Island Resort.

A third man, whose SCUBA gear was recovered near the public docks at the lodge, is being sought for questioning. John Lee Senelik, twenty-six, of Alexandria, Virginia, appeared briefly at the main lodge following the accident, but has not been seen since. Vacationing companions of the victims could not be located since they had checked out some time before the attacks were reported. Efforts are being made to notify next of kin.

O'Neill felt the perspiration running down his back. The sudden shock of hearing about his own death made his insides churn for a minute; he wanted to sit down. He tried to think of the implications, but his brain would not work.

He went back to the window. A hundred yards along the fence, a huge double gate swung open. Immediately, two Malaysian taxis rolled in and headed across the main lot, coming to a stop beside a small plane. O'Neill stepped back to the public telephone, his eye on the taxis, his hand on the receiver. The doors opened; two men got out of one taxi, one from the other, and they conferred by the back fender as the drivers pulled luggage from the trunks. Within seconds one was paying the drivers while the other two were standing on opposite sides of one of the cars. For a minute one of the men talked through the window to someone in the back seat. Then Christelle got out of the car.

She looked ragged, downtrodden. She stood with her eyes on the ground, her long-handled handbag nearly dragging on the pavement, all the life gone out of her body. Every instinct in his body made O'Neill want to charge through the plate-glass window, leap to the pavement, and tear into Christelle's abductors. He clenched his fists, fighting rage; then he picked up the telephone, dialed the operator, and began the process of a collect call to Alan Creighton in Missouri. While he talked to the operator, gave his number, and waited, the three men led Christelle up the stairs and boarded the plane. He realized one of her abductors had a folded newspaper under his arm. Had the report of the Tioman deaths made the newspaper? He thought for a minute, then relaxed. It was on TV, but this morning was probably too early for the story to be in print. It would show up in the *New Straights Times* tomorrow.

Undoubtedly, though, once they had some kind of official confirmation of his death, they would tell Christelle. Bloody sadists.

O'Neill recognized Christelle's luggage as two porters loaded suitcases through the cargo door. They had packed her luggage while she and Broc were diving! This was no opportunistic kidnapping. It had been planned in detail, even to the extent of closing out his resort account before the actual abduction.

The aircraft door was being fastened when Creighton came on the line.

"Christelle's here, Alan, at the airport. She's just been taken aboard a plane."

"Hang on, Broc, I'm dialing Hagan."

"By the way, this isn't Broc. Broc O'Neill is dead."

"So how is a dead man talking on the phone?"

"A bit of a mix up on SCUBA gear. It's too complicated to explain, but the official news is I'm dead. It said so on TV."

"Well, that may not be such bad news. It gives you an advantage chasing these guys since no one is going to track a dead man."

"Okay, you're right, but Christelle is likely to get the official version before she knows I'm alive."

"Damn! What a mess…! Okay, Brent's on the other line. He wants to know about the plane."

"Two jet engines, like pods on the fuselage behind the wings. It's small."

"How small?"

"About the length of three or four cars."

"How many windows?"

"Five on the side, triangular, points at the top."

O'Neill heard Creighton repeating information over the phone to Brent Hagan.

"Okay, Broc, Hagan says they've been watching that plane for several hours." O'Neill was surprised. "It's a North American Rockwell

Sabreliner, CT-39. It's often used by the U.S. Air Force for hauling military personnel, maybe a dozen at a time."

"What's a USAF plane doing in Malaysia?"

"Well, Broc, we doubt that this one is USAF. Hagan's got a line into the NSA. The satellite imaging records show it flew into Subang on Saturday from Nakhon Phanom base in Thailand."

Thailand… Nakhon Phanom… "Blazes! Alan, are you thinking what I'm thinking?"

"You guessed it! Secret Thai air bases during the Vietnam war. Air America."

Air America — one of several secret CIA 'proprietaries'. At its peak, Air America had sixty-five planes that ferried arms and personnel on secret missions from Okinawa to Indonesia in places unknown to the American people, unauthorized by Congress, unreported to the press. The CIA was supposed to have divested itself of Air America decades ago, but it was obvious there were remnants of the old network still intact. And someone in the CIA had managed to call out one of its planes to abduct Christelle Washington!

O'Neill stared at the Sabreliner moving off the parking pad toward the runway. CIA planes, like most aircraft linked to the intelligence community, could come and go in scores of friendly countries. Only minimal clearance was needed; no flight plans were filed; no records kept. It was only American surveillance itself that could reconstruct the flights, and only from the vast satellite imaging archives of the NSA.

O'Neill followed the plane with narrowed eyes. It was one more piece in the tangle of crime and corruption that just kept on growing.

"Broc! Broc! Are you there?"

"I'm here."

"Broc, Hagan's got instructions. He says we've got to get you out of there, and he's arranged a way. Catch a taxi to Kuala Lumpur. Tell the driver you want to go to Old Airport Road — The Royal Selangor Flying Club."

"I don't have a dollar to my name — or whatever you call them over here."

"Ringgits, their dollars are ringgits. But you won't need them. Somebody will meet you at the other end."

Thirty minutes later O'Neill stepped out of the taxi beside a low building with a sign in Malay and English: *Kelab Penerbangan Diraja Selangor* (Royal Selangor Flying Club). It was convenient that the sign carried its own translation, but then Malaysia was a former British colony.

Then everything began to happen with military precision. Captain Raymond Janson stepped out of the building in full uniform, introduced himself, paid the taxi bill, and led O'Neill inside. Within minutes he had signed papers for takeoff.

"We had a flight scheduled for later today," Captain Janson said in a heavy British accent, leading O'Neill across the pavement to the waiting aircraft. "Our weekly courier service to London. But it was rescheduled to get you airborne with speed. Special request through M15."

M15 — the British Secret Service. O'Neill gazed at the plane, a low-slung jet with a bubble cockpit, triangular wings, and a needle nose. It was like something from the movies.

"You like it?" Janson asked. "It's one of your American Talon T-38s, a near twin of the F-5 Tiger. Not quite state of the art, but there's not much wrong with them."

Within minutes O'Neill was in the cockpit seat behind Captain Janson, with earphones and flight jacket, taxiing toward the runway.

"Through M15?" O'Neill queried. "What was the origin of the request?"

"I'm not sure. Our instructions are to get clear of Malaysia ground radio and then tie in with Australia control. I'm sure there will be some answers then."

The Old Airport, Captain Janson explained, dated back to pre-colonial times when the defense of Malaysia was entirely in the hands of the British. The airport was now the principal base for the small Malaysian Air Force, which numbered just a handful of planes. But the commonwealth ties with the United Kingdom were strong; thus, the airfield remained a stopover for British military operations. The old Royal Selangor Flying Club retained the decorative colonial British atmosphere still evident in many of Malaysia's classier clubs. Its

325

members were primarily Brits with business appointments in Kuala Lumpur who enjoyed flying on weekends.

"Buckle up, Mr. O'Neill. We'll be at 40,000 feet in four minutes."

O'Neill felt the jets as the Talon revved up — a surge of raw power — and then they were roaring down the runway, acceleration pressing him into his seat, the plane soaring skyward at a breathtaking angle, arcing over the glass skyscrapers of the capital, Kuala Lumpur. Nothing O'Neill had experienced on commercial flights compared with the stunning speed of this. In no time, they were over plantations: endless rows of palm-oil trees and rubber plantations, and almost before he could fathom their speed, they were within sight of the coast, the blue waters of the Strait of Malacca and the distant gray-green mountains of Sumatra.

"Captain, you said London. What's our route?"

"Northwest across Southern Asia. India, Afghanistan, Iran, Turkey, and then half a dozen countries in Europe. If you blink, you might miss one. Even with refueling stops in Mumbai and Athens, we'll be in London in seven hours."

Seven hours! "How fast are we traveling?" O'Neill asked.

"Hang on, Mr. O'Neill; we're going over 650 mph. We'll be doing Mach I within seconds."

O'Neill felt the shudder, a strange ripple, as the Talon broke through the sound barrier and tore skyward, still climbing. There was a sudden strange silence as the roar of the rearward jets was left behind.

"You're going to see a lot of daylight, Mr. O'Neill. We took off at 10 a.m. We'll be crossing seven time zones, traveling with the sun in excess of 1,000 m.p.h. Your watch may say five in the afternoon when we land, but it will still be 10 a.m. in London when we land."

O'Neill heard the sudden crackle in his earphones. "Some of what you'll be hearing," Captain Janson explained, "is based on satellite surveillance, likely through the Australia monitoring station, relayed by satellite to us. It's encrypted information."

The radio came alive with greetings to Captain Janson, aircraft identification, a summary of weather over the Indian Ocean, and then a pause of several seconds.

"I think this is the information you want, Mr. O'Neill."

Please advise Mr. Broc O'Neill: Sabreliner CT-39 airborne from Subang International Airport at 0946 Malaysian time, fifty-two minutes ago. Location, four hundred miles northeast of Malaysia over the South China Sea. Possible course to Hong Kong, possibly Tokyo.

It was hard to take in. The plane was heading off on a Pacific route while Captain Janson was flying him west across Asia and Europe. The radio continued:

Sabreliner speed, 960 kilometers per hour, 598 miles per hour. If touchdown at Hong Kong occurs, likely route continuance across North Pacific, direct to L.A. If touchdown at Tokyo, likely route over Alaska... Canada... to Chicago.

O'Neill felt a wave of grief and fear. Christelle was on a plane somewhere over the South China Sea heading northeast while he was heading west to the far side of the world. Their routes were pulling them farther apart every minute. The agony was overwhelming. Whatever Christelle had to deal with included belief that he was dead. She had seen her abductors shoot at him; she had seen him sink below the waves and never appear again. She knew he was out of air. And then she must have seen the sharks.

O'Neill gripped the seat. He was shaken. Christelle... Christelle.

Captain Janson was speaking through O'Neill's earphones. "My understanding is you'll be met in London and transferred for a flight to the U.S." The radio came to life again.

Please advise Mr. Broc O'Neill: Sabreliner headed for Tokyo, then Continental U.S. Estimated ninety-five percent probability of Chicago touchdown. Registration of plane with CIA, indicates possible continuance to Washington, DC.

There was a brief pause.

Please advise Mr. O'Neill of his transfer at Gatwick International Airport then British Air flight to Washington National Airport. Estimated arrival time to be updated periodically. Now estimated at five hours ahead of Sabreliner. Please instruct O'Neill to meet Mr. Brently Hagan in Washington at the airport bookstore.

Brently Hagan — everything came clear. Brently Hagan, Directorate of Science and Technology, CIA. Alan Creighton, professor and historian of high-tech military hardware. Wally Matthews, entrepreneurial owner of the *Singapore Seabird*. They had done it. A phone call from Matthews in the South China Sea had so far sped him across Malaysia and launched him on his way to London. Soon he would be in England, then Washington, DC. Within hours they had constructed a network of support. Three Navy SEALs — explosive experts from the jungle wars of Vietnam — mobilized after a quarter century of military retirement. The efficiency of the platoon was evident. It was thorough and rapid, a model of military efficacy.

Chapter Thirty-nine

Gatwick Airport, London
Wednesday, August 21
11:18 a.m.

O'Neill paid the bill for his breakfast with the ten-pound note Captain Raymond Janson had shoved into his pocket as they parted company and sipped his coffee, his second cup. As instructed, he had provided identification for someone he had never met, bought the latest issue of *Time* magazine, and laid it on his table. Following the Republican National Convention the previous week, the cover featured Bob Dole and his running mate, Jack Kemp, Republican candidates for the upcoming November election. His mind wandering for the first time in hours, O'Neill wondered whether they could pull off a surprise victory. It was hard to imagine they could unseat Bill Clinton.

Within minutes an officer in airline uniform sat down across from him.

"Broc O'Neill?" He nodded. "You've got an hour until boarding time, Mr. O'Neill," the officer informed him. "Come with me. I'm sure you'd like an opportunity to shower." O'Neill nodded his thanks and accompanied the officer down the crowded corridor to a door marked 'Airport Security', then through a maze of hallways and into a room with lockers and benches. He gestured toward two leather suitcases and a briefcase by the lockers on a light aluminum luggage holder with wheels. O'Neill dropped his *Time* magazine by the briefcase.

"You'll find a change of clothing in the locker." He pulled a plastic garbage bag from his pocket and handed it to O'Neill. "I suggest you simply discard everything you're wearing. We'll dispose of them. You won't need anything from the suitcases until you get to the U.S., so just check them at gate 17 for your flight to Washington. Take the briefcase aboard as a carry on, I've been told it contains materials of interest. The combination is the first six digits of your American Social Security number. Once you've showered, but before you leave this room, you'll need to open an unmarked package in the inside pocket of the suit jacket."

O'Neill thanked the officer. "We're always glad to help," he assured. "M15 cooperates with your American intelligence agencies whenever possible. But we haven't had such a top-secret operation for some time. I have no idea what it is, only that it's top priority."

O'Neill thanked the officer, noting that he was impressed with M15 efficiency.

"By the way, Mr. O'Neill, I'm to inform you: there is a plane, a flight that I understand is of some interest to you. My latest information came in about ten minutes ago. The plane made a brief stopover in Tokyo and took off approximately two hours ago. Its present location is over the Bering Sea. It will be over Alaska in an hour. Its landing time at O'Hare International, Chicago, is almost the same as your landing in Washington."

Thirty minutes later, showered and dressed, O'Neill wheeled the suitcases through the crowds along the corridors to Gate 17. He was wearing a British summer suit, which fit him so well that he concluded Brently Hagan had wired his measurements to London. The package contained a new passport, which he handed over with his ticket as he checked the luggage. Within minutes, boarding began and O'Neill found his way to Row 4, First Class, a window seat. A small boy of about ten in the aisle seat immediately filled the seat between them with piles of stamps in plastic packages, which he proceeded to stick into a new stamp album.

As boarding continued, O'Neill studied his new passport. It was American, issued at Green Bay, Wisconsin, in 1989. It was stamped with previous flights to London in the summer of '91 and the Bahamas in the summer of '92. There were stamps dated late July for entry to Italy and one for the UK dated a week ago. The birth date was the same year he had been born, 1960, and the picture was his: the same photo taken two years ago for his passport stolen at Tioman Island. But the passport had been issued to Robert Brocford Winston.

O'Neill gazed at the stamps and markings. They had put together a new identity, including a whole past itinerary of travel, all of it fictitious.

The wallet contained a wad of bills — O'Neill estimated several hundred dollars — and a Wisconsin driver's license valid until 2000 with his photograph and the name Robert B. Winston. Half a dozen business cards listed Robert B. Winston as a 'Journalist', with an address, his mother's post office box in Eagle River, Wisconsin. The final item was a Social Security card.

O'Neill lay back in his seat as soon as the plane was aloft, resting, trying to think, feeling the fatigue of the past two days. It was scarcely noon, London time, but he had barely slept in the last forty hours.

Robert Winston — was that to be his permanent name or simply a cover to get him back into the U.S.? He said the name to himself several times, trying to feel a connection. Was Robert Winston the same as Broc O'Neill? He pulled out his passport and confirmed: Robert Brocford Winston. It had almost escaped him. Broc was buried in his middle name. That made a difference. Unexpectedly, he felt a link to the person he was, a connection with his past.

Christelle— She was somewhere over the Bering Sea nearing Alaska. His world had seemed to fly apart as he sped away in Captain Janson's Talon, but now things might be coming together again. He tried to visualize the globe. Soon she would be flying in over Alaska and the wilds of Canada's Northwest Territories. At the same time, he would be flying in over the northeastern wilds of Canada, their routes converging.

He slept. He must have been asleep for three hours because the plane was over the forests of Maine when he awoke. The boy in the aisle seat showed O'Neill his stamp album, flipping from France to Greece to Italy to show off whole pages covered with stamps. The boy grinned, wordless in his enthusiasm, and went back to sticking stamps on the Israel pages.

O'Neill retrieved the briefcase from under the seat and set it on his lap. Inside he found a bound folder with a wad of printed pages. Immediately, he realized he had the fruit of Alan Creighton's research in Missouri in his hands. The first ten pages listed various American organizations, arranged by state, which had received donations in excess of $300,000 in the past six weeks. O'Neill followed the numbers page by page, noting the totals for each state.

It was astonishing. The amounts were rarely lower than half a million dollars; most were in the $1 million to $3 million range. A few were higher. There were numerous research programs, scholarship funds, and artist grant funds, which were not particularly surprising. What was surprising were the huge charitable donations to public housing projects, teenage youth hostels, unwed mothers' shelters, abortion clinics, retirement communities, and nursing homes, free education projects for the unemployed, and a variety of placement services in Texas and California aimed at recent Hispanic immigrants from Mexico and other Central American nations.

O'Neill ran his fingers through his hair as he recalled the TVI debates he and Christelle had seen in Singapore. It did not make sense. The mood of the country was shifting. For middle-class Americans, programs supporting under-privileged sectors of the population were out of favor. The litany was continual: such programs perpetuated welfare dependency rather than encouraging self-reliance and employment. Funds should not boost a mediocre underclass; they should be funneled into investment and industrial development. Steps should be taken to reduce poverty by halting the endless influx of illegal aliens from south of the Rio Grande.

But there it was! Charitable assistance in the largest states ran as high as $140 million since the beginning of July — with the national total for July 1st to August 1st standing at $1.95 billion! All this had happened while he and Christelle were running for their lives! It was a stunning amount of money, enough to revive literally hundreds of faltering programs and funds and projects that were chronically cash poor.

O'Neill thumbed through the lists, more than fifteen pages of tables. The following pages listed charitable donors, except that none were precisely named. In each of thirty-five states, major banks were listed, holders of charitable trusts and foundations that dispensed donations. There were ninety-five such trusts listed, with actual dollar amounts disbursed over the past six weeks. O'Neill ran down the list to the state subtotals and then the national total. Even in today's economy, where millions and billions were reported on the news every evening, the numbers were stunning.

Money was coming from somewhere but not from the federal treasury, nor was it from the super wealthy. It was from trusts and foundations of unknown origin.

It was more than O'Neill could absorb. He needed time to think, and his thinking time was overwhelmed with Christelle. Their sudden separation pained him. Knowing that she thought him dead made his blood run cold. Thinking about what had happened sent him into a blind fury. The rage of five weeks in May and June came flooding back: frustration, anger, helplessness. And loss. The infuriating gall of whoever they were to destroy his life in a mindless act of violence serving some kind of vast corruption. And now they were doing it again.

Darcy... Christelle—

O'Neill clenched his fists and ground his teeth, ready to explode.

Broc stood gazing at the titles in the paperback book stand and wondering whether perhaps he should follow Christelle's lead and read a good page-turner for at least an hour before sleep every night.

"Broc, Broc O'Neill?"

The voice came from one side. O'Neill held his eyes steady, aware that he was now in Washington, the city where perhaps his enemies were concentrated, aware that a false move could send him to instant death.

"I can't use your new name because I don't know it." O'Neill turned casually, disinterestedly, and peered into the eyes of a complete stranger.

"We've never met. I'm Brent, Brently Hagan."

They hailed separate taxis from the airport to the Key Bridge Marriott. Hagan registered for a room in his own name and sent O'Neill ahead with his luggage. Minutes later Hagan came in. O'Neill had Scotch, gin, and rum with mixers waiting.

O'Neill shook the hand of the CIA man who had managed somehow to bring him back alive from the far side of the world. He appeared to be in his early fifties, though he had a trimness to his body, a well-preserved athletic tone that spoke of good eating, good exercise, care. His hair was jet black, his eyes gray, his jaw set and dark from his beard even though he was shaved clean.

Hagan set down a package the size of a shoe box wrapped and taped in brown paper. "You open this after I've gone. It contains things I don't know about, at least not in detail."

O'Neill stared at the package, wondering what else there could be. He was already carrying a wallet full of new identification, enough to allow freedom of movement, escape from detection, safety.

"At some point in the future, you may find it possible to reappear as Broc O'Neill. You now have exact replacement documents here for everything that was stolen. And, of course, you'll need your O'Neill documents for transfers of property. They're in this package in a separate envelope. For the time being, lock them in a safety deposit box until you need them. That could be months, even years, from now. Until then, remember that Broc O'Neill remains a target."

"Why don't we start," O'Neill began, "with you calling me—"

"Don't!" Hagan cautioned. "I don't know your new name, and I can't know it!"

"You created them; how can you not know them?"

"Our computers created them, Broc. Once the general parameters were set, an identity-creation program provided a name — actually two new names — printed the documents, and had them packaged without any human eye seeing them. As soon as we're done here, we're closing down this room reservation. You go wherever you want — next door, across the street, across town — and book a room under one of your new names. Once you walk out of here, no one in the world can trace you. There are no points of continuity. You may notice some; there are always some because we fed everything about Broc O'Neill to the computers. Your new names, birthplaces, etc., etc., were created as plausible alternatives for the person you are. Your education credentials will be close, but not identical. But no one can trace you. If they were to start with anything now in your wallet or that package, they could never trace you to Broc O'Neill. The moment the documents were complete, the computers were erased. There are no records."

"And why do I now have two new names?"

"One for each of your addresses in Michigan and Wisconsin. Whatever choices you make, you've got supportive documents."

"What about fingerprints?" O'Neill asked. "My prints will match."

"Part of detection-proof identity change requires altering, sometimes destroying, existing documents. All records of O'Neill's fingerprints have been erased or altered, all the way back to the vanity birth certificates hospitals create with baby's hand-and-foot-prints. Your actual fingerprints are now linked to your new identities. Of course, the standard registry records for O'Neill remain, but even they have been modified. If the time comes when you are sure it is safe to resume your original identity, use the username and password we've provided. This will automatically activate our computers and reset the records. For now, act as though Broc O'Neill is dead."

O'Neill got up and offered drinks. He mixed two gin-and-tonics and handed one to Hagan. "This is all very convenient," O'Neill maintained. "Officially, according to a TV broadcast, Broc O'Neill died in the South China Sea."

"I heard. We've had a *New Straits Times* story scanned and sent from Malaysia. It appeared while you were in flight. But how did they make this mistake?"

"It's like your detection-proof identity change. In the case of the mysterious death of Broc O'Neill, connections between ID recovered and those who actually died were erased — by sharks. Crucial facts were missing. Someday, maybe if we get together with Creighton, I'll tell you the whole story."

"The material in your briefcase — have you read it?"

"Most of it. The summaries. But I couldn't focus. But I'm ready now." O'Neill pulled the folder from his briefcase.

"You read. I've got to make a call."

O'Neill headed to the bedroom, propped himself up against the headboard and began reading the final pages in the file.

Ten minutes later Hagan came in. "This stuff is unbelievable," O'Neill asserted.

"We think you're the one to sort through it and find a way to—"

"The first thing on my agenda," O'Neill declared, his voice level and cold, "is to find Christelle Washington."

Hagan moved the chair by the dressing table and straddled it, facing Broc. "We've got an update on the Sabreliner. It landed in Chicago an hour ago. The plane was taken to a hangar, which suggests they won't be moving for a while. We had a surveillance team waiting; they saw Christelle Washington taken off."

O'Neill stood up. "You've lost her! What the hell went wrong?"

"Nothing went wrong, Broc, and we haven't lost her. What's happened is perfectly logical. Whoever's commandeering that Sabreliner knows it would be recognized in Washington. A routine check at Langley would uncover a clandestine operation. Whoever is behind this operation knows it would be scrutinized by their own people, CIA people like me. The stop in Chicago was a precaution."

O'Neill was confused and aggravated.

"Likely, the Sabreliner will be serviced and sent back to Southeast Asia. In all probability, a local plane will pick them up in Chicago in the next few days."

"The next few days! Christ, I've got to go—"

"Broc! Take it easy!"

Broc glared at Hagan as though he was crazy.

"We've got a surveillance team. We're tracking every move. We know exactly where Christelle Washington is at this moment—"

"Then you better bloody well tell me!"

"No, Broc! We aren't going to tell you." O'Neill could not believe what he was hearing. "We are not going to risk her life, your life, and maybe a successful breakup of this operation by letting you wade in alone. No more than we risked her life or yours in Malaysia."

"What the hell are you talking about?"

"Creighton put you up in a hotel at the Subang International Airport. Christelle was two miles away; she and her captors spent the night at the PJ Hilton Hotel. We even know the room number."

"You knew that!"

"We knew it two minutes after they booked in, two hours before you landed. We, Creighton and I, chose to keep both of you alive by making sure you did not know. You're shrewd, O'Neill. Anyone who reads your publications can tell that. And anyone who could stay alive as long as you have is very shrewd. But you're also impulsive, always in danger of wading into water too deep."

"What makes you and Creighton so damned all-knowing that you can decide what I can know and can't know?"

"Sit down. You'll hear me better."

O'Neill lowered himself onto the bed.

"You've got a trained mind, O'Neill, better than mine or Creighton's. Your research on intelligence has served you well. A trained mind, but not trained instincts. That's where Creighton is way ahead. Sorry to disillusion you, but you're just a kid, O'Neill, thirty-six years old with a career in a Midwest university. What were you? Still in grade school when Creighton and I and Wally Matthews were crawling through snake-infested swamps in Vietnam, setting explosives, wiring up bombs in the dark, stepping over sleeping Viet Cong? Do you think that was easy? Letting them sleep to blow up later when we were right there with a blade that could end it right then? Do you think keeping control was easy? And do you know why we're alive to tell you about it? Do you want to know how our platoon of Navy SEALs ran over a hundred, night raids into the Mekong Delta without a single failure, without a single lost life? Instinct. Knowing limits. Judging when the odds of failure are overwhelming. Burying fury with restraint. Then you find another way."

O'Neill stared at Hagan.

"This is no damned mountain river out west, O'Neill. It's not some whitewater rapids you can run in a kayak where you can pop out okay at the bottom. Lives have been lost. We want to prevent more. You've lost a wife. You know and we know you can't take another loss like that."

O'Neill sat silent for a minute, and then he demanded, "Have you finished? Have you said enough?"

"Not quite, O'Neill. You can say whatever you want, but we aren't telling you where Christelle Washington is. Not yet. That could happen in a few days. In the meantime, we've all got one hell of a lot of work to do. That includes you. And it's work that you can do much more effectively than anyone else."

"How is that?"

"Because you're dead. And you've got new identities. You can check in at hotels, make plane reservations, move around without detection. That gives you and all of us, the whole team, an enormous advantage."

O'Neill looked at him for several seconds.

Hagan spoke first. "We've got the evidence, and we've figured out what to do. Are you ready? Do you think you can leave Christelle Washington to us, to our judgment?"

O'Neill hesitated for several more seconds, then nodded.

Hagan reached into his jacket pocket, pulled out three folders—travel reservations — and laid them on the coffee table. "Don't open them until I leave, the flights are reserved under one or another of your new identities which — remember — I don't know. Alan doesn't know either, and he shouldn't."

O'Neill looked at the folders, then at Hagan.

"What I do know is that you've got three flights to make over the next week, to Bermuda, the Bahamas, and the Cayman Islands."

O'Neill leaned forward, his forehead wrinkled, his eyes on Hagan.

Hagan's face broke slowly into a broad smile. "Consider this a paid vacation with a little serious business to attend to on the side. We've worked out the perfect way to kill this monster. We're going to cut off its head, and you get to swing the machete. Now, if you're ready, I'll go over exactly what you need to do. Then it's up to you."

Chapter Forty

The Bahamas
Friday, August 23

Two and a half hours after takeoff from Richmond, Virginia, the Delta Air DC9 flew over the sprawling arms of Great Abaco Island on its way to Nassau, the largest city and business center of the Bahamas, situated on New Providence Island. Minutes later O'Neill felt the plane begin its descent as he gazed at the archipelago of the Berry Islands, with its dozens of uninhabited cays. The plane veered, gliding in over sand beaches and white roofs surrounded by tropical greenery on its way to the Nassau International Airport ten miles from the city.

It was four o'clock when he checked into the British Colonial Beach Resort, a stately tan-colored hotel that faced north across Nassau Harbor toward a line of expensive resorts on Paradise Island. As he laid his Mastercard on the counter — the third time he had checked into a major hotel under the name of Robert Winston — it struck him how liberated he had become with a new identity. For the first time since Darcy's death in May, he knew he was safe from sudden assassination.

In his room O'Neill folded his jacket over the back of a chair and looked out over the strait. The scene made him feel a sudden pang of grief. He watched a young couple walking along in water to their ankles — happy, playful, obviously very much in love, probably honeymooners. He turned away. He wanted Christelle to be safe; he wanted to tell her that he was alive, and that they would one day be together again. He wanted Christelle here, now.

A dozen times he had felt his stomach knotting up. Something might go wrong. Despite all of Brently Hagan's CIA resources, they might somehow lose track of her. It was more than he could contemplate. Struggling against fear, he turned back to the pages of numbers Hagan had given him at the airport. He had phoned Hagan again on Saturday;

there were more numbers. He and Creighton were slowly unraveling the tangled network of deception. But whatever they had found out since Thursday would have to wait. O'Neill had other things to do. He had to familiarize himself with a mountain of information.

Everything had worked out. O'Neill had stayed his first night in Washington in the room Hagan had rented. His new identity, Robert Brocford Winston, gave him confidence. None of them had figured out where the nerve center of Sparsum or Lignum was located, but even if it were here in the room next door, a new identity gave him complete immunity.

The next day he had moved to the Hyatt Regency on New Jersey Avenue, a preferred location that looked out on the dome of The Capitol. By noon he had arranged for money to be wired from Jefferson — from a new account under his new identity that had clandestinely received the remainder of Darcy's insurance money. The marvels of his new detection-proof identity were beyond anything he had imagined. He had paid the hotel for ten nights in advance, stashed most of his new wardrobe, driven a rental car south to Richmond, and caught a late morning flight to Bermuda.

It was mid-afternoon when he caught sight of the first of more than a hundred islands as the plane came in to land on a runway between Castle Harbour and St. George's Harbour. Within an hour, he was booked into one of the premier historic hotels, the century-old waterfront Princess. From his fifth-floor window, he stood watching the white sails dotting the protected waters of Hamilton Harbour.

Missing Christelle, agonizing over her trauma as a captive, he knew he had to trust Brent Hagan and his surveillance team to keep her in sight. Hours later, savoring a Bermuda Rum Swizzle ordered up from the bar, he forcefully drove away his anxiety as he watched the sunset over the Atlantic, reminding him of nightfall on the South China Sea.

What he had to do was done with astonishing ease. By three o'clock Friday afternoon, he had two vital documents in his briefcase and an extra day on his hands, so he spent Saturday wandering through the older sections of the city, visiting Fort Hamilton and the Bermuda Cathedral, then finishing the day with an hour in the fitness center. His Sunday morning flight returned him to Richmond, Virginia. He was on the ground no more than ninety minutes before he was in the air again to another offshore location.

Despite his new identity, he had one more transaction to make under the name of Broc O'Neill. This time it was in the Bahamas.

O'Neill followed the petite receptionist, a dark-haired brown-eyed woman whose skin glowed like copper as though she spent every spare hour working on her tan, exercising at her club, and generally living the good life, presumably with a devoted and wealthy husband. Her diamond rings were elegantly expensive.

O'Neill shook hands with the bank manager, took the offered chair across the huge mahogany desk, and passed him a business card. "Of course, Mr. O'Neill, we'd be more than happy to open an account. In your name, or the company name?"

"The company name will be fine." O'Neill pushed his papers of incorporation across the desk.

The bank manager examined the documents, which had been completed in the Bermuda registry office three days ago at a cost of just under $2,000. The documents included a Hamilton address administered through a Bermuda law firm, and bearer shares, with Broc O'Neill as the sole owner. "We'll need identification, Mr. O'Neill," the manager said.

O'Neill handed his passport and Indiana driver's license across the desk. "Of course," he added, "for obvious reasons I would prefer to sign the checks under another name." He passed across an Assumed Name Statement obtained less than an hour before from the Nassau registry office: a DBA authorization that allowed Broc O'Neill to do business as John O'Brien— a distinct entity legally entitled to open a Nassau bank account, write checks, operate a branch of a corporation, and conduct business in the Bahamas.

"Everything appears in order," the manager attested, folding his hands. "I assume you're an American." O'Neill nodded. "We would like to assure you that Regency of Nassau exercises the most rigorous privacy on all its accounts. Your Internal Revenue Service stays out of our business unless they suspect criminal activity. Then we are forced to disclose information." The manager picked up O'Neill's forms. "Your corporate registry in Bermuda obviates all that; American ownership is hidden. I assume you know this."

O'Neill nodded and the manager passed forms across the desk.

"This certificate gives us your company name. What we need is an address and your choice of design." As the manager passed him the catalog, O'Neill noticed that a Bahamas 'check' was still a British 'cheque'.

O'Neill wrote CR&R Limited, the usual designation for a British company. He added the Bermuda address on the second and third lines, added the word 'Treasurer' under the signature line and passed the paper back, then turned to the sample checks.

"I do have one other request," O'Neill began, as the manager filled boxes with standard bank information. He opened his briefcase and set three thick piles of American currency on the desk. "I'm a superstitious man, and I hope you won't mind, but I would like to have a bank account number that will align with my own personality."

The manager looked up at O'Neill, his face blank. His eyes dropped to the piles of money then back to O'Neill.

"It's difficult to explain, and I have stopped trying," O'Neill admitted. "Few people care about numeric arrangements and how they are related to one's own fate. However, I have here three possible account numbers. Any one of them would be sufficient." He pushed a notepad across the desk. On it were written three numbers:

450-003-1126
405-030-1126
405-003-1226.

"This is highly irregular. We usually follow the numerical sequence issued by head office. Let me tell you what your number will be, Sir—"

"But I really must insist." O'Neill laid his hand across the bills, looking the manager directly in the eyes. "Could you please check these account numbers?"

The manager turned to his computer screen, speaking as he entered numbers. "How would you describe your business, Mr. O'Neill? Or, shall we say, what level of financial transaction can we anticipate?"

O'Neill removed his hand and spoke carefully, avoiding the first question. "The deposit today will be $300,000, but this will be the minimum amount on deposit at all times." The manager glanced at him. Broc guessed the amounts would get him what he wanted. "The actual amount of money processed through the account will be many times that amount. It will be a very lucrative account for your bank."

The manager continued working at the screen. "I have good news for you, Mr. O'Neill. The second and third numbers are already taken. But the first number on the list is available. Will that be satisfactory?"

"Wonderful, Sir. That is most pleasing." He pushed the bills across the table. "Are there any more papers to prepare."

"None. The only thing left is the cheque design."

"I've already decided," he said, pointing to a sea-green design with tropical islands in the background. He clicked his briefcase shut and stood up. "There's only one more thing. I have a flight booked for 6 p.m. tomorrow. I would like to pick up my printed checks before closing time, say 3 p.m. Is that possible?"

"Most certainly, we can print up two hundred or four hundred. What is your preference?"

"I believe I'll need more, something in excess of four thousand, but I'd like to avoid having to reorder too soon. Could you please print six thousand checks?"

It was late Tuesday night when O'Neill caught sight of the lights of Grand Cayman, a twenty-mile-long island off the southern coast of Cuba. The beachfront resorts were visible as the plane slowly wheeled toward the runway. The night lights provided a dramatic display of wealth, the richest concentration of capital and the highest per capita income in the Caribbean. The plane landed at George Town. O'Neill checked in at Sunset House, a quiet hotel just south of the town, which seemed to be the resort of choice for SCUBA divers.

At nine o'clock Wednesday morning, O'Neill walked into a George Town bank housed in a non-descript low rise, converted enough American money to Caymanian dollars to pay for everything in cash, and asked to see the bank manager. In a few minutes he was sitting in a back office with a cup of freshly-brewed Caribbean coffee and a plate of donuts, the typical hospitality extended to well-heeled customers by any one of several hundred international banks with branch offices in the Caymans.

O'Neill passed his business card to the manager, Daniel Wicks, a well-dressed Englishman who sounded as though he worked in the financial district of London. The card was one of the many items in the detection-proof identity package supplied by Brently Hagan; it identified 'Robert Winston' as an officer of the Central Intelligence Agency. O'Neill had not asked Hagan for an explanation, assuming that his documents were similar to those supplied to bona fide CIA officers going under cover. He gave the manager time to read the business card, then flashed his CIA identity card.

"Mr. Wicks, we're in the midst of an investigation that involves one of your largest clients — Lignum Operations."

"Certainly one of our largest. Of course, we cannot divulge anything about the Lignum accounts — definitely not the actual funds on deposit — but we are confident there is no connection between Lignum Operations and the usual drug laundering cartels. We have made a number of calls to the U.S. We have had assurances."

O'Neill lifted his briefcase and pulled out a thick file. "You are absolutely correct, Mr. Wicks; our investigations verify what you say. However, we still have a problem with Lignum. While I sort through these papers, would you be so kind as to bring the Lignum account up on screen?"

Clearly dubious, the manager did what O'Neill requested, acting as though it was a fruitless but harmless exercise.

"Let's get the basics out of the way, first," O'Neill started. "Lignum Operations receives regular transfers of funds from the U.S. For example, let's consider the month of July. You've had transfers from four banks — in Los Angeles, Houston, New York, and Washington."

Wicks was obviously surprised by the accuracy of the information.

"For simplicity, let's pick one. L.A.? New York? Which would you prefer?"

"Houston, I guess," Wicks chose.

O'Neill thumbed through the file and extracted several stapled pages. "The account at Texas International Bank in Houston is under the name of Anatran Corporation. TIBH account number, 605-003-1296. Let's see; check your screen, Mr. Wicks. There were transfers from TIBH on July 2nd — $16.6 million, July 3rd — $39.6 million, July 7th — $22.8 million, July 8th — $25.3 million. I'm sure you appreciate that I am rounding the numbers, but just to be sure we're on the same page, let's be exact. July 10th — $19,467,920.64. July 11th — $13,166,200.26." O'Neill looked up. "Need I go on?"

Wicks moved his attention from the computer screen to Broc and back.

"Altogether, a little over half a billion dollars. To be precise, twenty-one transfers totaling exactly $506,690,615.85. Similar transfers from Manhattan National Bank, Jefferson International Bank in Washington, and Consolidated Capital Bank in Los Angeles add up to a total of $2.34 billion — all of it deposited during the month of July, in your bank, in the Lignum Operations account."

Astounded at what he was hearing, Wicks stared at O'Neill.

"This, of course, is not an isolated occurrence. During the month of June, $2.32 billion was deposited. In May, $2.3 billion. The fact is that you have been receiving regular deposits averaging around one billion per month from each of four U.S. banks, and this has been going on for nearly four years. Of course, the deposits were not so high at first, about half these amounts, but the steadily increasing deposits do concern us greatly."

Wicks stumbled, "Where... how did you obtain this... these figures?"

"American intelligence is able to pick up all bank transfers from the U.S. at source. You may also be interested to learn that we know precisely where all that money came from. For instance — this is not information that you would know — the July 7th transfer of $22.8 million was the sum of twelve deposits made to the Anatran account at Texas International Bank over the previous few days. We know the sources and the precise amounts." O'Neill held up a packet of computer printout nearly an inch thick. "And we have the same information for every one of the eighty-six deposits made to four U.S. banks and then passed on to your Lignum Operations bank. To be specific, account number BA567-842-1002."

Wicks was clearly alarmed at the scope of the investigation.

"Now, Mr. Wicks, on the last day of each month for the past forty-seven months, you have made electronic transfers of funds from Lignum to other accounts. On May 31st, the larger transfer was $2.3 billion. On June 30th, $2.32 billion. On July 31st, you transferred a record amount. It was you who did it, Mr. Wicks. Your own personal identification code is attached to the transactions, which totaled" — O'Neill rifled through his pages— "precisely $2,343,675,801.42. That amount is the sum of the July deposits we have just itemized, minus a small transfer elsewhere. On the surface, it looks like your bank is just a pass-through for massive amounts of money. On average, you have about a billion on deposit at all times. At a preferred-client interest rate of five percent, this account is earning somewhere around $3 million in interest a month, $40 million a year. It appears that Lignum is passing on the principal of its monthly deposits and leaving most of the interest earned with your bank. Our records show that this account is one of your largest. Interest earned has remained on deposit for over three years and has now accumulated to more than $115 million. That is a significant addition to the assets on deposit — and to the monthly total of interest earnings. That's what makes this account so lucrative for your bank."

Wicks stared at O'Neill, who, after a pause of a few seconds, added: "Judging by your salary — and annual bonuses — this account, which is entirely under your care, has been very lucrative for you, too."

O'Neill watched Wicks, who fidgeted with a paperweight on his desk, moved a notebook, picked up a pen. "Is there... any criminal activity... in any of this?"

"None in anything that you've done. In fact, it would be very difficult for you or anyone else to locate precisely where the criminal activity lies. Actually, it's far back in the supply chain before the funds reach Regency. They're disguised as charitable donations, but they've been obtained through extortion, bribery, harassment, and awards of massive government contracts to cooperative American companies — all crimes of the highest order. Recently, there have been some nasty developments. Arson has been used to persuade certain wealthy 'contributors' to make payments. The list of crimes, and of laws broken, is still being compiled. The guilty parties add up to several dozen."

O'Neill leaned forward. "Mr. Wicks, I believe we can break this with no repercussions to you or your bank. But we will require your cooperation."

Daniel Wicks looked at O'Neill, uncertain of his role. He appeared afraid to ask.

"First of all, this case of money laundering is like almost every case ever investigated by the CIA or the FBI. The account owners in the U.S. typically develop a series of shells, which shield them from direct tax liability. In the case of Lignum Operations"— O'Neill mentally drew a breath and plunged in — "the ownership has been concealed by other corporate names established in offshore tax havens—"

"That's right," Wicks confirmed." Ironwood was incorporated in Curaçao."

Bull's-eye! That was what O'Neill wanted to know. Curaçao. Another offshore business center — Caribbean tax haven… capital of the Netherlands Antilles.

O'Neill nodded, and then leaned forward. "Mr. Wicks, how often do you get back to England? You know, for a vacation, quality time with your family?"

"Not nearly as often as I would like. My wife especially misses England."

"That's what we suspected. Mr. Wicks, we are in the process of arranging a long, fully-paid vacation — say for four months, maybe to the end of the year — to England, or wherever else you would like to go. Arranged this way, your absence will not arouse any suspicion. However, you may need protection well beyond that. So, the British Secret Service, M15, will be in touch as soon as you arrive in England. It will be in everyone's interest if you disappear from public view. You and your wife could remain in England or do some traveling. We've discovered you have advanced degrees in economics, enough to qualify you for what we suspect you would like most: a position in the prestigious British Institute for Economic Research — BIER for short — which is very private about its membership. It's connected to the London School of Economics. So, we've arranged for your retirement from Regency to become effective at the end of your vacation. Your retirement income is guaranteed of course, for life, at fifty-percent higher than your current salary, which should be sufficient, especially when supplemented by the stipend earned from BIER."

Wicks stared at O'Neill, astonished. "What... what do I need to do?"

"When you get back to England, file papers for your own LLC, a Limited Liability Company, where the business climate is congenial. Wyoming would work. Then open a bank account in the name of your LLC. Pick a place you might like to go for vacations; Jackson, Wyoming, is not far from the Grand Tetons and Yellowstone National Park. Or, if you would prefer someplace closer to home, the Isle of Man in the Irish Sea would work. Whatever you choose, that's where your retirement salary will be deposited. Send me the bank, branch, LLC name, and account number once it's in place." O'Neill passed a paper to Wicks with his e-mail address. "Of course, you won't ever have to go near the bank. You can arrange for automatic transfers to your British account."

Wicks pondered a minute. "What else do I have to do?"

"We need your cooperation in the transfers scheduled later this month. Normally, you transfer the Lignum Operations funds to the account of Sparsum Operations — let's see, Account Number 405-003-1162 — located in Regency of Nassau in Barbados."

O'Neill handed a piece of paper across the desk. "These are additional instructions." Then he passed an envelope to Wicks. "These are plane tickets."

Chapter Forty-one

Chicago
Wednesday, August 28

Christelle moved slowly. Everything was gray like dirty fog drifting across the water. The water was iron gray — hard, metallic, as though it had been covered over with engine oil. The boat rocked and turned as waves rolled under the hull, jarring everything, throwing the hard gray waves out of focus. Everything waved and drifted. Then slowly the darker gray settled and came into focus. Iron-gray metallic waves under a stormy gray sky.

Christelle turned over. She felt herself rolling. She was floating on iron gray waves. Sickness poured through her body, waves of nausea moving from her stomach, through her chest, until they reached her head and she felt wretchedly dizzy. She must have opened her eyes because she felt a blinding gray-white light from the window pierce her head. Pain shot through the nausea. She heard herself moaning as she rolled away from the light, lying as still as she could until the pain slipped away.

The water lay all around — iron gray, ugly, ominous. But wasn't it blue before, a perfect tropical blue? Why was it gray? Without warning, the waves erupted in a violent maelstrom as an immense, blunt-nosed beast broke surface. She saw the steely eyes, the half-open maw, the fragments of human life trailing from the jagged teeth; and she cried out again, her body tensing up in a violent convulsion that made her pull her knees up to her chest. She saw the blood streaming from the teeth, staining the iron-gray water — the precious blood of life. The agony made her shudder and convulse again, and then she was sobbing uncontrollably, weeping for Broc O'Neill. The slicing pain made her want to run into walls, tear down doors, crash through the window until she plunged down into some dark alley where grief and pain would come to an end.

They had rushed her from the dive boat in her bathing suit with nothing more than a towel and her handbag. Any one of them could have held her, but there were three. Within minutes they had walked her along the beach — too far from the Tioman Resort to cry out for help — forced her onto a hotel luggage cart, and taken her over the hill to the waiting aircraft. Somehow, her luggage was already there, thrown behind the seat.

Then she broke down. The plane, with four people crammed into a cockpit smaller than a Volkswagen, soared from the Tioman runway over the water above Tulai Island. Screaming, hysterical, blinded by tears, she clawed at the windows, staring frantically at the water around the island where they had fired their guns at Broc — where he had been attacked by sharks and died a violent death. Then the pain started up in her head. They had brought her to the surface too fast. She clawed at the man beside her, doing everything she could to tear out his eyes, creating so much turmoil in the cabin that the pilot was bumped and jostled, until the other two constrained her — biting, clawing — and forced something into her mouth. She screamed and kicked and scratched, drawing blood she was sure, until she felt a blank emptiness sweeping over.

Everything was muddled, tangled days and nights without order, light and darkness that did not make sense. She remembered standing up, walking, riding elevators, climbing steps, and then the memories came flooding back: the iron gray waves, the sudden eruption of the water, the bloody human remains. Again, and again, she went into a fury, attacking her captors, tearing, scratching, clawing, biting, until they held her down and forced something into her mouth again. Then the white emptiness began.

She woke up on another plane. She was sleeping on the floor at the back, sandwiched in the aisle with a pillow and blanket. There were passengers ahead, and no more than the length of a room away an open door, and through the door the pilot. She heard conversation. It was drowned by the roar of engines. The plane was small, like the twenty-passenger tourist plane she and Broc had ridden to Tioman Island.

Broc... The pain started up. Christelle stifled her sobs, trying to keep still. She did not want to be drugged again. She had to think. She had to figure out what was happening. She moved her hands slowly under the blanket. She was wearing a blouse and denims and socks. But they had caught her in her bathing suit. Bastards! They had removed her bikini and dressed her while she was drugged. Damn them! That must have given them a big thrill!

Christelle squeezed her legs together and felt around her abdomen, then between her legs. If they had raped her, she would have been bruised; she would have known. But she wasn't sore, no discomfort. In the seats ahead she could see only shoulders and arms. They were big men, but they didn't look like thugs. They were well dressed. She had scratched one of them rather badly, enough to infuriate most men. But other than nasty drugs, they hadn't done her any harm. She squeezed her sides and her ribs, her arms, and then her breasts.

The plane touched down. She lay still with eyes closed and listened to them. They were in an airport in Japan, and then they were in the air again. Japan? Why Japan? Where were they taking her? She tried to imagine a map. She and Broc had flown from Los Angeles non-stop to Singapore, but you could get there with a stopover in Japan. Maybe they were on their way to the States!

Oh, dear God! Malaysia and Tioman Island were so far behind. Christelle pulled her legs up and lay in a ball. *Broc... Broc O'Neill...* She couldn't help it: the deep sobs started to come again. She lay on her side, struggling against the grief, crying, tears flooding out on her pillow.

"Hey, the bitch is awake!"

"Check her out, Wade."

Christelle heard sounds of feet. She lay still, trying to stifle her sobs.

"Okay, bitch, sit up!" She didn't move. She felt a hand grip her shoulder, not painfully, just firmly. "Sit up or we'll tie you sitting up."

She had to keep calm. Slowly, she moved onto her stomach and pulled her knees under her — the only way to get up in the narrow aisle. She got up on her knees, feeling a sudden wave of nausea. She felt like she would vomit.

"Get up on the seat," he ordered. She glared at him, feeling the icy glare in return.

He had a BAND-AID on his cheek and another on the side of his neck. "You bloody bastard! You're lucky I didn't get your eyes!"

"You're the lucky one, bitch! You try that again and we'll get out the pliers. You'll wake up with those claws torn away to the quick. Now get the hell into that seat. If I have to put you there, it will be with handcuffs." He dangled them in front of Christelle.

Glaring at him as nastily as she could manage, Christelle slowly climbed into the seat. She felt nauseous and weak, and when her captor shoved the yogurt at her, she snatched it. "Are you going to give me a spoon, or do I have to throw this stuff in your face?"

"Such bad manners," he said, pulling a half-sized white plastic spoon from his pocket. "Now, Miss Washington, you've been without food for hours, and you're full of some nasty dope. That's why you're feeling ready to barf. The only cure is to eat. If you behave, you'll get your meals. In fact, for all I care, you can pig out until that little bottom pops right out of those jeans."

Christelle leaned forward until her face was about a foot from his. "You bastard with balls for brains," she said, her voice low and level. "Mr. Wade Whoever-You-Are, who the hell do you work for, the federal screw department? You can dream all you want about this little bottom, but you lay a finger on me again and you'll have holes in your head for eyes!" She moved like lightning, snatching the spoon from his hand before he could blink. "Now get the hell up to your seat and leave me to eat in peace."

She stared him down, and after a few seconds he moved away.

"Testy little bitch," she heard him say to the others. There was a minute of mumbling and then they all turned eyes front and left her alone.

It was a good thing for them she didn't have that Colt 45 or they'd all be dead.

She ate the yogurt and, half an hour later, a ham-and-cheese sandwich they pulled out of a Styrofoam cooler. She found her handbag, dug through her paperbacks, found her brush, and did what she could to fix herself up.

By the time they were over Alaska, her stomach felt better. She stared at the immense glaciers winding down from the mountains while struggling to control herself, pulling her mind away from Tioman Island.

She tried to think. Who were these guys? They must be the ones who were after Broc. She felt her stomach jerk, like a violent hiccup, as she realized sharks had done their dirty work. God! What a way to die! But why hadn't they killed her? Why had they hired some kind of private plane to take her back to the U.S.? They couldn't link her to the car that went off the road in Vermont or to the murder of Colonel Spiker in Allentown. Or could they?

Christelle kept silent for another six hours as the plane flew its long arc, she guessed down over the Canadian wilderness. She watched the endless forests and lakes roll by, and then the beginning of farmlands, and finally the vast Canadian prairies squared off in fields of grain as far as the eye could see. She had slept almost every minute on the flight to Japan; she was wide awake now, even though all three of her captors were asleep. Only the pilot was awake, and she was not about to tangle with him.

Hours later, she saw a huge body of water stretching away to the east. Within minutes she heard the crackling of the radio, from stations in Duluth and then Green Bay, and she knew they were coming in over the Great Lakes. Another thirty minutes brought them over Milwaukee, and then they were circling, waiting for instructions for landing at O'Hare International Airport in Chicago.

Christelle managed to hold her fury for another hour while they landed and were led through a huge hangar to a waiting car. Then she lost it. They had slowed for a corner at the edge of the airport when she saw a police station. Enraged, she lashed out at her captors and did everything to scratch the man beside her and throw the driver out of control. She yanked his hair back and clawed at his neck — and then they had her by the hair and were forcing her down and forcing something into her mouth.

Christelle rolled over again. Her head was aching, splitting with pain. She felt the pain of the light from the window. There were two doors, both ajar, one to a small bathroom, the other to a hallway. The room had an insipid modern painting on the wall like the ones in cheap hotels. She heard the low sound of a TV set through the open door.

She struggled to sit up. It was difficult because she was in handcuffs. She stared at the nasty metal rings connected by three links of chain.

Damn them, anyway! In front of the closet stood her suitcases, bulging full as they had been on their way to Tioman. They must have broken into their hotel room and packed up everything while she and Broc were diving. Bastards!

Queasy in her stomach, she tested her legs. She moved across the carpet without mishap and went into the bathroom, pulling the door closed behind her. She sat fighting nausea, then stared at herself in the mirror. She looked wretched. Dark circles under her eyes. Tangled hair. She needed to clean up.

She stood by the bedroom door listening to the low conversation, then moved out and down the hall and stopped in the doorway to the central room of the suite. Four men looked up from a game of cards, obviously thoroughly pissed. There were BAND-AIDs now on three of them.

Bastards! Give me half a chance and I'll scar all four of them. "I need something to eat."

The man called Wade checked his watch. "Get the hell back to your cage, bitch; dinner is another hour and a half."

Christelle felt her stomach churning. Whatever dope they had forced into her was worse than the first time.

"You look like shit, bitch! You'll have to clean up before you can eat with us, so get your clothes off and get the hell into the shower."

Christelle gave him the dirtiest look she could manage. "Mr. Wade Whoever-You-Are, let me explain a simple middle school geometric principle to your retarded little brain. It is not possible to remove one's clothes while in handcuffs."

Wade got up, went to the counter, got her handbag, and ordered her back to her bedroom. "Lie on the floor, bitch. On your stomach."

Christelle lowered herself awkwardly to her knees. "What is this? Another of your filthy little fantasies?"

"On your stomach, hands over your head."

She was desperate to get off her feet before the nausea made her fall, but she took her time obeying him. She lay still, waiting. Wade walked across the carpet and stood over her, and then she heard the click of a key in the cuffs, and the rough metal scraping her skin as he pulled them off. She did not move. A minute later, she heard the door close and a key turn in the lock.

Chapter Forty-two

Caloocan City, the Philippines
Wednesday, August 28

Willy Rand stood in the shadows near the docks. It was ten minutes past midnight. He gazed into the darkness on Manila Bay, which was lit by a few scattered lights, deck lanterns of anchored ships waiting for offloading. He pushed the button on his watch. Two minutes and forty-two seconds since his last signal. He waited, watching the second hand, tick slowly, second by second. As it reached the twelve, he pointed his flashlight into the darkness. One quick flash.

He stared into the blackness. There would be no returning signal, only darkness. but in exactly three minutes, he would signal again. Seven signals in eighteen minutes.

Willy Rand: Fifty-six years of age. Employed in one of the largest electrical installations in Hawaii. Ex-Navy SEAL. Veteran of the Vietnam War.

He had signed up exactly thirty-two years ago. His father had watched the Japanese bombs fall on Pearl Harbor and so had served against Japan at Guadalcanal, the Marianas, and Iwo Jima. They lived in Honolulu. Every December 7th, his father drove them to the harbor, where they could see the blasted hulks of American ships. Family pride made the military the obvious choice for Willy. He was too young for the Korean War; he had signed up for naval duty in Vietnam.

He gritted his teeth. Now he had the wisdom of age and history. A couple of months ago he had picked up a book by Robert McNamara, Secretary of Defense during the Vietnam War, who had admitted that Johnson and Nixon and the rest of the Administration knew this war was unwinnable. But they had kept on sending troops — young men caught up in the draft. It was a costly, senseless war spiraling through one mistake after another: an Asian independence movement misperceived, another attempt bred in the parlors of America's brightest strategists at containing communism, financial backing for the French in Indochina gone sour, a failed foreign policy under three American presidents. It had led to a war that never should have happened. McNamara's book had generated a tempest of anger from people who had lost sons and relatives because Johnson and Nixon had followed a philosophy of 'escalation' — it was the fashionable word of the times — sending wave after wave of service men to fight in Southeast Asian jungles while knowing victory was out of reach.

Willy Rand had known none of this. He was eighteen years of age, a drop-out student who had read Jack Kerouac's *On the Road* and dreamed of roaming California with the last of the Beats or the first of the Flower Children. His blood was hot; the adrenaline was pumping. He had surfed Hawaii's biggest waves. And then he felt the lure of adventure and the pride of serving his country. He had volunteered.

The way to military excellence was narrow focus. Attend to the immediate task at hand. Willy Rand was focused; he was also like a fish in water from long summers spent on the Hawaiian beaches. They discovered him; they sent him to train for the Navy SEALs. At Camp Benning, and later during the final phases of the Underwater Demolition training, he met some of those he would be with for the next five years: Brently Hagan, who became the Officer-in-Charge, and his partner of choice; Wally Matthews, who became the Second-in-Charge; and eleven others in the fourteen-man platoon, including Alan Creighton.

The record of the Navy SEALs was impeccable, but it was a disillusioning war. For every mile gained by the SEALs, two others were overrun by the Viet Cong. By the time it was over, it had cost President Johnson his job. It had brought Robert Kennedy into the 1968 presidential campaign and had seen him assassinated. Hundreds of thousands of college students and millions of ordinary Americans were angered. Those who ran off to Canada to avoid the draft chastised those who had fought, an ugly reversal of the pride among World War II veterans.

Willy Rand served, survived, and went back to Hawaii, managing to take along what he valued most — a lovely Vietnamese girl whose family had been killed by American bombing raids. She was a reminder of those

357

terrible years, both his and America's, yet her smiling face and dimpled cheeks and the three beautiful children she had borne him in the next ten years had made his life worthwhile. Now, nearly a quarter century later, they lived together, very much in love, two of their offspring in college, the eldest a new graduate in engineering with a successful position in Silicon Valley, California.

Rand pushed the button on his watch, counted down the last twenty seconds, and flashed his light into the pitch darkness of the bay.

Two years ago, an invitation to a platoon reunion had somehow found its way to his mailbox. He had set it on his desk and never replied. Months later, a newsletter had reached him, listing the members of his platoon who had attended the reunion and where they were now settled. Rand had thought about it for a year and a half. Then he wrote to Wally Matthews, a permanent American expatriate living in Singapore.

Rand admired Matthews. Wally had turned a disastrous series of family tragedies during the war into things of the past. He had struggled through, crawled out from the darkness, and started a new life. Rand had photographs of his platoon on his desk. One showed Wally with his Malay wife and two sons, who would soon be attending the National University of Singapore. In the background floated a magnificent blue, white-trimmed tourist boat that Matthews owned and operated among the islands of Southeast Asia.

Willy shifted against the warehouse wall. The darkness along the crowded bulkheads was almost total. The waterfront north of Manila was comprised of docks, but they still lacked the modern facilities of the U.S.: the harbor lights, offloading cranes, mechanized handling facilities.

A week ago, he had received an express mail letter from Wally. Something big, something enormous, was afoot. A criminal network beyond the scale of Watergate or the Iran-Contra subversion of Congressional Law. It was the first time, Matthews considered, that anything going on in the States had concerned him, and now the prospects excited him. He had met someone at Tioman Island, an American called Broc O'Neill, who had stumbled into the midst of the conspiracy and somehow teamed up with two members of their platoon: Brently Hagan and Alan Creighton. Together, they were determined to break the back of this monster. It was a new war, Wally declared, and he was in it, too. Was Willy willing to help?

Willy had flown from Hawaii to Manila two days ago. Now, after spending the daylight hours exploring Caloocan City and the layout of Teleconic Electronics, he was ready. He flashed his light and watched. There were no sounds, nothing more than the quiet lapping of waves against the piers a few feet away.

Rand shifted again, and then walked out onto the broad cement platform. Ambling slowly, he moved toward the closest dock. A freighter had pulled out in the afternoon; the next one would probably pull in tomorrow. It was a long pier; he estimated 350 to 400 feet. He knew he was virtually invisible at more than ten yards. When he got to the end, he was within five seconds of the next signal. He flashed his light seaward and lowered himself into a seated position, hung his feet over the end of the dock, and waited.

Two minutes later, he heard a splash. He stared at the surface ten or fifteen yards away. Another splash, a little closer; and then someone was below him by the pier.

He gave his light one brief flash. Immediately, he heard another splash and words out of the darkness. "Willy... Willy Rand?"

"It's Rand. Here, I'm lowering a rope."

A minute later, he felt the jerk and hauled up the rope, untied the waterproof satchel, and lowered it again. This was repeated six times. He waited. The rope jerked again. He hauled it up and dumped the bundle on the dock; a cluster of goggles, fins, BCDs, and other SCUBA equipment. Two more hauls brought air tanks onto the dock. A minute later, two men came over the edge.

"Willy," a voice said, "I'm Kareem. This is my brother, Samir. Our father is on the boat."

"Your father?" Rand asked the tall shapes in the darkness.

"Wally Matthews."

Rand shoved out his hand, stunned at the appearance of Wally's sons, who were taller and more powerfully built than their father.

"The boat's a half-mile out," Samir said. "Father wanted to come, but we persuaded him to stay. Even for an old Navy SEAL, some jobs need to be passed on to the young."

"My God! He's trained you up to be like him!"

"He sure did. He's run us through sessions he calls 'Hell Week'. He said you'd know what that was all about."

"Sure do." Rand picked up one of the duffle bags.

Five minutes later, they had made three trips and transported everything from the docks to a dark passage between the warehouses. Within another minute, Samir and Kareem had pulled out clothes and dressed. Then the three of them picked up two duffle bags each and headed into the city.

They boosted him in the shadows. Within seconds Willy was on the roof at the west end of Teleconic Electronics. Within another minute he had hauled up the duffle bags. He moved carefully, but there was hardly any need; the roof was solidly constructed of corrugated steel over closely spaced joists. A hundred feet along, he came to a narrow gap where a three-foot alleyway separated two buildings. He had walked past in daylight and spotted it through the fence, a crowded impassable space where trash made the alley unusable. He pointed his light down, cupped his hand around the lens, and turned it on. Directly below sat a half dozen empty barrels. Along a twenty-foot stretch of wall, he picked out three resting against the wall of the other shed.

Rand pulled out a piece of paper from his pocket and spread it out under his light. It was a photocopy of a sketch — the interior of the Teleconic complex — which Broc O'Neill had given to Wally at Tioman Island. According to the sketch, the space immediately adjacent to this alley, right where the barrels were standing, was where the sensitive Teleconic computer chips were made and stored.

Rand worked quickly, opening three duffle bags packed with explosives. How easy it was to bring these materials ashore in the middle of the night; how impossible it would have been to bring them in any other way.

The explosives were more compact than anything used in Vietnam, but knowing that Rand would be working in the dark, Wally had installed a familiar Vietnam-era mechanism to each. Cautiously, Willy attached a twenty-foot length of wire to each, then partially zipped up the duffle bags and lowered them with lengths of rope one at a time into the barrels.

He scraped off the rubber covering from the ends of the wires, twisted them together, and attached them with a copper clamp to a single wire, which he ran along the roof. He did a quick check of the diagram again, angled the wire over the peak of the roof, and headed for a gable over the central loading yard. From another duffle bag, he brought out a small antenna, which he laid out on the roof with a direct line of sight to the office windows across the loading yard. Now all he had to do was set up some way of triggering a signal to the antenna. It was hardly necessary to place the explosives next to the workplace where the chips were made; there was enough power, now concentrated near the center of the complex, to blow the entire factory to bits.

Rand looked around for a place to attach a rope, then spotted a pile of crates against the wall of the next shed. The gap was six feet, an easy jump, and within another two minutes, he had followed the roof around, lowered himself to the crates, and dropped to the ground. The front office window was unlocked.

Within a minute Rand was inside with his last duffle bag. The window was hidden from the street; he could risk a light. He saw the telephone on the desk. It had six extensions, numbered 10, 20, 30, 40, 50 and 60. Rand followed the wire away from the phone to the wall three feet from a door. He went through to the other side. The wire came through the wall, followed an uncovered stud to the ceiling, where it was stapled to a rafter across the ceiling, then ran through another wall to a storeroom stashed with old computer equipment.

Picking a spot where the wire ran behind some shelves, Rand cut it, installed a coupler on each end, and clicked the plastic parts together. Now he had a place to connect another wire. He went back to the office to test the phone; the dial tone was strong. Back in the storeroom, he clicked another coupler in place and ran eight feet of wire down to the floor, dropping it behind the stacked boxes to a spot in a corner. In a few minutes he had the black box out of the duffle bag and wired up. In another quarter hour, he had run fifty feet of copper wire from the box back to the office, shoving it into crevices and running it along baseboards. The windows were badly fitted; there were cracks where the wire could be run to the outside of the building.

Rand climbed out the window, found the wire, ran it below the windowsill to a spot about fifteen feet away from the door, and wound it around a projecting nail. He checked the line of sight to the copper antennae across the yard. Perfect.

He climbed in the window again and went back to the storeroom. The cover of the black box was easily unscrewed. Inside it were five dials with settings from 0 to 9, which allowed for a hundred thousand possible combinations. He turned the dials one at a time, setting the numbers for an easy sequence — 3-4-5-6-7 — then tightened down the lock nuts. He held his breath as he connected the final terminal, loading the device. In another minute he had screwed the cover back in place, pushed the device out of sight, and shifted some boxes an inch or two, completely hiding the box without altering the appearance of anything. He paused another minute to check the course of the copper wire; nothing was visible. Rand stood in the office for a minute. The telephone now had six known extensions, each with two digits, and now an added secret extension of five digits. A phone call from anywhere in the world, to the new extension would trigger an explosion. Teleconic Electronics would disappear from the face of the Earth.

Satisfied with his work, Willy shut off the lights, climbed out the window, pulled it back in place, and headed for the pile of crates. Minutes later he had climbed back onto the roof, worked his way back to the west end of the factory, and dropped to the sidewalk with two empty duffle bags in hand. Kareem and Samir came out of the shadows and the three started back to the docks.

They stood on the wharf. Wally Matthews' sons were suited up again with BCDs, fins, masks, and air tanks. The empty duffle bags had been discarded in trash bins; there was nothing to take away.

"Give my best to your father. I would like to have seen him tonight. But I understand. We're a little too old now for long swims hauling explosives. By God, we did enough of that."

"Father wanted to come," Samir avouched. "He says he'll be out to Hawaii for a visit within six months. And, of course, he wants you to come to Singapore."

"I'll do it, once this thing is over." Rand shook their hands. "By the way, what's next on the agenda?"

"Dad has planned a little visit up to Penang. It's a little more accessible. He thinks we can handle it without assistance. We'll let you know how it goes."

Rand stood on the wharf as Matthews' sons dropped to the water. He heard splashing for a minute and then silence. He pointed his light out into the darkness and signaled with two rapid flashes. Immediately, two flashes came back from the darkness of the bay. He looked at his watch and then waited. Exactly three minutes later he flashed his light again, twice. The signal for returning swimmers.

It had been a fruitless war, an obstruction in the independence the Vietnamese had wanted for decades. But Rand was elated with this one. Another war, this one against the Enemy Within. And they were going to win this one.

Chapter Forty-three

Broc stared at the numbers on his laptop in his hotel suite. Within minutes he had worked out the modem connections with Brently Hagan; now their computers were linked. His 'Robert Winston' identity package included a network access code that allowed him, as a legitimate intelligence officer under cover, to tap into the CIA computers at Langley.

The unsorted numbers were too much to deal with. O'Neill got up and paced around, stopping by the tenth-floor window of his hotel. He gazed at the towering dome of the U.S. Capitol, seat of the most powerful legislature in the world. It had an aura of majesty, a sacred quality reminiscent of the domes over great cathedrals in Europe. It was difficult to believe that anything but a perfect governance could come from such imposing power. But over the past few days, as the murk slowly cleared, he had discovered a surprising cluster of names. Corruption had oozed into every crack and cranny of the government. Gazing at the massive Grecian pillars, he realized how deceptive appearances could be.

He was unable to concentrate. Christelle was captive somewhere in Chicago. Her absence left him empty. He could barely control himself. A team of agents under Hagan's orders was keeping her captors under surveillance. Nothing had changed in the eight days since the Sabreliner had landed. Four days ago, with a new crew, it had headed back to Southeast Asia.

O'Neill gritted his teeth. For every clandestine flight that was known, there were dozens more that never reached the light of day — off-the-record trips, illegal movement of weapons, abductions — all arranged by power brokers with their own agendas, all funded by the innocent American taxpayer. Calling those responsible to account seemed virtually impossible. The corruption went on: secret Pentagon operations, illegal sales of American technology, thefts from the government by retiring senators. The whole system was laced with the self-serving projects of those alleged to be in power to serve the people. A secret government behind the visible façade.

The phone rang. It was Alan Creighton.

"You've had quite an adventure, I hear."

"I'll tell you about it some time. Right now, there seems to be too much to do. One hundred twenty thousand phone calls to sort. I've got information overload, and a splitting headache—"

"That was happening to me a week ago, Broc. But the last three days I've made some progress. A colleague at Southern Illinois worked on this for a few hours with some freelance programming. We've started to generate some data. Are you interested?"

O'Neill squeezed the bridge of his nose. "I am, and I'm not. I wish it would just go away. But I guess we have to keep pushing on this stuff. What have you got?"

"A new file, a simplified approach to the data. I've loaded it into Christelle's computer account at JSU."

"Hang on a minute," O'Neill paused, as he punched things into his keyboard.

"Hold up a minute, Broc. You won't be able to get the data by modem while we're talking, so let me summarize. We started with the phone records for Colonel Spiker and Joe Terrence. Then Hagan added the three agents who abducted Christelle. Six months of telephone calls, a bloody maze, but this computer whiz went to work."

"What can you generate from a tangle like that?" Broc wondered, still massaging his forehead. "I've been searching through some of those records. It seems impossible."

"My colleague looked for repeat calls. First, he sorted calls by number, from the most frequently called numbers to the ones that turned up only once or twice over the past six months. Then, we traced the numbers. It turns out that each of these guys makes regular calls to Worldwide telephone users. Soon the pattern was clear. Spiker, for instance, had a bunch of numbers he called in Atlanta, part of Tennessee as far north as Nashville, and Georgia as far south as Montgomery. And every one of them is an owner of a Worldwide telephone."

"So… he is… he was the contact."

"Right. Wade Bracket phones Worldwide customers in Michigan and Ohio. John Bradshaw, the NSA guy who was in Malaysia, calls customers in Southern California, New Mexico, and Nevada."

O'Neill had the phone stretched across the room to the bar, where he had managed to get out a Coke and bottle of Bacardi. "So, they've got the whole country parceled into territories. That's all very nice, Alan, but how can we turn a list of calls into evidence of crime? A hotshot Washington lawyer would say we've got no case." He poured a dollop of Bacardi into a glass, then another half dollop.

"Maybe not, not yet. But there's more. My computer friend started doing crosschecks for frequently called numbers common to Joe Terrence, Wade Bracket, John Bradshaw, Colonel Spiker, and the other kidnapper, Steven McClosky. Interesting stuff started to come up. We found a couple of numbers that were common in the phone records. We checked some of them out. One of them is particularly interesting, calls to a guy by the name of John Orchard, a counsel in the Department of Justice. There were calls to his office, a lot to his house. He lives in Washington, Kenwood Acres."

O'Neill scooped ice cubes from the freezer and dumped them in his glass. "People in the Justice Department have connections. Maybe Orchard has a lot of friends."

"Maybe, but there are all sorts of things here. Take Joe Terrence. He made calls on the 8th and 23rd of May, the 8th and 23rd of June, the 8th and 23nd of July. Always the same two-week spread. Wade Bracket, the same. Calls to Orchard on the 11th and 26th nearly every month."

O'Neill poured the Coke. "Sounds like a regular reporting system."

"Then we examined Orchard's calls. Here the pattern is entirely different. He doesn't call any of these guys on a regular basis, but when he does, he calls them all at once."

O'Neill listened in silence. Creighton continued.

"March 23rd. In a space of three hours, Orchard called all five of them. In fact, he made calls to sixteen numbers in the same three-hour time period. Same thing May 10th, May 22nd, July 9th, July 14th—"

"Alan! Say those dates again!"

"May 10th, May 22nd—"

"Jesus! Alan, my article in *American Documentary History* was published on the 9th of May; Darcy died on the 22nd." There was silence on the other end of the phone. "What was the next date, Alan?"

"July 9th—"

"A couple of guys chased us up a mountain road in Vermont on July 8th. They burned when their car went over the edge. What was the last one?"

"July 15th—"

"My God, I talked to John Randolph on the 15th; they nearly got us at Pennsylvania Produce on the 17th. They succeeded with Monahan and Randolph."

"Then we've got it! These guys are part of some committee. John Orchard must be the chairman. An emergency comes up; he calls everyone to decide what to do."

Broc could feel the blood pumping in his neck. "There must be more."

"There are two recent ones: August 11th and August 13th, and, let's see, Orchard's phone record includes calls to Bracket, Bradshaw, and McClosky—"

"Looks like preparations. Those three flew into Subang International Airport on August 16th. Planning sessions for an assassination in Malaysia."

"It's there; the pattern is there!"

O'Neill stared out the window. There were people by the huge reflecting pool, others taking pictures on the grass. The space in front of the Capitol was busy with tourists. Everything was falling in place. The pattern. "Alan, what about the others Orchard called?"

"We ran them down three days ago. Martin Atwater, chief assistant to Senator Jacobson, New Hampshire. Leopold Hudgeons, a judge from Maryland, served a term in the state legislature, 1984 to 1990. Samuel Jensen, House Representative from 1986 to 1992. Sam Whiterock, House Rep for Virginia a few years back. Dwight Blakeney, head of the Indianapolis branch of the FBI. There are more, some new ones phoned on August 11th and 13th: Craig Ramer, Richard Swentz."

"What a lineup! They're all powerhouses. I've heard of two or three — members of Congress. I know one of them: Sam Whiterock. He's retired, runs a foundation in Virginia. He invited me to do a stint with his research team."

"Did you consider it?"

"I put him off. Never gave it another thought. I was caught up in a funeral and getting out of Indiana."

There were a few seconds of awkward silence, and then Creighton went on. "There's more, Broc. We've tracked off in other directions. Listen to this list: John Adamson, Henry Kramer, Robert Shiner, Ross Tabbitt—"

"U.S. senators! Holy blazes!

"You've got it! How about these? David Myerson, Janick Bronson, William Waggoner, and another half dozen."

"State representatives on the Hill!" O'Neill stared at the symmetrical Capitol steps leading from the chambers of the Senate and House of Representatives.

"It's astonishing, Broc. Every one of them has a territory; every one of them is making regular phone calls to Worldwide cell phone customers. Henry Kramer has four monstrous electronics and computer companies in his territory out in California, all suppliers of high-tech stuff for military aircraft. And Janick Bronson, the longest serving member of Congress from the Midwest, a real dove during the Vietnam War. He's in contact with vehicle manufacturers with huge government contracts for military stuff."

O'Neill screwed up his forehead. It didn't make sense; a pacifist as far as the military was concerned. Yet here was Bronson, the icon of Democratic pacifism, in constant contact with manufacturers of war vehicles. Except… they were somehow the enemy."

Icon of Democratic pacifism — O'Neill stood at the window with narrowed eyes, the phone at his ear. The whole thing was gross, unbelievable. A massive extortion ring, with money being laundered through the Cayman Islands and the Bahamas. But the sudden realization had just struck him.

"Alan, you remember that memo I sent you from Penang, the one about all the owners of Worldwide telephones, the victims?"

"You mean about them all being Republicans?"

"Have you noticed anything about these guys — Orchard, Adamson, Bronson, Shiner, anyone you want to name? Hudgeons, Spiker?"

There was a long silence on the other end of the line, and then Alan Creighton said, "Yes, they're all Democrats."

It was a Democratic conspiracy to raise money in truly obscene amounts from companies run by chief executive officers who were, every one of them, Republicans.

"Alan, what have you done with all this information?"

"I talked to Hagan. He said a pattern of calls was not enough. We need conversations. He delivered it to a judge Monday morning. By afternoon, they had the wiretaps in place. Hagan's got a dozen guys monitoring phone conversations. But he says they're overwhelmed; it's all they can do to keep up. They're taping everything, and already they've got stuff you wouldn't believe. Coddling, bribery, promises, reminders, threats, extortion. In spades!"

"Alan, I'm going to download that file from Christelle's account, and then talk to Hagan. I'll get back to you tomorrow."

"It's nasty stuff, Broc. Worse than reading horror novels. You'll get the idea in an hour, but it will wreck your sleep for a week."

"Thanks, Alan. My sleep's already been wrecked for a week. That's just what I need!"

Alan Creighton laughed at his irony. "By the way, Broc, when you get a moment, you might call your secretary at Jefferson State to clean out your phone mail. Sounds like the recorder has gone haywire."

O'Neill dialed into Christelle's JSU account. Creighton's file was exactly what he said: a summary, a highly usable distillation of the data that had poured out of the telephone records after their first query — one hundred twenty thousand phone calls, over the last six months. And another thousand were pouring out of Hagan's computer every day. But Creighton's summary, a neat twenty pages, displayed the patterns of relevant calls, laying bare the way John Orchard's fund-raising committee worked. John Orchard... *Lignum* Operations... *Sparsum* Operations.

Lignum... Sparsum... what the hell were they? He had a smattering of Latin, one college course, but he had never run across these.

O'Neill printed out Creighton's summary and then logged onto the Internet, a simple dictionary search. Latin. *Lignum* — something gathered, firewood. *Sparsum* — something dispersed. Something gathered in, something scattered. Lignum Operations was gathering money; *Sparsum* Operations was giving it away. And somewhere, behind both, was someone or something called Ironwood.

It was getting late. Brently would have left his office. In another hour he would be home. But O'Neill had a massive headache. If Hagan called him, he would talk, but O'Neill would not call tonight; he would wait until tomorrow.

Clean out your phone mail... the recorder has gone haywire—

O'Neill picked up the phone and dialed his office at Jefferson State. He waited until his voice came on — "This is Broc O'Neill" — then punched in his code. There was a reminder from the Department of History secretary of the meeting to be held the Friday before classes began in September. A student wanted to know something about the course he was scheduled to teach in the fall; O'Neill jotted down the name and number. Another student wanted to query the B-minus she had received in the History of American Intelligence course he had taught last spring. The final message led into a long sequence of beeps. It sounded like the message tape had picked up someone dialing.

He had better not erase it, not until the department secretary figured out what was wrong. The message system was four years old; occasionally it went haywire. O'Neill's headache was getting worse. He dug out a bottle of aspirin, one of the many things Brently Hagan had put in his suitcase, though he doubted that Hagan personally had anything to do with it. O'Neill drank them down and turned on the shower. The CIA obviously had a procedure for producing everything: replacement documents like his new driver's license and passport; detection-proof documents that had recreated him as 'Robert Winston'; pre-packed suitcases for people who had lost all their luggage.

Except it wasn't quite that simple. O'Neill was amazed. The two suits that were ready when he got to Washington had been made by his tailor in Jefferson, Indiana, who had taken his measurements months ago.

O'Neill climbed into the shower and let the hot water beat down on his head for several minutes. Between the aspirin and the heat, that ought to do it. He felt better as he dried himself; his headache was nearly gone.

He sat on the bed and dug into the box containing his identity papers. There were things here he hadn't seen. A birth certificate for Robert Winston. A high school transcript from a school a few miles from where he had grown up. Four copies of each of his college transcripts, all the way up to his doctorate at Yale University. The courses and grades were his, but the degree had been awarded to Robert Brocford Winston.

O'Neill dug a little deeper. He found a voter registration card and various consumer credit cards: Hyatt Hotels, Western Auto, Exxon. There were even long out-of-date identity cards: things from college, library cards. In every case, it was O'Neill's picture beside the name of Robert Winston. There were two bank accounts, both in the name of Robert Winston, with checkbooks and the latest monthly bank statements showing a total of nearly fifty thousand on deposit. At the bottom of the box, he found the title for a car and the 1995 registration papers. It was Darcy's BMW, but the owner's name was now Robert Winston.

He lay back against the pillows. Christelle was somewhere in Chicago, still captive, still sure that he was dead. Broc O'Neill was not dead, but he was disappearing; Robert Winston was taking his place. O'Neill was not sure how he felt about it, but it was clear that it was necessary. He, Creighton, and Hagan were assembling what was needed to smash up Lignum and Sparsum, the whole operation, but it was too big. There were too many of them. They could never be sure whether they got them all. And while there was one left, Broc O'Neill could not be sure he would survive. *Ironwood...*

Chapter Forty-four

Washington, DC
Thursday, August 29

O'Neill followed the official at the bank, the branch closest to Washington National Airport. The woman turned the master key in the lock. O'Neill pulled out his own key, the only thing overlooked by Christelle's abductors on Tioman Island, and unlocked the safety-deposit box. As the official disappeared around the corner, O'Neill pulled out the oversized drawer and headed for a booth.

The box contained what he and Christelle had stashed there before boarding their flight to Singapore: the Colt 45, the Hi-Power Browning, and several clips of ammunition for each. O'Neill wrapped each weapon in a T-shirt and packed them into his briefcase. In an envelope he found credit cards and photographs from his wallet that he had known would be of no use in Singapore, keys to the apartment in Kalamazoo and Darcy's BMW. The final item was Christelle's designer key ring to her Grand Am, which included the key to her sister's cabin in Vermont.

O'Neill caught a taxi to the airport remote parking lot, found Christelle's car, and turned the ignition key. The car had been parked for five weeks, but the engine fired up. He put the vehicle through a car wash and headed back to the Hyatt Regency near the Capitol. Christelle would be pleased; her favorite possession looked as good as ever.

Christelle... He hardly saw anything as he drove the last three miles. The traffic was snarled as it always was on the streets around the nation's capital, but O'Neill could not stop thinking about Christelle. He could hardly stand it any longer. Once he got the next task out of the way, he would talk to Hagan. It was time to go after Christelle's captors.

The central room of his hotel suite had undergone a transformation that morning. Three Insta-Business secretaries were busy at computers, writing letters and processing long lists of names that O'Neill had supplied. He went into the bedroom and put through a call to Hagan. There was no news from Chicago, only round-the-clock surveillance where Christelle was being held. O'Neill lost his temper for a minute and then, with a massive effort of will, calmed himself and relayed the real purpose of his call: additional papers he thought should be filed in connection with his identity change.

"They'll probably be ready soon. You are due some more documents that take a little time, but I'll call Kay; she'll take care of it."

"Who's Kay?"

"A wonderful woman; you must meet her sometime, Broc."

"This is a serious request, not something to be handled by a girlfriend."

"She's only a girlfriend on the side. She works downstairs in the CIA center of new identity development. She's the one responsible for your box of new ID. I'd guess she'll have this handled before closing time tonight, if not, by Monday noon."

"You've got your NSA friend monitoring the banks?"

"The banks, yes, and also going through their records. You won't believe what we're finding."

"Can you give me some clues?"

"Not over the phone, but I'll have a sample delivered this afternoon. Broc, what are your plans today?"

"A little private business."

"Nothing dangerous, I hope."

"Nothing dangerous, Brent. I just need to get out and walk. It's better than cabin fever in this hotel room."

O'Neill set out on foot, walking east along Constitution Avenue to the National Museum of American History, a collection he had wanted to visit for years... and would have visited this summer with Darcy during their stay in Washington. He felt a surge of anger flaring up as the memory of Darcy came back, but he managed to suppress it and keep his attention on the exhibits.

After a sandwich in the museum cafeteria, O'Neill continued west. He stood gazing for several minutes across the grass at the White House, contemplating its power, its grandeur, its secrets, and wondering whether the network of corruption that was slowly unraveling penetrated this far. None of the records they had excavated appeared to reach to the Administration, but then there was no reason they should.

It was Congress that was of concern. It had become solidly Republican in '94 and looked as though it would remain Republican in the election in November. Democrats had dominated for decades, but now the overriding concern was what this Republican dominance might mean for Democrats and Democratic legislation that had begun with Franklin D. Roosevelt in the thirties and had since become compacted into a kind of federal bedrock. In the past four years, desperate over a perceived threat to their programs, indeed, their entire way of life, Democrats all through the government — the House, Senate, Department of Justice, CIA, FBI, NSA, and God knows how many other departments and agencies — had set out to protect their favorite social programs, assuring that somehow the funds would keep flowing even if the new Republican Congress somehow managed to slash them all.

It was panic and paranoia based more on fantasy than fact, O'Neill thought, because social programs could take years to repeal. And there would be injunctions. The kind of thinking dating to FDR's New Deal somehow remained intact. Americans were attached to programs they were accustomed to, even while they still screamed about big government and high taxes. The wealthy kept giving away inordinate amounts of money for assured tax deductions. The technological revolution — computers, cell phones, Internet — was pushing up income, the stock market, and thus the size of charitable donations. There had been talk from the Federal Administration about the Social Security system going bankrupt, and various plans had been fielded to convert to other retirement income plans, but in the end, the matter had to be dropped, and the Democratic sacred cows remained.

The result was, it appeared, that dozens of welfare institutions the Democrats were afraid might fail had survived, and now they were thriving. For several years, four or five hundred million dollars a month had somehow found its way to charitable causes. And the amount was growing, a steady increase of a few tens of millions every month: $2.32 billion dollars "donated" to Lignum Operations in June had been disbursed by Sparsum Operations to hundreds of Democratic projects in July. An additional $2.34 billion collected in July had been donated in August, and now the August collections were nearly complete. According to the latest update, Lignum had $2.35 billion in its Cayman Island account, with millions being added daily.

And in two days, David Wicks would put through an electronic transfer.

O'Neill ambled along the edge of the reflecting pool. To the east, its still waters caught the high tower of the Washington Monument; to the west, the Lincoln Memorial. Both were reminders of dignity and power, milestones in the history of the oldest democratic government in the world, reminders of ordinary men who had risen to extraordinary influence and power.

O'Neill circled the west end of the pool and walked in front of the massive Greek columns of the Lincoln Memorial. As he came through the trees, he was standing before the Vietnam Veterans Memorial. The reflection from its black walls struck him, and then he went up to examine it, moving along its south wall as dozens more were doing.

Its impact was overpowering. The names were engraved but not in marble, which would somehow glorify the cause they fought for. They were engraved in black granite, which seemed to symbolize the bedrock importance of the people, those from whom the power of the American government flowed, those who gave their lives even if the American government abused its power. O'Neill followed the names, fifty-eight thousand men and women who had made the ultimate sacrifice for a war that should never have happened. The polished black stone reflected his face, his own image mirrored among the names of the dead.

A couple stood before the stone. O'Neill stopped and watched. The woman reached out and touched a name. She ran her forefinger over the letters, one by one, and O'Neill could see her hand was shaking. She was a woman of at least eighty, and her husband was gray; his shoulders were stooped. O'Neill did not have to ask; he knew she was tracing out the name of a son, and he knew that they had lived under the shadow of this loss for nearly thirty years. It must have been a terrible loss. It put his own loss in a new perspective. Neither should have happened.

O'Neill turned away. He felt the same overpowering emotion he had felt in Manila as he stood before the endless white crosses of seventeen thousand graves from the Pacific War. Men who perhaps did not need to give their lives, except for the corruption that infected the men charged with leading them into battle. His mind flashed again on Wally Matthews, a Navy SEAL who had decided to remain a permanent expat and make his life elsewhere. He was a survivor, one of a whole platoon of survivors, fourteen men who had done their duty and lived to remember, but what they remembered was a war that should not have happened, a war they did not win, a war that would plague each of them to the grave.

O'Neill got up Saturday morning after a sleepless night. He showered and dressed and went downstairs for breakfast, but he was unable to read the newspaper. Back in his room by eight forty-five, he waited for the Insta-Business secretaries to arrive for their second day on the job, and then left them to their work. It was all so time consuming, and there was nothing to do but wait. But he could not stand the waiting, so he went out again, this time, to satisfy his curiosity.

He drove Christelle's Grand Am, caught Pennsylvania Avenue running southeast, and drove until it turned into Maryland Highway No. 4. Thirty minutes later, twelve miles out of the District of Columbia at Forestville, he pulled up in front of a low, newly painted building. He checked the stapled sheaf of computer offprints, verified the address, and pulled into the parking lot.

Two women greeted him as he got out of the car. "I'm sorry, Sir, this is not a facility open for male visitors."

O'Neill unfolded a letter of introduction and handed it to them. "I understand that these women need to be protected. Even the sight of a man, can send them into hysterics. Perhaps you could simply show me the facilities and describe the services."

The older of the two women read the letter, an impressive looking document Hagan's girlfriend, Kay, had produced. They looked at O'Neill and then motioned him inside, leading him to the offices and inviting him to sit down. "I think we can assist you, Mr. Winston. South

District Women's Shelter is four years old." The other woman offered him a cup of coffee. "It was funded privately in 1992, initially with twenty-five rooms."

She pointed to the pictures on the wall, a series of framed enlargements of a lounge O'Neill guessed would measure thirty feet by fifty. There were clusters of furniture, two TV sets, a ping-pong table, a floor-to-ceiling bookshelf, contemporary magazines, and two telephones. One picture showed a cluster of women talking in front of a fireplace.

"We provide shelter for battered women — women who have been abused by fathers, boyfriends, husbands, women whose lives are considered in danger if they are not removed from their home environment."

The woman handed him a floor plan. "The Trauma Center is the most modern in the state of Maryland. It's like a hospital emergency room. This morning, for instance, a woman came in after a beating, one eye black and swollen shut, her clothing torn, bruises on her arms, her baby's arm broken. "She handed O'Neill a Polaroid photo. He felt his insides knotting up. "She couldn't even tell us what happened, how it started. That was three hours ago. She's calm, now, sitting up, talking. Her baby's arm is set."

She handed O'Neill an album of pictures. He thumbed through. By the time he got to the end, his hands were shaking.

"We began with twenty-five rooms. Two years ago, we opened sixty-five more, along with an extension on the Trauma Center and added therapy facilities."

"Where did the money come from?"

"We had promises three years ago, signed commitments that guaranteed funding. It was a godsend, prayers answered. We were able to procure short-term bank loans and begin construction in '93. Permanent funding came through. We were able to pay off the loans, which means no debt. We now supply advanced medical treatment, emotional rehabilitation, legal counseling — even though most of the women who come here are without medical benefits of any kind."

"Do you have any idea of the cost of the facility?" O'Neill asked.

"It was in the millions. But we had generous funding, with over $300,000 left over after we had paid off all the loans. That meant we were able to upgrade every aspect of our services. And we've had additional grants, $80,000 every month. We're taking in and helping three hundred women a month from Maryland and Virginia, and there's no shortage of funds. We provide every service a young battered woman might need. We've even managed to fund apartments for women while they file for divorce or complete courses at college."

"Do you know where the funds are coming from?"

"Oh, yes, there's a new Maryland foundation. We understand it's funded by charitable donations. And we're just one of the shelters they're helping. There are eight more around the country, and I've heard more are being planned."

Manassas, Virginia

Twenty-five miles southwest of Washington, O'Neill parked in the shade of the dense hardwood forest that ran along the front slope of the property. He gazed for a minute at the trees, a forest of gray-trunked ironwood, then proceeded up the steps through the tiered rock gardens, six acres of some of the best maintained institutional grounds he had ever seen. The building occupied the crest of a low hill with a spectacular view in all directions.

"We've come to be seen as the most advanced senior-citizens' facility in the state," Mr. Ronald Kent highlighted, as O'Neill turned to look again at the building. "We've had awards; we've been cited for advanced design, our health services, the extra care. We've got a waiting list."

O'Neill pointed toward one wing of the building. Layers of ivy clung to the brickwork; only the windows were clear of greenery. Scarcely noticeable, the windows were all protected by black wrought ironwork. "Somehow it appears decorative; it's tastefully done, but I don't understand why a senior citizens' nursing facility needs window bars."

"That's one of the features that's been cited over and over, Mr. Winston. Some seniors are suffering from one or another form of cognitive disfunction or emotional trauma. They're suffering from schizophrenia, paranoia, or delusions. They don't sleep well; they wander; they get lost."

"So this facility is distinguished for its safety?"

"Absolutely. Our record of protecting the aged and infirm is sterling."

It was a side of senior citizen care that was new to O'Neill.

He climbed the stone steps with Mr. Kent. They ambled through the foyer and then toward the west wing. As they rounded a corner, they came upon a barred hallway.

"This is the entrance to the security wing you saw from the outside," Kent said, as he pushed a series of numbers on a wall panel. The door opened and they went through.

"It's as secure as a prison," O'Neill noted.

"All for safety. Do you know that there are dementia patients who escape — thirty or so every year around the country — and some die before they are found? They get lost; they get struck down on the highway; they wander into construction sites; they try to go swimming in surf they used to play in as kids. We've managed to eliminate this hazard entirely."

"It must cost a lot. Where does the money come from?"

"Private donations. The extra security on that wing cost $985,000, but that's only part of it. We're receiving monthly funding, enough to add five acres across the road. We're in negotiation for loans to add another two-hundred-room facility. Meanwhile, we've increased the ratio of employees to patients. We've got better care, better beds, better rooms. You'd be amazed how far $150,000 a month can go with a facility like this.

O'Neill glanced into the rooms as they passed. Suddenly, he stopped by an open door. The blue patient sign read 'EARL WHITEROCK'. O'Neill stepped to the doorway and observed an aged, emaciated man sitting motionless, looking vacantly into space.

"A tragic case. His brother was a senator, you know—"

O'Neill nodded. "I've met the former senator." He glanced at his guide. "How long has he been here?"

"Nineteen years — our longest surviving Alzheimer's patient." Ronald Kent shook his head sadly, almost as though to deny the truth. "His father was here, too. He still holds the record for survival with this disease. He lived in that tragic, uncomprehending state for more than twenty years."

It was half an hour later. O'Neill stood on the curb by Christelle's car. Gazing up the slope at the massive facility, he was awed by the level of care that could be provided if the funds were available, stunned again by the tragedy of the Whiterock family. He stared at the sign by the path, and then turned again to regard the thick stand of hardwoods along the lower slopes.

His thoughts were churning as he drove away.

Baltimore, Maryland

"Take a look across the street, Mr. Winston. A sentence complete, another release. That prison releases four or five a week. That one, Jason Powell, has turned down our help, but forty percent of prisoners paroled from that prison come to us. It helps, in fact, it's strategic, that we're located here, right across the road."

O'Neill gazed around the front foyer, an attractive environment with the appearance of a large family room: soft lamps, comfortable chairs and couches. Wilson Rehabilitation, one of a chain of such establishments spreading through the northern states, provided up to eighteen months of free societal adjustment counseling and training to paroled convicts.

"It's a new concept, Mr. Winston. I'm sure you know today's prisons are a revolving door. Within six months, twenty-five percent of parolees are back in prison. Within two years, sixty percent. Take a look there; you can see the reason why."

Across the road a battered 1980s Chevrolet sat at the curb, engine running.

"When prisoners are released, they rarely call their families. The guys they call to pick them up are the ones they were with when they were arrested. Within hours they're back with the same crowd, a gang of law breakers outside jail who probably should be inside. We try to break that cycle. If they agree, we bring them here. Six weeks in this facility and most of them want nothing to do with their former partners in crime.

"We pay for courses and on-the-job training. We arrange for post-training consultation and interviewing. You know the problem, Mr. Winston. Employers are reluctant to take on people with a prison record. We've developed a network of companies who are willing to make exceptions in exchange for our assurances. We keep a continuing relationship between the parolee and Wilson Rehabilitation. Our goal is to place them and then keep them on the job."

O'Neill studied the map of the facility on the wall. There were over fifty apartments where parolees could stay during the first weeks after release, three classrooms, two gymnasiums, a weight room.

"What does all this cost?"

"We were able to borrow on the basis of charitable pledges. Between four and five million. We opened three years ago. We've got pledges of continuous funding of at least $180,000 a month."

O'Neill stood at the door of the gymnasium. Two teams of men were playing basketball. Another fifteen were sitting on the sidelines.

"What kind of success? Is this something you can measure?"

"We think it's working. We've brought nearly two hundred released prisoners here, trained them, got them into jobs. We've cut relapses by seventy-five percent. I'd say that's better than you'll find anywhere else in the country."

Chapter Forty-five

Tuesday, September 3

The three Insta-Business secretaries were within two hours of finishing their assignment when they came in Tuesday morning at 9 a.m. O'Neill had set them up in his suite Friday morning. Insta-Business assistants had brought in portable tables, computers, and supplies. The secretaries, all willing to work four days — Friday through Monday, right through the Labor Day weekend — for triple pay, free meals, and a bonus, had worked eight hours a day, Friday to Monday, and were about to finish up six hours early. O'Neill had agreed: the earlier they finished, the bigger the bonus.

O'Neill wrote out their checks, an even $4,000 each, which made them squeal with delight and ask him when they could work for him again. He took requests for a feast — $375 for the best luncheon entrees on the menu for the secretaries and their boyfriends — then phoned in the orders and shuffled them off to the eleventh floor Capitol View Club Restaurant.

O'Neill surveyed their handiwork: mountains of mail, over four-thousand letters addressed, stamped, and sealed, each containing a letter and a check. Within two hours they would be in the mail, special delivery. Some might be delivered tomorrow, the rest by Thursday.

O'Neill stared at the piles of mail, enough to fill several suitcases, nearly $6,000 in postage alone. He walked to the window and stared out at the Capitol for perhaps the hundredth time since he had checked in five days ago. The roof gleamed white against a cloudless blue sky.

The New Deal... Camelot... the Great Society... the War on Poverty... A kinder, gentler nation...

The telephone rang. It was Brent Hagan. He began talking immediately. "Broc, the August 31st bank transfer went through. Wicks authorized it Saturday; it showed up in the Bahamas account about ten minutes ago. In case you want the precise amount, it includes every August deposit to Lignum until the bank closed Saturday at noon. Altogether, let's see. $2,368,555,930.72. As you directed, he included all the interest earned in August, plus seventy-five percent of the back interest."

O'Neill penciled a row of jagged lines across a piece of hotel stationery.

"Broc... Broc, are you there?"

"I'm here, Brent."

"What the hell's the matter? Are your secretaries finished?"

"They finished up a few minutes ago." O'Neill ran a parallel set of jagged lines alongside the first. "There's a ton of mail here. The suite's flooded."

"Broc, what the hell's the matter? You sound like—"

"Hell...! and I feel like hell. Yes, it's all done, four thousand five hundred eighty-seven letters ready to go." Hagan did not reply. "Brent, do you know what's going on out there? Do you have any idea?"

"Crime, kick-backs, bribery, extortion, money laundering, arson, murder—"

"Damn it, Brent! I've been out there for the past two days. I went to see where the money's going. There are ninety-five trust accounts around the country fed by Sparsum Operations, every one of them funneling money to special projects. I went out to see firsthand. To be exact, eleven different facilities within fifty miles of here."

"My God, Broc, you sound upset."

"You'd be upset if you went and had a look. Brent, there are things going on out there: convict rehabilitation programs, education programs for new immigrants, free job training programs, shelters for battered women, medical research start-ups — stuff you would not believe!"

"We know that, Broc. What's new?"

"What's new is this: the most extensive social welfare revolution in seventy-five years! What's going on is better than anything Roosevelt or Truman or Kennedy or Johnson or Carter or Clinton or any Democratic Congress ever dreamed of. What's going on is the first sign of societal renewal among the poor, the disadvantaged, in the past five decades. It's a new world. It's astonishing, Brent; it's like nothing we've ever seen before. It's grassroots; it's direct funding, no damned red tape, no bureaucracy eating up the funds, no streaming off the top for project administration. Do you know there's not a sign that any of these guys — Orchard, Bracket, Spiker, senators, representatives, judges — is lining his own coffers? Not one of them! This is a social revolution American liberals have been dreaming of for most of this century,"

"Jesus, Broc, what are you saying?"

"I'm saying that what's happening is what's needed, what all of us have known is necessary at the poorest end of the social spectrum. It's like a revolution in our midst, a new political party without election campaigns, without left-minded politicians having to pour millions into bullshit ads on TV to get into office, without giving people power that leads to corruption. It's a renewal that's accomplishing what massive amounts of federal spending has never accomplished. It's relief for those who need it without raising new taxes. It's the wealthy finally reaching out with something."

"Broc, you sound like you've gone over some kind of edge. What are you going to do? You're going to mail those letters, aren't you?"

O'Neill stared at the mountainous piles of envelopes. He glanced at his watch; special delivery pickup would end in two hours.

"I don't know what I'm going to do, Brent. I don't have any idea what I'm going to do," he replied, and then he hung up.

Broc went up to the eleventh floor to the Capitol View Club Restaurant. His three secretaries and their boyfriends were having a rollicking good lunch party over by the window. Two of the girls and one of their boyfriends were already tipsy.

O'Neill sat in the farthest corner from the window. The waitress came by with a drink list. He struggled against the overwhelming urge to drown his thoughts. It was difficult, but he finally won and ordered a club sandwich and iced tea.

His mind empty, he ate looking down at his plate.

At ten minutes after two, he paid his bill, went back to his suite, and dialed the postal service. They were there in five minutes. O'Neill invited them in and watched them pack up the envelopes, which filled several

384

bags. He gave them a generous tip as they loaded the bags onto a luggage carrier. As they pushed it off down the corridor, three employees from Insta-Business arrived for the computers and furniture. Within a quarter hour his suite was back to normal. Empty.

O'Neill had one hand on the phone, ready to confirm the mailing to Brently Hagan, when it rang. It was Alan Creighton.

"Broc! Jesus, Broc, they've lost her."

"What the hell are you talking about?"

"Christelle. They lost her! Hagan's men somehow let them get out of the building. She's gone; they didn't see them leave."

O'Neill felt his whole body go cold. "How do you know? Damn it, Alan, how do you know?"

"Hagan called. He tried to call you. There was no answer. He was scared to death, relieved you weren't there. He asked me to phone—"

O'Neill threw a glass across the room. It shattered against the wall scattering shards on the floor. He raged across the room, ready to pick up something and hurl it through the window. Of all the damned stupidity! Why had he let Brent Hagan talk him out of going to Chicago? All this secretarial work could have waited.

O'Neill stood at the window, his fists clenched, wanting to tear out of the hotel and burn it all down — the Capitol dome, both chambers — and then storm up to 1600 Pennsylvania Avenue and burn down the White House, and on to Langley to burn down the Pentagon, and maybe the NSA after that.

He made himself a drink, a triple header with enough whiskey to down an elephant. Now what? After all this, Christelle was gone.

Christelle...

Oh, Jesus no! He couldn't take it again, not another loss like Darcy.

Her face kept swimming in front of him. He saw her sitting across the tiny table at the Rasa Singapura Food Center, her chin in her hands, her eyes meeting his; he saw her spinning around in her little Filipino dress; he saw her hazel eyes and water-green jade earrings as she touched the brim of her cowboy hat. And then he saw her walking along a beach at Tioman, hustled along by three abductors. And he saw her — the last time he had seen her — standing on the pavement at Subang Airport in Malaysia, her eyes on the ground; her whole body seemingly beaten up, defeated; her handbag hanging limply, almost on the ground —

Handbag... *handbag!* O'Neill felt something click.

He ran to the phone and dialed, made a mistake, dialed again. Halfway across the country in his office at Jefferson State University, machinery kicked in. "Broc O'Neill." He punched in his identification number and listened to the messages again: from his secretary, from two students, and a long series of beeps.

Sounds like the recorder has gone haywire...

O'Neill hung up. He walked to the window. Phone Hagan? Hagan had the equipment to figure out what was happening. No, Hagan would obstruct things. Phone Alan Creighton? Creighton knew someone in St. Louis who knew electronics. No, Creighton might call Hagan.

O'Neill dashed to the telephone, got Information and found the number for Bell Communications in Vermont. It was two thirty in the afternoon, working hours. In two minutes, Dillon Shaver was on the line.

"Dillon, this is Broc O'Neill, I've got an emergency. First, before you ask, your ID is gone, stolen, destroyed. Second, before you ask, I'll get replacements."

"No problem, Broc, no prob—"

"Dillon, I'm sorry to interrupt, but this is an emergency! Maybe life or death. Have you got a pen? Take down this number." He read his office phone number and ID code, and then his hotel number and extension. "Dillon, get some sort of company machinery on the line and record what you hear."

O'Neill's phone rang ten minutes later. "I've got it, Broc. Someone phoned your voice mail and then just pushed a bunch of buttons. We've recorded them—"

"What the hell can you make of it?"

"I don't know, Broc. The machinery has translated it all into numbers, that's all it is."

"Read them to me!"

"There are interruptions half-way through. Somebody has phoned in two or three times. Here goes."

O'Neill wrote what Shaver dictated:

284878... There are spaces, the beeps are grouped, so write these out in groups: 24 3327 2526 2278483 46 2442246 2762 47 3323 430430430.

Shaver paused. "Is that it?" O'Neill asked.

"That was the end, they hung up. But there are more. Do you want to copy them down?"

"Okay... just a minute... Wait! Are those last numbers right — 430430430?"

"They're right—"

"That's Christelle's password. She created one she wouldn't forget. It's the password to her university e-mail account. Alan Creighton would recognize it. That's got to be her signature."

"Hell, Broc, this is easy. We play like this around the telephone company when there's nothing to do. These are just letters off the telephone dial. I can almost read this: 2 is A, B or C; 8 is T, U or V; 4 is G, H or I; 7 is P, R or S. August, the first word is August. August 24. Hang on." O'Neill looked at the buttons on his phone and started writing. Two minutes later they had it:

August 24 Dear Alan Captive in Chicago Broc is dead — 430430430

"It's a message to Alan Creighton. She thinks I'm dead; she's sure she saw me die. They captured her in Southeast Asia. She's got her handbag with her. Full of novels. They never looked; they never checked. She's got my Worldwide cell phone in her handbag. Jesus, she must be sending messages on the sly."

In another five minutes they had the rest transcribed:

August 26 Alan Nothing happening Four guys Wade Bracket Steve McClosky John Bradshaw Ron Sandy Leaders Admiral Veil and Ironwood — Christelle

August 30 Alan I am sick of this I need to get out of here I dont know whether you are getting this No way I can't find out the address Hell damn shit — Christelle

August 31 Alan These guys are suspicious They think they are being watched Things are not good — Christelle

September 2 Alan Somethings happening. Orders from Ironwood Getting ready to leave Dont know where — Christelle

Fuming, furious, O'Neill paced the suite for three hours. He had not phoned Brent; Brent had not phoned him. It was a good thing. O'Neill was ready to blast him through the telephone. His agents had stood around too long in Chicago, waiting until all the evidence was pieced together before they struck. That made sense. But then they had been spotted. Christelle's captors had panicked and somehow found a way out of wherever they were staying. And now they were gone,

The telephone rang. It was Dillon Shaver.

"There's another one, Broc. I must have phoned in minutes after she left a message. I guess you don't need the numbers, only words.

September 3 Time seven Alan Something has started panic These guys have gone nuts Rough handling Just landed at Bolling I hope you figure this out one day — Christelle

Time seven. O'Neill glanced at his watch; it was 7:30 p.m.! Her message was only thirty minutes old! They were on her trail, but where on Earth was she?

"Where in hell is Bolling?" Shaver questioned. "I've never heard of it."

"No idea. Keep me posted, Dillon. I'll stay here until I hear from you."

Chapter Forty-six

Christelle caught the full name of the airport as the limousine pulled onto the highway: Bolling Air Force Base. She was sandwiched between Steve McClosky and John Bradshaw, whom she had figured out over the past week were intelligence agents. Ron Sandy, the pilot of their plane all the way from Malaysia, sat in the front middle seat with Wade Bracket — damned pervert! — with the driver and a newcomer in the front.

She watched the signs: Saint Elizabeth's Hospital, an exit to Fort McNair, the Potomac River. Realization — Washington, DC. As the car swung onto the bridge, she pointed at the tall spire. "Is that the Washington Monument?"

"It doesn't matter what it is," Wade Bracket retorted, turning in his seat. "Don't expect any fancy tours, bitch. All you're going to see tonight is a county museum, and we may leave you there as an artifact for archaeologists to dig up."

Christelle feigned claws in his eyes, making him pull back, startled.

"Why don't you sit still, bitch?" Bradshaw demanded, grabbing her by the elbow as McClosky did the same with her other arm. "Wade, where the hell are your handcuffs?"

Ron Sandy spoke to everyone in the vehicle. "Bracket let the bitch throw them out the hotel window."

Wade Bracket said nothing. If it weren't dark, Christelle thought, we'd all see the color running up your neck. As uncomfortable as she was, she couldn't help laughing inside. None of them thought much of Wade Bracket. She waited a good ten seconds and then yanked her elbow free of Bradshaw's grip, turning and glaring at him in the half light, then did the same with McClosky. It was a calculated move. They left her alone.

She knew they would. She had had their stupid little plane pitching halfway on its side with her antics over the South China Sea and managed to get her nails into every one of them before the week was out. None of them wanted to tangle with her again. They held her captive by only dint of numbers; if they made the mistake of leaving one of them alone with her for even ten minutes, he would regret it very much.

She saw the signs for Arlington National Cemetery, Falls Church, and soon the boundary of the District of Columbia, and then the limousine was roaring into the evening dusk along Interstate 65, heading west. She watched the signs: Highway 15, the city of Gainesville, the ramp to Highway 211, the boundary of Rappahannock County. That was a difficult one; Christelle went over its landmarks and its spelling in her mind. One day when she got out of this stupid mess, she would need to find her way here. She would come back and get these guys. And it wouldn't be with any imaginary handguns.

Broc—

She felt the little jerk in her stomach, like a hiccup, and was scarcely able to control it. She felt the sobs gathering in her throat. She struggled to control herself. This was no time to show her weakness. There was nothing she could do about Broc now. But she remembered their plan: if one should be killed, the other should go after the killers.

The car turned onto a dark country road, then onto a gravel road. They were right; they were on their way to a County Historical Museum. This must be the Rappahannock County Museum.

The building loomed up against the dark sky; there were no lights, no other cars in the lot. They led her toward the building, down a long ramp, into a dark basement, then a conference room with a long table and at least twenty chairs, and nearly every one of them was already occupied. They set her at one end of the table where she could see everyone and everyone could see her. She had never seen so many hostile faces.

Their attention shifted as someone else came in. A minute later three more came in. Someone went out and brought back folding chairs. By now there were murmurings of subdued conversation. Cigarettes were being lit.

Christelle leaned toward the man nearest her on her right, a stranger. "I wonder, is there a ladies' room?" she entreated in a low voice.

He nodded down the room. "I don't think we've ever had a lady here before, so I guess you'll just have to use the mens'."

Christelle pushed back her chair and made her way past the other chairs, trying to remain as dignified as possible while they all watched her with expressionless fantasies in their eyes. Meanwhile, she suppressed her own fantasies of scratching out all their eyes, slowly, one by one.

"We've got a crisis here," the man at the other end of the table declared. "I didn't stop to get details; there was barely time to get all of you here as a matter of joint concern for both Lignum and Sparsum."

Christelle recognized the names from Broc's research.

"I think," the man at the other end of the table continued, "we should begin with Sparsum since that apparently is where the crisis lies. So let's give this over to Craig Ramer."

A sandy-haired man halfway down the table leaned forward. "We might as well report on the minor issue first, then we can forget about it. You met Troller and Senelik about three weeks ago. There's been a bit of a crisis at Langley down in Special Ops. Officially, no one knows what happened to them. They applied for a few days' leave, disappeared, and haven't been seen since. Special Ops has been pursuing defection, with no success. They left no records of where they were going."

"Is there a problem? We know where they are: they flew out to Malaysia under secret cover, didn't they?"

"There's no problem with that: their mission and destination are buried—"

"Then what's the problem?" someone countered.

"Troller died off the coast of Malaysia — a shark attack. It appears that Senelik survived and then disappeared."

Christelle felt the sudden jolt of remembrance. She had known it but hardly thought about it, and this was the first time any of her captors had mentioned anything about what happened that day at Tioman.

391

No one uttered a word for a few seconds; then Craig spoke: "We don't know what's become of Senelik, but at least the mission was successful."

"As you can see," Wade Bracket interjected, "we have Miss Washington." He tossed a newspaper on the table. "This is the *New Straits Times*. Our man in Singapore mailed it. You'll find Broc O'Neill's obituary on page 3."

You bloody bastard. You've probably had that newspaper for days and never showed it to me! She felt her insides knotting up as memories flashed across her mind. The shark, its bloody teeth, the trailing human remains. Forcefully, she willed herself not to think about it. Concentrate. *One day you guys will pay—*

Craig Ramer redirected, "The other matter is a way bigger crisis."

The door opened and someone else came in. Several of those present greeted him and motioned him to a chair.

"You're just in time, Shane," Ramer continued. "I was just about to summarize. To put this simply, the bank transfer did not go through."

Christelle saw the sudden stirring all down the table.

"We sent to Grand Cayman for the records; this is the return fax;" Craig held it up. "The manager, Daniel Wicks, made the transfer at 6 p.m. Saturday, the usual last-day-of-the month transfer. It didn't show up in Nassau this morning."

The new man called Shane sat forward. "Actually, it did show up. I've spent the day tracking it; that's why I'm late. It showed up, but not in our account."

There was another stirring down the table. Someone butted a cigarette.

"Wicks put through the transfer, but two digits of the account number were accidentally transposed. Instead of being transferred into the Sparsum Operations account, number 405-003-1162, the funds went into another Nassau account, number 450-003-1126."

"It's an easy mistake," someone else said. "It should be easy to fix."

"One would think so," Webster conceded, "but there are problems. First, Daniel Wicks could not be reached. He was not in the Cayman Islands this afternoon. It seems he flew out to London on the first flight Sunday morning."

"London?"

"London, England. He's a Brit. He's got family somewhere in the English countryside."

"Surely someone else at the bank can—"

"That's what we thought," Webster agreed, "but it's not the case."

"What about correcting it at Regency in Nassau?"

"That's where we went next," another man said. "But we were informed this afternoon that the transfer was quite proper."

"Then we have to get to the owner of the account."

"We spent most of the afternoon on that angle, too. The account is under a company name, CR&R, Ltd., with signing authority in the hands of someone called John O'Brien. We tracked John O'Brien. It's an assumed name registered in the Bahamas. We tracked CR&R; it's a company incorporated in Bermuda."

"And presumably, the same person who is doing business as John O'Brien in the Bahamas owns the corporation in Bermuda? Who is it?"

"Broc O'Neill."

Christelle couldn't believe what she had just heard, nor could anyone else at the table. Someone grabbed for the newspaper and tore it open to the third page. Everyone was in an uproar. Christelle felt herself swimming in confusion.

"Gentlemen, gentlemen," the first speaker of the evening broke in, "I think Mr. Webster has more to say."

The noise settled. Webster looked around. "Naturally, with this contradictory information, we were at a bit of a loss. So we tapped into the records at O'Neill's university, Jefferson State. There was nothing unusual. But then we got into city records, and something came up."

The silence around the table was absolute. Christelle stared at Webster.

"It's not his real name. 'Broc O'Neill' is also an assumed name. It was filed a good while ago, the year he started teaching at JSU. As you know, an assumed name is good for ten years. The filing was renewed earlier this year."

Christelle sat in stunned silence, staring down the table, unable to comprehend what she was hearing. Broc O'Neill... Professor Broc O'Neill... She had known him for three years. She had attended his classes. He was married to Darcy O'Neill; they owned a house in Jefferson; she had shopped with Darcy. She had stood by Darcy's grave in Jefferson. She had seen his picture in the paper. Her teacher, her advisor, the man she had traveled with, the man she had made love to at Penang, on Tioman Island — Broc O'Neill... was not real.

"Christ, didn't he graduate from Yale, and before that from Green Bay?"

"We pulled the records at Green Bay. He filed an assumed name long ago. He's been 'Broc O'Neill' since he was twenty-one. He filed again in Connecticut when he entered Yale graduate school."

"Shit! Who filed an assumed name document?" someone roared.

"It doesn't matter! Some guy by the name of Bob Smith, who was born the same year as O'Neill, but it doesn't matter. We really don't know who. Bob Smith died in a family auto accident at the age of six."

Christelle's insides were turning upside down. She felt dizzy. The scene in front of her had turned into a smoky dreamscape. Nothing made sense. It was more than she could comprehend. Broc O'Neill, dead at the bottom of the South China Sea, and now this!

"Miss Washington!"

Christelle felt herself dragged back to reality, not sure what was real any more. Everything since Tioman Island was a shambles, a tangle of things she could not comprehend.

"Miss Washington, what do you know of all this? You spent the past two months with Broc O'Neill. What the hell is going on?"

Christelle sat motionless, staring down the table at her gray-haired interrogator.

"Miss Washington, my name is Hudgeons — Judge Leopold Hudgeons. We'd like you to answer some questions for us."

Judge Leopold Hudgeons. This was getting more unreal every minute. It was a courtroom, some sort of hellish inquisition.

"There's way over two billion dollars missing from our corporate account. It's in the account of someone by the name of Broc O'Neill. At least one of his names is Broc O'Neill. You've been with him most recently. What do you know about this?"

"I... I don't know anything..." she spluttered. "I saw him... I saw him... die."

"Don't know anything!" The room flew into an uproar again. She saw angry faces, blazing eyes, snarling teeth.

"How did Broc O'Neill open an account in the Bahamas? It was opened a week ago?"

"I don't know... I saw him... I saw him die. At Tioman Island."

"How did Broc O'Neill find out about Teleconic Manufacturing?"

"Why was he talking to John Randolph?"

"Why were you in Penang?"

"Come now, Miss Washington, you know about these things. Why was Broc O'Neill visiting Walter Monahan in Allentown?"

Christelle was confused. She looked from one questioner to another.

"Miss Washington, silence will do you no good. You were with Broc O'Neill in Allentown. You were with him in Pennsylvania. Why did Broc O'Neill visit Walter Monahan?"

Christelle said nothing.

"Damn it! Show her the video!"

"Miss Washington," the Judge shouted, "we have you and Broc O'Neill on video on the night of July 17th. Why were you at Pennsylvania Produce?"

Christelle felt herself slipping. Everything was running together, a blur of confusion and tangled memories. And Broc... Broc O'Neill. Was it Broc she was with that night? He wasn't who she thought he was. She stared down the table.

"Miss Washington," the Judge continued, "we have you on video firing a gun. We have you blowing out the windows of Colonel James Spiker's automobile on the night of July 17th. Colonel Spiker died that night. Why were you and Broc O'Neill in Allentown?"

"We ought to put her in thumbscrews," Wade Bracket suggested. Christelle glared at him. "That bitch and her damn professor evaded us for weeks. She was with him; he was traveling on a stolen passport. She knows a whole lot more than she's letting on."

"We can take her downtown and throw her to the DA or take her out in the woods to rot—"

"She's a murderess. Blakeney, have you got enough to take her in?" Christelle saw another sinister-looking bastard nod. "Give her over to

Blakeney. Let the FBI deal with her; she'll spend the rest of her days in prison—"

Christelle could feel her anger rising. This was intimidation, a trial with no jury, a verbal lynching without the benefit of a defense. And they were only getting away with it because they were all bigger than she was. One woman surrounded by twenty crooks.

"I say we stick her feet in concrete and dump her downstream. Let her meet the same fate as Broc O'Neill, whoever he is." The judge glared at her. "Same question again, Miss Washington — who opened a bank account in Broc O'Neill's name in the Bahamas?"

Christelle was furious. She sat forward and glared down the table. "You bloody excuses for men! You think you killed Broc O'Neill, but you don't know. He's got you all by the balls. He's a sorcerer; he's doing magic; he's come back as a ghost; he's stealing your stolen money from the other side. The whole damn lot of you are haunted, and if you try out any of your threats with me, I'll help him haunt every one of you to the grave—"

Gunshots at the side door. Blasted away, the lock flew across the room, barely missing Orchard. The door frame cracked and splintered and the door crashed open.

Broc O'Neill stood in the doorway with both pistols level, smoke rising from the barrel of the Colt 45.

Chapter Forty-seven

Broc moved down the room toward Christelle. His eyes went from man to man.

"There's enough ammunition in these to finish every one of you," O'Neill affirmed. "If you get out of this room alive, consider yourself very lucky. If any of you moves, consider yourself dead. Now, I want every hand flat on the table."

Christelle was staring at him, incomprehensibly, the look in her eyes frightening him. He moved to her side, watching them, and touched her shoulder with his arm, reassuring her, knowing he had just walked into her life from the land of the dead. He felt her hair, the pressure of her head against his forearm, and knew that she would come through.

One of them was standing by the water cooler at the end of the room. O'Neill's Browning roared and the cooler exploded. "Get to your seat!"

Terrified, the man moved quickly and sat down. Every hand was in sight, palms flat on the table. Every eye was on him, a walking ghost.

Christelle stood up. "Broc, give me a gun!" she demanded. "I've got some scores to settle. The 45 will be just fine. It will make a bigger mess."

O'Neill handed her the Colt. Take it easy, Christelle. The look in her eyes alarmed him, but not as much as it alarmed the men at the table. She moved back to the corner where she could see everyone and glanced at him. My God, she was like a rock.

"Now, gentlemen," he resumed, "it's time to do some accounting. We've got $2.36 billion collected in August, almost as much in July — a total of thirteen billion in the past six months, roughly $110 billion in the past four years. All of it extracted from prominent companies, all from Republican CEOs, all of it obtained illegally."

"That's a lot of bullshit!" one of them shouted. "You haven't got a shred of proof."

O'Neill walked down the table and stood beside him, his Browning stuck against the back of his neck.

Christelle introduced him. "His name is John Orchard. He's the chairman."

"Well, Mr. Orchard, I'm pleased to meet you. Department of Justice, I believe."

Orchard said nothing. "Let me explain a few things about the way American intelligence works. It's clear that there are a few things you don't know. For instance, I'm sure you've heard of the case where the National Security Agency recently broke the codes of some encrypted messages from World War II. Do you know how that was done? Mr. Orchard, do you know how that was possible?"

Orchard said nothing.

"Perhaps our two NSA men could help here. Mr. Bradshaw, Mr. McClosky." Christelle pointed them out with the barrel of her gun. "Mr. Orchard, those messages were decoded because they were archived, for forty years. Nothing the NSA intercepts is ever thrown away. Is that right, Mr. Bradshaw? Mr. McClosky?"

Neither man moved.

"These two gentlemen were in charge of your COMINT sector in the NSA. COMINT has been monitoring messages on over four thousand Worldwide Communications cell phones for the past several years. Surely, you don't think they've been sitting up late with earphones."

O'Neill could see the fear in Orchard's eyes.

"No, that is not how it works. The NSA has got over five acres of computers. They've got as much computer memory as the whole rest of the country combined. And you know what, Mr. Orchard? Every one of the conversations you had — you and these gentlemen around the table, and a number who aren't here — every one was recorded. There are seventeen agents down at the NSA right now — agents on our side — pulling out your recorded conversations at about a hundred an hour."

O'Neill pulled a cassette tape from his pocket and waved it around.

"Ninety minutes, thirty-five bits of conversation. At least ten of you are on here." He pulled out another cassette. "Here's another one, twenty-eight conversations. You know something, Mr. Orchard? This is the tip of the iceberg. They've already got enough on tape to make Nixon's Watergate tapes look like a B-minus history documentary."

O'Neill pulled the gun away from Orchard's ear. "So, you see, your own colleagues, Mr. McClosky and Mr. Bradshaw, have collected enough evidence to put all of you away for a long, long time."

"You damn fake," one of them shouted. "You talk big—"

"What's your name, Sir?" O'Neill demanded, pointing his gun.

"Joseph Terrence."

"Ah, Joseph Terrence. A man I've been waiting to meet ever since I left Manila. O'Neill glanced around and then strode to the other end of the table. I see we have a telephone here: how convenient! And a long extension cord." O'Neill carried the phone down the room and set it in front of Terrence. "Of course, I see you also have a cell phone, Mr. Terrence, but we need to make some long-distance calls, and I don't want to run up your bill. Would you like to dial, or shall I?" He smiled.

Terrence did not move.

"I guess I should dial," O'Neill decided. "Here, Christelle, you take both guns, and shoot anyone who moves. Okay, we will first dial 011 for an international line; then the country code for the Philippines, 63; area code for Caloocan city, 2." O'Neill punched in the numbers. "Then the phone number. I'm sure you recognize Mr. Tong's office number at Teleconic Manufacturing: 67-4592. And now. Ah! We have a recorded message. It says there are six extensions: 10, 20, 30, 40, 50 and 60. You recognize all this, Mr. Terrence? You've been in Mr. Tong's office. After all, you're seventy-five percent owner of Teleconic. Now, let's try Teleconic's newest extension. Well, maybe you didn't know they had a new extension. But you need to know this one: it's 3-4-5-6-7." O'Neill punched in the numbers and shoved the receiver against Terrence's ear.

Four seconds later, Terrence's head jerked away. Those who were closest heard the explosion from the receiver, and then the line went dead.

"Well, Mr. Terrence, that's the end of Teleconic Manufacturing. Blown up. Gone. I think the value of your overseas investment just hit rock bottom."

Stunned, everyone around the table was staring at O'Neill.

"Let's try Hai Phong Electronics. International code, 011; country code for Malaysia, 60; area code for Penang, 4; then the phone number 31-7074. Now, let's see, who will have the honor? Maybe Mr. Bracket, you have an interest in Hai Phong Electronics."

O'Neill walked around the table and set down the phone.

"Extension 3-4-5-6-7." O'Neill punched in the numbers and shoved the receiver against Bracket's ear. Everyone around the table knew what had happened when Bracket's head jerked away.

"By the way," O'Neill said, glancing at his watch. "It's 8:55 p.m. Tuesday here; that's 7:55 a.m. Wednesday in Southeast Asia. An hour and five minutes before starting time, so nobody is at work yet. But just to be sure no one would get hurt, we padlocked both buildings last Thursday night. Mr. Tong has been sent a check for his twenty-five percent share of Teleconic: $1,240,000, I believe; and every employee of both companies has been sent a check for $2,000 in U.S. funds — severance pay. Of course, that's courtesy of Lignum funds, transferred to the account of CR&R Ltd in the Bahamas."

Wade Bracket's temper flared. "You'll never get away with this! Your grad school bitch will never get away. We've got her on videotape—"

Christelle strode down the room and pushed her Colt against Wade Bracket's head. "You are so stupid! I can't believe the CIA has any use for you at all." She shoved the barrel against his skull, making him wince. "This is the gun you saw me firing. You won't find more than six shells among the ones collected at Pennsylvania Produce that match this gun, and none of them will match the machine gun bullets in the bodies of Colonel Spiker and Walter Monahan—"

They heard the sirens.

Christelle grabbed Bracket's hair and pulled his head to one side, the barrel of the Colt against his cheek. "You damnable pervert!" She pulled open his jacket and yanked her bikini out of his inside pocket. "I should have pushed you out the window with your handcuffs."

O'Neill and Christelle stood by the door as the police officers filed in.

"How the hell did you find us, O'Neill?"

"You ask hard questions, Judge," Christelle smiled, rummaging in her handbag, "but I know the answer to that one. The way you found Dr. O'Neill is the way he found you."

She held up the Worldwide Communications cell phone.

Christelle's Grand Am roared east on Interstate 65. She clung to his arm as he drove, her head against his shoulder, speechless, until the lights appeared, and then she sat up and looked around, dazed by the tall spire of the Washington Monument and then the monumental façade of the U.S. Capitol. She stared at the lights, the towering hotels, the spreading lawns in front of the steps; she sat in silence when he pulled the car up in front of the Hyatt Regency. She gazed at the lighted buildings and walked as though in shock as he led her into the hotel to the elevator.

The porter followed with her luggage loaded from the limousine into her trunk at the museum. Speechless, she stood in the middle of the suite, looking around at the suitcases, the laptop computer open on the desk, the piles of computer printout, and Broc O'Neill.

He held her against him, wordlessly taking in her presence, her face against his neck, her hair cascading over his shoulder, her body crowding him as though there were no other place to be but exactly where he was. He held her, stroking her hair, feeling her trembling, feeling her whole body shaking. He held her, not believing she was there, not believing they had found each other, unable to grasp that they were somehow together again.

She found a nightgown from Singapore with the tags still dangling from the collar. They went to the kitchenette. He poured two glasses of orange juice. They sat looking at each other across the coffee table, neither of them knowing what to say or where to begin.

"That was quite a vacation you arranged, Professor Broc O'Neill." She lifted the glass and sipped her juice. "All except the last part. I didn't get to finish my dive."

She was coming back.

She was coming back to him from the shock of the past two weeks. He understood what she had gone through. And now she was coming back — the same Christelle he had found and fallen in love with, irretrievably, irrevocably — coming back with everything he loved about her intact. He walked around the table and pulled her to her feet and kissed her, and then led her over to the window. The Capitol dome glowed against the night sky. "This is a new ending to the vacation, a couple of days in the national capital."

"How come just a couple of days?"

"That's how long it will take to finish this. But there's still a lot of cleanup to do. Until then, we need to lie low, stay out of sight until it's safe to leave."

"Like getting out of Dodge City — maybe I can wear my cowgirl hat and boots." She smiled at him.

"I thought all that stuff was gone—"

"That's one thing I've got to say for those guys. They packed up everything: hat, boots, laptop, everything. Anyway, disappearing shouldn't be hard for you — John O'Brien, Bob Smith, Robert Winston — Broc O'Neill. They'll never figure out who you are. And, incidentally, I'm not sure either."

O'Neill drew her to him and kissed her again.

"There's no mystery to who I am, Christelle, but it will take hours to explain. Just a lot of fabricated documents and carefully arranged identity changes." He kissed her again. "All you need to know now is that we're here together."

She put her arms around his neck and held him fiercely. "Let's go to bed," she whispered against his neck, squeezing her body against him.

He stroked her hair and twisted a tail of it in his hand. "Is this an emergency situation?"

"If you're anywhere but right here beside me anytime for at least the next six months… that's going to be an emergency situation." She kissed him. "Since you're here right now, I guess it's not." She kissed him again and gave him another fierce hug. "But you're welcome to pretend it is."

Chapter Forty-eight

Susquehanna Valley
Pennsylvania

William Kaiser stretched, luxuriating in the early afternoon warmth. His cruiser had been drifting from the dam downstream for over an hour. He rolled over, enjoying the sun. After another five minutes he sat up, pulled a bottle of Heineken from his cooler, and lit up a cigarette. He was opposite the house; Betty was knitting on the back deck.

Kaiser watched a red, white, and blue van come down the driveway and stop near the house. Betty went down the steps and talked to the driver; then the van backed and turned. Betty stood waving on the beach.

Kaiser butted his cigarette, started up the engines, and headed the cruiser slowly toward the shore.

"It's a special delivery letter. It's for Kaiser Shipping, but it's addressed to you and marked 'Personal'. They brought it out from the office."

Kaiser tore open the letter as he walked slowly toward the stairs to his deck. It was addressed to William Kaiser; c/o Kaiser Shipping; York, Pennsylvania. He opened the letter and sat down on the steps. The check, drawn on an account in the Bahamas, was made out to Kaiser Shipping and signed by John O'Brien.

Capital Recovery and Return, Ltd
Hamilton, Bermuda

Dear Mr. Kaiser:
You are one of over four thousand executives receiving a letter today. Enclosed, please find a check in the amount of $1,680,000, the exact amount that you donated to Maryfield Charity Trust in August. All these donators have one thing in common. Their primary

403

"crime" is their commitment to the Republican Party. If great wealth or spectacular corporate profits is a crime, this was the second reason they were targeted for donations. Other reasons are embarrassing mistakes, poor decisions, marital infidelities, and other indiscretions. Most of your fellow donors were willing to pay to prevent disclosure.

The total amounts donated over the past six years by you and others adds up to $110 billion. While all of this capital was used to construct, restructure, and enhance institutions that Americans can be proud of, the funds were obtained illegally, by threats, bribery, and extortion.

Capital Recovery and Return, Ltd., is unable to return your donations made prior to August 1st. These funds have been dispersed, and those who received them do not have the resources to repay, even should you wish to lodge a lawsuit for recovery. On a positive note, your funds were used for admirable, humanitarian goals. Our advice is that Kaiser Shipping should be wary of any further attempts to encourage or extort donations from your company.

As part of our service, CR&R, Ltd., wishes to replace a defective cellular phone, which you acquired several months ago. You may return it to the nearest outlet of Worldwide Communications for a free replacement.

Sincerely,
John O'Brien, Treasurer

William Kaiser looked at the check. A handwritten note was held to the upper left corner of the letter by a staple.

Dear Mr. Kaiser:
Extortion is a crime, but victims of extortion are vulnerable because of their own earlier crimes. Among the 4000+ victims, your family is guilty of the worst atrocity I have ever encountered. Your grandfather's treasonous activities during World War II — shipping munitions for the Japanese on American ships — is now far beyond the statute of limitations. You've been amply punished for your

treason by the extortion of some $60 million; moreover, Kaiser Shipping was punished more than fifty years ago by the loss of thirty-eight freighters during the American bombings in Manila Harbor in 1944. However, if you and the company feel you are still vulnerable to blackmail or extortion, you might consider shedding the Philippines division of Kaiser Shipping.

Your collection of German and Japanese weaponry must be worth a substantial sum. Preserving it with truly obnoxious and overbearing pride reveals a loyalty to despicable activities of your forebears. While this devotion to artifacts of past treason remains, it is difficult to feel that you have moved beyond their reprehensible symbolism. Your collection of weapons betrays a devotion to ideologies quite at odds with the pacifist Quakerism you espouse.

Within a few weeks the National Firearms Museum, Fairfax, Virginia, will call to discuss an appraisal of your collection and its acquisition for its growing international collection. We suggest donating your collection as the final step past a despicable egotism and treasonous past.

Incidentally, William Penn did not found the Quakers. It was George Fox.

Sincerely,

John O'Brien, a.k.a. Jacob Wallace

The U.S. Capitol
Thursday, September 5

Senator Robert Shiner came out of the Senate Chamber and stood at the top of the steps for a minute. Several colleagues stood at the bottom of the steps.

"Mr. Senator—"

He found himself looking into the hazel eyes of a woman with auburn hair. She was wearing a dark brown business suit and carrying a briefcase. She stepped forward and discreetly grasped his arm. "Come this way, Mr. Senator. There are things we need to discuss."

"He stood firm. I don't need to discuss anything, not with you or anyone else."

Christelle faced him. "Mr. Senator, look down on the grass. You will see Judge Adams with several police officers. He is looking this way and wondering what you will do. Now" — she held up a folded paper — "this is a warrant for your arrest signed by Judge Adams. But it's conditional. Your choice. If you refuse to follow me, you will be arrested and taken to jail. So, what will it be?"

Speechless, he followed her down the steps. John Adamson, Henry Kramer, Ross Tabbitt, and three others were standing in a cluster at the bottom. Their faces remained starkly rigid.

"What is the meaning of this?" Tabbitt growled. "And who do you think you are—?"

"I don't think this is a time for you to be asking questions, Senator. It's time you and your colleagues did some listening."

Senator Roberts, directed down by one of the Senate ushers, stopped a few steps away. "It's been a long day with a difficult vote. I'm leaving"

Christelle turned and glared at him. "As I just pointed out to Senator Shiner, I have a warrant for arrest if you try to leave. We're having a little meeting in a couple of minutes. After we're finished, you can tell those reporters your side of the story. You'll have front page space in *The Washington Post*."

Senator Roberts did not move.

Christelle saw Broc with members of the House of Representatives. "Follow me, Senators." They followed her, meeting Broc on the main steps into the Capitol.

"Gentlemen, let me introduce Professor Broc O'Neill." She saw the startled countenance on every face.

"It seems, Gentlemen, that you are surprised," he acknowledged. "Perhaps that's because you heard I was last seen being torn apart by sharks in the South China Sea."

O'Neill looked them over, amused at their shock. "Maybe some of you feel neglected. Your phones have been silent for the last forty-eight hours. The chairman of the committee is in shock to discover that I am alive. He's also in shock that he's in jail. You won't be hearing from John Orchard again."

The effect of his words was clear.

"I believe you were told I was the main obstruction for your programs — programs that are hidden under the names of Lignum Operations and Sparsum Operations. Programs that take funds from Republicans and give to causes traditionally supported by the Democratic Party. And all of this under the secret code name of Ironwood."

"What is this all about? Why do we have to listen to this garbage?"

Christelle stooped to set her briefcase on the steps, released the clasps, and exposed several cassette tapes.

"Senator Kramer," O'Neill explained, "one reason you have to listen to this 'garbage' is because the police, and members of the FBI who have already been pointed out, will send you back here if you walk away. A second reason is that if you don't want to listen to us — alone, here, now — then you will get to read transcripts of these tapes in tomorrow's *New York Times*."

Christelle handed O'Neill the tape player and a cassette. "Let's listen to this from June 13th". He inserted the tape and pushed the play button.

Voice: This is an outrageous situation. Margins of profit are not what they used to be twenty years ago. There are regulations —

Senator Kramer: Let me remind you that forty percent of your profits are from government contracts, which we procured. They are up for renewal next February, but it would be easy to delay further funding within the next thirty days.

Voice: Johnson Tramways cannot afford donations of $350,000 every month. That amounts to ten percent of profits.

Senator Kramer: Why not call it tithing? Of course, if you're not interested, then I suppose Johnson Tramways should begin downsizing for the cuts, which, according to my calculations may bankrupt your company.

O'Neill shut off the tape recorder and held up a sheaf of paper. "It seems, Senator, that Johnson Tramways was persuaded. On June 17th, they made a donation of $350,000, and they followed it with the same amount on July 17th and August 17th."

O'Neill glanced from face to face. "Would anyone like to hear some more of what Senator Kramer calls 'garbage'? That briefcase is full of cassette tapes — at least one for each of you."

"That money was not used to—"

O'Neill cut him off: "It was not used by any of you for any reprehensible purpose. That is true. No one here personally benefited from these donations, which now add up to billions of dollars over several years."

"You don't know anything about how those funds were used—"

"You're wrong, Sir. This briefcase has records of every one of the hundreds of institutions and programs that benefited. I can list twenty off the top of my head. I've toured several—"

"Haven't you got a heart, O'Neill?"

"Haven't you got any honor, Mr. Senator? You were elected by the people. This money has been coerced from the people."

"What people! Rich Republicans who earn hundreds of thousands in salary, in command of companies that earn billions—"

"That's their right. They've built their companies; they've found ways to excel in their chosen businesses. They've made a lot of money and then invested it well, and so they have made more. I think I learned once that the American system is based on capitalism. I didn't think I would have to point that out to members of the U.S. Congress!"

"The problem is, Dr. O'Neill," Senator Roberts pointed out, "that massive amounts of money are needed to provide all the services and correct all the problems that need urgent attention. It may be true that companies and wealthy executives have made their money honestly, but they don't pay their fair share in taxes —"

"And," Representative Waggoner added, "there are too many loopholes for corporations to reduce their taxes. Some practically avoid taxes altogether. You could regard the donations we encourage as additional tax revenue directed to worthy causes. That's what Senator Kramer referred to as tithing: donating a regular part of income to charity. But tithing occurs in churches, and corporations with the resources to tithe don't go to church —"

"Also, as you know," Senator Roberts interjected again, "the American people bitterly oppose increasing taxes. Republicans run for office on a low taxation platform. Remember what George Bush said at his acceptance speech, with millions of viewers watching: 'Read my lips. No new taxes!' We are simply trying to get past this funding logjam by motivating those who have the funds to pay and to help build the kind of America everyone wants."

"Democrats were in power for forty years," O'Neill said. "You had your opportunity to introduce new tax legislation—"

"Except," Waggoner added, "government funding for social programs was always shot down. Whenever we proposed directly funding for social improvement, it was labeled redistribution of income. Republican rhetoric claims that the poor needed to be taught to stand on their own two feet. Welfare has always been a dirty word. It leads to laziness. It undercuts self-reliance. Economic efforts to correct wrongs are labeled socialism, which is considered right next door to communism."

"Undoubtedly," Broc admitted, "there are formidable barriers, but you need to find ways to get around them. Pretending that bribery and extortion are ways to correct an inadequate tax code undermines the legal and ethical foundations of American society."

"O'Neill, where are you coming from? The Republicans have taken control; they've taken power. We may never find a way to build the Great Society that President Johnson promised. Instead, the Republicans are slowly dismantling everything we've built. Decades of Democratic programs are underfunded. It's wrong; it's damnably immoral."

"Senator Tabbitt, when were you put in charge of what's right and wrong?"

"I'm an elected—"

"Election has nothing to do with right and wrong. It has to do with passing laws, to promote programs legally. It has to do with building this country according to a vision, a plan—"

"That's what we've done. We have a vision, a plan."

"Plans and visions take place within political parties. Political parties are subject to something higher, the will of people, the framework of the law, the Constitution, the Bill of Rights. You've violated every one of these."

"Tell that to the Republicans—"

"Damn it, Senator, I'm not telling it to the Republicans. I'm telling it to you! I, too, represent the people of this country. I'm a citizen; I cast my vote. We all live within a structure; we have principles; we have laws. These include a legal and appropriate place for both Democrats and Republicans. And also, Independents if they choose to run. All are subject to the law. They are not authorized to decide what is right or wrong. The people decide that. The truth is not what Democrats think any more than what Republicans think. It's somewhere in the middle, not simply what they want or what you want, but the combination that comes out of the debate, the struggle, the dialogue."

They glared at him as though he was some sort of pariah.

Senator Shiner implored, "Don't you want to see something happen in this country? Don't you want something new in the world?"

O'Neill looked at him, then began to speak slowly, deliberately. "Senator, I was only a toddler when Senator Robert Kennedy was assassinated. He was a senator who served where you serve, who climbed these steps where you're standing. When I was seventeen, I found an old paperback of his book in a secondhand store. Have any of you read it? *To Seek a Newer World?*"

No one answered him.

"Perhaps that's why you've lost your vision... one of the reasons. All you do is watch election commercials on TV. Well, I read it, and though you may not believe it, from that day forward, I was and I remain a Democrat. Yes, I want what you want: a newer world. I've been watching this country's politics for a quarter century, waiting for the newer world to happen. And... yes! I've seen what you're doing." O'Neill held up a printout. "I've got the full list of every one of your benevolent projects — every one from Hawaii to Maine, Alaska to Puerto Rico. I've gone out and looked. I've seen your shelters for battered mothers. Absolutely astonishing. I've seen your readjustment centers for paroled convicts. They are inspiring. I've seen the improvements in care

410

for the aged, training centers for new immigrants, homes for unwed mothers. And, damn it, you're right! It's the closest thing I've seen to a newer world in my lifetime."

They stood on the steps, motionless, silent.

"But we've also watched this government run its secret wars — in Laos, for instance. We've watched while it attempted to assassinate leaders who did not do things our way, like Fidel Castro. We've seen this government destroy another country because their people wanted to be free — Vietnam, in case you've forgotten. We've seen this country commit crimes to advance what were seen as worthy causes. We've seen whole administrations go down; we've seen whole departments of this government break the law. We've all seen these things, they're so much a part of the political scene that the American people no longer believe in government or those who govern. And no matter what kind of better world you can build, if it comes out of the kind of corruption running rampant in this city, it will not be a better world."

"You know, Professor," Senator Kramer extolled, "for decades the Democratic Party has stood for broad-based, people-serving programs that promoted health care, assisted battered women, trained prisoners on release for trades, extended educational opportunities. These are the long-term ideals of the Democratic Party. The new programs we have funded address the concerns of our historic base of supporters."

"There's no doubt about that," O'Neill conceded. "But your historic base of supporters doesn't know how you did it?"

"You must live in another world," Professor O'Neill. "If we published all the social programs we have repaired, extended, and created — if we announced them here, from the steps of the Capitol — we have a base of fifty million voters who would cheer us on. We'd sweep every election for decades. Democratic votes would go through the roof."

"Yes, but those votes wouldn't be worth having. Voters often consider the ends but overlook the means. They would be little more than a base of voters as corrupt as you and your operations. A demographic base that cheers on gains based on threats, bribery, extortion, or torching a warehouse to force donations is a base without values on which this nation was built.

"Every one of you would castigate a Republican base who cheered on a Congress or President for repealing wilderness reserves for commercial development, deregulating protections on polluting industries, or ignoring Native American rights in order to build a superhighway through their historic lands. You'd call that base a crime syndicate, not a democracy."

"Why the hell are you so steamed up, O'Neill? What's all this to you?"

O'Neill grabbed Representative William Waggoner by the front of his coat. "You bloody bastard! Because an order went out to kill me. Because this organization planted a car bomb and blew my wife to kingdom come! You want to see?" O'Neill shoved his open wallet in front of them. "You are looking at Darcy O'Neill. Killed by a car bomb intended for me. Oh, no, it wasn't you who set the bomb. It was one of your sleezy mercenaries you've teamed up with — ruthless thugs, part of your Sparsum and Lignum that most of you have never met, committing atrocities you would not choose, but the stuff they do sullies all of you. That's what you've set loose. And my wife, Darcy O'Neill — she was a citizen of America, one of the people of this nation who did her job and cast her vote to build a safer world. And she was carrying our baby, a future citizen of America. And she was one of you — a Democrat!"

No one spoke. Someone shuffled his feet. Three or four lowered their gaze toward the sidewalk. One of the representatives wiped his eyes.

Senator Adamson resisted the accusations. "We may have made the calls, raised some money, but these kinds of orders — we had nothing to do with them."

"I know that, Senator. All of you were pawns. Under all the brazen political stuff, most of you have ideals. You want to build something better; that's why you ran for office. Then you got up here on the Hill and found out how difficult it is. You saw an opportunity: a chance to build a grass-roots organization that would transcend the red-tape nonsense of party politics. A secret government. Someone well hidden, someone who is still well hidden found a way to get to you, persuade you, and set it all up. I know, I understand. The guys who did the dirty work — the heavies, the ones who tried to kill me and who slaughtered John Randolph and Walter Monahan, and one of their own, Colonel Spiker — they're elsewhere, scattered around a dozen federal agencies. And now they are in jail. And you... you were all just too damned eager! You saw Ironwood as a quick fix. So you forgot your principles."

O'Neill could see the pain as they shifted on the steps, gazing up Pennsylvania Avenue, staring down at the reporters who had gathered a hundred feet away.

"What are you going to do with this, O'Neill?"

"It's not what I'm going to do with it, Senator, it's what you are going to do that will make a difference. The Democratic Party had over forty years to do its work, and it did its work well. The Republicans got control of Congress in 1994. It could be that they have their own half century. But remember, they had to wait around while you guys were running things, and now it may be your turn to sit on the sidelines. That's not a reason to give up your vision of what is best for this country. Some of them have visions, too, and what's finally right is the system we're all part of. It's what comes out of the debate, what happens when the parties work through it together."

They stood silently. The cluster of reporters had grown into a crowd of several dozen. A van with TV cameras had pulled up.

"I think," Christelle summarized, "that Professor O'Neill is calling for you to build a newer world a better way."

"Just who are you, Miss—?"

"My name is Christelle Washington. I'm a student, an American citizen, a voter. I'm someone who would cheer what you have done if you could have accomplished it the right way. I'm someone who is young enough to have ideals and would like to see men like you help to build them."

"You seem pretty sure of yourself for someone who's never been beyond the ivory tower—"

Christelle's temper flared. "First of all, I've been way beyond the ivory tower. I've been accosted sixty feet underwater, brought to the surface too fast to clear the nitrogen from my blood. I've been drugged, held captive by goons you don't even know have been coopted into your illegal program without knowing a thing about it. My car and I have been

413

shot at with machine guns. I've come close to losing my life at the hands of idiots in the trenches — high-school dropouts who abuse good citizens and know nothing of your high ideals."

She turned. "Senator Adamson from California, correct? From San Diego, correct? That's where I cast my vote, every election since I could vote: — '88, '90, '92, and '94. As I recall, you came out a winner in '88 and '94. You are pretty insulting to one of the voters who sent you here!"

Adamson looked at her, speechless and humiliated.

She went on: "Senator Adamson, and all the rest of you here, it's time you started doing something. This is a party of great possibilities that has lost its way. Where is this party, anyway? There are one hundred ninety-five million voting adults in this country but only a miniscule number who are members of the Democratic Party, and their average age is over fifty! Pretty poor for the party alleged to represent the people. Men like you came of age when John Kennedy challenged you to ask yourselves what you could do for your country. You began your careers running campaigns for Eugene McCarthy. You were fiery young men who marched in the streets to bring an end to the Vietnam War. But what have you done since then? The last challenge to the youth of this country, whom I represent, was the Peace Corps, begun nearly fifty years ago. The last great project launched under a Democratic president was a space program to land men on the moon; that happened when I was a year old! The last piece of major legislation from a Democratic administration was the Civil Rights Act of the sixties. Then, finally, when you decided to do something, you did it by illegal surveillance and extortion. And now you are all soiled with violence, arson, and murder."

They stood before Christelle, withered by her fury. For a long minute no one moved.

"No," O'Neill disburdened them somewhat, "even though you all deserve to be behind bars — and we could send you there — we're not going to do anything... just send you back to your jobs. We're going to tell the TV camera operators to take a walk and tell the reporters there's no story. The tapes of all your conversations, the telephone records — they've been collected, deposited in safe places — four copies of them. If any remnant of this conspiracy should reappear or if anything happens to either of us, we've left instructions for all the evidence to be hauled out and released to the press. And you can be sure you'll go down. The whole Democratic Party will go down!"

"You'll go down, O'Neill, you'll go down as long as Ironwood goes free. None of us knows who he is. No one knows who he is—"

"That's right, Senator," O'Neill agreed. "Ironwood is the lynchpin who's managed to stay out of sight."

Out of sight. O'Neill felt the same apprehension from months ago at Darcy's funeral — the sense there might be eyes hidden nearby. That somehow, they might be watched.

"He knows what's going on. You'll never get Ironwood behind bars. He's too smart to get caught."

"Most of you thought you were too smart to get caught."

"He's beyond you. Give it time. He'll get you and you'll go down, and this whole thing will go away."

"Maybe. But I made a choice and a promise when I escaped from sharks in the South China Sea."

Senator Williams spoke for the first time: "You said these records were being deposited in safe places. Do you mind telling us where?"

"Not at all, Senator. One set here in Washington. The others were all sent by Federal Express two days ago. They've already arrived: one set in Missouri, one in Hawaii, one in Singapore."

They looked at him with disbelief.

"I guess we can assume," O'Neill added, "that these records will be safe for the foreseeable future. Especially in Singapore."

There was a long pause in the conversation. The sun was low in the afternoon sky, almost below the trees.

"Dr. O'Neill, you didn't do this by yourself. Who helped you?"

"One of the people who helped is right here: Christelle Washington. The young woman from the ivory tower. She saved my life; she helped me penetrate to the heart of the organization. She led to the capture of your leaders. The others, four Americans from a platoon who fought a war that should never have been fought, a war they didn't win. Four Navy SEALs. And now they've just finished fighting a new war that had to be fought — and they've won."

Chapter Forty-nine

Friday, September 6

Christelle sat in her Grand Am. She looked as though she was going to cry. Broc stood by the open window, put his hand on her shoulder and squeezed.

"I don't want to go, Broc; I'm afraid to leave you here alone."

"There's nothing to fear," he said, with more bravado than conviction. He was eager for Christelle to be on the road and out of harm's way and to follow her as soon as possible. I've got a couple of days of business, then I'll be catching a plane out of here. You need to phone your mom and dad, make contact."

She reached out the window and grabbed his arm. "Please, please, Broc, be careful."

"I'll be okay, but... are you going to your sister's place in Vermont?" She nodded. "Are they back from Spain?" She shook her head. Broc opened his briefcase and pulled out something hard wrapped in a sweatshirt: the Colt 45. "I had it cleaned. I don't think anyone could tell it was ever used."

"Wonderful! I can sneak it back into Roy's trunk. He'll never know."

"And, if you see Dillon Shaver, here are replacements for his Canadian passport and driver's license, courtesy of the CIA Printing Office."

He kissed her and then pulled out his wallet. "Here's some cash, enough for food, motels, and maybe some treats. When you've driven a hundred miles up the road, find some place where you can sit for a while. There's a package in your trunk, and a map."

She wrinkled her forehead at him.

"The package is from Brently Hagan. The map is from me."

"What are you going to do?"

"A guy offered me a position last spring. I told him I'd let him know this month. His foundation is just across the river."

She smiled up at him, eyes glittering. "I love you, Broc O'Neill."

He kissed her again, grasping her face, his hands in her hair. "The same. You have no idea, Christelle."

Alexandria, Virginia

O'Neill pulled his rental car into the tree-shaded driveway of the Whiterock Council on Foreign Policy. In the parking lot there were two cars, six spaces. The building was an old mansion, dating, he guessed, to the early part of the century — a solid three-story Edwardian structure immaculately kept.

Samuel Whiterock came out on the verandah as O'Neill walked slowly up the brick walkway.

"O'Neill? Is it Professor Broc O'Neill?"

O'Neill came up the steps and shook his hand, gazing along the spacious shaded porch. "It's a fine structure, Mr. Whiterock; it must be one of the premier pieces of real estate in Alexandria."

"Please, Professor, please call me Sam. And don't be deceived. This grand old house is where I grew up, but I don't live here now. My father acquired it at the height of his business career. But we were about to lose it until I formed the Whiterock Council; there are certain tax advantages for non-profit organizations. But still, we barely make it financially. Won't you come inside?"

O'Neill had checked his computer printouts. There were half a dozen institutions in Alexandria that had benefited from grants from Sparsum Operations. The Whiterock Council on Foreign Policy was not one of them.

A long room was lined with bookshelves. O'Neill stopped and gazed at what was possibly the most impressive institutional library outside the Library of Congress. The shelves went all the way to the twelve-foot ceiling. He did a quick estimate: fifteen, maybe twenty thousand volumes, mostly history, economics, and politics. He stopped in front of a couple of shelves of books with bright red dust covers. He noted the authors: Cicero, Suetonius, Tacitus — Roman historians.

"My undergraduate major was classics," Whiterock explained. "Greek and Latin, but I preferred the Roman historians. The Greeks, Herodotus and Thucydides, were so far back that their histories are marred by legends. I prefer solid facts." He turned and headed down the hall. "Come into the office."

O'Neill stopped just inside the double door and gazed at a huge room that measured at least thirty by forty feet. Sunlight streamed in a bank of tall windows along the east wall.

"You grew up in this house?"

"Yes, but it's been much changed since then. Cramped little rooms done away with, walls removed to make more space."

O'Neill followed, passing a woman polishing brass." Come in; sit down, Professor O'Neill." Whiterock motioned to a chair by his desk.

The room was paneled in dark wood, some kind of tropical variety, O'Neill guessed. It was furnished with plush sofas and two large work tables piled with dictionaries and various reference books. What caught O'Neill's eye, however, was the solid west wall. Its entire forty-foot length was made up of tall doors about eighteen inches wide, with brass handles. The lower set rose to six feet; and upper set of doors went to the ceiling. A library-style rolling ladder stood toward the back corner.

"Are you interested in something to drink?" He noticed Madeline was still working by the door. "Madeline! Please, I wonder if you could polish the brass later!"

Startled, the woman stood up and hurried out of the room.

"She doesn't seem to know when she should make herself scarce," Whiterock alleged, crossing the office. He put his key in the lock and turned the bolt. "Sorry. Where were we? Oh, yes, drinks?"

"Whatever you're having, I seem to remember you served a very fine Scotch in Indianapolis."

"Cutty Sark." He opened a cupboard, brought out a bottle, and then got a container of ice from a mini-fridge. O'Neill watched him work, efficiently, methodically. The office had the stately air of an eighteenth-century English mansion.

"So, you've decided to take me up on my offer, Dr. O'Neill," Whiterock assumed.

"If I thought the offer was a sincere one, I might."

Whiterock turned to him, his brow furrowed.

"I don't see," O'Neill wondered aloud, "how the Whiterock Council on Foreign Policy can afford to hire anyone. You said yourself you can barely make ends meet."

Whiterock poured the glasses half full of Scotch over the ice, then added water. "What are you driving at, O'Neill?"

"I just wonder why you made the offer last spring."

Whiterock sat down in the leather chair behind the desk. He seemed puzzled. "I thought that adding you would boost our reputation for procuring funds."

O'Neill paused for a second, then surveyed the spacious office. "This is a major institution with a great reputation," he affirmed, "even if it is poorly funded. What stops me... I just can't believe you want to spend precious resources on a project like investigating the election of 1980 or, for that matter, any party irregularities that happened years ago. And even if it did involve questionable negotiations with a foreign government, it's too long ago to matter. It won't provide any traction in the present."

"So, it doesn't interest you," Whiterock concluded.

"It interests me because I think the offer was a cover. Your proposal was a smokescreen. What was it that was really on your mind last May?"

"You're a very puzzling man, Professor O'Neill."

"On the contrary, I'm a very simple man. I always assume the obvious. Occam's razor, if you will. When I see something out of the ordinary, I am immediately suspicious. For a man who prefers solid facts, you should understand. As I asked, what was really on your mind that morning in Indianapolis?"

Whiterock glared at him coldly.

O'Neill continued: "Why would a man of your influence and stature fly all the way from Alexandria to Indiana, along with two associates, to tender an offer to an unknown professor of history for a year in a think tank?"

"You're not an unknown professor of history."

"Not after I published an article on the founding of our intelligence agencies in *American Documentary History*." O'Neill watched him. Not a flinch.

O'Neill probed. "How come you haven't asked me about my summer, Mr. Whiterock?" Not a flinch. "How come you haven't asked me about my wife?" O'Neill caught it, a minor change in expression, which was gone in an instant. "Is it because you're not interested?"

"Of course, I'm—"

"Or is it, perhaps, because you already know about my summer? And about my wife?"

Whiterock set down his drink and looked at O'Neill. "You're talking in circles, Professor O'Neill."

"Am I? Uh-uh! Don't move that hand!" O'Neill leveled the Browning across the desk at Whiterock. He stood up and stepped around the desk. "We'll just remove this," he asserted, lifting the Beretta from the top drawer of the desk. "I remember you said you were a gunman."

O'Neill moved slowly back to his seat, keeping the Browning on Whiterock. "You made three mistakes when you came to Indianapolis. You gave away your fanatical hatred of the Republican Party. Since you haven't asked about my summer, I'll tell you. I've spent my summer dodging people with a fanatical hatred of the Republican Party. Your second mistake was that of the killer who wants to look his victim in the eyes before he completes the kill. That's why you were in Indianapolis."

"You're not dead, O'Neill—"

"Don't insult my intelligence! Every attempt on my life came right after I made a phone call on a Worldwide Communications cellphone. The car bomb meant to blow me to bits was planted after I left that meeting in Indianapolis... after I had phoned and arranged to meet my wife for lunch at the Jefferson Chicken Diner. And since you continue to feign ignorance, I'll inform you that the bomb killed my wife instead."

"I'm sorry; I never heard about that."

"You're a liar who must take me for an idiot. The two goons who came with you to Indianapolis — Boatright and Sawyer, whom you introduced as your vice president and secretary — were nothing of the sort. They were your dirty assistants who got to Jefferson in tine to set the bomb in my car."

420

"You're crazy, O'Neill—"

"No, I'm furious? Why don't you ask me your third mistake?"

Whiterock stared at him. O'Neill could tell he would not ask.

"It was when you decided there was little left in life — not with a family history of long-lingering Alzheimer's running in the family. Do you remember what you said?"

Whiterock said nothing.

"You don't remember? I see no signs that Alzheimer's has struck you. But you don't remember?"

Whiterock's face flushed with fury. He was about to explode. "Damn it, O'Neill! I don't remember!"

"Then let me remind you. You said one of your few pleasures in life was a couple of trips a year to Curaçao. That's in the Netherlands Antilles, isn't it, Mr. Whiterock, near the coast of South America? An offshore business center for those seeking absolute financial secrecy."

"What of it?"

"Do you think I'd still be alive if I were as naïve as you suppose? I must admit I was not sure you were the head of this extortion network... not until I got here."

Whiterock stared at him, puzzled.

"Those red volumes on your shelves. Caesar, Ovid, Plutarch. Twenty or thirty out of several hundred volumes in the Loeb Classical Library. Latin on the left, English translation on the right. I'm a historian, so I have a few on my own shelves. Anyone who has learned Latin would make the connection. You hid your identity in plain sight under Latin names. Huge amounts of money gathered like so much firewood — *lignum* — laundered through the Cayman Islands and the Bahamas, then disbursed — *sparsum* — to institutions in need, and to new institutions formed with the sudden flow of cash. All controlled by a network controlled by Veil, also called the Admiral, and directed by a company incorporated in Curaçao. Of course, it all began small. A minor piece of extortion — enough to fund renovations on a nursing home, enough to insure the best care for a doomed victim of Alzheimer's: your brother. And it worked, beautifully."

O'Neill watched as Whiterock began to crumble.

"Suddenly there was money, a steady flow of it. So why not do it again… and again, and again? Why not pull in others, create a network, expand nationwide? A supersized Democratic program for remaking America. A vast program of extortion and money laundering linked to an equally vast redistribution network. Why not rebuild all of America's service organizations — institutions in danger of budgetary cuts because of the ascendency of the Republican Party? And the whole thing was code named after your first success. Ironwood."

"You'll never prove it, O'Neill."

"I will if I have to. We've had a tap on your telephones for the past ten days. And taps on transferred calls from other places." O'Neill glanced at the bank of telephones by the window." Transfers that ended up here. Veil, the Admiral, Ironwood, they're all the same person, aren't they? A conspiracy, a network, a mystery, a man, one man, Mr. Whiterock. But never mind; I'm not inclined to prove it. That's not necessary."

Whiterock stared down at his hands.

"Have you noticed, Sam? The calls have stopped. No calls for three days." Whiterock looked up, startled. O'Neill could tell, he didn't know. "There haven't been any calls because a dozen members of Congress have been neutralized and eighteen of your thugs are in jail. It was a silent raid. No reporters, no press releases. Your network is broken, gone."

Whiterock looked trapped.

O'Neill swept his hand in a broad arc, gesturing toward the west wall. "I'm going to make a guess, Sam. Behind those doors are several hundred file drawers. My guess is that they hold your research, years of information gathering that led to founding of Lignum and Sparsum and a steady flow of cash now amounting to billions every month. My guess is that there are at least four thousand incriminating files behind that wall. They would rival the files of J. Edgar Hoover. You have spent most of your life digging — sifting the past of every wealthy Republican in America, every personal slipup or scandal since World War II; looking for precise facts that could be used for extortion. How else can we explain your rather astonishing knowledge of Republican skeletons in the closet?

"It must have taken some remarkable sleuthing to discover that an American firm, Kaiser Shipping, was transporting weapons for the

Japanese in the Philippines during the war? That's treason from more than half a century ago. It never made the news here; it's not in any list of commonly known conspiracies. I would never have discovered it if I hadn't dug into military records in the Philippines. But you found it! Just the right kind of scandal that William Kaiser would pay anything to keep buried."

O'Neill leaned forward. "Go ahead, Sam, open up those doors and prove me wrong. Show me four thousand files full of innocent information."

Whiterock stared at O'Neill like an animal caught in the glare of headlights. "So, what is all this about?"

"First, it's about my work. The publisher has had queries from subscribers of *American Documentary History*. When will my copy arrive? And reports from libraries of copies that have disappeared. As an academic, I'm incensed. Suppression of information violates my First Amendment rights."

"Your argument," Whiterock contended, "your call for a Senate investigation is irrelevant. The replacement, the final NSCID No. 9 that became law, did away with Truman's early draft idea of allowing domestic surveillance. I have a copy. You can look for yourself."

"Which defines your entire Worldwide Communications telephone surveillance network as illegal. But if the final NSCID clarifies the issue on surveillance, there's another issue. I have a right to publish both the initial discovery of the early draft, which reveals something so far unknown about President Truman, and the retraction in the final NSCID. And that issue of the journal your henchmen stole from subscribers and libraries included other articles. You violated the rights of their authors, too. That's just a small example of the massive violation of rights your crimes have perpetrated. It's a minor violation compared with extortion and murder, but we'll start with it. I've ordered a reprinting of the pilfered journal, along with a remailing, at your expense. Here's the invoice. You can write out a check; I'll mail it to the printer. Let's do it now."

O'Neill held the Browning on Whiterock, who fumed as he wrote out a check for $7,952. "Are we done, Professor?" Whiterock demanded, as he handed O'Neill the check.

"I don't think so. Apart from intimidation, fraud, illegal surveillance, extortion, and kidnapping, you are responsible for the murders of at least five people who got in the way. It's about how we should see justice done."

"Why don't you take me in, O'Neill? If you've got legal wiretaps"

"Have you got children?"

"I was never married."

"Nephews, nieces, heirs?"

"None."

"The Whiterock Foundation on Foreign Policy has an impressive history, a record of real accomplishment. And, contrary to your claim of empty pockets, it's got substantial assets in this property and library resources. What's going to happen to all that?"

"I haven't thought about it."

"You've got about two minutes to think about it, Sam, and while you're thinking, get out the company formation papers."

"What on Earth for?"

"Because you're going to sign it all over to me."

Disbelieving, Whiterock stared at him. O'Neill put the gun down in his lap. Whiterock picked up his drink and drank the rest.

"If you want another drink," O'Neill offered, "go ahead and make it. I can wait."

O'Neill watched him get out ice and pour the Scotch, then fill up the glass with water. He came and sat down. His hands were shaking.

"Why? Why would I want to sign over the Whiterock Foundation to you?"

"Because you have no heirs, because you don't want to go to jail. Because you know I'm a Democrat with ideals like yours and you want your work to continue."

"And how would you fund it?" Whiterock asked.

"Over six years, your Lignum account in the Caymans earned a lot of interest. In return for immunity, the bank official in charge of your account agreed to transfer not only all of your August donations but also seventy-five percent of the accumulated interest. It's now in my account. The interest added up to something in excess of $190 million. Of course, there are some expenses. Replacing four thousand rigged cell phones.

Severance pay for several hundred employees of Teleconic Manufacturing and Hai Phong Electronics. Retirement pay for Daniel Wicks. Postage, envelopes. There should be a least $180 million left over. Right now, it's earning over $20,000 in interest every day. We'll leave it invested. That should fund the Whiterock Council in perpetuity."

"And what would you do with it?"

"First, I would burn all those files. Then I would table the Senate inquiry since we now know that domestic surveillance remains illegal. In its place I would frame new goals — total dedication to rooting out government corruption. I would rewrite the charter to define the Whiterock Council as the finest guardian of American freedom and human rights this country has ever seen. In addition, I would identify an additional goal, a positive project that would help to build the new world you imagine. It would carry through your great ambition, but it would be done within the system, legally and ethically."

"I'll get the papers, Dr. O'Neill. You may want to form your own foundation."

He walked over to a cabinet and opened the door. Inside were two drawers with brass locks. Whiterock felt in his pocket, then walked to his desk. Then he walked over to the bar, his hands fishing in his jacket pocket. "Where are my keys?"

"In the door where you left them."

Whiterock walked to the door and retrieved his key ring, fumbled for a minute, and then opened the cabinet. A minute later he sat down at his desk and laid out the papers on his desk. "Do you want to look at them?"

"I want you to sign this letter." O'Neill passed an envelope across the desk. "It transfers the Whiterock Council and the Whiterock Foundation to Broc O'Neill, effective immediately. And this letter, too." He passed another envelope to Whiterock. "It transfers all your property and assets to Broc O'Neill."

Whiterock flattened out the letters. He read them and then looked up, thunderstruck, at O'Neill.

"No children, no heirs. Who else have you got, Sam? Do you want to go to jail? Your father languished for twenty years with Alzheimer's. Your brother is a vegetable. You've got it in your blood. Do you want to sit in jail with Alzheimer's? Think about it. Of all the institutions funded by Sparsum, not one was a prison. They're all rat holes. There isn't a correction facility in this nation that would do more than leave you to rot in a corner. A convict with no mind, no dignity. You'll be brutalized and sodomized out of your mind — whatever mind you have left. Can you face that? A lingering pathetic vegetable, a mindless lump of humanity?"

O'Neill could see the terror in Whiterock's eyes.

"You haven't got long, Sam, you know that. A few minutes ago, you lost your keys. How often has that happened?"

"I... I'm not... not sure—"

"It's happened before?"

"Yes."

"You know this disease. How long have you got? You've watched your father, your brother. How long have you got before you lose it?"

"I'm not... not sure. Six, maybe seven, years. Newer treatments might stretch it to ten."

"Is there any chance you'll be cured?"

"Probably none."

"So after a few years of slowly sinking into mindlessness, you'll go through another ten, fifteen, maybe even another record-setting twenty years more in jail as a vegetable."

Whiterock was shaking. "What... what do you... want to do?" O'Neill watched him breaking down. "If... if I sign these... what can... what can you do?"

"Extortion, bribery, money laundering. Am I right, Sam? You deserve to go to prison? But somewhere in all those taped conversations, there's proof of your ordering elimination, assassination, murder. That's different. Virginia still retains the death penalty. If you were lucky in court, you might get life without parole."

Whiterock was shaking. Slowly, his head sank forward onto the desk. "Yes, dear God, yes, I've made terrible mistakes."

"I'll help you, yes. And I'll tell you how first. And then you can decide whether you want to sign."

They pulled into the parking lot. O'Neill got out, opened Whiterock's door, and then opened the trunk. There were two suitcases. A porter came down the walkway with a luggage dolly, stopped beside the car and proceeded to load his luggage.

O'Neill walked beside Whiterock. He stared up at the magnificent brick building with its tiered rock gardens, mounting stone steps, and the ivy-covered west wing with its decorative security bars.

They climbed the long flight of steps among the flowers. As Whiterock climbed the last dozen stairs, O'Neill glanced back at the dark green hardwood forest of ironwood trees for which the facility was named, and then at the white sign with black letters by the entrance:

IRONWOOD RIDGE NURSING HOME
Founded 1957 Remodeled 1993
"The Best Care in the Nation"

They sat at the desk across from the manager, a woman in her late forties who was new to the position, replacing the manager who had toured O'Neill through the facility the previous Saturday.

"I understand you will be responsible for Mr. Whiterock," she confirmed.

O'Neill glanced at Whiterock and nodded. "I have power of attorney over all his assets. I will be the primary contact, with full financial responsibility. "He passed a pile of checks across the desk, two years' worth. This one's dated September 6th, the rest are postdated the first of each month thereafter for twenty-four months.

"Mr. Whiterock, I understand you are signing up early."

Whiterock nodded. He was shaking. "We have a family history. My brother is already a patient."

The manager leaned forward with the papers. "This is an unusual opportunity for you, Mr. Whiterock. It gives you control over your care while you are still able to choose. With this much lead time, we will be able to observe things that normally are lost to medical research. Perhaps, we can test new preventative drugs. I have prepared the papers. And, of course, once you sign yourself in, we become responsible — and fully liable — for your care."

"I understand the procedure. I have been visiting family members here for thirty years."

"Then you understand about our maximum-security protection. We've earned our reputation from renovations that make this facility impossible to escape. Once you've signed in, any attempt to leave or any request to be moved must necessarily be regarded as a symptom of dementia. Your signature places all future care and security in the hands of Ironwood Ridge Nursing Home, in consultation with Mr."— she checked her notes — "Mr. Broc O'Neill."

Whiterock nodded, his eyes downcast. "Please, if you have the papers—"

They stood in the hall by Whiterock's door. O'Neill looked him in the eyes. They were clear, steady. In a few years his expression would be empty. Dead. For now, they were eyes filled with the burden of something that had gone out of control — a vast criminal network that had spread far beyond what he had wanted, much more than what he had hoped for.

It had started as a simple attempt to fund a facility, to provide the best care that could be offered to his brother who was lodged in the terminal wing, insensible for the past fifteen years. Whiterock had accomplished that, and then he had gone on to build his vision of a newer world. He had almost succeeded.

O'Neill shook his hand. "There are things you should know. You were a member of the inner circle. Your disappearance will be noticed. It will lead to a search. Although you didn't make any calls last night, your phone records now show calls to airlines and a credit card purchase. You bought a ticket and showed a boarding pass. You landed in a Midwest city several hours ago. I have no idea where. Anyone who tracks you this far will find transfers to three different flights out of the U.S. Since you won't be on any of them, the trail will go cold."

Whiterock stared at him in disbelief. "Where am I going?"

"I don't know; no one knows. Your necessary disappearance was fed into CIA computers; the records were created and filed, but they were never seen by human eyes."

Whiterock stood silently, shocked at what he heard.

"I'm the only one who knows or will ever know where you are. Forget your friends; you can't talk to anyone. If someone we haven't caught discovers where you are, this facility, with you trapped behind bars, will be burned to the ground."

Whiterock nodded understanding.

"The Whiterock Council will do well, Sam, it will thrive. It will be your memorial. We'll make sure of that." He paused a few seconds, then continued. "You're in the best facility in the world; you made it that way. You did it yourself. I'll be back to talk," O'Neill confirmed. "I'll need your advice, the wisdom of your many years of work with the Council."

Whiterock shook O'Neill's hand and nodded, and then turned slowly toward the window that would provide his only view of the outside world for the rest of his days.

A window with bars. Complete isolation. A prison cell of his own design.

A life sentence with no possibility of parole.

Epilogue

Land o' Lakes, Wisconsin
Sunday, September 15
3:10 p.m.

Oaks and maples towered above the roadway, yielding to a solid stand of pines and spruce as Broc drove the last quarter mile before the cabin. He slowed the BMW to fifteen miles an hour, nursing it over the rough ground among huge trees and boulders. The temperature had cooled into the low seventies — enough to tell him autumn would soon be coming on. In a few days the maples and aspens would start turning color. He remembered the brilliant splash of red fireweed against the gray rocks. It was a hidden wilderness world he had known all his life.

He came around the last bend in the road. The cabin sat as it always had, dark brown stained logs with lighter brown shingles, half hidden among the pines. O'Neill pulled the BMW alongside Christelle's Grand Am parked under the carport and got out. On her dashboard lay the map to the cabin he had drawn.

The place was tranquil with the ancient peace of the northern woods. Overhead, a pair of geese honked, early southward migrants. The pines moved with a whisper from the breeze.

Broc carried his suitcases inside, looked around, and went back for his briefcase and a few groceries: milk, bread, cereal, apples, cheese, a case of Coke. He walked around, looking in the bedrooms. The windows were open; a breeze from the lake was blowing through the screens. A vase of wildflowers stood in the middle of the kitchen table. Christelle's laptop computer stood open on the table by the bay window. There were books on the table and a boxful on the floor.

Broc read the titles. Some were books she had been reading at the cabin in Vermont before they left for Singapore. But there were a dozen new titles — biographies of presidents, a history of recent political change, an analysis of political parties since World War II — most found in discount bookstores in Cleveland and Minneapolis. He picked them up, recognizing both: mint-condition hardbacks now long out of print. One called *The Puzzle Palace* was about the NSA — "America's Most Secret Agency." There were yellow Post-it notes sticking out, and a bookmark near the middle of the book. The other, *Cloak and Gown*, was subtitled *Scholars in the Secret War, 1939—1961*. O'Neill remembered it as a fascinating history of Yale University professors involved in early American intelligence.

Broc walked into the kitchen and unpacked his groceries. On the counter he found a cluster of spice bottles with pale green labels. Turmeric, Cinnamon, Ginger, Coriander, Cumin, Fennel powder, Nutmeg, Cloves. A paperback called *Hawker Recipes from Singapore and Malaysia* lay nearby. Inside the refrigerator stood a plate of sliced apples covered with plastic-wrap. A jar of brown sugar and a big baking pan sat by the stove. His mother's *Fannie Farmer Cookbook* lay open at a recipe for Spicy Apple Crisp.

O'Neill walked to the window and peered toward the lake. He moved his head to search the water through the pine boughs, and then he saw her. He went to the closet and found the binoculars.

The canoe was drifting a quarter mile away. Christelle was wearing a straw hat and dark glasses. He watched her take a stroke and then lay the paddle across the gunwales of the canoe while it drifted slowly along for a quarter minute. It was as peaceful a scene as he could imagine.

He went back to the table by the bay window and opened a letter that had come through the mail from the Department of History at JSU. It had the same informal brevity of all the chairman's letters.

August 28, 1996
Broc, the College Dean has approved your request for a year's leave of absence. We've hired adjuncts to cover your scheduled courses. Best of luck — Bill

A fat bundle from Regency of Nassau addressed to John O'Brien lay on the table along with a thin envelope from Daniel Wicks, postmarked from London. Christelle had found the keys to the post office box and collected the mail. He glanced at the summaries and dropped them on the table.

He went to the window. Christelle was still drifting along in the canoe.

He opened his suitcase, pulled out his new laptop purchased in Kalamazoo, and set it up across the table from hers. In three minutes, he had the phone jack plugged in and files booted up. In another two, he had tapped into his computer account at JSU. There were half a dozen e-mail messages. He read them through — mostly communications from former students, colleagues in history at other institutions, and professional queries related to various ongoing projects around the country. He stopped and read one.

TO: Broc O'Neill
FROM: John Bailey, Political Science
RE: Christelle Washington's dissertation
DATE: September 10, 1996

Broc, Christelle has asked us to send along this query. She's put in a request to write her dissertation off campus. Of course, this is a little different from our usual procedure, but she's an excellent student. It seems okay to me. I've advised her to drop into the department at the end of the fall semester to discuss her progress. She's ready to go ahead as soon as she gets your approval for her topic. She proposes to send drafts of her chapters in by mail. Should we forward them to you, or can she send them directly?

O'Neill typed out a brief note indicating his post office box number, and clicked on "Send Message," with a copy to Christelle. Then he punched in Christelle's e-mail address, typed another message, and copied it to her dissertation director:

Dear Christelle,
I read your proposal this summer. It looks good. See the copy of my memo to Dr. Bailey. You can send your chapter drafts simultaneously to Dr. Bailey and me. Send me your address. If you

have any questions, please write. I've found a bunch of books on your topic; they're sitting here by my computer. Real bargains — mostly from second-hand stores in Cleveland and Minneapolis. Good titles, good prices. I'd be happy to send along the titles. I think you've found a wonderful project — Best of luck. By the way, how was your summer?

Sincerely,

Broc O'Neill

As he closed his laptop, he spotted the Worldwide cell phone, disabled, he knew, because Christelle said she would get it to Dillon Shaver to make sure. *Worldwide*. A lot of mileage, secrets uncovered, a conspiracy broken, a violent death, a life saved. It lay by her books, a remembrance of their summer, and so much more.

O'Neill got up and looked out the window. He caught sight of Christelle through the trees. She was pulling the canoe onto the shore. He watched, catching only glimpses of her bare arms and legs, and flashes of her hair through the leaves. A minute later she came out of the shadows into the sunlight.

He watched as she came up the path. She was wearing a black bathing suit, with a wide panel of sheer net that dipped between her breasts well below her waist. A sheer black skirt, tied at one side, clung to her hips. O'Neill caught his breath.

She came in the screen door. "My golly, a stranger in the cabin."

He tried to keep his eyes on her face.

"Quick," she dared, "prove you're not a stranger! What's my name?"

"Is this a trick question? Christelle Washington."

"Wrong." She walked over to the counter, dug in her handbag, and pulled out a wallet. "That package you gave me — this driver's license says my name is... let's see... Annie Christine Walker. You want to see?"

She showed him, then pulled out a MasterCard and VISA. "See, I'm a new person." She smiled up at him, her hazel eyes glittering. "By the way, I love this place." She motioned around. "I need a quiet spot to work. Would it be okay if I stayed here through the winter?"

"You have a dissertation to write."

"I've got permission to write it off campus."

"We'll get snowed in—"

"We? I mean me," she corrected. "Can I stay here through the winter? You have classes to teach!"

"I've asked for the year off; it's been approved. So, it's both of us who'll get snowed in if we stay here."

She beamed. "Sounds wonderful—"

"But as soon as we see snowflakes, I suppose we could pack up. I've got an apartment in Kalamazoo."

"That sounds wonderful, too. I've never been to Michigan."

"That's Michigan right across the lake. The Upper Peninsula."

Christelle tried to see the other side through the trees. "Well, could we drive through it to get to Kalamazoo? I've heard there are great views of the lakes."

"It's the shortest way to the rest of Michigan, so, yes, we can go that way."

"Here," she directed, handing him a towel, "this Wisconsin water has given me the usual spiral perm. I couldn't find a hair dryer. Would you mind?"

O'Neill kissed her on the forehead and motioned her to sit on the couch. "I should warn you," she prefaced as he got ready to dry her hair, "this does things to me. I'm not very good at controlling myself when someone plays with my hair."

"I'm not very good at controlling myself around a woman wearing a bathing suit like that. Sort of like cowgirl hats and Texas boots."

"You like it? I got it in Singapore while those guys were following me through Lucky Plaza."

"Lucky Plaza? That sounds interesting." O'Neill rubbed her head for three or four minutes; then she got her brush and comb. She sat for a minute smoothing out her hair, and then got up and walked over to the table. O'Neill watched her. He could not tear his eyes away.

"What do these statements mean?"

He walked over and pointed over her shoulder. "Well," he explained, "it looks like Daniel Wicks transferred this amount to Nassau on August 31st. That included millions in interest. "He pointed to the Nassau bank

434

statement: fifteen pages, dated September 12, stapled at the corner. "Turn to the summary on the last page. There's the deposit. Then there were four thousand nine hundred fifty-four deductions. That's the exact number of checks sent out by CR&R. Four hundred thirty of those, a total of $860,000, were sent to Southeast Asia, to employees of Teleconic and Hai Phong. Severance pay, while they find new jobs. Another check went to Mr. Tong in the Philippines to pay for his twenty-five percent share of Teleconic. Total, $7,480,000, which came out of the interest on the Lignum account. This amount of interest — $184 million — is left over."

Christelle was puzzled. "What are you going to do with it?"

"I tried to turn it over to someone, like spoils from a crime, but no one had any idea who. So I checked with the Justice Department. They said to keep it. They said it's enough to fund a foundation."

"And what's this?" Christelle pointed to the pouch he had laid on the table.

He opened it and showed her the paper; it listed the initial deposit of $535,000 in a joint account in the names of Broc O'Neill and Samuel Whiterock. He opened the checkbook with its carbon copies of checks, a whole book.

Her brow furrowed.

"It's a long story. If I try to tell you everything now, you won't get your dissertation started until after Christmas—"

"I plan to have it half done by then. See" — she held up a sheaf of handwritten pages — "I've been taking notes."

"Maybe this will entice you." O'Neill went to his briefcase and pulled out an airline reservation envelope. "We're going to take a vacation: four weeks — December 27th to January 18th—after you go home to see your parents for Christmas. I've got some friends I want you to meet."

Beaming, Christelle reached for the envelope. "Another vacation so soon! That's wonderful, Broc; I've lost touch with everybody. Who are they?"

"Alan Creighton and his wife Annie. Brently Hagan and his fiancée, Kay Brennan — she works in the documents department at Langley. A guy by the name of Willy Rand from Hawaii. He's got a Vietnamese wife he took home with him after the war. Wally Matthews and his wife, Rozita — you met them."

Christelle's eyes widened in disbelief.

"And a young couple I met at the National University of Singapore. John Chen and Susan Wu. They've invited us to their wedding in the botanical gardens."

"Botanical gardens?" Christelle tore open the envelope and checked out the tickets.

"Singapore!"

O'Neill nodded. "New Year's in Singapore, then a week at Langkawi. A cluster of islands up the coast of Malaysia, north of Penang. Six couples — a party of twelve."

"I can't believe it! But, oh my golly, four weeks. I've got to get at least half my dissertation done before we go or I'll never finish by May."

"A minute ago, you were sure you'd have it half done by Christmas."

"It's a plan, a hope, but it's going to be a lot of work!"

Broc took her by the shoulders and turned her toward him. "Everything's cleared away: the proposal has been okayed by Dr. Bailey. I sent in my approval."

"I've got to get going right away or I'll never get it done! I'm a whole summer behind on my reading."

He held her face and pushed his fingers into her hair. "I have something to point out to you, Miss Washington. First, I'm really happy you can write your dissertation off campus. This is a great place to work, so yes, you may stay here for the winter."

"I promise. I'll make it worthwhile. I'll stay home and bake!"

"Second, this is only September 15th. The fall semester doesn't start until the 22nd. You can plan to work on double-agenda politics after that, and I will read every word you write. But for the next week, I'd like to stick to a single agenda."

"I'll bake while I'm finishing the dissertation. See, in that book, I've got this wonderful new recipe for Spicy Apple Crisp—"

O'Neill scooped her up into his arms and kissed her. "There are other ways to make it worthwhile. Let's do the Apple Crisp later. I don't think this agenda can wait."

Afterword: The Author and the Book

A back-to-school gathering of York University students in Toronto on Friday, August 7, 1964, turned into a contentious discussion and debate that lasted through most of the night. Earlier in the week President Lyndon Johnson had ordered a reprisal bombing raid on North Vietnam, marking the beginning of a conflict that would last for nine years. What had begun as a war of the Vietnamese people to end European domination across French Indochina was now recast as a war against communism.

Throughout the night, opposition, condemnation, and speculation on the consequences dominated student discussion. The nebulous event of the so-called Gulf of Tonkin incident on August 4 that precipitated the bombing was already under suspicion as a convenient fiction to begin a war. Seventeen years later, our suspicions were confirmed in *The Pentagon Papers: The Secret History of the Vietnam War* (1971): covert plans under the code name Operation Plan 34A had been drawn up six months earlier with clandestine military sorties against North Vietnam beginning in February 1964. The Gulf of Tonkin incident, ambiguous to this day, provided a way to turn a war already underway from clandestine to public.

Our long August night of debate in Canada serves as a reminder that American projection of power has always occurred within an arena of world opinion. For me, the genie was out of the bottle; politicians and governments had to be watched.

Moving to the United States four years later, I arrived in that fateful year when President Johnson realized that the war America had joined was beyond his control; thus, he withdrew from running for a second term. A few weeks later Robert Kennedy, the presidential candidate on whom hope for an end to the war was conferred, was assassinated.

In 1972, the Watergate burglary revealed the length to which a sitting president might go to retain power. A few years later, murmurs of secret negotiations with Tehran to assure a victory for Ronald Reagan in 1980 highlighted the struggle for political power. To this day, what may have occurred to subvert a Jimmy Carter "October surprise" remains a mystery that may never be solved. In 1987, a secret Iran-Contra arms-for-hostages conspiracy came to light, revealing clandestine activities hatched in a simmering "deep government" hidden in the back rooms of Washington. A nine-year secret American war in Laos left behind more than seventy million unexploded bombs with continuing casualties now more than 20,000. Every new discovery increased suspicion that there were more.

The loss of long-standing Democratic control of Congress to Republicans in 1994 revealed a new anxiety: how might a paranoid political party respond to loss of power and control? *Ironwood Ridge* was written soon after this Republican takeover. Then, diverted by other matters, I set it aside. Perhaps the story was too dated. Perhaps the anxiety of this shift in power was temporary. Then, as the struggle for party control continued through the next dozen elections, intensifying in the new millennium, I took the manuscript off the shelf to look again at a plot imagined twenty-five years ago. The story was set in the 1990s, when decades of party cooperation descended to contention, conflict, and desperation.

Today party and administrative control is the dark subplot of every congressional vote, investigation, confirmation, court decision, and executive order. Its outliers are dozens of lawless groups promoting extremist causes. Uncertainties over traditional policies and their future fate concern voters across the entire spectrum of political persuasion who yearn for some version of American stability, predictability, and moral authority. That yearning goes on amid apprehension that the higher ideals of the American experiment will ever be achieved. I felt that a story set in the time when political uncertainty first appeared was still the story I wanted to tell.

Barry Wood

BARRY WOOD, a Canadian by birth, is a naturalized American citizen with a doctorate from Stanford University. He teaches English literature, American literature, and interdisciplinary studies at University of Houston and has had visiting appointments in Canada, England, and Malaysia. *Ironwood Ridge* is his first novel.

CPSIA information can be obtained
at www.ICGtesting.com
Printed in the USA
JSHW052114210222
23164JS00003B/11